Helena
Thorfinn

Before the River Takes Us

This book is dedicated to my parents, Inga and Magnus Thorfinn. They followed this writing process as long as they could. Their love and warmth was with me all the way.

In memoriam

Before the River Takes Us
Originally published in 2012 by Norstedts in Sweden as
Innan Floden Tar Oss

TallestTreePublishing

Paperback ISBN: 978-91-519-3118-0
Ebook ISBN: 978-91-519-3119-7

Translation by Agnes Broome
Cover design by Anders Timrén
Book design by Sarah E. Holroyd (https://sleepingcatbooks.com)

1

The small, hyper-efficient wheels spun in the air as Janne tilted the pram to get on the escalator leading down from the upstairs restaurant at SkyCity. Teo kicked his legs and hooted with delight. For the hundredth time since morning, Janne worried this had been a serious mistake. Travelling alone for over twenty-four hours with two children had seemed realistic back in May, when the Ministry for Foreign Affairs had booked their tickets. He had even looked forward to it, vaguely envisaging a journey spent reading and doing jigsaw puzzles with the children. He had imagined there would be lots of things to do during their stopover in Bangkok. Oh yes, the stopover. It was nine hours long: an eleven-hour flight plus nine plus three. What had he been thinking? What had Sofia been thinking?

'I'll travel on ahead, make sure the house is habitable,' she had mused. 'It might be a good idea for one of us to be there for a few days before everything kicks off.'

It had seemed to make sense. Her emails over the past week had informed him that the house was 'amazing', 'a palace, though maybe a bit austere', and described a garden overflowing with fragrant flowers, fruit trees and palm trees, as well as a chef who knew how to make lasagne and Swedish meatballs.

'You're going to love the house!' she had written just yesterday. 'There's a mango tree outside the window in your study. We have an enormous patio with bamboo furniture.'

Janne squeezed Noella's sweaty little hand and helped her off the escalator while simultaneously manoeuvring the pram onto safe ground. Everything was still under control. The children were fed and happy. Nappies had been changed and their hand luggage crammed full of biscuits, bottles, wet wipes, the Nintendo, picture books and stuffed animals. But then again, they were only forty minutes into the twenty-three-hour journey.

Down in the international departures hall, Janne quickly scanned every nook and cranny. Nothing child-friendly in sight. He needed a place to sit for about an hour until they could board. If the people at the Swedish Civil Aviation Administration were stupid enough not to install a play area – some slides, a jungle gym – they had only themselves to blame. He turned the pram towards an indoor garden area, hoisted Teo out and parked him next to some potted yucca plants. The two-year-old quickly made the best of the situation by transferring clay pellets from the planters onto a toy truck, which he then proceeded to push around on the floor. Six-year-old Noella sat down next to him with her Barbie doll.

The past few months had been the most intense of Janne's life. Their everyday existence had felt like an endless series of emergency measures. Things just had to work out. Since Sofia had been offered the SwedeAid job in March, everything had been a blur. Fortunately she had been on maternity leave since then, and had done most of the organising. It wasn't her first international move, and like a seasoned pro she busied herself with booking the moving firm, subletting their apartment, cancelling their phone contracts, and spending their entire relocation grant. At the start of June the movers had come in and packed their container with everything a family of four might need for three years abroad. Except for furniture, which the state was providing. But everything else: clothes, toys, bikes, helmets, a trampoline, linens, lingonberry jam, twenty bags of Swedish sweets, Swedish Christmas decorations, Änglamark detergent and a new computer. All their worldly goods.

Suddenly it had looked paltry to Janne. Was that his life? All their needs and experiences in a handful of boxes? Their shipment had only just filled one small corner of the giant container, and he wondered what was wrong with their packing. Or their life. How did other families manage to fill thirty cubic metres? Had he and Sofia forgotten something essential? He had tried to raise the issue with her, but she had just sighed and rolled her eyes.

'Janne, sweetheart, isn't that the very definition of a non-issue? Isn't there enough to worry about without obsessing about what other families might bring? Or not? Wouldn't it be better if you focused on what still needs to be done? I mean, have you written to the Council? Made sure Teo doesn't lose his spot on the nursery waiting list?'

The night before the movers came, Sofia took a call from Dhaka, from a woman whose husband worked for the telecom equipment company, Ericsson.. She wanted to ask if her mother could come by with a few bottles of balsamic vinegar, emphasising: 'I can't get by without it.'

Sofia had been understanding, and obliging, and very early the next morning accepted several crates of both olive oil and balsamic vinegar. The most exclusive brand.

'You get hung up on certain foods when you're out there, you'll see,' she had told Janne. 'I reckon you'll be recruiting a mule or two to bring you Swedish snuff when you run out in October.'

The memory made Janne smile and think affectionately of Sofia, even as he attempted to prevent their energetic son from swallowing too many clay pellets. His beautiful, driven goat woman – wilful as a goat, wise as a goat. She was his jackpot and sunshine, everything he had ever dreamed of during his years in the wilderness that was single life.

They had been slightly older when they met, or at least that's how it had felt, even though they had actually been, by urban standards, of the fairly average ages of thirty and thirty-five. A friend who worked for the newspaper *Dagens Nyheter* had invited Janne to the launch of South Reporting, a new freelance agency focused on international development. At the party, almost as soon as he'd stepped through the door, he had noticed the thin, blonde woman standing by one of the desks, a glass of red in her hand as she browsed through online images. She was tanned, with long silky hair that cascaded down to the middle of her back. Her high cheekbones and her ears, accentuated slightly with the hair tucked behind them, had at first made him think of a creature from *Star Wars* or an elf from some fantasy film. It was only much later he detected the goat in her – lean, strong, sinewy, sexy. Her determination, her energy: hop, hop, ever onwards, upwards, to new vistas and tufts of grass, following some unerring guiding star he was often utterly unable to discern. And always with that calm obstinacy he himself lacked, and which he always admired when he encountered it in others. Later, when they had started dating, they had been like two magnets, impossible to pry apart. He had just wanted to be near her, touching, asking, learning. She had laughed and her sky-blue eyes had looked at him and him alone while she gradually softened and opened up. And their conversations – wondrous, meandering conversations that never ended and inexorably brought them closer to each other's positions and perspectives with a kind of ease he had never experienced before.

Yet they were fundamentally different, and had always moved in different circles. She had grown up and studied law in Uppsala, specialising in human rights, before quickly landing an internship with the UN in Geneva, spending only a few years back home before moving to Dar es Salaam in Tanzania to work for SwedeAid.

Janne had also studied at Uppsala, but had moved in very different circles. A typical teacher's son, Janne had passively gravitated towards that same profession as if by default, studying a term or two of this and that, eventually settling on history and social science before almost reluctantly capping off his education with a year of teacher training in Stockholm. Even though he loved photography, and even though his happiest time at university had been the semester he took advanced photojournalism as an elective, it had never seemed viable to turn his hobby into a career. Photography had to remain at best a part-time gig.

His career soon took him to one of the newly established free schools, south of Stockholm, where the head teacher had seen his potential and soon made Janne his deputy. It was said about Janne that he had a way with young people that bordered on perfect pitch, that the way he approached them was unique, but he was aware that he was also known to be a little undiplomatic vis-à-vis his colleagues and his boss. He was not a strategist. Several times he had promised himself to impose clearer boundaries between himself and his students, to not get so personally involved in their lives.

In that, he was Sofia's polar opposite. She was always able to remain professionally detached. She weighed things objectively and guarded her privacy, even when she was in Rwanda collecting evidence for the court in Arusha, interviewing relatives of missing persons. Time and again he had asked her how she could bear it – what was going through her mind? What had she seen? But she had just explained that she had made a conscious decision to be a camera, to document, to record, nothing more.

An important humanitarian assignment. Just a job? Janne couldn't wrap his head around it.

Teo had lost interest in fiddling with the planter and Noella wanted help undressing her Barbie. What's more, the six-year-old had spotted an ice cream sign and was now demanding an ice lolly.

'Not right now, sweetheart, OK? I'm sure there'll be something yummy on the plane. We're going to have so much fun, aren't we? You'll have your own little table that you can fold down. And we can watch the Alfons film.'

Teo caught the word ice cream and, spotting the ice cream stand, dashed off towards it. Suddenly both children were standing over by the freezer. This is exactly what is not supposed to happen, Janne thought to himself, but nevertheless felt obliged to follow them. Which is worse? Saying no to ice cream and causing a row, or flying long-haul with two children on a sugar high?

Out of the corner of his eye, he noticed passing businessmen eyeing the clay pellets scattered across the floor, and had to turn back to pick them up. There! No harm done, right? He pushed the empty pram over to the children, pulled out his wallet and took comfort in the fact that he was treating Noella and Teo to the last Swedish ice cream they would eat for a year.

He and Sofia had been given a week to consider SwedeAid's offer, and went back and forth on the issue of relocating. Janne had played devil's advocate, pushing Sofia with his concerns and fears, looking for holes in her reasoning. He had also played the 'good parent' card several times. Sofia had calmly answered all his questions and argued that the timing was perfect, both with regard to the children's ages and to Janne's career. He needed a break from the school, he had said so himself on numerous occasions. Maybe he should explore new opportunities? Try something different? And wasn't it, in fairness, his turn to care for the family?

They had argued this way and that about it, always within the parameters of what a normal, Swedish family with children had to consider before emigrating. The quality of the schools. Economic circumstances. Leaves of absence. Health care. And Janne thought Sofia had turned over a new leaf. That she had decided to forget, to let bygones be bygones.

He had brought up leaving their flat and their ageing parents and the loss of pension, missing the slow shifting of the pieces on the board, the glint of steel behind Sofia's back. When he thought she had finally given up, accepted limiting her career to Sweden, she stated what they both knew was true.

'You owe us, Janne. You promised. You have a family to save.' And then, as though nothing significant had been said: 'We're moving to Bangladesh.'

*

Nazreen ran through the breaking dawn along a high bank between water-logged rice paddies. Her bare feet barely touched the ground, she seemed to be soaring, her sky-blue sari like a sail behind her. She was afraid. Afraid and in shock. While she ran, thoughts struck at her like a cobra.

If someone had seen her from afar, they might have described it as an unusual, beautiful scene. The young woman in the blue sari, reflected in the still water, against a backdrop of mighty palm trees swaying gently in the wind. Somewhere ahead of her were huts and the shadows of animals. Perhaps the observer would have been surprised at the girl's speed – running is not common in Bangladesh – and wondered what was so urgent it could not wait until after morning prayers.

She had been roused from her sleep by her mobile phone. At first there had been nothing on the other end but a long moan. Even so, she had instantly known what had happened. It was Nilufar, Mokta's sister-in-law, defying her family by making the call.

'He did it, Nazreen, I couldn't stop him. They did it together. Nazreen, don't go to the police. We're poor, Nazreen. Come here, right now, if you want to see her. But, Nazreen, it's too late, everything's too late. We're just miserable women, Nazreen, it's the will of Allah, inshallah. Please don't be angry with me, Nazreen. What could I do? Nothing, I could do nothing. What will your parents say? Nazreen! Why did they let her come here? *Inna lillahi wa inna ilayhi raji'un.* We belong to Allah and will return to him.'

*

Ambassador Moberg was wondering whether it had slipped Babul's mind that he wanted his afternoon tea slightly earlier than usual today, at two. He stretched his remarkably long limbs and went over to the window to look out past the entrance to the embassy and down into the kitchen, noting with satisfaction that Babul was, in fact, busy making his tea.

The entrance to the embassy compound was in the middle of a large, two-storey brick building flanked by two wings, one housing the Swedish embassy, the other the Danish. The front of the building was fenced off by tall iron railings and imposing gates, but once you made it past that you were welcomed by lush, low bougainvillea and an impressive Banyan tree. The tree's strange, snakelike branches reached down, as if to wanting to ensnare the embassy jeeps being polished by one of the drivers armed with an oversized feather duster. A handful of guards were dozing in the nearby huts.

Yet, although charming, the entrance was not entirely secure, as the ambassador was all too well aware. The whole idea of sharing a building with the Danes had felt unpleasant, to say the least, while the so-called Muhammad caricatures were making headlines. Angry mobs had gathered outside the gates and the embassy staff had needed military protection and over seventy bodyguards to make it in to work. Even with those precautions, a rotten egg had found its way onto the ambassador's jacket, and the news cameras had zoomed in on the Swedish flag while the journalists reported on the cartoons. The Danish ambassador had, moreover, failed to straighten out the mix-up in a timely manner and delayed making proper clarifications to the press, in Moberg's opinion. This was, after all, a Muslim country they were working in, and there was every reason to respect people's hurt feelings. Even if Bangladesh remained secularised, for now, extremist elements remained present. In Jakarta they had been unable to subdue the angry mob, and the Danish embassy had been burned to the ground.

Politics and conflicts were not actually Moberg's forte. In his heart of hearts, he had been surprised at his appointment; the ambassadorial route had not seemed like his calling. Even as a child he had loved languages and sounds, different types of sounds. The son of a Swiss mother and Swedish father, he had come into contact with several languages at an early age, and by the time he had turned eight he was already fluent in Swedish, English, Swiss German, German and French. During his military service he was assigned to the Armed Forces Interpreter Academy and learnt Russian in a record-breaking two months. The process had been familiar from his childhood – it was listening and mimicking, not cramming grammatical rules, that had been the key to his fluency.

A diffident knock on the door and Babul appeared with the tea service. The servility and mild smiles of the Bengali man had at first set Moberg on edge. But he had soon grown accustomed to it and after four years he barely noticed the nervous politeness of doors being carefully opened, cups refilled and the nodding smiles offered, all of which served to make his life easier.

'*Assalamu alaykum*, Ambassador,' Babul bowed deeply and took a few quick steps across the room, setting the teacup down on Moberg's desk.

'*Dhonnobad, thik ache*, Babul,' Moberg spoke Bangla with the local members of staff every chance he got. Now that he had thanked Babul for the tea, he was keen to have a bit of a chat. He often discovered some dialectal nuance in their language that fascinated him, and he was keen to practise his pronunciation. Unfortunately the locals invariably seemed uncomfortable with his attempts at making contact. An ambassador ought not deign to speak to them, that much was obvious.

'*Kemon achen*?' Moberg tried asking Babul how he was.

Babul blushed and waggled his head. '*Thik ache*, Ambassador, *thik ache*,' he managed, before backing out the door with obvious relief.

After the Interpreter Academy, the Foreign Ministry had approached Moberg with the offer of a traineeship. Because he had not had time to look for work as a translator of Russian literature, which had been his original plan, he had taken the entry exams for the job and, to his surprise, been accepted. Classic fluke, in other words, but a fluke that had taken him all around the world, from Moscow to Madrid, via Vienna and now, most recently, to Dhaka. Dhaka, the name alone was heavy with associations, with the third world, foreign aid and misery. Not his specialities. Bangladesh: one big, wretched delta. Constant cyclones, floods and famine. And a level of corruption that permanently ensured the country's top ranking on Transparency International's list of the world's most corrupt. Why would he have wanted to relocate to Bangladesh?

Now, four years later, he was happy he had made the move. It had actually enriched his and Vanja's lives. Because Vanja had quickly found friends who didn't find her too eccentric, and since Arthur had settled in nicely at the American International School, Moberg had asked for an extension every year, when appointments were up for reconsideration. The way he saw it, Bangladesh had a stabilising influence on his family. And the human resources department at the Foreign Ministry had been grateful. Recruiting for Bangladesh was no easy task. Moberg performed his ambassadorial duties well, and for him personally, the posting had made it possible to dedicate himself to his passion – languages. By now he could add both Standard Bengali and street Bangla to the list of languages he had mastered, and on the Internet forums he frequented his views on the development of Bengali from Sanskrit were always warmly received. Right now, for example, he was waiting for a comment on the ongoing changes to the simple past tense of verbs from a researcher in Delhi he had met on a linguistics forum.

Having finished his tea, Moberg checked his inbox again. Nothing from Delhi. Instead, it struck him that people should be awake back home by now and might have sent him instructions on how to formulate his response to the European Union's delegation's proposal for increased coordination of the response to the Rohingya refugees. The signals coming from the Ministry indicated that more coordination and unity were needed, especially within the EU framework, but that the Swedish profile must nevertheless remain a priority.

But no messages from Stockholm, yet. Good. At least the ball was not in his court.

There was, however, an email from the incoming Head of Development Co-operation, Sofia Paulin, who had arrived in Dhaka just over a week before. The blonde woman, whose resumé had appeared in his inbox no more than a few months ago, had already turned some heads. She had quickly got to grips with the complex political situation, even though her work related primarily to the foreign aid side of things. Without any real involvement from Moberg, she had drawn up appointment lists for herself, ordered reports and evaluations of the aid programme from the archive and generally given the impression that she was both competent and level-headed.

As soon as he saw the email's subject header, however, Moberg had a sinking feeling. It read: 'Re: furniture inventory'.

He instantly knew the email was about Siv. During the past couple of years, Siv, the Head of Administration at the embassy, had caused constant friction. Friction that sooner or later provoked conflicts that inevitably ended up on Moberg's desk. Moberg cursed the idiot at headquarters who had sent her back into the field with good references, even though the staff at her previous two embassies had, or so Moberg had heard, written directly to HR to openly discourage further international postings.

Siv was a typical panjandrum, a former economic administrator who had been granted her own fiefdom to rule when she was promoted to Head of Administration. She meddled constantly, revoking established decisions in favour of her own capricious whims, altering routines for no conceivable reason, extending and withdrawing privileges on obscure, arbitrary grounds. If it were not the drivers feeling threatened because she wanted to curtail their lunch breaks, it was the Swedish staff wondering why their mobile phones had suddenly stopped working. She also unabashedly interfered in the personal affairs of the Swedish staff, and regularly berated the local employees.

Siv had been one of the reasons Sofia Paulin's predecessor had chosen not to extend his stint in Bangladesh, and in his final conversation with Moberg he had expressed – in the bluntest terms – his disappointment regarding the ambassador's failure to put his foot down when it came to Siv.

His harsh words were still ringing in Moberg's ears:

'Karl-Otto, just so we're clear. For two years, this woman has obstructed and impeded the work and lives of the Swedish staff, not to mention the locals. My premature departure is a direct consequence of your lack of integrity. The least you can do is file a report, make sure no other embassy is subjected to her in the future.'

But Moberg had delayed reporting Siv to the Foreign Ministry in Stockholm, and was hoping he would be able to avoid it entirely. He was counting on Siv grasping the severity of the situation, and the unwritten agreement that existed between them. Having her sent home would benefit no one. A failure of that magnitude would be a blot against his own name, his own ability as a manager. If she would just curb herself during this, his final year, he would refrain from filing a report regarding the situation in Dhaka. Let some other ambassador deal with the mess.

But the subject line of Sofia Paulin's email was ominous. Moberg took a deep breath and opened the message.

'Dear Karl-Otto, Good morning. I'm sorry to trouble you with this but I feel I must raise the issue, better now than later. After a number of attempts at getting in touch with Siv, I feel I must now contact you directly, as Head of Mission. The matter at hand is the furniture in our house in Baridhara. Let me say first that we are very happy with the house, so close to the school and the embassy, but I'm wondering if there's been a miscommunication regarding the furniture? Siv had emailed us before we left Sweden to say that the house was to be 'furnished to residency level', which is not in itself uncommon these days, and which suits us because the furniture from our 1000-square-foot flat could never have filled the 4000 square feet of this house! For this reason, we chose not to ship any furniture at all, only some bedding, a few of our possessions, and pictures. As it turns out, however, we have been allocated a jumble of furniture, everything very old and in poor condition. It would have been nice if the furniture had been dusted, and in some cases washed, but Siv informs me that this is not the Embassy's responsibility.

'More urgently: Janne and the children are arriving tomorrow, and we still have no bed for Noella or crib for Teo. Siv is now saying that children's beds are not included in "residency furnishing" and that we should have brought them with us ourselves. Why were we not informed of this? And are there no furniture inventories detailing what we have a right to expect? Siv is very defensive, and refuses to provide clear information.

'I would be grateful if you would look into this as a matter of urgency. Best wishes, Sofia.'

Moberg sighed, but was soon pleasantly distracted. The researcher in Delhi had sent an email confirming what he had long suspected: there was an emerging tendency in street Bangla to swallow the last syllable in the simple past form of active verbs.

*

An hour before Mokta was murdered by her husband and mother-in-law, she had been squatting next to the *chula*, the fire pit, stirring the flames that would kill her.

She worked quietly, focused, crouching low, her knees bent, her arms and hands the only tools for grasping, pressing, poking, turning, cleaning, discarding. Her movements occasionally made her clay-coloured sari slip down her back. Whenever that happened, she quickly pulled it back up over her hair. To veil, hide and make herself invisible had quickly become second nature.

Anxiety flickered inside her, making her breathing shallow and rapid. Too much fuel? Not enough twigs? Was she going to be able to keep the *daal*, the lentil stew, warm until they returned? Had she made enough? Would they notice yesterday's leftover rice? She squatted even lower, as though anticipating a kick from her mother-in-law. No, there was too much fuel, she had to pull some sticks out of the chula. But that made it too cool. Stirring, stirring, making sure the daal did not stick.

Mokta had been married to Faruk for almost three years. Every day for three years she had looked after the household they shared with his parents. Every day she had swept the hard-packed dirt floor and every night she had rubbed her mother-in-law's aching feet. Every night and every day she had been reminded of the shame brought upon her as a result of the fifteen-thousand taka still missing from her dowry.

'Money, when are we getting the money?' her mother-in-law Rahima would shout at her every now and again. 'Money and a grandchild, until then you're *bhalo-na*.'

Bhalo-na. Bad, not good. They told her she was useless, just another mouth to feed, a member of the family who had not even contributed the one thing expected of her – a child. She thought about her own, worn-out, worried parents. About their joy and relief when Faruk's mother had approved the match, even though the whole dowry could not be paid before the wedding had taken place. Twenty-thousand taka was enough to get things started. Everything would be all right, Mokta would be married to a man from a poor but industrious family, and that precarious time when she was neither a child nor a married woman had come to an end. Her father had made ten-thousand taka from the sale of one of his two rickshaws, the other ten he borrowed from family, and the remaining fifteen thousand he would have to earn over the next two years. Everything was going to be all right. They had found a good, honourable match for Mokta, their eldest, pale-skinned daughter, and had thus discharged their parental duty. Faruk and his family had now assumed responsibility for her, for her honour and upkeep.

Mokta got to her feet. There now, the fire was burning well and the daal no longer needed stirring, just to be left to simmer. She went into the house and walked over to the brown uniform hanging on the wall on the family's only hanger. She had spent all morning down by the pond, washing the family's clothes, lingering over the scrubbing and rinsing in the hope that some other woman would climb down the laundry stairs to join her. She longed to make friends of her own here.

But it almost seemed as if the other women turned on their heels when they saw her. The only woman she sometimes felt close to was Nilufar, Faruk's sister. But of course they were only able to speak properly when Rahima and Faruk and all of Nilafur's younger brothers were out. As soon as anyone joined them, Nilufar treated her like air.

Faruk worked as a security guard at the docks outside one of the neighbouring villages, his uniform was provided by the company. He was guarding some westerner-owned containers, and thirty-five thousand taka was really too small a dowry for a husband of his calibre. A man in uniform was a trusted man, a man who had left the fields and begun building a real career. Who knows, maybe he could be a police officer one day? Or a UN soldier?

Faruk and Rahima had visited Mokta's parents' house twice before the wedding. The first time, Mokta had worn her most beautiful sari, the pink one with gold trim. Her younger sisters, Nazreen and Meena, had painted her hands with *mehndi*, henna. Nothing ostentatious, but just enough, intricate branches climbing up her arms. She had rubbed coconut oil in her hair, combed it thoroughly and coiled it into a tight bun. She had smelled sweetly of neem oil and her body had hummed with anticipation, even though she knew she would not be allowed to meet her husband-to-be.

It grieved Mokta to think about how she had sat there, so hopeful. So innocent. Her pulse racing and her cheeks flushed, fragrant and dressed-up, stock-still on the bed inside the house while negotiations took place outside. His mere presence, his voice, his eyes which would maybe, maybe search for her between the cracks in the boards of the house walls. All the hopes she had had for her adult life. Maybe even love. She had not dared to think beyond that.

After that first meeting, she had tried to ask her mother about Faruk, the man they wanted to marry her off to. How had he seemed? Was he handsome? Where had he been sitting? Farida had been evasive, but did show her where he had sat. Mokta did not know why, but that spot became important to her. She tried sitting in it. She looked for signs in the sand. She tried to imagine his body, there, in that place. A body that would soon be closer to hers than any other. Sometimes, prospective husbands left poems for their brides, but nothing at all had come from Faruk. But she did have the spot. There, right there, was where he had been sitting.

The next time Faruk and Rahima had visited, half the dowry was paid and the negotiations entered a more intense phase. Mokta had worn her pink sari again, smelled of neem again and mehndi had once more adorned her arms. But this time she had positioned herself so that she could look out through the gap between the broken doorjamb and the sheet-metal wall. She would be able to see him. If he sat in the same spot. And if she remained absolutely still. She remembered barely breathing, her pulse racing and a strange exhilaration spreading through her body.

Later on, Mokta had spoken to her mother about it. About Faruk belonging to an inferior family. Mokta had seen it straight away through the gap. His manners, his clothes, his dark skin, the words he used. It was clear she was more educated than he was. Her English. Her mother had told her over and over that she must not think about it, not seem like a *kotto borro*, a woman who thought herself above others. After the river took their land, they had no choice. In the delicate dowry negotiation, everything was taken into account. Level of education, the reputation of the family, skin colour, and the family's ability to pay.

'*Meye manusher kaaj hoilo shojja kora*', her mother reiterated as she swept the yard. And Mokta knew what she meant by it. A woman is born to bear everything. 'Now you have to prove that we taught you the most important lesson of all – *meye manusher kaaj hoilo shojjo kora*.'

The dowry required to consolidate the match between Mokta and Faruk was modest. Faruk's family wanted the Bhuias's good reputation and were prepared to forego a large dowry. That way, their son would have a wife who spoke some English and who was famed for her beauty and pale skin. For Mokta's family, the marriage meant settling their daughter with a husband on the cheap and, given his job as a security-guard, that her future was now tied to the fortunes of a man with good prospects.

She had been in shock the first few months in her new home. Having always been able to giggle and play with her younger sisters and roam freely about the village, pretending to herd goats while fantasising with the other teenage girls about what it would be like to be married, her world had suddenly shrunk dramatically. Rahima, her mother-in-law, had transformed overnight, it seemed to her. Before Mokta and Faruk's wedding, she had thought Rahima could be a friend and ally, and she had expected to transfer her close relationship with Nazreen and Meena onto her mother and sister-in-law. She had not thought that getting married would entail drastic change. But it soon became clear that an equal relationship had never been in the cards. With Mokta joining the household, Rahima had secured herself a servant, someone she could boss around and who could do the chores she herself and her daughter Nilufar preferred to avoid.

And Faruk, the man she had counted on falling in love with, was rarely around. Uniformed, he disappeared every morning and spent his free time with friends up by the roadside tea stands. At night, he would come at her roughly and quietly and leave her sore down there, her thighs sticky and wet. Rahima often observed their coupling. Her mother-in-law's eyes glinted through a gap between the metal sheets. Unmoved.

Mokta knew a son was expected. She prayed for Allah to bless her with a child so the attacks would stop. Every night, she dreaded Faruk's savagery, the moments that made her feel like pieces of her soul were slipping away. She ceased to be Mokta and became a thing: a piece of furniture, an animal, a cockroach on the floor. A vessel to be used.

She could not understand how Allah could allow her own husband to mistreat her so brutally. But Faruk had his own pact with Allah. During the violent interludes, he murmured prayers about a son.

The son he had to have and that Mokta had to bear him.

After the assaults Faruk usually fell asleep next to her. If the whole house were quiet, she would get up, gather up her sari and go down to the river, the only place in this strange village that reminded her of home and of her own, beloved family. The river in her hometown was the same as this one, the mighty Padma, which regally wound its way across the Bengali plain. Tiptoeing down to the river and placing her palm against its surface made her calm and still.

'Not just you,' it seemed to whisper. 'Not just you and not just now. A woman has to submit, that is the only thing that matters. Bear it, bear it, bear it – that is what women have always done. Eventually, the pain fades.'

2

Janne opened his eyes and for a few seconds he was confused by what he thought was fog blanketing the bedroom. Then his brain made the leap from 'fog' to 'mosquito net', and he realised he was sprawled on a double bed cocooned in the middle of an enormous room. An enormous room in Bangladesh. He closed his eyes again and noticed the sound of unfamiliar birdsong floating in through the open terrace door. Bangladesh. Dhaka. Baridhara. A completely blank, fresh page to start doodling on, a new phase. A new start for Janne and Sofia.

He could hear Sofia playing with Noella on the other side of the door. He hoped Teo was still asleep. What time was it anyway?

They had arrived at Hazrat Shahjalal International Airport in Dhaka the day before, exhausted. Sofia had been waiting for them, a vision of light amid the unfamiliarity, the chaos. Old men with long beards and what seemed to him like nightshirts shuffling around, youngsters in white hats crowding together in clusters, and women in shimmering swaths of fabric snatching at bulky parcels as they arrived on the baggage reclaim belt. The parcels, held together with plastic rope, were wrapped in blankets and sacks that only barely concealed everything from television sets and bicycles to foot baths and armchairs. Their own Samsonite bags, standing anxiously at attention, had glided towards them on the carousel.

'How conventional, suitcases,' Sofia had joked as the henna-haired man from the embassy sprang forward to collect them. Janne had stood next to her, bewildered, watching his fellow passengers struggle with their parcels.

Someone was pushing past them with a trolley carrying an elderly lady wrapped in shawls. A young boy ran after them with a crying baby in his arms. A girl, slightly bigger than Noella, but wearing heels and several layers of makeup, asked to hold Teo. Before Janne had a chance to react, she had carried the boy off and was placing red lipstick kisses all over his face.

And then, at long last, they were ushered towards the exit. It turned out the hennaed man, Mr Hossein, was the embassy's go-to guy, he had their papers and stamps sorted in the blink of an eye.

'That was the official arrivals hall,' Sofia told him with a wry smile. 'Now there's the unofficial one. Have a look at the exit, but don't let it scare you.'

Janne looked up. At first, he could see nothing but a dark wall blocking the daylight outside. After a few seconds, he realised the wall actually consisted of hundreds, possibly thousands of human bodies, pressed against an enormous fence separating the new arrivals from the parking lot on the other side. People were standing on each other's shoulders, hanging from the fence, holding out their hands, shouting and whistling. One or two waved.

'Hey siss-ter, brother . . . what's your name? Which country? Do you love me? Please, please, do you want to marry me?'

Sofia smiled and shook her head, waved to somebody and immediately twenty hands waved in response.

'They're here to greet relatives, or fellow villagers, coming in from Dubai or Malaysia or wherever, where they've gone as guest workers,' she explained while rescuing Teo from further displays of affection, this time from an older man in a filthy *punjabi*, a type of long shirt. 'They go away for years. Their salaries help support whole villages. When they finally return they're given a royal welcome.'

The embassy jeep had managed to squeeze through the crowd to a loading platform, and in just a few short minutes Mr Hossein had made sure all their bags were safely stowed, that they were all on board and that Teo had been carefully strapped into a car seat. Noella wanted to sit on Janne's lap to have a better view.

The car slowly pulled out of the airport and the driver skilfully steering his vehicle around women in burqas and a group of young men in loincloths who stared at them with undisguised curiosity. Dirty little boys clung to the car's side step until their driver rolled down his window, shouted and banged his hand against the door to make them let go.

Twenty minutes later, they turned off the main road and entered a lush residential area, where stately villas could be glimpsed between palm fronds the size of suitcases. Sofia took Janne's hand and squeezed it.

Their house was, as Sofia had told him, magnificent. A white-stone palace ringed by a high wall enveloped in a cascade of rustling bougainvillea. Later on, Janne realised the hot pink flowers concealed rusty barbed wire and crushed glass embedded in the concrete but that was later. Now, he pointed to the flowers with delight.

'Noella, look, pink flowers! We get to live in there!'

A massive iron gate was opened by a uniformed guard and the jeep pulled up in front of a sizable entryway. Grandiose pillars of blush-coloured marble flanked the front door on either side.

Janne inhaled sharply. The front door of their new home was worlds away from the standard, modern Swedish door they had left behind in Stockholm. This one was made of dark, lacquered wood. It was at least eight feet tall and wider than Janne's outstretched arms. The middle of it was skillfully carved with a circular menagerie of animals.

Once inside, Janne was met by a sweeping marble staircase, under which he could make out a fountain in the shape of two dancing bronze fish. A bright living room – or was it a hallway, or a drawing room? – surrounded the staircase and through the windows more rooms and verandas were visible. Brass grates covered the inside of every outward-facing window, iron bars shielded the outside.

Janne walked to the middle of the hallway, his eyebrows deliberately raised, his mouth ajar. He dropped his bag on the floor with a theatrical thud. Sofia came over to join him and gave him a hug and a kiss on his ginger stubble.

'Welcome home. Will this work as a substitute for a semi-detached in the suburbs? At least for now?' She ran a few steps up the staircase with the children in tow. 'Think Bollywood. Imagine me, in a sari, gliding down the stairs.' She laughed, made a sweeping gesture with her arm and posed. 'We're in the middle of a Hindi film, get it? This aesthetic is aimed at Bangla millionaires, all the prestigious things you can think of have been crammed into this house. Fountains, pillars, marble, flourishes, flash . . . '

She noticed Janne's hesitation and continued.

'It's a Bollywood house, that's how you have to look at it. It's not a house for trendy Europeans, or Americans, or Thais. And that's what's so cool about it, right? To have the chance to live in a Bollywood film?'

'Sure, why not? Perfect for an aid worker in one of the world's poorest countries,' Janne retorted archly and looked around, astonished. 'This is one proper gilded cage, huh?'

He stepped into one of the living rooms and climbed a few steps to reach yet another room beyond it. At the back, a veranda opened out onto a lush garden. The hibiscus, he noted, was in full bloom.

'Think of it this way,' Sofia was hard on his heels. 'It's the world that's messed up, not us. We just happen to be living next door to these absurd injustices. Your life won't be any easier for being full of pillars and marble. There's no in-between here, it's the slum or this. Go down to the market someday, and you'll see why we need a cook. I would trade the cook for a Swedish supermarket any day. We won't live better here than in Stockholm. Not really.'

'Wow, wow, wow, feeling defensive, are we?' Janne turned and took her face in his hands. 'So you mean to say there are no nice semi-detached terrace houses here? Preferably with a working fireplace?' He kissed her forehead and then her mouth. 'Don't worry, I'm sure I can get used to this. I just don't want us to start thinking this is our real life.'

*

It had been a long time since Mokta had been to the river. It was as though the comfort it brought her had become too difficult to accept, and as though the soothing flow of the water had morphed into something that called out to her in a way that frightened her. Instead, she had tried to focus on her chores, making sure the house was in order, cleaning, preparing vegetables and looking after Faruk's uniform. She had made sure never to give them a reason to scold her and had stayed outside by the chula, trying to make herself as invisible as possible. Rahima had decided Mokta was never to go to the market by herself, or even to the well, unless it was necessary. One of the boys could fetch water. She had prayed in accordance with the Koran, or at least she had performed Fajr at dawn and Maghrib at sunset. And that was more than anyone else in Rahima's household did, Mokta had noticed.

No, the river was too painful. It demanded her attention, asked questions and awakened old dreams. She had memories that were closely associated with the river, and those memories hurt too much to think about. Like when they had been little she, Nazreen and Meena. Always the three of them. Always so close, like clouds drifting in and out of each other, never truly apart. How she had loved her younger sisters. Teaching them to swim in the soft water, they had hung their clothes on the bushes and slipped into the river, giggling and naked, as dawn broke.

She had shut the river out now, avoided it. It was dangerous. After her parents told her they couldn't, wouldn't take her back, after the punches and kicks from Rahima had gone too far, and after Faruk's contempt and abuse had scraped a hole in her soul. That's when the river had become dangerous.

Her parents had Nazreen and Meena to think about now and Allah had, after all, given her a husband. She had to find a way to live with him. She was an adult now, and no longer welcome in the home of her own family.

That is when the river had come to embody a promise of release and liberation. She could just walk out into it. Straight out, to the deep part, and then just keep walking until she lost her footing and her heavy sari pulled her down. Later on, they would find her, like they had found her aunt, back when she was just seven and had not been able to understand. Now she understood all too well.

She knew her mother, Farida, had grieved and cried over her daughter's fate, but she could also see that her parents were hard pressed on all sides. How would they ever be able to marry the younger girls off if she ruined the family's reputation by not having children and running away from her husband? They had never been able to come up with the money for the rest of her dowry; there just wasn't any. Her father pulled his one rickshaw himself, even though the pain in his knees was so severe he whimpered all night long. The family's situation had worsened since Mokta moved away.

The last time she had returned, seeking shelter, her father had lashed out at her. 'You get to eat, don't you? You get rice and fish, don't you? And thick daal? You eat three times a day, don't you? Do you think we do these days? Do you?'

He was a broken man, but had done what he could for his eldest daughter. He could do no more for her. The river had taken his land, but at least Mokta had been married off before the family was plunged into utter destitution.

Meye manusher kaaj hoilo shojjo kora. A woman is born to bear everything. She had to live the life that was hers.

The sisters had nevertheless continued to meet, in secret. Even though Faruk's village felt like a different world to Mokta, her childhood home was in fact no more than a few miles away. After nightfall, either

Nazreen or Meena would come running on scrawny legs and gingerly scratch at the wall where they knew Mokta slept. Mokta would get up quietly and meet her sisters behind the outhouse where no one would follow her. If Rahima noticed, and thought she was taking too long and came to look for her, her sisters would quickly slip away in the dark. Their meetings sustained Mokta. Her sisters brought gossip and news from home, and gave her the tenderness and intimacy she craved. Her younger sisters caressed her, comforted her, combed her hair, tried to make her laugh or at least smile. They needed her as much as she needed them.

One night a few months back, Nazreen had been upset, sitting with her threadbare *dupatta*, the long scarf that forms part of the Bangladeshi traditional dress, wrapped around her legs. Her large, dark eyes flashed in the gloom and her wheezing voice had stuttered and sobbed.

'Dearest, sweetest, loveliest,' Nazreen had sobbed. 'I don't want Amma and Abba to marry me off. Now they're talking about Nasty Ali. Can you imagine? Nasty, Nasty Ali. He's asking for just five-thousand taka. But he's at least forty, and he smells and his beard is gross. Let's run away, you and me? Meena can come along later, she can look after Amma and Abba for a while first. Amma and Abba would be relieved, even if they'd never admit it. Three girls is a curse.' Nazreen had held up three trembling fingers in the dark and stared at them as though they frightened her. Then she continued: 'Three! And a little brother who's ill! No family can pay three dowries, they couldn't even manage yours! We'll do what Taslima did, earn our own dowry, we'll show them what we can do! Or we'll get a job in Dubai, like Malaka, or we'll go to Kolkata. Yes! Just to Kolkata. Or anywhere in India. We can work as maids, maybe in America. That's it! We could buy tickets to America! Or to Dhaka. You're old enough to work in a factory, all the garment factories want girls like you, Mokta! And we speak English, everyone says they want you to know how to speak English in Dhaka. A bit of English, and I can clean, or do whatever. Dhaka, Mokta, let's run away to Dhaka. We can stay with Cousin Babul. I'll sell vegetables to make enough for the tickets. Please, Mokta, run away with me. We'll come back for Meena later.'

The thought of running away with Nazreen had swept into Mokta's life like a cool breeze. It felt like the arrival of the summer monsoon. Relief. Change. Maybe, maybe. Even though the sixteen-year-old's fantasies were not entirely realistic, or so Mokta suspected, there was suddenly a way out. Maybe. Babul was their second cousin, he worked in an office in Dhaka. In the village it was said he earned a fortune, and that he had a fancy flat on the outskirts of the city. When he had returned home for Eid two years ago he had joked with the girls, saying they could come to Dhaka and stay with him. Babul had married a girl from a neighbouring village who worked in a Western household, and it was said about the couple that they were even postponing having children until they had put some money aside.

Mokta's and Nazreen's dreams were only just beginning to take shape when a large box of rat poison suddenly appeared in the kitchen. The house had never had a rat problem. Mokta had gone cold when she first noticed it. She knew very well what it was in aid of, and in some strange way she felt caught red-handed. Had Rahima realised how seductively the river was calling her? Had she felt that Mokta was about to break inside, and that it was time? The rat poison was in the first instance an exhortation, and in the second instance a threat. More than anything, however, it was an irrevocable declaration of the family's plans for her. As long as she was alive she stood in the way of a new marriage for Faruk and another dowry for Rahima. Since neither money nor children seemed to be forthcoming, her role in the family was played out.

And so it was that powerful emotions and a difficult decision tormented Mokta on the night of her murder. She was waiting for her executioners. She moved silently and unnoticed: between the *chula*, where she stirred the daal, and the room, where she stood in front of the uniform on its hanger. She tried to think about her life. She thought about her sisters and what they were actually capable of. She tried to ignore the pull and call of the river.

*

Ambassador Moberg and his wife, Vanja, had been invited to a dinner at the residence of the British High Commissioner, Chu. Chu had bought one of Vanja's watercolours a year ago, and was generally positively inclined when it came to the Swedish ambassadorial couple. Moberg was hoping for a nice evening, even if the Brits were otherwise hardly known for their interest in building relationships with the Swedes. Sweden was uninteresting, from a purely political perspective, not a country that mattered much in terms of the UK's dialogue with the Bangladeshi government.

Bangladesh was of central importance to the British, that was just a fact. The number of Bangladeshis in Dhaka in possession of a British passport was roughly equal to a small English town. British politicians frequently travelled to Dhaka to meet the voters and campaign. And vice versa. Events in Dhaka were closely observed by a growing English-born middle class of Bangladeshi extraction. A well-educated middle class residing in the increasingly affluent areas in the east London borough of Tower Hamlets, and the traditionally Bangladeshi streets around Brick Lane. It was imperative for British politicians to be familiar with the Bangladeshi political scene, and crucial for British Secret Service agents to follow developments within the militant Jamiat-ut-Tahir and the outlawed Hizb-al-Islami-Bangladesh.

All of this had dawned only gradually on Moberg, who initially had a hard time understanding the intensity of the British interest in 'the Land that God Forgot', as someone had dubbed the country where he was stationed. Bangladesh was his first posting to a former British colony and his first encounter with the Muslim world. The colonial heritage that dominated British foreign policy was fuelled by an internal logic that was difficult for an outsider to fathom. At least that is what Moberg told himself. To understand British geopolitical thinking, you simply had to be British.

Be that as it may, tonight's event was set to be a friendly get-together, and for some reason the Swedes had been invited. Moberg hoped Vanja would be on her best behaviour, and that she would moderate her alcohol intake.

Vanja had not even made it all the way downstairs before Moberg sensed the evening might become difficult. She had chosen one of her more eccentric ensembles, a Southern Indian skirt with a matching, embroidered top, and she had plaited thin, colourful ribbons into her long, red hair. She smiled her introverted, dreamy smile and seemed not to notice that Arthur was calling her from upstairs.

'Can I go over to Aziz, Mum? Can you send the driver back? Hello, Mum?' Arthur bellowed in the breaking voice of the adolescent male. 'When are you going to be back? Can I have some of those sweets Dad got from the new Swedes?'

An ominous smile curled the corners of Vanja's mouth, but it clearly had nothing to do with their son. Moberg had to reply himself.

'Yes, you can have some Swedish sweets! And text the driver when you want to be picked up. Saleha knows where we are if you need us.'

Moberg hated shouting in the giant residence, it made him feel idiotic. The semi-detached on Lidingö had been a different story, there you could keep up a conversation even between floors.

Meanwhile, Vanja had carefully applied her lipstick in front of the big hallway mirror, and now she spun around dramatically and wrapped her arms around him. The ten or so thin glass bracelets jangled around each of her wrists.

'So, my love, what instructions do you have for me tonight, then?' She smiled and planted a kiss on his chin. 'What may I not call by its rightful name?'

Annoyed, Moberg pushed her away and rubbed at the lipstick smeared in his well-trimmed beard. He sighed and began to dread what promised to be a taxing evening ahead.

Vanja and he had met at university in the mid-seventies. She had been one of the most beautiful girls on campus, with the kind of charisma and grace that made both men and women turn. Women out of envy and men out of lust. She had been called the 'hippie princess' and had surrounded herself with an air of Indian mystique. She had studied art history and later been accepted to Stockholm's prestigious University College of Arts, Craft and Design. But it was not until much later, when he was long established at the Foreign Ministry, that they met again and fell in love.

'Vanja, not instructions, per se, you know I don't like thinking of it that way. But maybe . . . ' He took a deep breath, how much did he dare ask for? 'Maybe you don't have to talk politics or aid. At all? Please?'

'You're referring to what I said at the dinner on Saturday, yes? About how you and Hans Christian believe the British take up too much space at the table? Or is this about how the UK refuses to work within the EU framework, and won't attend you're delightful Head of Mission lunches?'

She pretended to zip her mouth shut, and Moberg felt his anxiety level rise. Had she already been drinking?

By now, their driver had pulled the car up and Moberg decided not to argue with his wife. He simply noted, yet again, that she had overheard more than he would have wished during the dinner with the Danes the other night.

Out on Gulshan Avenue and over by the traffic lights by the Gulshan-2 roundabout, street children crowded the car. They knew who was inside. Vanja pointed and waved and pressed her nose against the glass until the children fell over themselves laughing. But no money, that's what they had decided. The street kids learnt to recognise the cars, and it would become unmanageable if they thought they might get money, *baksheesh*, every time they spotted their Mercedes. But Vanja knew a lot of the children from her work at the local slum school.

'Feruza,' she scolded through the closed window, 'take your brother home this instant, he's too young to be here. Come on,' she motioned, 'off with you! *Jao, jao!*' She turned to Moberg. 'They bring the toddlers out with them, it's insane. Feruza's younger brother isn't even one yet, and he already knows how to beg. You know,' she mimicked, putting her hand out, 'tilt of the head and the little hand. And that boy over there, see? He's such a bright child, but his father won't let him go to school. Do you understand what I'm saying? Won't allow him! Instead he has to beg, to earn money for his family. But he still plays hooky and comes to school sometimes.'

Meeting the children had cheered Vanja up, and when they reached High Commissioner Chu's residence, she was alert and charming.

The dinner was a grander affair than the invitation had suggested. The entrance to the High Commissioner's tasteful residence was covered in thousands, no, tens of thousands of tiny, tiny lamps – fairy lights – a common party decoration in South Asia. Moberg could never fully shake the feeling that fairy lights were a Christmas thing, but he had to admit the thousands of little stars set against the tropical night always lent a festive air to proceedings. His own residence had been adorned in much the same way on the Swedish national day, so he knew it must have required somewhere between seventy and a hundred thousand little lights to make the High Commissioner's garden look the way it did.

'Well, well, here comes ABBA', the High Commissioner quipped when he spotted the Swedish Ambassador and his wife. 'Make sure you get yourselves a drink. What a night, eh? Great, lovely to see you. Vanja, you look radiant. Welcome, welcome.'

Professionally pleasant, he kissed Vanja on both cheeks, gave the Swedes a few seconds of attention and then turned to the next guest.

It was not the first time the Mobergs had been called ABBA by their international acquaintances. There was something about Moberg's neat beard and aura of decency, in combination with Vanja's long hair and often artistic outfits that immediately brought the famous group to mind.

A young man, dressed all in white, serving drinks from a bamboo hut in the garden expertly prepared two gin and tonics for the Mobergs. The ice clinked and Moberg noted anxiously that Vanja positively guzzled her cocktail.

High Commissioner Chu was originally from Hong Kong but had grown up and gone to school in England and was now one of those eminently well-qualified second-generation immigrants from the former colonies who were taking over the Foreign Office. He was driven, quick, socially astute and took instruction directly from Whitehall and the British government. Moberg attempted to suss out the purpose of the dinner party – dinner parties always had a purpose – by making the rounds.

It soon became clear it had something to do with aid. It would have been the perfect opportunity to introduce Sofia, their new Head of Development. But Sofia had her hands full at the moment, getting her family settled in.

Three people from the managing team of the British equivalent to SwedeAid were present. Peter, who was ultimately in charge of the half a billion pounds the Brits bestowed on Bangladesh every year, and Rebecca and David, two of his department heads, in charge of private sector development and support for civil society, respectively. The Danish Ambassador Hans Christian was there as well, as was the Dutch Ambassador, Anna Mieke, and her Head of Development, Antje. A number of Dhaka-based consultants were also roaming the garden, as were a handful of others Moberg did not know. From the conversations about the queues at Hazrat Shahjalal International Airport, he surmised they must just have flown in.

Suddenly Chu was at his side.

'Karl-Otto, allow me to introduce Dr Malcolm Davis from the London School of Economics and Professor Ahmadiya from Harvard. They're in Dhaka to draw up guidelines for a study we want to conduct on the subject of the Islamification of the rural population.'

Moberg greeted them politely, and as he did so the Danish Ambassador joined their little group.

Chu continued: 'We have clear instructions from Whitehall to do what we can to map and investigate how serious the dissemination of militant Islamification is in Bangladesh. You've probably heard from the Americans that some extremist groups are run remotely by members of the Bangladeshi diaspora in London and Birmingham. The High Commission aims to approach this problem holistically, with the aid of both scholars and field studies. Dr Davis, would you care to comment . . . '

Dr Davis cleared his throat and swirled the ice cubes in his gin and tonic round and round for a few seconds.

'Well, as diplomats you're familiar with the concern raised by the events in 2005. Five hundred bombs exploding simultaneously across the country. It implies a certain amount of coordination.'

Moberg nodded. The bombs had been discussed and analysed both in Bangladesh and abroad. The Swedish authorities had come to the conclusion that the Islamist groups were likely considerably more organised than previously thought. The Danes, who had been forced to deal as best they could with the consequences of the Muhammad caricatures at the same time, had been very insistent ever since that any aid given by them had to serve to counter violent extremism in various ways. To Moberg's mind, however, it had always been more than a little unclear how exactly this was to be achieved. Hans Christian had applied himself to the task with a level of dedication that to Moberg's mind often tipped over into aggression and verged on islamophobia, and he had given countless speeches to donors on the theme of 'countering religious radicalisation'. Moberg suspected these speeches would now be recycled as comments to Chu and Dr Davis. And he was right; the Dane could barely contain himself:

'Finally someone takes this seriously! Thank you! For our part, we're keen to be able to look our taxpayers in the eye. We can't risk our aid money ending up in the pockets of violent Islamist organisations – and we all know how difficult it is to keep tabs on civil society and all these grassroots organisations. We give money to networks that are linked to other networks, which may in turn be connected to just about anyone. It's a nightmare. Just the thought of feeding the hand that's constantly biting us.'

Moberg felt ill at ease. Partly it was because he could not see what was in Vanja's glass. She was talking to Antje. If the content of her glass were brown, he would be able to relax. That meant it was Coca-Cola. If it were clear, on the other hand, it could well be her second G&T of the evening, or possibly still her first? And partly it was because the Dane's trite rhetoric, and its superabundance of platitudes, riled him, even as it left him at a loss of what to say to really put him in his place.

'We Danes are for diversity in all its forms, and religious freedom is one of the pillars of our constitution, of course. But,' at this point he made a dramatic pause to make sure he had everyone's attention, 'when it comes to certain forms of Islam, what we're seeing flies in the face of everything we believe in. I can't emphasise enough how important it is to map the extreme Islamists. It's crucial that we international donors contribute to that work. This is about the war on terrorism.'

He said the last part with an indignant vibrato and turned to High Commissioner Chu, as if seeking praise.

Diversity and Denmark? Well, that was certainly not an unqualified truth, Moberg thought to himself. His own cousin, who lived in Åkarp in the south of Sweden, had Danish neighbours who had married Pakistani partners and consequently been obliged to relocate across the Sound to Sweden. They were no longer welcome in Denmark. The fact that the Muhammad caricatures had appeared in Denmark and not somewhere else was hardly a coincidence, Moberg mused.

Chu was quick to chime in with the Dane's indignation, but he also smoothed things over, like the much more skilled diplomat he was.

'Most Muslims are good people, of course, but the Americans are putting a lot of pressure on us to find out more about the British-Bangladeshi diaspora in terms of their contacts with extremists. I'm hoping that over the course of the next few months, the Davis-Ahmadiya team will be able to create a platform for future dialogue, based on a study of rural communities and civil society. And we'd love for the report to have the support of Sweden, Denmark and the Dutch.'

Chu looked round his garden, searching until he located Peter, one of the British senior aid managers.

'Peter, would you mind joining us?'

The Brit obeyed his boss and extricated himself from the discussion he was involved in.

'Peter, could you possibly expand a bit on our ideas regarding a future platform. Our colleagues and neighbours are curious.'

'The idea is still in its infancy,' said Peter, 'but the main thrust is to develop tools that can be used to screen organisations before granting them financial support. As things are, we don't know where our grassroots organisations stand on the issue of violent extremism and groups that may be receiving funding direct from the Gulf States. What's happening in the rural communities? A closer examination of the ideological influences present in villages will be crucial to any effort at conflict prevention and to the ongoing work of strengthening human rights and equality.'

Vanja had sidled up to the small clutch of people gathered around Chu and was listening with the hint of a smile on her lips. Moberg noted that the contents of her glass were clear and, judging by the fullness of the glass, that it must be her second drink. Or maybe third? Anxiety washed over him.

Hans Christian, the Danish ambassador, picked up where Peter had left off.

'And that's what's so damn frustrating. One day these organisations take money from us, and the next they go off to some al-Qaida training camp.'

'Pardon a regular taxpayer,' Vanja cleared her throat and wobbled ominously. 'Hans Christian, are you planning on creating small networks of informants within your organisations on the ground? I mean, is going after impoverished peasants visiting their local mosque the best way to stop terrorism? Is there no difference between Islam and terrorism?'

Hans Christian shot Vanja an exasperated glare.

'We just want information. And it might be an idea for you to update your understanding of what a modern intelligence service does. To assess the severity of the threat, we need knowledge –'

'But isn't it bad enough that Muslims aren't allowed to be Muslims in Europe? This is their own country, after all, isn't it?' Vanja asked, slurring slightly, swaying, then looking down at her now-empty glass. 'This is the kind of talk I remember from when I was in San Francisco in the seventies. McCarthyism was still pervasive and there were spies at our peace gatherings and . . . '

Moberg could feel his toes curl in his shoes. She was drunker than he had realised. She must have had some at home before they left. Thankfully, everyone chose to ignore her and she promptly lost her train of thought. Moberg quietly slipped away from where he was standing.

Peter took it upon himself to provide a diplomatic summary: 'Times have changed, with the general radicalisation of Islam since 9/11, but also as a result of the islamophobia back in Europe. There's a lot of talk, for example, about Taliban values being taught in the madrasas here in Bangladesh, according to models imported from Pakistan. That pamphlets are being handed out –'

'Pamphlets?' Hans Christian did not miss a beat.

'Yes, pamphlets handed out after Friday prayers. Apparently they incite their readers against the US and the UK –'

'and Denmark, it's safe to assume,' Hans Christian finished Peter's sentence, took a deep breath through his nose and shook his head.

While the discussion continued, Moberg had been circling the group until he reached Vanja. He put a hand on her shoulder and tried to guide her away from the group. She stumbled, but Moberg deftly steadied her and whispered: 'Vanja, that was a very interesting observation, but I think we should be going soon, don't you? I'm certainly not having any wine with dinner anyway, remember that we have to get up early to watch the tennis match.'

'Darling, everything's under control, don't worry! I'm having a good time! Peter's here, and Antje. Amigos. Friends with bright auras.'

And so they stayed. Moberg ended up sitting between none other than Peter and Antje at the dinner table. Vanja, he saw, was deep in conversation with Dr Ahmadiya who seemed to be drowning in her dark brown eyes and watched, enchanted, as her bejewelled arms waved about enthusiastically as she spoke. She laughed and purred like a cat in the warmth of Ahmadiya's attention. At least he, a Muslim, had not been offended by Vanja's comments.

'By the way, Karl-Otto,' Peter had turned to him, 'how's Alor Desh coming along? I assume the final audit is almost complete?'

Antje replied, while Moberg felt like a big question mark.

'Oh, yes, my god. Isn't it horrible? I would never have thought that about Khadija Anam. But now we have to move on. Will you put your new Head of Development on it straight away? If the rumours are true we'll have to act immediately. Alor Desh is primarily Sweden's responsibility, so the rest of us will just follow your lead.'

Moberg looked back and forth between them.

'I'm not sure I'm following. Alor Desh is the organisation we're working with, with you? In the char area?'

'Exactly. We support their work with the people in the river delta, the poorest of the poor. Khadija Anam's outstanding programme. We initiated that audit last summer? Remember?'

Antje looked at Moberg and Peter added more information in an attempt to jog Moberg's memory:

'There were anonymous tip-offs that spring, alleging severe corruption, and now Ernst & Young have published their preliminary findings, did you see them? It seems the accusations are true. We're talking court bribes, ghost employees, big sums to accounts we didn't know about. They're more or less accusing Khadija of eating babies for breakfast. Did Sweden not get the report? That's odd . . . '

Moberg had a think. Sofia's predecessor had left the embassy in a huff after Christmas and since then Moberg had half-heartedly tried to fill the position himself. He had not quite had the time to get into all of it. An auditors' report, had there not been something like that in the pile marked 'Urgent', which he had meant to ask Sofia to have a look at? He apologised.

'Mea culpa, mea culpa, I have to blame the fact that my new Head of Development hasn't had the time to get settled properly yet. Her name is Sofia Paulin, by the way, specialises in human rights and equality. Could you give me a quick run-through? I'm not the resident aid expert, as you know.'

Antje set out the background.

'We were hoping against hope that this was all down to some disgruntled employee with a bone to pick with Khadija. You know this place is a hotbed of gossip and spurious accusations. The programme is, to put it plainly, one of the best we have, a unique way of reaching the people who are by far the most vulnerable in this country, maybe in the world. Now we'll have to have a think about how to proceed,' Antje said, and then switched back to the subject of Sofia, clearly aware that Moberg's limited experience of – and interest in – international aid.

'This Sofia, are you going to appoint her Sweden's Dev-Com representative?'

There was a sudden hush, or so it seemed to Moberg. Peter turned and studied him intently. The question of who got a seat on Dev-Com, the Executive Development Committee, was a delicate one. Dev-Com was the agency coordinating international development efforts. It was the organ the Bangladeshi government engaged with directly. Every donor country or multilateral organisation, such as the UN or the World Bank, was allowed *one* representative on Dev-Com. It was a power hub, really the only one in Dhaka, apart from the poorly functioning government.

'I don't know,' Moberg played for time. 'This is Sofia's first posting as Head of Development. I'm not sure she's . . . '

'The rest of us would be grateful if she were nominated,' Antje broke in, her tone friendly but firm. 'I depend on being able to coordinate with both the Swedes and the British. Isn't that right, Peter?'

'It is, Antje. Think about it, Moberg. You EU ambassadors have your Head of Mission meetings every week. Isn't that enough?'

Moberg mumbled something indistinct and glanced across the table. To his surprise he noticed that Dr Ahmadiya had laughingly placed his hand over Vanja's wine glass. The Muslim academic pointed heavenward – to Allah? – and shook his head with a troubled look on his face. Vanja tilted her head imploringly, but the man instead offered to top up her glass with Coca-Cola. Astonished, Moberg relaxed a little. Surely she would take the hint when it came from another guest? At least now there were two of them trying to keep the evening from spinning out of control.

*

No one was awake the night Mokta was burnt to death, or if they were, they were probably at the mosque by the river, listening to the prayers of righteous men. But if anyone had been awake, they would have seen a determined Rahima walking towards the little shed, a cudgel in her hand. They would have seen her son, Faruk, following her, trying to talk her down. They would have seen an argument that quickly escalated into screaming and struggling. They would have heard Rahima call out to Faruk to fetch the petrol, and seen the man-boy slouch off to their neighbour's house for a bottle of kerosene. They would also have witnessed Rahima pinning her daughter-in-law to the floor, spitting in her face and scratching her with dirty fingernails, and then, a few minutes later, they would have seen Faruk return with the bottle and start dousing his wife's sari with its contents. And then the screams, the screams tearing out of Mokta as her sari burned. Isn't it odd that no one woke up? She tried to escape from the house, but her mother-in-law's cudgel stopped her. She burnt, ablaze like a torch and the neighbours, had they been there, would have seen how both her husband and her mother-in-law made sure the fire caught properly before they let her escape, only to hurl herself, howling and smouldering like a charred branch, in the direction of the pond.

But everyone must have been fast asleep on this otherwise beautiful Bengali night, even Faruk's younger brothers and cousins. Because when the sleepy police officer from Goalpur arrived at the scene a few hours later, finding a weeping Rahima wringing her hands and tearing her hair, there were no witnesses to be found. Nineteen-year-old Mokta's body lay twisted and charred in the middle of the yard. Parts of her yellow sari have melted into her flesh, the smell of her burnt hair lingers in the air. Someone has covered her face with a dirty sack.

No, no one had seen how Mokta was murdered by her mother-in-law and her husband. Mokta was cooking rice and daal, as usual, and must have fallen into the fire. That's how it must have happened, they said. And now Faruk is to be pitied, the poor husband who lost his beloved wife. Thankfully, there were no children, and no other belongings. The police officer takes notes. They will come for the body in the morning. The police are welcome to inform her parents, Faruk and Rahima are too distraught to do it themselves. Poor souls.

Inna lilahi wa inna ilayhi raji'un. We belong to God and shall return unto him.

3

It was taking Janne a while to get over the jetlag. Thankfully, a Norwegian family had issued a standing invitation for the children to come for play dates until school began in earnest. Sofia had arranged for the Norwegians' *ayah*, their nanny, to look after Noella and Teo as well, for a few hours every day, until they could hire their own.

So far, the days had been full of people coming and going, furniture being moved and rearranged and cables and plug sockets being installed and set up. No one had paid much attention to Janne, and he had wondered to himself if the Bengalis were being ironic when they insisted on calling him 'Boss'.

The real boss seemed to be Siv, the domineering woman in her fifties who strode around their house as though she owned it, ordering around reedy little men in loincloths and turbans. Shelves and air-conditioning units were put up, the children's beds had arrived, and every once in a while Sofia called from work to check on progress and ask how he was. Today she had decided they would have lunch at the Nordic Club, or 'the Nordic', as she called it. The cook, Hanif, grabbed him by the arm and put him in a rickshaw.

The rickshaw Hanif had hailed was of the bicycle variety, pedalled by a young man in a filthy shirt and a loincloth around his hips. Hanif gave him instructions in Bangla and Janne plunked himself down on the seat.

The rickshaw itself was spectacular with its bright colours and sparkling hood, quite unlike any vehicle Janne had ever seen before.

The seat, decorated with Bollywood motifs, would have fitted hand in glove in any hip Stockholm café, and the whole idea of a bicycle was at least environmentally friendly, Janne figured.

'But the Nordic Club,' he muttered as the rickshaw pulled out, 'so fucking colonial.'

The rickshaw raced through the streets and Janne begrudgingly felt his mood lifting. There was a world outside the air-conditioned house and, my god, what a world! Fifty feet from their house he discovered they were neighbours with a whole village, a slum with tiny sheds dominoed against other tiny sheds, where two women fought over a sack of twigs, where a few children were using a water-filled barrel to wash their laundry and where skinny goats picked their way through the jumble. A few yards on, the rickshaw passed high walls, behind which he could make out a white stone palace with enormous windows and crescent-shaped balconies. Next to the palace was a lower fence hiding a hacienda-like building embedded in verdant greenery. And then another waterlogged ditch, lined with ramshackle sheds, and after that another half-finished house where you could see twenty, no fifty, no a hundred emaciated, half-naked men in loincloths balancing on bamboo scaffolding, carrying baskets of building supplies on their heads.

Janne thought to himself that this must have been what it looked like when they built the pyramids. Bare hands and the power of thousands of backs and legs bending and bracing. No advanced equipment here. Human bodies and ropes and pulleys. When he let his eyes roam up the many open, bare floors of the half-finished buildings he saw to his surprise that people seemed to be living in them. There were naked children playing, people cooking and chickens scratching at the floors. Laundry hung from the rebars, stacked dishes were drying in the sun. And then the palaces again, a pink one, a yellow one and a white. Pools, grand driveways, marble pillars and fountains. The images flitting past were so unexpected and disjointed that Janne literally felt his chin drop and he sat in his rickshaw, open-mouthed.

People lived . . . there? And there?

So this was Baridhara, one of Dhaka's three diplomatic zones, where Sofia had said they would be spending most of their time. 'And it's more or less like back home' he even remembered her saying. 'Suburbia.'

Janne had been to The Gambia as a child, but as an adult he had never been very interested in travelling. There was enough injustice and misery to be found in Sweden, he had reasoned, and he had never felt an affinity with the group of colleagues who always wanted to get involved in international development and ran school twinning projects with Africa. He had spent most of his vacations on Gotland, every once in a while going as far as Cyprus, and had never given much thought to the fact that his points of reference were rather limited. It was not until he met Sofia that his eyes were opened to other things, that he understood how she moved through the world, around it and with it and for it, in a way he had never even imagined possible. To Sofia, capitals like Lusaka, Managua, Kabul and Phnom Penh were workplaces, characterised by growth rates, developmental indicators and the level of access to ministers. And they were populated by friends, or former colleagues, or former lovers, all of whom spent more time with Sofia than he did, he would sometimes think with a pang of jealousy. But that was all changing now. She would travel less, stay here, in Dhaka. Together with him and the children. A second chance.

With a few quick jerks the rickshaw crossed a violently chaotic intersection and sped towards a roundabout. Cars, dinky moped-like miniature cars and standard-sized jeeps were coming at them from every direction. Janne took a deep breath once more and wondered if he had lost his mind, sitting so unprotected in the middle of traffic. Without a helmet.

If I fall off now, I'll die, he thought and dug his fingers into the rickshaw's colourful seat.

'Careful, OK, careful,' he said and the driver bobbed his head.

'No problem, Boss, no problem. *Thik ache.*'

At the roundabout they ran into a sea of other cycle rickshaws, all ringing their bells and blithely going every which way. Stuck among them were three giant jeeps. One of them bore the familiar blue UN logo, another was marked as belonging to Save the Children. In the middle of all this were also a handful of mini-buses, jam-packed with passengers and with more people riding on the rooftops. Everyone was leaning on their horns and ringing their bells and shouting and no one could move an inch. Inside the jeeps, he could make out air-conditioned Westerners who, unperturbed by the bedlam, shuffled their papers and talked on their mobile phones.

Janne wanted to get off. This was not right. He might die. Why should he die like this? Besides, all the rickshaw drivers were ogling him and shouting things to his rickshaw guy. And what was up with this roundabout anyway? The whole point of a roundabout is that everyone moves in the same direction, this free-for-all was just demented.

'Nordic Club, Nordic Club, no problem, road fifty-five,' the rickshaw driver said cheerily, looking back to smile reassuringly at Janne. When he noticed Janne's apparent distress, he seized the opportunity to start a conversation.

'No problem, Boss. No problem. What is your country? First time in Bangladesh? Need some focky-focky? Some hashish? How many years are you?'

When Janne shook his head and told him to pedal and keep his eyes on the road, his driver laughed uproariously.

'Some problem? No problem. Paris, New York, Dhaka! Same, same!

When the worst of the commotion had died down and the cars at the roundabout had scrambled loose, the rickshaw lurched forward again, across a stream that threatened to flood the street, and onward towards a clutch of ramshackle high-rises. This area was more built up and signs and stands and shops fluttered at him.

Everything was so chaotic, so random and incoherent. Fragments next to fragments next to fragments, separate worlds with no intention of becoming one. This was a crude way of life, no frills, Janne thought. Everyone goes about their business. All the time. And then the vegetation, the almost suffocating, snakelike vegetation that embedded buildings and brokenness and joints, the lushness oddly evocative of holidays and luxury.

Suddenly the rickshaw pulled up short and the driver turned around.

'Nordic Club. Two hundred taka, Boss.'

Janne thought twenty kronor, sure, sounds reasonable, and then Sofia was suddenly by his side.

'Two hundred taka, I don't think so, no more than fifty taka, maybe actually just twenty. You were about to be had there.'

Janne looked at her while she handed the rickshaw guy a crumpled note. He pulled a box of Swedish snuff, *snus*, from his back pocket. He felt it was exactly what he needed.

'Two kronor. Two kronor to lug almost sixteen stones of Swede around for half an hour?'

Janne moulded his snus portion meticulously, noticing that the rickshaw guy was studying his hands. After a while, the guy pointed to the box of snus.

'*Paan*?'

Janne laughed and turned inquiringly to Sofia, who answered: 'Not paan, or maybe Swedish paan. He thinks it's some kind of betel, and I guess it is, in a way. Same function, I mean.'

'Well, whatever it is, I need it. And, hey, the water? There's water everywhere, almost at street level? Are we going to be flooded?'

'No more so than at the end of every monsoon. There's a reason all the cars have their exhaust pipe on the roof.' Sofia pointed to some jeeps that were parked outside the club wall. Indeeed, the exhaust pipes looked like little chimneys attached to their roofs. 'That's the thing about Bangladesh. Sooner or later there's always a flood.'

The Nordic Club was, thankfully, not a flashy place. Quite the opposite, actually, it was simply an old villa that had been converted. Janne noted a tennis court and a pool, well-kept and clean but not brand new. In the garden there was a thatched-roof restaurant and, over in a corner, a small playground and paddling pool. Perfect for Noella and Teo: little people, small world.

A familiar silhouette stepped out of the shadows under the thatched roof: Siv. Janne had seen how she treated the Bengalis who had helped with their move. He did not like her.

'So, Janne, you've finally braved the outside world. How did you like the sofa they delivered yesterday? Where are you going to put it? I was think—'

'Thanks, but the sofa was broken. I think you're going to have to take it back to the shop. We can't put it anywhere in that state. What's more, I would have preferred if we could have picked our own furniture. Isn't there a storage unit somewhere?'

Sofia tried to stop Janne's outburst and turned to placate Siv, since they had no choice but to place any number of decisions in her hands.

'The thing is, Siv, it's a bit collapsed, you know? And that will hardly be helped by the children no doubt jumping on it before long. Kids, you know,' Sofia ventured, smiling. 'But thank you for getting us beds for the children. Noella is crazy about hers. Right now there's just one problem, the A/C in Teo's room doesn't work. Could you ask Mr Hossein to have a look at it this afternoon?'

Siv took the bait and chose to be helpful and pleasant. She ignored Janne's comments and gushed at Sofia instead.

'You're a counsellor after all, Sweetie, of course you shouldn't have to put up with a local Bangla sofa. You can have one of the big, blue ones. An Ektorp, fresh from Ikea. I hid one from your predecessor in the storage unit. I wouldn't let him have it! But you take it!'

Sofia thanked her and Siv looked pleased and left. Janne watched her as she walked away. He had picked up on the way Siv had said 'Bangla sofa', dripping with contempt, but also had to acknowledge once again that Sofia was a master at dealing with troublemakers.

'Why should we be grateful to her? She acts as though she's giving us her own furniture and we should walk around expressing some kind of gratitude. It's her goddamn job, isn't it? Making sure things work? Or am I wrong? Don't we have any rights? Tell me, you work with human rights . . . '

'Calm down, Janne. She's going to sort it out now, isn't she?'

Sofia had noticed Janne's mood getting worse with each day he spent cooped up in the house. She hoped she had not misjudged him, that he was up for being here with her. Not all men could handle having no professional identity or network, and she knew she had not really given him a choice. She had pushed on, overruled him, gone where she wanted. She knew that. But he deserved to be in the doghouse for a while. His betrayal still stung, even though she was genuinely trying to leave the past in the past.

Since the meeting with Mike, her old boss from her UN days, a year ago in a hotel bar in Nairobi, the decision to go for an international job again had seemed increasingly natural. It had been just before the deadline for SwedeAid's Head of Development job postings. He had listened to her babble on about the kids and Janne and Stockholm and SwedeAid and then, in his American way, delivered a series of platitudes.

'That all sounds great, Sofia. But what about you? When are you going to take the next step and follow your dreams? You're a winner, you know you are, Sofia. You can make a difference, the world needs people like you. Take the ball and run with it, Sofia!'

Very American, to be sure. But also the push she needed to apply for one of the jobs, despite Janne's concerns. In the end, it had seemed fairly straightforward to her: either she stayed in Sweden, frustrated and unable to try her wings in the field and advance her career, with Janne a burnt-out head teacher surrounded by swooning female admirers. Or she could be in her element, in the right place, running with the right ball and the right job, with Janne as a potentially frustrated 'trailing spouse'. Potentially frustrated. Some spouses actually loved the life and saw it as their chance to try something new. That would mean that, in Dhaka, the odds were more in favour of them finding a way back to each other after everything that had happened. She had painted a picture of what their life would be like out there: housekeeping staff, including a nanny – an ayah – who could babysit whenever they wanted, their finances more secure, and of course regular holidays around exciting Asia.

Once the decision had been made, Janne had, at least outwardly, played his part flawlessly.

'It's Sofia's turn now, she's done a great job with Noella and Teo for so many years. I look forward to supporting her career, playing second fiddle for a while,' he had explained to their family and friends.

But even so, the fact that she – and her job – were now the centre of attention made him grumpy. But did he even see that connection?

Sofia watched Janne, the large, blond man who sat himself down across from her. The bohemian who had so unexpectedly fallen head over heels for her, and whose intensity and warmth had won her over. Just now, he was scratching at his three-day stubble, scrutinising the restaurant's child-friendly menu with a certain scruffy enthusiasm. His long hair fell across his face and he quickly tucked it behind his ears.

'Fish fingers, pizza, shit, they even have *falukorv*, my god, Noella won't notice she's in Bangladesh! Is there nothing Asian here . . . let's see . . .'

Those sweeping gestures and his unguarded facial expressions, so different from the stiff correctness of her colleagues. That wide-open, throbbing heart that always wanted to be loved and was so poor at protecting itself from disappointment. The life in him, the love that spilled out in every direction and was not always overly discerning. The warmth everyone could sense and that people wanted to get close to. Too many people.

Right now he was slightly agitated and overenthusiastic, Sofia noted. Before long, he would become angry at something. A smile played on Sofia's lips while she waited.

'Damn it, Sofia, there's no Bengali food here at all! Is this some bloody reservation? Remoulade, Danish, *fiskekaker*, Norwegian, *pytt-i-*

panna, Swedish. Look! I thought we were supposed to be in Bangladesh, right? Right? Is there like no contact with the outside world here, or what?'

Sofia had actually brought along a To-Do list of everything they needed to discuss today, but for the moment she decided to leave it folded in her pocket.

'We'll have Asian food at home instead. I've been told Hanif is one of the best chefs in Dhaka. Hey, what do you think about meeting with some of the ayahs by yourself? And we need a driver. And do you want me to go curtain shopping with you?

But Janne was in no mood to discuss to-do lists.

'Brief me. So H&M are here? Indiska? Swedish Save the Children? I spotted an Ericsson logo?'

'No, not Indiska, they're just in India. But Lindex, Kappahl, Ikea, Hemtex, I think. And in telecoms there's Ericsson and Norwegian Telenor, which is part-owner of Grameen Phone, which is a new branch of Grameen Bank, which netted Dr Yunus his Nobel Prize. Microcredit somehow morphed into mobile phone networks, don't ask me how.'

Their food arrived and Sofia felt Janne's questions unleash a wave of stress about all the things she had to get to grips with in her new role. She tried to summarise:

'Anyway, it's a big and growing economy, a growth rate of six, seven per cent. So many companies are here, and more are arriving all the time. Bangladesh is known as Asia's Boomtown. There's no cheaper labour anywhere. It costs three times as much to produce a T-shirt in China, for instance.

Janne nodded, and added: ' . . . and so they pay people fuck all, but they get the growth rate up and turn all Bengalis into happy-go-lucky consumers of mobile phones and plastic crap and eventually cars that ruin the environment. Unregulated, laissez-faire capitalism and exploitation of human beings and the environment.' Janne was now waving his glass around. 'The flipside of growth, the place where the market finally triumphs over reason, is that how I should think of Bangladesh? I read an article in *The Economist* –'

'Hold on a minute,' Sofia felt a need to add nuance to Janne's rant, 'flipside, I'm not sure –'

Their discussion was interrupted by a large man who had sauntered over to their table from the tennis court to introduce himself.

'Bjarne Jensen, more commonly known as Papa Bjarne here at the club. I don't think we've met?' He extended a hairy arm and shook their hands whilst studying them curiously. 'I guess you must be the new embassy Swedes, eh?'

Sofia and Janne nodded. Sofia glanced at her watch, stressed because she wanted to use this time to go over things properly with Janne. And they still hadn't ordered lunch. But the big Dane was impervious to rejection. He pulled up a chair and sat down at their table. He wiped sweat from his brow with a towel a young Bangladeshi boy then unobtrusively removed from their sight.

'So, new, huh? You know what they say? "You cry when you come to Dhaka, and you cry when you have to leave." ' He laughed heartily and continued, 'Thank god I didn't know about the second part. We just haven't really got around to going back home, the wife and I. But I don't mind telling you that I've stopped crying, long time ago. Life here in Dhaka is really, really sweet, actually. The wife and I own a garment factory, and we've lived here for eight years. So there's no reason to cry, none at all. I run the factory, and she runs around on the tennis court. So basically, we've divided the chores fairly.'

He let out another raucous laugh, nodded toward the tennis courts and then turned to Janne and shoved a conspiratorial elbow in his side.

'Sometimes she has a few rounds of manicure and pedicure as well, so she keeps herself busy. And sometimes she fills in for the aerobics instructors. As I always say: It's never over in a Land Rover.'

Sofia was relieved to see Janne declining the opportunity to do some male bonding. Instead he said: 'Right, I see. Someone told me there were three Ms in Dhaka, as far as Westerners go – misfits, missionaries and money-makers. I guess you're a money-maker.'

Bjarne let out another laugh, loud and appreciative.

'Misfits! That's so fucking spot on! It's brilliant, money-makers, missionaries and, what was the last one? I'm definitely using that! And I certainly hope I'm a money-maker rather than a misfit! And you, well, you must be a missionary, working with international development, I guess that's pretty much the same thing,' he said, nodding to Sofia and then looking directly at Janne: 'And that makes you the misfit!'

He gave Janne a friendly nudge and laughed uproariously. Janne and Sofia exchanged glances across the table and when the Dane's laughter had died down, Janne tried again.

'I'm sorry, but a garment factory? We were just talking about that. Do you work for Swedish and Danish companies? H&M?'

'Hardly, no thanks! We don't work for such . . . shall we say . . . particular buyers. Only the really big factories out in Ashulia and Savar can handle the giant orders H&M and Kappahl place. We work on a smaller scale, taking orders from China and the Middle East, focusing less on finesse and more on quantity. Big volumes, no frills. I have four hundred girls in my factory, just here in Gulshan. And we're thinking of hiring a thousand more out in Naragonj. All thanks to Danish aid money!'

He turned to Sofia, got up and and bowed theatrically.

'I tip my cap to the upstanding international development lot, your colleagues on the Danish side. Some peppy little case worker at the Danish embassy figured we Danes should invest in the private sector and, well, we had to go while the going was good and, hey, presto,' he snapped his fingers in the air, 'a factory for Bjarne!'

Sofia didn't know what to say. With his reddish body hair and in his half-naked state, Bjarne looked like a big, ginger cat that had suddenly taken over their lunch. He dominated with the effortlessness of an alpha male. Sofia was fascinated. Were there really people like him in real life?

Now he was laughing again, leaning in toward Janne, rubbing his fingertips together.

'Seriously. It's really big money, my friend. Big profits. You know there's a Bangladeshi gold rush going on, don't you? No reason to go back home, no reason at all. You should get into business, too, if your wife insists on working.'

He leaned back in his chair and studied Janne for a moment, but then he changed his tone.

'Did you say your name's Janne? Do you play tennis?'

'Tennis? I did play a bit when I was younger, but –'

'Excellent, then it's settled. We need another player for the men's B-team on Saturday. It's just for laughs. Do you have a racket? If you don't, I'll see to everything, just be here by ten and make sure you have proper footwear! And hey, there's no excuse not to play tennis if you know how – we need all the good men we can get. There's really nothing else to do for fun around here!'

One of the young girls Sofia had seen by the pool was approaching their table. Her hair was dyed jet black and she had a silver ring in her nose. She went straight for Bjarne.

'Hi there, Papa Bjarne, the money for Stig's fiftieth birthday party, you're the only ones who haven't paid. One thousand taka, please!' Then she turned to Janne and Sofia. 'Hi, are you the Paulins? Are you the new Head of Development?' She looked at Sofia and extended her hand. Her fingers were adorned with black nail polish and several silver rings. 'My name's Charlotta, I volunteer for a charity here, Alor Desh. I've been looking forward to talking to you.'

'Charlotta is one of those good people, you see,' Bjarne broke in and put a friendly arm around her. 'She gives her money to the poor and prefers to live in a mud hut. Check out the halo. Did you shine it today?'

Charlotta retorted without missing a beat.

'It's lucky someone thinks about someone other than themselves, Bjarne. You can't even spell solidarity or dignity. Or minimum wage for that matter.'

Bjarne laughed delightedly at her comment, and then turned to Janne.

'One of our boys is the same way. He graduated from the American School a couple of years ago, and now he works as a nurse for Medecins sans Frontiers in Sudan. As a parent you have to ask yourself where you went wrong.' He laughed loudly, shook his head and gave Charlotta a fatherly pat on the back. 'But, seriously, Charlotta, you know I think the world of the work you do, you young people. Someone has to make this world a better place, right?'

Charlotta and Bjarne continued their verbal sparring until someone called Bjarne back to the tennis court. Charlotta lingered, studying Sofia intently.

'So how are you liking Dhaka?' She directed the question to both of them.

'To be honest, I've no idea,' Janne answered truthfully. 'So far I've only seen the real Bangladesh for about ten minutes from my rickshaw. Does that count?'

'My knowledge of Bangladesh is mainly theoretical', Sofia admitted. 'I haven't had time to –'

Charlotta interrupted her.

'Sofia, I don't want to come on too strong, but god, you've landed a dream job. At least my dream job. With your resources! I've really been looking forward to you coming and sorting things out at the embassy. You know what's happening with Alor Desh, right? Khadija Anam, you know? You have to come out into the field with us before you make any insane decisions. Promise you will!'

'I'd be happy to meet with you for a briefing soon. I just need a chance to get my bearings first. Really. Give me a week or two.'

Sofia was interested in hearing more about the legendary Alor Desh, one of the many NGOs, Non-Governmental Organisations, active in Bangladesh. They were the grassroots organisations that took a bottom-up approach to development. But right now, she sensed Charlotta's enthusiasm risked hijacking her whole lunch break. She really needed to have a chat with Janne about a few practical things.

Charlotta took the hint.

'Sure, I'll ask my boss Khadija to get in touch.' She turned to Janne. 'You're both welcome to come have a look at the villages once you're sick of hanging out by the pool. Bring the kids! It usually takes about a month to outgrow this bubble. Give me a call when it happens!'

Sofia breathed a sigh of relief when Charlotta left, but her extremely undisguised expectations made her feel even more stressed than before.

They quickly ordered food, and then she launched into it:

'OK. Janne. I've made a list. A To-Do list.' She pulled the note out, unfolded it and smoothed it down against the tabletop. The first order of business a matter of urgency.

'You have to ask our security guards to stop spitting.' Sofia had noticed the guards leaving big puddles of saliva in their driveway. Since Janne was now in charge of the household, she thought it was reasonable to expect him to deal with this issue, as a priority.

'I'm sorry?' Janne looked at her quizzically.

'We have three guards, Janne, and they spit all day long. The children might pick up some disease. It's disgusting.'

'What are you talking about, disease? Come on, Sofia, that's where I draw the line. Are we supposed to just waltz into their lives and tell them to –'

'To stop spitting. That's right. They could have TB or some strange flu strain. Teo and Noella will be playing in the garden where they've been spitting. You're going to have to bring it up with them.' Sofia looked at Janne and realised he needed more convincing. 'It feels like a man thing, you know. The women don't spit. And you're supposed to take care of things around the house. They're spitting around the house.'

'"A man thing?"' Janne pulled a face. 'What else do you want me to ask them to do? Wash their hands when they've been to the bathroom?

Isn't this compromising their integrity? God, Sofia. I don't know. It makes me feel really weird. You're the diplomat, and the concerned mother. Can't you?'

They sat in silence for a few minutes until their food arrived. Sofia sighed. She would have to deal with this herself. After they began eating, she read aloud from her list, he wasn't going to get out of the rest of the chores.

'Fine, never mind the spitting then, but you'll see what I mean. Maybe we could ask Mr Hossein to have a talk with them. But the rest . . . ' She counted off the points on her fingers. 'Ayah, driver, jeep, gardener, day care, drinking water, furniture, school fees, alcohol licence, curtains, field clothes, weekly menus for the cook.'

She smoothed the paper down again and put it in front of Janne. There. It was his turn to deal with all things domestic. They had to pull together if they were to have any chance of making a good life for themselves in this land of floods and crowds.

*

The clicking of the ceiling fan stopped, the blades that had been slicing the air into cool ribbons slowed. At the same time, the computer died. Khadija Anam cursed loudly. A lizard bolted across the ceiling. The electricity always gave out when she needed it most. Internet banking was convenient, but the whole idea was contingent on access to electricity, and the Internet. But then, pretty much the whole world had access to those things, apart from the idiots who insisted on living their lives beyond the reach of civilisation, she grumbled to herself. Now her son in London would have to wait a few more days for money, and this would confirm his opinion that she was wasting her life in a hopeless bog among the dregs of this world.

She heaved an exasperated sigh and supressed an impulse to light a cigarette. Maybe she could sneak in a few puffs on her way to the meeting? The villagers must not see her smoke. In the village, only *maagi*, whores and fallen women, smoked. If they knew she sometimes had a glass of wine with dinner they would probably stone her.

Her little office was dark and cool, furnished simply with a table that doubled as a desk, three chairs and in one corner a threadbare sofa she had shipped over when her headquarters were first built on the island. Her Right Livelihood Award diploma, 'awarded to PhD Khadija Anam for her innovative and pioneering efforts to empower some of the world's poorest people', hung on the whitewashed wall. She had been so proud that day, and it had opened so many doors. The diploma had protected her. Until now?

Suddenly Siraj appeared in the doorway.

'Are you ready?'

She nodded and slipped a packet of cigarettes into her purse. With the help of a small hand-held mirror, she made sure her bindi was centred. She couldn't do anything about the burns on her face, people got used to them after a while. She adjusted her sari and made ready to leave. The last thing she did was unlock her desk drawer and pull out a thick envelope.

'I'm ready. Are you? How many women made it out? How many *dais*?' he said, referring to the traditional midwives.

'Six women and five dais, two women are using the same dai. They're due any day. They'll be OK. The day before yesterday ten women went in from Barikhali district. We really ought to be negotiating with more clinics, Khadija.'

'Not right now. The audit, you know. I've no idea what's going to happen.'

Siraj nodded and together they set out on the short walk down to the riverbank, where a rowboat was waiting for them. The boat would take them to the nearest village, where they were due to have their monthly meeting with the District Chairman. The Chairman, Mr Basum, embodied the civil service in the char area of Lalpara, where Alor Desh worked. The char areas were more or less temporary islands that alternately emerged and disappeared in the mighty flow of Bangladesh's rivers. These fertile but unpredictable landmasses provided temporary havens for the poorest in a country under constant threat of flooding.

Mr Basum belonged to the local elite. He lived off tightening or loosening threads in the social web his family had spent generations weaving, through a combination of clever marriages, job offers, bribes and threats. Farmers in the area often joked that no rice grew in Barikhaldi district without the Basums' say-so.

Likewise, Alor Desh would be utterly unable to operate without the consent of the local elite, so Khadija always felt ill at ease before her meetings with Mr Basum. Being a woman, moreover, meant she was barely taken seriously and had to be accompanied by her Head of Programmes, Siraj.

Khadija gathered up her sari and stepped into the boat. She opened a big, black umbrella to shield herself from the sun and offered the shaded seat next to her to Siraj. A young man wearing a *lungi*, the traditional loincloth, piloted the boat with his single oar.

The idea behind the pregnancy boats had been Siraj's and he remained enthusiastic about it. Every week, boats went around the villages, picking up women who were about to go into labour or who were experiencing complications in connection with their pregnancies. The char women were terrified of going to the clinic on their own when their time came. They preferred giving birth at home with their dai, a traditional midwife, by their side and their female relatives in attendance. If they lost their lives, it was the will of Allah. In Bangladesh, hundreds of thousands of children had lost their mothers for no good reason, as Khadija was well aware. Mothers died from simple infections that could have been cured with a round of penicillin, if only they had been diagnosed in time.

When Alor Desh, on Siraj's initiative, began paying the dais directly to accompany the women to the clinic, resistance to the clinics had decreased among both dais and the women. Everyone had benefitted: the women, who survived; the men, who were not widowed; the infants; their siblings; the dais, who received recognition; the honest doctors, who were given a chance to help their patients. The World Health Organisation, also benefitted, struggle as they did to reach the Sustainable Development Goals. Sweden benefitted, too, as did the Netherlands and the UK, who could point to returns on tax money invested. And of course, Alor Desh, which had brought about the change. The only ones who might be losing out were the crooked doctors who performed caesarean sections on perfectly healthy women, for a fee of six thousand takas. And the mullahs, the clerics. Could it be irking them? To see the women leave the home? And how much exactly did it irk them? Khadija found that difficult to judge. There were progressive mullahs and reactionary mullahs, mosques that pulled in the same direction as Alor Desh and mosques that felt threatened. A good rule of thumb was that the more money they received from the Middle East, the more reactionary they tended to be. And all this talk about a new caliphate? It had been brought back by returning guest workers.

An hour later Siraj and Khadija were seated in a bare room, on the floor above the District Authority offices. The electricity had gone here, too, but the man sitting across from them seemed unperturbed by the heat. His face was covered in a sheen of sweat, the oiliness smudging the thick lenses of his glasses. The frames were big and square, seventies-style, and he was absentmindedly chewing his long, white beard while he counted the money. A calendar depicting Mecca was hanging askew on the wall behind him. It was from October 1998. Khadija studied him with revulsion. He was practically drooling on the notes.

'We have over forty outstanding cases,' Siraj said. 'Mr Chairman, if you would be so kind as to make sure the court –'

'This is not all of it. The transaction fee is missing. And the stamp duty. And you promised alms for the mosque. I think you're getting stingier all the time.'

The man smiled, revealing teeth blackened by a lifetime of betel chewing.

'That should be enough,' Siraj replied curtly. 'As I said, forty outstanding cases in this district alone. The farmers need to have their lands registered in their names. Immediately, preferably before the autumn harvest. Both the man and the woman. It can only be done with a court judgment. We also have –'

'Oh, my. The court is so busy,' the man broke in and started complaining. 'We have our hands full in this district. We have visitors constantly.' With a studied air, he started playing with a pen, then pulled a lever on his chair, angling it back slightly. The money was still on the table.

Khadija and Siraj waited silently.

'As I've said, many rich and important visitors. Visitors who also pay good money for the court to look at their cases. Very good money. In fact . . . ' he leaned forward, once more looking and pawing at the pile of notes, 'in fact, they pay ten times more. And the imam approves of them.'

'I beg your pardon?' Siraj retorted. 'What are you implying? Alor Desh meets with the imams on a regular basis.'

The man smiled again. Then he started rocking back and forth, complaining.

'So much to do. Who has time for it all? When the rice is so expensive? When the schools are so expensive? I can't push the courts any more than I already do. So many people want the land, you know this. So many. And there will be more. Oh, my. If you only knew . . . ' he trailed off.

'Our landless farmers have been waiting for six months. We have come to you every month,' Siraj replied.

Khadija was becoming aggravated now, too, and added: 'Your brother is the magistrate. That's why we're here, let's not pretend otherwise. Your brother's a magistrate, your cousin's the Chief of Police and your children work in the district administration. Everywhere, everywhere the Basums.'

The man peered at her and chuckled. He discovered his beard had got stuck in his mouth and slowly pulled it out. He was in no hurry.

'You don't say?'

'What's changed? What's happening?' Khadija wanted to know. 'The stamp duty we pay has always been enough. You know the farmers have a right to that land. Why these delays?'

'Right and right,' the man's face darkened and he swept the money into a desk drawer. 'Many people are hungry. And many wonder how the Alor Desh farmers always manage to fill their stomachs. We have had visits from . . . ' he opened a drawer and pulled out a grimy jumble of cards, bits of rope, elastics, broken pencils. He peered at the array on the table and then abruptly singled out one of the business cards and held it up to them. 'This man. And his friends. What do you think I should tell them when they come back?'

Siraj took the card and showed Khadija: Ernst & Young Auditing, Kolkata.

'They ask questions, of course. How do you think we should answer them? I barely make enough to pay my employees in the district. The rice has become so expensive, hasn't it?'

Siraj and Khadija made no reply. Afterwards, they discussed what they could have done differently, but every imaginable course of action would have turned out wrong. To sit quietly was as good a strategy as any. In the end, Mr Basum had both rocked and spun in his chair and then wiped his glasses, all the while thinking out loud.

'Did I mention the mullahs in the new mosque in Barikhali? Twenty cases and more coming? Was that what you said? Such a shame there's not enough money, such a shame. The rice is so expensive, the schools are so expensive. Inshallah, we'll see how it goes. It's not in my hands, it's in Allah's hands.'

After the meeting, Khadija slipped out onto a narrow terrace at the back of the house and pulled Siraj with her. She hurriedly got a cigarette out. Her hand trembled as she lit it.

'What's happening?'

*

Nazreen reached the village before sunrise, before the first prayer rang out from the mosque. She had to see Mokta one last time, had to know it had really happened. She had arranged to meet Nilufar, Faruk's sister, on a path outside the village. Nilafur would take her to her sister, and after she had seen things for herself, she intended to leave quickly, escape plans were already hatching in her head. There was no time to lose.

Nilufar emerged from the shadows behind a tree when she spotted Nazreen.

'Nazreen,' she said. 'I'm so sorry. I've prayed for her soul all night. You must pray, too. Pray to Allah that he has mercy on her soul. *Inna lillahi we inna ilayhi raji'un, Allah mohan.*'

Nazreen responded by murmuring the same prayer, as a sign of respect for the dead. 'We belong to God and shall return unto him. Allah is the greatest.' She closed her eyes for a second before turning to Nilufar. She had no great desire to comfort Nilufar, who was part of the family that had tormented and killed her sister. But for the moment, she needed her.

'Where's Mokta?'

'In the shed, over there, she's under a sack and they're coming for her soon. Are you really going to go in there? She –'

'Do you think Faruk's going to morning prayers?

'No, that lazy man never goes to the mosque. No, no one will be up for another hour. Come! If you really want to see her?'

The scene that greeted Nazreen was horrifying. She backed out, stumbled away from the shed and threw up against a wall. There could be no question that the corpse was her adored older sister. Even if her body was transformed and charred, it was definitely Mokta lying there. Her beautiful, pale-skinned sister.

Nazreen's felt herself tremble, a shiver ran through her, and she rounded on Nilufar.

'Why didn't you save her? Why didn't you pour water on her? Why didn't you stop them? What kind of people are you? This is murder, everyone will know it. Mokta was so unhappy. And your family needs another dowry! For your dowry, Nilufar, so someone will take you! This is your fault! Everyone will know.'

Nilufar carried on whimpering and tearing her hair, making no attempt to defend herself.

'We're just wretched women, Nazreen, don't you understand? None of us can go against our brothers, our mothers! Especially not against Rahima. She's said it's the will of Allah! Otherwise he would have stopped it, right? Your sister's time was up, inshallah. She may be happier where she is now, inshallah. I don't know how to –'

'You,' Nazreen hissed, 'this isn't about you. Mokta is dead and your mother murdered her.'

Nilufar let out a drawn out moan. She dug at a crease in her sari. 'You hate me, I understand, I understand. But I'm just a wretched woman, too. Nazreen, you can hate me, but take this.' She thrust a small plastic box into her hand. 'It's for you. Take it, just take it. It doesn't belong to us. There's blood on the money, I don't want it!' Then she ran off, crying.

Nazreen lingered for a moment, then turned and ran in the opposite direction. From the mosque came the sounds of the first prayer of the day, the ancient lament lonelier and more desolate than ever.

Nazreen followed the river towards her own village, running with the plastic box pressed against her chest. Seeing Mokta's body stiff and twisted, nothing but the empty, blackened husk of someone she had loved, had been so brutal the shock of it made her insides churn and her legs buckle, again and again. In the end, she collapsed in a small bamboo grove just behind the house where her parents were still sound asleep. Her breath came in shuddering gasps and she had to forcibly supress an impulse to vomit again. She had to stop thinking, stop seeing what she had just witnessed. Mokta was gone, dead, that was enough. Questions about how and if she had suffered were more than she could bear.

'Just be with me, Mokta, I have to live our dream without you,' she mumbled and slowly opened the box Nilufar had given her.

The box was full of creased, dirty notes: five-taka notes, twenty-taka notes and a few hundred-taka notes. She had never held this much money in her hands before. It must be Nilufar's dowry, which probably contained money from Mokta's dowry. Why else would anyone keep this much cash in a plastic box?

As she smoothed down the notes, one by one, and twenty was added to fifty, to a hundred and a thousand, a possible future began to take shape in Nazreen's mind. They would not have to beg or steal or lie to afford bus tickets to Dhaka.

When she picked up the last note, Nazreen discovered a bright-green hairband at the bottom of the box. She recognised it instantly. It had belonged to Mokta. Nazreen suddenly remembered that Mokta had said the colour reminded her of the first spring mangoes. The idea that there were always new mangoes, regardless of how difficult the year had been, had given her the strength to go on living with Faruk.

Nazreen slowly pulled the green hairband onto her wrist and realised she had to make her choice quickly.

She had wanted to run away from her family and the village for a long time, she did not feel as if she belonged there. She was seventeen and still unwed, but since her family was unable to scrape together a good dowry, her marriage arrangements had been postponed. Her father and uncles had made no effort to hide the fact that it was a matter of finding anyone – anyone at all – to take her. Her parents wanted to be rid of the duty of protecting her virtue and supporting her financially. And then the same thing would happen with Meena.

Nazreen hated the humiliation of people thinking she walked around waiting to be married off to some stranger. When she was younger, before the river had taken their land, several highly regarded families with sons of an appropriate age had expressed interest in her. And she had thought and fantasised about various second cousins and neighbour boys. She knew her family enjoyed considerable status and her skin was quite pale, if not as pale as Mokta's. Her mother had been a teacher before their little brother was born and with nine years of schooling Nazreen was well-educated. And, most important perhaps, she was pliant, calm, and obedient. If her family could have afforded a proper dowry, she would have had many suitors. She knew her worth.

Sometimes she thought about the lady from the organisation called BRAC. She had come to the school once to speak to the girls. She had claimed dowries were illegal and that the most important thing for them as girls – in fact, she had used the word *nari*, women, which had felt significant and special – was to make their own money and decide how that money was to be used. The whole thing had sounded peculiar. She couldn't imagine it ever working in the village. Yet, still, it had changed the way she looked at things. Sometimes she thought she caught glimpses of that other world, like on the television set they watched at the market in Rajigonj. It sometimes showed girls who seemed different. They probably made their own money.

Some of them looked just like Mokta, pale-skinned, elegant and beautiful. Over the past year, she had started thinking they should be those kinds of girl, she and Mokta and later Meena, too. Not the kind of girls who stayed in the village and married for a paltry dowry, a dowry their parents couldn't afford. She had whispered and giggled with Mokta about bundling up their things and taking off. Getting away from Nasty Ali who smelled, and who was widely known to have beaten his previous wife so badly she had lost a baby and moved back to her parents. Now he was looking for a new wife. Most parents of girls Nazreen's age had already found suitable husbands for their daughters, or could afford to reject Ali. But lately Ali had been spending many evenings with Nazreen's father, and Nazreen feared the worst. All the girls in the village knew what was happening. Nazreen felt like they were whispering and eyeing her with pity.

And now that Mokta was dead, Nazreen instinctively sensed that her death boded ill for her. As soon as the news reached her parents, which it would within the next few hours, her marriage to Nasty Ali would draw nearer. She knew it. It had to do with things Nazreen only half-understood, things that were not spoken of. A sense of balance and security for the family. She knew the noose had suddenly tightened. Her father would need to palm Nazreen off on someone else after the shock and failure of Mokta. It had to do with honour and respect. Through her marriage, Nazreen would replenish the family's stock of cash and goodwill among neighbours and acquaintances, depleted by the shame of losing Mokta. And so Ali would be there, ready to marry Nazreen and save the family's good name on the cheap.

Nazreen felt a fluttering of panic in the pit of her stomach and put the money back in the plastic box. She had to leave. Now. She quickly got to her feet in the early morning coolness of the bamboo stand. Determined, she flipped her blue sari back over her shoulder and hurried towards the family home.

Everyone seemed to be asleep. One of their chickens was scratching around the neatly swept yard and a stray dog, which had got it into its head that it lived with them, barked feebly until it realised who she was. She had maybe ten minutes to find everything she needed and pack it. Then she would wake Meena and tell her to come with her to school, but instead she would take her sister along with her, straight to the bus.

She methodically collected four *shalwar kameez*, long shirts with matching trousers and scarf – two sets each – her neem oil, talcum powder, a bar of soap, a comb and a handful of hair clips. That was all she owned and all she needed. Babul's address and phone number were written on a note in the tin box by the front door. She knew that because she had been the one who had jotted them down a few years ago. Some papers from school? Her eighth grade certificate? And that text about Bengal tigers she had written in English? All important documents were in the tin box. Quietly and resolutely she pulled out the ones pertaining to herself, and to Meena.

She could hear her father whimpering in his sleep in the other room and realised she had to light the fire, else it would seem strange that she was rummaging around like this. How was she going to let them know why she and Meena had disappeared? Maybe . . . Mahmoda . . . Hope suddenly surged through Nazreen. Of course, how could she have forgotten about Mahmoda? Her great aunt who was semi-shunned by the family, but who at this juncture could help Nazreen and Meena.She lived on the very corner where the bus to Dhaka stopped. If they could speak to her, Mahmoda would be able to explain things to her parents.

It was time to wake Meena.

'Little sister, Meena-shona', Nazreen said, gently shaking her thirteen-year-old sister, who was sleeping in the same bed as their mother.

'Quiet, come with me!'

'What?!' Meena sat up in bed and was about to object to being woken up when she noticed Nazreen's stony expression.

'Put on your uniform and come with me. But quietly.'

When Meena had dressed in her school clothes, and gathered her things, the girls tiptoed out of the house. Meena, still bleary-eyed, blinked in the early-morning light.

'Come on, we have to hurry,' Nazreen said. 'I'll explain later.' Then she took Meena by the hand and led her away from the house. The girls ran for a good long while, out of the village and up onto the main road, where they managed to persuade an early rising rickshaw driver to give them a lift all the way to Rajigonj. Since the rickshaw driver would be able to overhear, Nazreen did not tell Meena what had happened, just yet. She just asked her to be quiet, and trust her.

The little town of Rajigonj was waking up as they arrived. Several men were rushing from the mosque after morning prayers and women carrying bundles of kindling and wood for breakfast fires were trudging alongside the road. Nazreen pulled her sister in behind the bus stop, where they found a rickety bench to sit on.

'It's like this, Meena,' Nazreen began, taking a deep breath. 'Mokta's dead.'

Meena stiffened, grabbed Nazreen's shoulders and shook her. Her voice rose to a falsetto, her pupils dilated, her eyes wide with alarm.

'That's not true, Nazreen, that can't be true. Who told you?'

'I saw her, Meena.Early this morning. Nilufar rang me. I've seen her body. It's true.' Nazreen held out her wrist, showing Meena the hair-band. Meena recoiled.

'How?'

'She was burned to death, Meena.' Nazreen almost choked on the words. She could only whisper them, then looked away, tears welling. 'They set fire to her. Her sari . . . '

Meena cried out and kept shaking her.

'Tell me you're lying! You're lying!'

Nazreen started crying. Meena kept shaking her, while a sound as from a wounded animal erupted from her throat, and tears streamed down her face.

'I'm not lying. She's dead. Mokta's dead. It's just you and me now.'

Nazreen wrapped her arms around her sister and squeezed her tight. They clung to each other, as if to keep themselves from drowning. Eventually Nazreen tried to talk to Meena.

'Meena-jaan.'

She tried to lift Meena's head up, but the girl just pressed her open mouth against her shoulder even harder, as though screaming soundlessly. Tears and snot and saliva soaked Nazreen's shalwar while she soothingly rocked her little sister.

'There now, calm down, Meena, calm down, and let me tell you something. I have a plan. We have to leave, listen.'

Nazreen knew her sister so, so well. The three sisters had grown up like a trefoil leaf, always connected at the root and always with Mokta in the middle. Watching their beautiful, wise Mokta being broken and turned into a cowering shadow of her former self had frightened and confused both Nazreen and Meena.It had not really been possible for them to judge the severity of Mokta's situation, but while Mokta's death was a shock, it was not a complete surprise.

'Meena-jaan. We have to stay strong now. For Mokta. Everything has changed . . . I don't know, Meena, but I feel like we're the only ones who can decide how . . . it will be. With our lives, I mean. Amma, Abba, no one cares about . . . us. Sure, they love us, but they loved Mokta, too, after all. All the old stuff, Meena, it's not right. The mosque, dowries, Ali . . . we don't have to. Girls don't have to . . .

Nazreen sobbed and searched for the right words, the ones that could find their way deep into her solemn little sister, and make her feel the same kind of conviction she herself felt.

'Mokta and I talked about running away. You don't have to . . . always obey. Meena, we're the ones who own our lives, we can't live them for someone else. Do you see what I mean?'

She knew how emotional Meena was, but also that she could turn her feelings off when she needed to. There was an irrepressible strength in Meena, a will of iron. Of the three of them, Meena was actually the best at rising above things and spotting patterns no one else had noticed. While people in the village were distracted by their everyday lives, Meena was observant, putting two and two together in an almost eerie way, predicting the course of events. She somehow knew, when no one else suspected, that Faruk and his family were violent. She had warned the family about the marriage. She had been the one to arrange for medicine for their little brother to be brought from Dhaka. Nazreen needed to reach that part of Meena now.

'Meena.Look.'

She glanced around quickly to make sure no unwelcome eyes would see the contents of the plastic box and then opened it. Meena inhaled sharply and wiped away her tears.

'It's four thousand eight hundred taka. We can go to Dhaka today, now. Because if we don't . . . '

' . . . one of us has to marry Ali,' Meena quickly finished her sentence.

Nazreen nodded. Clever little Meena had figured it out. They were both pawns in a game of honour now. One of them would have to marry Ali, unless they could find a life for themselves elsewhere.

'But Amma and Abba . . . '

'I know, Meena, I know . . . We're going to see Aunt Mahmoda.

We'll tell her we're setting off to earn our own dowries, and that we'll be back. We'll tell her we'll come back for Eid next year, whatever happens. That way Amma and Abba won't feel as if they've lost us. What do you think? What do you say?'

Meena went quiet, weighing the options in her head. Nazreen sensed she needed to give her little sister a push in the right direction.

'Amma and Abba are a bit old-fashioned, sort of. Lots of girls have to earn their own dowries these days, why not us? Our family can't afford, well . . . obeying Allah. You know? And I have Babul's address here. If we take the bus to Dhaka now, we can be there by tonight.'

Meena started crying again.

'Nazreen, will I never see Mokta again?'

'Little sister, believe me, you don't want to see Mokta again. She didn't look . . . '

Nazreen felt the back of her throat contract in a violent gag reflex. 'She didn't look like our Mokta-jaan. We'll do Namaz for her tonight, in Dhaka. We will pray for her soul.' She raised her palms to her face in a soft gesture, and quiety recited '*inna lillahi we inna ilayhi raji'un, Allah mohan*'. We belong to God and shall return unto him. Allah is the greatest.

4

The man standing in front of Janne was thin, short and dressed in a white shirt with a collar that was much too wide for his neck. Under his hairy nose sprouted a thin, neatly trimmed moustache. His hair was meticulously combed and parted, and he was doused in cologne faintly reminiscent of the pomade Janne's great-grandfather had used. A smell from a different era. According to his crumpled papers, it appeared that he had worked as a lorry driver for Exxon for five years, and afterwards as a chauffeur for both the Canadian ambassador and the head of Oxfam; he had excellent references.

'So you know your way around Dhaka?' Janne asked rhetorically, mostly to have something to say.

'Yes, Boss.'

'Feel free to call me Janne. I'm Janne.'

'Yes, Boss.'

Janne glanced up to see if the man was smiling. He wasn't.

'Have you ever been involved in an accident?'

'No, Boss.'

'Do you like children?'

'Yes, Boss.'

Janne sighed, uncomfortable with the whole situation. So far that morning, he had interviewed five potential drivers, and there were more waiting outside the gate if required. Five was enough for now, at least two of them had seemed nice and decent. He took out their CVs and went over his notes. He was going to do this right.

Suddenly he jumped. Two of the drivers had worked for Exxon. At the same time. He scrutinised the certificates. Yes, and with the same certificate. A closer look revealed that another driver had the exact same certificate as the man who had worked for the UN. They hadn't even changed the date of birth.

Janne flung himself back on the blue Ikea sofa and called out for Hanif, their cook.

'Hanif, look at this! Huh? All these references and certificates floating round? They just copy them! How cheeky is that?'

Hanif, who had become something of a guide to everyday life in Dhaka to Janne, laughed at him.

'Boss, no problem. This is Bangladesh, they can probably all drive your car just fine. Only one in ten drivers has a real licence, the rest just buy theirs at the market.'

Janne looked at the pile of creased CVs, as if for answers. He did not feel right about choosing a driver who used counterfeit documentation. He figured that if they forged their papers they would probably cheat him in other ways, too.

One of the drivers had a job that was – allegedly – coming to an end. The Japanese employer listed as a reference was about to leave the country. Janne decided to rely on bona fide, oral references and dialled the number listed.

Fifteen minutes later, he had been told all about the congeniality and reliability of thirty-five-year old Nizamuddhin Beza. The Japanese man and his wife had employed him for over three years and he had never been late and had never been in an accident. Janne went outside to ask Nizamuddhin back for a sit-down and another chat.

The man sat down in their big armchair, but looked very ill at ease. When Janne reached for his papers somewhat abruptly, he shot to his feet and practically stood at attention. He told Janne he had a wife and two children, a girl and a boy, and that it would make him 'very, very maximum happy' to work for Janne.

'Your happiness is my happiness and my happiness will be big if you consequently ride maximally happy in the car while I drive comfortably,' he explained, his head bobbing vigorously up and down. 'People that are definitely happy can make other happy people even happier.'

The man's enthusiastic Bangla-English fascinated Janne. None of his papers seemed forged and Janne had no real idea what to ask him. But by the end of their meeting, Nizamuddhin had been hired. The family now had a driver.

Sofia cheered at the news over the phone.

"Can he start straight away? Ask! I was thinking I should take some time off and we could go down to Chandni Chowk together to buy fabric? Shjuli can stay late for once. Then we can go grab some dinner afterwards." Before hanging up she remembered to add, "Bring a bottle of wine. Restaurants don't serve alcohol, but since we're bideshis, foreigners, we can bring our own."

Janne smiled. Finally. He had felt increasingly annoyed about Sofia's late nights, by how she almost demonstratively left him in charge of absolutely everything to do with the house. And then still could not stop herself from meddling. When she left for the embassy at seven each morning, she left long lists of things she thought he should 'see to' and yellow Post-its reminders. 'Don't forget the alcohol ration!', 'Call Norwegian Emma about playdate!', 'Can we do dinner Friday?', 'Doubles tennis Saturday with the British?' Every night for the past week, she had come home at 10 p.m. and gone straight to sleep.

Consequently Janne felt enlivened by the prospect of a few hours' audience with her. He missed their intimacy and their conversations when the responsibilities of the everyday came between them. He felt so needy, and hated himself for it. Sofia, she was more independent. He really had been trying to give her space, but he still couldn't help feeling as though she thought him too clingy whenever she was home. But when was she going to make him a priority? The whole idea of moving to Bangladesh had been to have more time with the family, right? Time to mend, time to find paths leading forward, together.

It took a good long while to get into central Dhaka. If traffic seemed stressful in the diplomatic zone, it was completely irrational, not to mention lethal, outside it. When they left Gulshan, crossing the railway tracks, Janne realised just how dense and sprawling the slum really was. In Gulshan and Baridhara there were just patches of slum, but here he suddenly saw block after block of corrugated-iron shacks, dirty market stands and throngs of people who all seemed to be on their way somewhere. Any alleyway between the houses – if there was one – was muddy and narrow. He was desperately curious about the glimpses of human life whizzing past him. He was for ever wanting to stop the car, get out and interview the women in dirty saris with children on their hips. Who are you? Who do you live with? What do you do for a living? What are your dreams? Will your child be going to school? How do you sleep at night? Do you have a pillow and someone who holds you and loves you? Who do you trust? What do you think about us? About the people like us, passing by in our cars and jeeps?

It also struck him that this – the slum and what to his eyes looked like squalor – was an order onto itself, a system infinitely more organised than he was able to discern. People really were on their way to things. To a sister who had just been married, to a part-time job as a hotel guard, to the doctor because the children had such terrible coughs. Some of the shacks were probably better than others, some stands outperformed others, and he assumed someone made sure they were in a position to control every single water pump.

As soon as the car stopped for a red light, or whenever the traffic simply ground to a halt, they were thronged by beggars: elderly, bearded men in Punjabis and white skullcaps; mothers of young children with sleeping infants in their arms; and the children, all those children, chirping and laughing and smiling and waving. All calling out to them in broken English.

'Hello, Madam, how are you? How are you? Please, please, some little money, please.'

They get really excited to see *bideshis* – Westerners,' Sofia explained. 'Outside Gulshan there aren't many white people.'

'What are you supposed to do?' Janne started digging around for his wallet.

'Oh, Janne, I'm not sure. Were you going to give them something?' She put a hand on his wallet.

'Everyone at the embassy says they're organised, and that we shouldn't encourage begging, because they make so much money begging, their parents take them out of school. I don't know if it's true . . .'

He sighed and let his eyes rest on a little girl who looked to be about Noella's age and was dragging her little sister around. The girl sensed she had achieved eye contact and had soon climbed onto the jeep's side step. She was adorable, and beamed at him, revealing a row of the oversized white teeth of a typical seven-year-old. She wore a tiny butterfly clip in her matted hair, but that was the only splash of colour on the otherwise filthy, drab siblings.

Janne took out a fifty-taka note and hid it in his hand. He thought to himself that he didn't give a damn if she belonged to Fagin's gang in *Oliver Twist*, he could make her full and happy right in this moment. Just as the car began moving off, he rolled down the window and handed her the crumpled note. The girl beamed at him and shouted: 'Thank you! Thank you!' and waved and kissed the note with such genuine gratitude it both moved and unsettled him.

They sat quietly for a while until Sofia mumbled.

'Right, it's the vinegar of Sabadilla, isn't it . . . ?'

It took Janne a second before he knew exactly what she meant. In one of Noella's favourite films, Astrid Lindgren's *Mischievous Mardie*, which both he and Sofia had watched with her at least thirty times, little Mardie's mother decides to delouse the impoverished neighbour kids, Mia and Matti, with vinegar of Sabadilla. Mardie's father finds out about her intervention and teases her, somewhat pointedly, saying that 'the noble lady at Junibacken is caring for the penniless'. The way he saw it, the other, larger injustices were so much more pervasive and insidious, important.

In the film, Mardie's mother is upset and runs to the children's bedroom, asking Mardie, 'But surely Sabadilla is better than nothing?'

'Right, exactly, surely Sabadilla is better than nothing,' Janne quoted.

'Precisely. I'm sitting up at the embassy, doling out millions in an attempt to change the underlying structures, but not a penny goes to what is called direct support – which is to say poor people here and now. Vinegar of Sabadilla. And that's how international development works. It has to tackle the structures, otherwise you end up in a disgusting charity situation, and we don't want to go back to that.'

'So you mean, how do we act as individuals?'

'Yeah, something like that. You can't just give money to every beggar who comes along either . . . '

Janne felt the last of his frustration with Sofia dissipate and remembered that he loved her and respected her thoughtfulness. He tried to help: 'But we employ people and pay them a decent wage. That's good, right? And I might be able to come up with something in due course.'

Sofia sighed curtly and cut him off.

'We can't shoulder the weight of the world's misery either. We'd be crushed. Just because we happen to see it every day doesn't make it our problem. All the people back home and in the West share the responsibility. Morally speaking.' She kissed him on the cheek. 'You're lovely. The most important thing might be that we can bear to stay and do what little we can. Right?'

The hustle and bustle around Chandni Chowk, one of the world's largest garment markets, was unlike anything Janne had ever seen. It was slightly unclear where one thing started and another ended, as was so often the case in Bangladesh. The market had probably originally meant to be contained within an enormous, many-storied building with cloth merchants crammed into every nook and cranny, but it had clearly spilled out into surrounding streets and houses, taking over whole city blocks. If there were order to it, it escaped Janne and Sofia.

Nizamuddhin pointed to one of many openings in the wall.

'Go in there, straight into the dark, there you look and find. Call me on the mobile when you are done. You are my biggest, maximal treasure and I always find you.'

Sofia and Janne smiled at their driver's eager outburst and got out of the jeep, jumping over an open sewer and up on to a high pavement consisting of crooked, cracked slabs of cement.

They were immediately surrounded by four or five merchants keen to pull them into their booths and stalls. Janne and Sofia could not see the ends of Chandni Chowk's long, narrow, claustrophobically winding aisles. Fabric everywhere. Occasionally displayed so you could see it properly, but more often than not stacked in tightly, tightly packed bundles where things like colour and quality could only be vaguely made out.

'You have to have some kind of . . . attitude here,' Janne raised his voice to be heard over the din made by the many whirling ceiling fans.

Sofia gave him a wan smile in response. She was being dragged into a small booth where an enthusiastic young man was unfurling elaborate saris, holding them up against her pale skin. In many of the booths, only really big enough for one person, several people sat, ate and slept at the same time. When potential customers passed by, the inhabitants of the booths were shaken out of their slumber or driven away from their meals.

In one booth, they came across a man surrounded by children and older women. A big, green parrot was hopping back and forth between his shoulder and a wooden perch, picking tiny, dirty envelopes from the man's hand with its beak. People seemed to be paying a few paisa for an envelope.

'Future, your future,' the man tried to explain, smiling at them. The bird flapped and hopped around, nabbing an envelope and extending it to Sofia. 'The Koran, your future, what advice from the Koran?'

Sofia laughed and grabbed the envelope. Inside was a tiny note with a few handwritten lines in Bengali. The man snatched the note back and read it.

'Ah, very, very good', he switched over to Bengali and read the note aloud several times so the crowd that had gathered around them could hear. They all stared wide-eyed at Sofia.

'Very good. Allah loves you. No problem. Two hundred taka.'

Janne paid, declining taking an envelope for himself.

'That's an insane amount of money!' Sofia fumed. 'But it's too late, now. I can't very well ask for it back, can I?' She pulled a face and Janne quickly ushered her away, further down the aisle. 'But I'm definitely going to ask Moberg to translate it,' she turned to him and winked, grinning. 'Maybe it's something pivotal?'

Sofia started pointing at some of the saris, feeling the fabrics. A young man who seemed to know English tugged and tore at the massive piles of cloth to get to the ones she wanted.

'We said we could use saris as curtains upstairs, didn't we? Or what do you think? And then maybe something more conservative in the downstairs living room?'

Janne had spotted a hot pink sari liberally embroidered with mirrors and rhinestones. Noella would die to have it.

'What about this for Noella's room?'

Janne and Sofia shared a certain unease about their daughter's extreme interest in anything pink, and had taken the principled stand of not foisting traditionally girly things on her. Society and school did such a good job in that area anyway, they reasoned.

But Janne did not mind making a one-off exception. Sofia, however, gave the sari one look and shook her head.

'Oh, no, that's not happening. Put it back.'

Janne grumbled, and reluctantly capitulated.

The rumour that bideshis were shopping in the market must have spread, because people were waiting around every corner, staring openly at them.

'Hello, hello, what's your name?' and 'Only look, please, look, beautiful saris'

A dirt encrusted, barefoot little girl led the way to a flight of stairs that took them up to the next floor. Up there, the heat was almost unbearable. The smell of slightly mildewed fabric blended with fragrant spices fried in oil. The sweat of strangers mixed with their own effusions and the remnants of that morning's deodorant.

Janne had never been gawked at this way before. From every booth and heap of garments, he was followed by friendly but unabashedly curious eyes. And as he passed a mirror hung between fabrics, he realised how different he looked. Next to the slim, terracotta bodies and jet-black mops of hair surrounding him, he was grotesque. A swollen pink hog of a man. Six feet five inches tall, pasty skin, with ginger-haired legs sticking out of a pair of shorts. His green T-shirt read: 'Never Mind Stockholm – We are Hammarby Södermalm' and stretched over his gut. And then his puffy face, his stubble and on top of that the long blond strands of hair that were damply clinging to his skull. No, he was not a pretty picture and, lo and behold, the children let out terrified little shrieks and dashed into the booths as he made his way down the aisle.

Suddenly Sofia pulled up short, and with her the troop of Bangladeshis trailing them.

'Look, Janne!'

In a messy corner hung a fabric that sent a wave of emotion through Janne. Their very own cloud sheets from Ikea, which always had Noella say she was flying.

'I'd forgotten! Ikea's big here. It feels just like home. Sheets, towels, curtains. A lot of it's produced here.'

A few hours later, when they tumbled out of the garment market, soaking with sweat, they had found almost everything they needed, and Sofia noted with satisfaction that several items on her list could be crossed off.

'But you forgot about the item: "Give my husband some attention",' Janne pointed out. 'It's going to require at least that bottle of wine and two hours of intense wooing to finish the job properly.'

*

Their great aunt Mahmoda was at home and in bed. She sat up when the girls entered. Mahmoda had been a handsome woman once, large and imposing, her hair always neat and her bindi always meticulously centred between her eyebrows. She was still handsome, despite the aching hip that kept her mostly bedbound. Her blouse strained across her chest and folds on her arms and stomach bulged out from under the draped layers of her sari. The people in the village sneeringly claimed she spent most of her time in bed, getting fat off the sweets, *mishti*, she bought using her generous pension. Now she shooed the neighbour girl, who had come to make her tea, away, telling her to fetch two more cups.

"Girls, girls, what are you doing here? Aren't you in Goalpur?"

For a split-second, Nazreen wondered if she had misjudged the situation. Maybe Mahmoda would be angry with them, yes, of course she would be. At first. But then? Great Aunt Mahmoda wasn't quite like the other old people in their family. She had worked as a teacher for years, before being hired by a local NGO that gave loans to poor people. She was considered intelligent and modern, but people were also slightly afraid of her. People said she was possessed by a *pari*, an evil spirit, because she spoke so freely. Her oldest son had become a teacher, too, but in a madrassa, a religious school, and now disavowed everything his mother had tried to talk about in the village. He had announced she wouldn't be allowed to live under his roof until she rejected all Western ideas and obeyed Allah. That was why she had been forced to move and now lived in shame and humiliation with her sister in Rajigonj.

Nazreen quickly told her what had happened, and the old lady started rocking back and forth in her bed.

"Girls, leave, leave now!" she exclaimed when she'd heard the whole story. "You have to get away from this village and these people. Poor Mokta. Inna lillahi wa inna ilayhi raji'un. We belong to Allah and will return to him. I don't understand what's happening. Why can't people see what's happening to their girls? Sweeties, I have no money to lend you."

"Diddi, money's not a problem," Nazreen cut in. "We just want you to tell Amma and Abba that we're not gone forever. We just have to get away, neither one of us wants to marry Ali."

"Not him, nor anyone else either," Meena added.

"No, girls, you should marry someone of your choosing, or at least someone you can accept. That's how they do it in Dhaka, well, or at least in America. Everywhere, except maybe India. I think having your own money is the only way to have your own life as a woman, at least that's what they told us at BRAC. But that was so long ago now. You know I was the local chair of one of the first micro credit programmes, don't you? It was in 1988 and your father . . ."

"We know, we know, and you met Dr Yunus in the eighties and he said you did Bangladesh proud."

"Exactly! Back then, no one thought I was possessed by a *pari*, back then, people listened when I talked."

Nazreen had heard the story several times before and wanted to keep their aunt from going off on that particular tangent. What she needed to know was if their aunt was willing to help them, for real, so she decided to risk rushing her elder.

"Will you go to Goalpur and let them know?"

"Yes, but I won't make it there now, before the funeral, which must be today. But of course I will tell them you were here. And I have to make sure to go for the memorial forty days from now. I wouldn't miss Mokta's *chollisha.* I will tell your parents then. Though I don't think they will understand. Your father's not strong, his heart is full of fear. They're simple people who want to live close to their maker, inshallah, it's just that I believe Allah doesn't want women to be so poorly treated. Do you think he wants to torture women?"

While they spoke, the neighbour girl came back with tea for all of them and the girls drank theirs eagerly.

"Would you like some breakfast? The bus to Dhaka takes three hours, at least. You can't do it on an empty stomach. Wait another fifteen minutes and I can give you breakfast."

The girls greedily wolfed down their fried eggs and chapatis, and Mahmoda ordered them some food for the road. She was certainly able to spare them a bag of dried crackers and a bunch of bananas. They discussed how the girls could send money back to their parents from Dhaka.

"They need every paisa. Some good must come of your leaving. Your father will probably have to pay the mosque not to put a fatwa on you. That alone will be a thousand taka. You're going to have to learn how to send money with your mobile phones." Mahmoda limped over to a drawer and pulled out her own phone. Her eyes were sparkling and her cheeks were flushed. "Learn how in Dhaka. I can receive the money and go over to Goalpur once or twice a month. The lady next door gets a hundred dollars from her son in Dubai every month via phone. Imagine that! A hundred dollars, that's eight thousand taka. What a son, what a blessed son!"

Just as they were about to leave their great aunt's, Meena signalled to Nazreen.

"What? Your stomach hurts?"

Meena blushed and leaned forward to whisper.

"Blood, I'm bleeding. It's my unclean period. I can't spend several hours on a bus. You know how much I bleed."

Nazreen looked at her little sister and then back at her great aunt. This was not a time to be coy.

"Auntie, Meena has her unclean period. We can't get on a bus to Dhaka."

Nazreen whispered the last part and Meena averted her eyes. The girls were not used to spending any length of time away from home, particularly during their monthly flow. At those times, they didn't leave the house.

For the first time since they entered the small house, their great aunt seemed angry, muttering darkly to herself. She leaned down and pulled a box out from its place under her bed.

"There's always something. Yes, indeed, always some obstacle when girls want to travel. Let me see . . ."

She pulled out long strips of fabric and some rough linen cloths. She held one of the swaths of fabric up to the light, nodded slightly and then tore it into thinner ribbons.

"Go wash, Meena-jaan. Cleanse yourself, but then you should go. You need to leave today. I will sort out pads for you and show you how to keep them in place when you're on the road. You can't let little things like this stop you."

She looked enlivened and smiled at the girls.

"You'll have to leave all of that behind. You're going to become modern women."

*

"Alor Desh!"

The yellow post-it he'd put on his computer screen drew his eyes. Right. The accounting. Maybe he should give it a quick glance before handing the file over to Sofia.

The report was complex, full of columns and summaries in bold. Moberg let out a weary sigh and thought to himself that Sofia needed to be brought in on this as soon as possible. The British charity probably expected a meeting immediately. Khadija Anam was internationally renowned and in a worst-case scenario, the British press might catch wind of the allegations.

Being the head of an embassy in an aid recipient country was completely different from being the head of an embassy in, say, Vienna. Granted, he was the senior diplomat in Dhaka, too, but because the government had decided SwedeAid's field offices would fall under the remit of the local embassies, diplomatic entities had suddenly been obliged to let foreign aid people into their midst. The reform had not been welcome. Not by the traditional diplomats in the embassies, who were suddenly forced to sit back and watch as colleagues with more resources and contacts in the recipient countries began to play increasingly central roles. Nor by the foreign aid people, who found working at the embassies difficult. They felt the Foreign Ministry's understanding and knowledge of their issues was lacking. There were also likely many foreign aid bureaucrats who felt the Foreign Ministry people's job descriptions and duties were vague. The diplomatic corps was obsolete, according to a lot of people at SwedeAid. Since the global networks woven these days were so much more sophisticated and refined than back when diplomacy was the only means for two countries to communicate, diplomats had now been reduced to cocktail and reception pros.

Furthermore, it was the rule rather than the exception for embassies in developing countries to be torn in two. A number of pivotal ones were led by two equally senior managers who lived to contradict each other and made sure to do so often. Indeed, it wasn't uncommon for the ambassador and the foreign aid counsellor to stop talking to each other altogether. "The ambassador says X and the counsellor Y," sighed the employees, who inevitably ended up in the middle.

Ambassadors technically had seniority, but counsellors were in charge of distributing the foreign aid money and consequently had a mandate to act fairly independently.

That kind of conflict was not going to rear its ugly head in Dhaka, if Moberg had anything to say about it. He had his hands full handling Siv and preferred to spend the year he had left in Bangladesh not rocking the boat.

Sofia Paulin's CV had been flawless, he had to admit as much. An undergraduate degree in law from Uppsala, with honours, a minor field study funded by SwedeAid at a Rwandan court, a trainee position with the UNs Junior Professional Programme in Geneva, human rights and civil society caseworker for SwedeAid in Tanzania. Then gender equality advisor at SwedeAid's headquarters in Stockholm. Everything suggested a competent and adept individual who had made sensible, intelligent career choices.

"She's not a wild-eyed feminist, I promise," a friend from his university days in Uppsala, who was listed as her manager in Geneva, had assured him when he called to anxiously ask about the "gender equality" bit.

"Sofia's a professional. She's systematic, deliberate, even a bit rigid. She's an expert at gender equality the way other people are experts at roads or water. I never got the feeling she was . . . angry, you know. Don't worry. She's good. A proper workhorse."

Moberg had also asked Vanja to check with their former head of admin, who had worked as a secretary at SwedeAid's headquarters in Stockholm. And he'd had nothing but praise for her either.

"Nice, if a bit impersonal, a careerist, in a good way," had been his assessment. And that last part, *careerist*, had settled it. Without being able to formulate it clearly, Moberg knew a careerist wouldn't stir the pot. A careerist would be more interested in good relations and future letters of recommendations than in forcing issues down people's throats.

An efficient knock on his door made Moberg look up. It was Rickard, one of the foreign aid caseworkers.

"Hi there, Mr Ambassador. Listen, I don't know, but check this out."

Rickard held out a sheet of paper signed by Siv. A memo directing all foreign employees to sign a document committing them to returning all furniture provided to them in mint condition, or pay for replacements.

"I don't know how you feel, but after moving halfway across the world and being set up in poorly furnished flats by the state, we're now supposed to pay for normal wear and tear that happens while we live there, too. Is that okay?"

Moberg sighed inwardly. It was clearly moronic. Siv marking her territory again, to demonstrate that she was a heavyweight at the embassy. The memo might have something to do with the fact that Sofia had requested a proper inventory of her accommodation. This was Siv's revenge. That was often how Siv operated.

"Let me take a look."

Moberg skimmed the memo.

"Well, as you can see, Rickard, I haven't signed it and I have no intention to do so."

Rickard's smile was what Moberg had several times thought would best be described as "winning". Rickard was, generally speaking, fairly winning, Moberg reluctantly admitted to himself. A dark young man in his thirties, carrying a few too many pounds, but compensating with freshly-laundered shirts and polos. Hiring Rickard hadn't strictly been in line with the embassy's needs. They had advertised for a senior water expert or a senior poverty expert, but due to the difficulty of recruiting staff to Dhaka, they had instead been sent a young man more or less fresh out of university.

A quick glance at his short CV had convinced Moberg Rickard was a person who would do his job without any real zeal or skill, but also without making a hash of things. Good enough.

*

Janne thought he'd misheard.

"Barbecue at the archive?"

He was bathing Teo, who was slippery as an eel, and could only hear part of what Sofia was talking about in their bedroom. Noella was running about, brandishing her pyjamas, singing a song in Bangla their new *aya* Shjuli had taught her.

Sofia appeared in the doorway.

"Yes, apparently tonnes of old documents from the archive have to be burnt, and these things have to be done a certain way," she explained. "Swedish citizens have to be present and it can only happen at certain times and you have to sign a letter saying you witnessed the destruction of the documents. So Anna-Lena suggested we burn it all in the residence garden and use the fire to cook hamburgers. Sounds like fun, no? But we were thinking of making it a family thing and get everyone together. What do you reckon: Thursday, after work?"

That Thursday night, Janne brought Noella and Teo to the residence, which was yet another handsome, oversized villa in Gulshan, not too different from their own. The garden was magnificent, a park with rows of fuchsias, giant jacarandas and an ancient mango tree. Palm trees lined the lawn and bougainvillea and climbing roses jostled for space on the walls behind the tree trunks.

Box after box brimming with good old Swedish Esselte binders had been carried out and piled in the middle of the lawn. Flames were dancing in a number of metal drums. Janne looked from the mountain of binders to the fires and realised destroying documents was a time-consuming activity in Dhaka.

"You have to incinerate them properly, which requires some active participation. If we were to just toss it all in, these documents would come back to haunt us in the form of forgeries and other kinds of fabrications," a fit, middle-aged man who introduced himself as Erik explained and then mumbled something about "consular business". He seemed to be in charge of the conflagration.

"I figured we keep the fires going for about an hour, then there'll be some good embers and we can slap the burgers on."

Ambassador Moberg and his wife Vanja seemed happy to see Janne and greeted Noella and Teo warmly. Janne liked the ambassador, who appeared to be a humble, almost shy sort of person.

"Kemon achen, Janne. Khub bhalo? That means 'Good day, how are you?' Have you had a chance to familiarise yourself with Bengali yet? Or Bangla, as they call the spoken language. Fascinating, don't you think?"

"So far, the script alone is enough to baffle me. Can you read Bengali, too, Mr Ambassador?"

"Of course. It's challenging, but absolutely necessary for a deeper understanding of the language. Besides, thousands of Bangladeshi have died for the right to use their language and their alphabet. Back when the country was called East Pakistan, the central Pakistani government tried to ban Bengali, so the alphabet is closely linked with the Bangladeshi national identity."

He fell silent, pondering this. Janne was just about to formulate a question about the war with Pakistan when Moberg lit up again.

"Did you know, by the way, that the Swedish word for nose, *näsa*, is directly related to the Bengali *naakh*, and the Sanskrit *nas*? Moberg seemed to pronounce the words phonetically correctly, Janne noted, and he'd raised his hand to his mouth to underscore the sounds of the words. "Since time immemorial, there has been an exchange between Sanskrit, modern Bengali and Europe . . ."

Moberg launched into a passionate lecture about the linguistic roots of Bengali while Janne listened politely. The previously grey-looking man's cheeks flushed and his eyes twinkled when he sensed Janne's interest.

"Take the suffix -pur, for instance, which you're going to encounter in so many village name, Mirpur, Mahendipur, Pirpur. It's an example of an ending that means village, cluster of houses. You can see how close it is to our Swedish *by*, can't you?

After a while, Anna-Lena joined their conversation and contributed anecdotes and terminology from the world of Bangladeshi theatre, which apparently was her specialty.

Sofia had described Anna-Lena as a "classic foreign aid woman" and Janne could see what she meant. Anna-Lena had a short bob, a slightly stern face and was dressed in a shalwar kameez. Large wooden earrings in the shape of parrots dangled from her earlobes and she seemed perpetually entangled in the long shawl that went with her outfit. Her ex-husband was a famous professor of developing economies, Sofia had told him, and after the divorce, she had decided to stay in Bangladesh with her two teenage girls.

Young Rickard, whom Janne had so far only seen in a bathing suit at the club, had brought a young, pretty Australian girl to the barbecue and he introduced her to Janne.

"This is Charlene, she's a water case worker at AusAid. But I'm sure that's just a cover and she's actually here to purloin our secret foreign aid casefiles from the mid-eighties," Rickard joked. "Isn't that right,

Charlene? If you're really good, I'll let you read a land strategy document from 1995 before its devoured by the flames!"

Charlene laughed brightly at the joke, and Rickard proceeded to ask Janne whether he played golf.

"In Dhaka, you play tennis or golf or bridge. Nothing else. So – your choice! Golf with me in the verdant beauty of the Kurmatola Golf Club or tennis with the Danes at Nordic? Or bridge with Moberg? Should be a no-brainer."

Janne laughed politely, but then he had to chase after Teo who was toddling around dangerously close to the burn drums and their dancing flames. He noted with annoyance that Sofia was standing with her back to them. Her back was often to Teo these days, Janne mused. Or was that all in his mind? It was as though she took every opportunity to signal that Janne was responsible for their family life, even on her days off. Surely, they'd shared that responsibility on days off before?

When he got back, carrying Teo, Rickard had another question for him.

"Are you going to the Glitter Ball?"

"Not that I know. Is that something Sofia's supposed to attend? Calm down, sweetheart." Teo wanted to get down and was writhing in Janne's arms.

"The Glitter Ball, the ball to end all balls!" Charlene clapped her hands at the mere thought of it. "The parties are the main reason people want to be stationed in Dhaka, and this is the best one. You should sit at our table!"

Janne was just about to decline, but Charlene carried on enthusiastically.

"Everyone dresses up according to a theme and performs. Last year, I was a penguin! Our table's theme was climate change." She laughed excitedly. "I was a penguin looking for ice for my drink!"

Rickard laughed at her enthusiasm and turned to Janne.

"Imagine six hundred guests at a crazy, over-the-top fancy dress party. I've never experienced anything like it. It's like Hollywood, or Cannes!"

"Blimey. Well, we haven't really given it much thought yet." Janne felt sceptical. Teo wanted to get down and was writhing like a snake.

Suddenly, Vanja appeared, holding Noella by the hand, looking to take Teo as well. She held her arms out to him and Janne handed the boy over.

"I want to show them my crystals," she said. "Did you know, Janne, that I have the biggest collection of crystals and charged stones in Dhaka? Come see!"

As if to illustrate her statement, Vanja was wearing a long necklace with a large crystal pendant and around her slim waist was a belt bedazzled with ice blue amethysts. Crystals dangled from her earlobes as well. Janne concluded it wasn't entirely to his taste.

He noticed both Noella and Teo could sense this lady was different, and he thought he could almost see Noella scrolling down her cast of fairy-tale characters to place Vanja. Fairy godmother? Witch? Queen? Elf?

Janne followed Vanja and the children into the residence and was greeted by a ceiling height of about fifteen feet. They saw the first signs of Vanja's collection as soon as they entered' an enormous, shimmering, apricot-coloured piece of quartz was sitting on a small table. Several crystal mobiles hung from the ceiling and each and every table in the government-furnished residence was adorned with a sea-shell still life.

Hideous, absolutely hideous, Janne thought, but Noella was ecstatic.

"Look, daddy, it's so pretty," she exulted. The fact that her tastes appealed to a six-year-old didn't seem to offend Vanja in the slightest. The children flitted around the large room in wonder.

"You know, Janne, when I first moved into the residence, I could feel there was a lot of frustrated chi here. The sofas were in crazy places, blocking all the energy and I think an insane person must've hung the paintings on that wall!"

Vanja pointed to a wall that was now completely bare. Janne couldn't quite see the problem with hanging paintings on it.

"I want to tear it down, the whole wall," Vanja explained. "But the National Property Board won't have it. They don't care that we get headaches and can't sleep. I've asked Karl-Otto to write to them, explaining the problem, but . . ." she chuckled quietly. "Well, you can guess what the outcome is."

Her eyes sparkled with good humour and she took a few challenging, theatrical steps toward Janne.

"You can feel it, can't you? The power? There's power in this country, Janne. You can see it in the eyes of the children! I'm convinced there's such a things as global feng shui. Look at the delta, look at all the water flowing through Bangladesh. Nine hundred rivers. Nine hundred. That means power, energy! Can't you feel it? Here!"

She grabbed Janne's hand and put it on her stomach. Janne yanked it back in alarm and confusion.

"I'm sorry. I just wanted to show you which chakras we're talking about. I scared you. I'm sorry, my friend."

"Don't worry about it." Janne got ready to head back out, but Vanja reached out and held him back. She tilted her head to the side and watched him for a few seconds.

"You can see it too, can't you? That Bangladesh is like Mother Earth, like Gaia? An amazing, green place, overpopulated and poisoned. Where are we humans supposed to go? When the flood comes, the land will be swept away, there's not much time left."

Janne cleared his throat, unsure how to respond.

"Yes, I've heard that. Thirty million people are about to lose their land, someone said. Terrible. An apocalypse."

Noella and Teo had been studying the large apricot crystal and now Vanja turned her attention to them.

"Tell you what, Noella, I will let you pick a crystal from my special collection. And your little brother, too. Come on. I keep my prettiest stones upstairs."

Janne hung back in the official parts of the residence, while Vanja dragged the children up to the first floor, chatting warmly to them. If this was the official collection, he shuddered to think what her private one looked like. Speaking of which, wasn't it some sort of crime to mix elegant Swedish design and Josef Frank prints with a bunch of rocks? What was the official policy? Janne mused. Wasn't there some kind of government agency overseeing things like that?

Janne wondered what kind of person Vanja really was. She was strikingly beautiful with her red hair and big, dark eyes. Janne pondered what a woman like her saw in a man like Moberg. The chakra manoeuvre had been a bit unexpected, and earlier that week, she'd come up to him at the club and insisted he teach at a slum school she was involved with.

"We need someone like you, Janne! We need to become more professional, do better by the children. They need access to the energy flows and they can only get that if they're given the right tools. Why don't you come have a look?"

So far, Janne had managed to elude Vanja's persuasion. After all, the whole idea of moving to Bangladesh was to give him time, to find himself, both professionally and as a person. And as a father and husband. That's what he'd told everyone when they asked.

The fact was, he'd worked out a whole spiel concerning their move to Bangladesh. He'd spent the spring in hanging out in cafés with other fathers of young children. Sipping lattes and eating sourdough rolls with brie. Nibbling the pepper that came with the brie and explained.

"I've been a teacher for almost fifteen years, time to try something else for a bit. You have to be brave enough to quit sometimes. This is Sofia's big break."

His friends had nodded and stared out at the slush on Hornsgatan. Seeing them long to get away, he'd suddenly began to like being the person who was leaving. The person who was going on an adventure for a few years. He'd refilled his latte glass with regular coffee and kept going.

"It's good to change things up every now and then, for the kids and for us. My god, there's a whole world outside the city limits. It's going to be good to get away from the Gore-Tex for a while."

He'd been surprised at the power a move abroad held, the kind of yearning it seemed to awaken. Apparently, lots of people in their mid-thirties and forties were questioning their life choices, that much had become clear. This was the time if they wanted to quit and do something else. Soon, it would be too late. He for his part had actually always been rather happy and content with his life at the Lindeberg Free School and wouldn't have minded staying on, enjoying the routine.

The only one he'd told the truth about their decision to move was his older brother Mikael in Jönköping.

"I've let Sofia down, you know. It just sucks, to be completely honest. I haven't been myself. This Bangladesh thing . . . you know, the oxygen mask that falls down in the plane cabin? It could be like that!"

"Or maybe just a hair shirt for you?"

"No, not at all." Janne had been annoyed with Mikael. Big brother with his perfect marriage and catalogue-like knowledge of Janne's life and previous relationships. Mikael had dubbed Janne's catastrophic mistake with a colleague Camillagate.

"I adore Sofia, you of all people should know that. She's the one for me, my soulmate. We've gone through a rough patch, okay? I've been a big, fucking jerk. It's her turn now, and we need this time. Maybe I shouldn't be a teacher anymore? Maybe we should have another baby?"

"Another baby? Or just a chance to erase and rewind? You'd do better to make sure you're there for her *now*, Janne. For a change, I mean."

Vanja and the children were coming back down the stairs. Janne could see his daughter's eyes beaming with wonder at a gigantic pink crystal.

"Daddy, look, the lady gived me this. She *gived* me it."

Vanja was holding the little girl's hand and carrying Teo on her hip. They walked out through the elegant patio door, into the heat.

"We're going to hit the trampoline. That's okay with daddy, isn't it? The big kids are going to have to make way!"

She nodded for Janne to go back to the fires and walked off with the children.

Janne accepted the cold beer he was handed and took up position next to Anna-Lena. She was flipping through some old binders that were probably slated to be incinerated and Janne thought there was something familiar about her efficient, slightly jerky hands.

"Look, Janne," Anna-Lena opened the binder and read: "Funding for vocational training for garment workers. Skills training for girls. Mahendipur, 1998". A vocational programme I started in Stockholm and raised fifteen million kronor for. I'd completely forgotten about it. That was how Bjarne – you know, Danish Bjarne from the club – started his factory. The Danes still work that way, big foreign aid money is funnelled to private companies in the hopes that it will eventually trickle down to someone poor. We're heading down that path in Sweden, too. Private enterprises are up and coming in the foreign aid world. Completely incomprehensible, if you ask me. Aren't they busy trying to make a profit? I feel a bit odd, seeing the old paperwork again."

It dawned on Janne why she looked to familiar. The teacher type, yes, that was it, with her down-to-earth fashion sense and slightly subdued appearance. Like some of his older colleagues at Lindeberg. Idealists: highly educated, efficient, well-intentioned, knowledgeable. Slightly worn down and disappointed that their work never received the attention it deserved. Was he going to end up like that?

"Here!" Anna-Lena read, her fingers tracing a line on the yellowed page. "Five hundred girls were educated each year to enable them to work in the garment factories. Ha! You never get investment like that in the culture sector. And now, the garment sector's red hot."

"Makes you wonder where those women are today, I mean . . . did all that foreign aid improve things?" Janne said tentatively. Until now, foreign aid hadn't been an interest of his and he didn't fully know how to strike the right note in these discussions. Was it possible to be critical without sounding like a neo-liberal think tank, for example? He'd asked Sofia that very question several times, but had never been given a straight answer.

"Improved, well, I guess that's the kind of thing you ask yourself during long, dark winter nights. Some are doing better, that's for sure. Dhaka has a skyline now, with new skyscrapers, and there are super markets and a growing middle class. When I was first here in the seventies, there was *one* freezer in all of Dhaka, and what the mullahs said was law. Now there are women on the streets and someone has to live in all those high-rises, right? But the question is whether foreign aid was what made the difference. And if it still counts as improvement when you factor in the environmental damage done and the rise in consumption levels."

"But you can definitely see a difference?"

"Oh yes, a big difference. But personally, I'm not sure if this particular type of aid is such a good idea," her hand slapped the open binder. "The owners of the garment factories ought to educate their own workforce and build their own factories Why should foreign aid go to the private sector? We should be educating the masses, making sure people are healthy and know how to read and write. Or supporting civil society, like with Alor Desh . . ."

She turned to Janne and peered at him over the rims of her glasses.

"Don't you think? Rather than helping companies turn a bigger profit."

Sofia overheard them talking and came over to look in the binder.

"Can I see? Oh, right, that must be what Bjarne was talking about at the club. It was back in the late nineties when we were supposed to work with private sector development, and preferably bring Nordic companies over here in joint efforts with the Danish and Norwegian foreign aid agencies. Interesting."

"That's right, and now the question should be what if any obligation the Danish state has to the girls working there today," Anna-Lena snapped. "From what I hear, Bjarne's a proper slave driver and his factory's falling apart. When it comes to their working conditions, I mean. Who's caring for those girls today?"

Sofia looked up at her colleague and nodded.

"Good question. And I don't know the answer. Or rather, we might be burning the answer."

5

Babul had been in a good mood all afternoon, ever since some street boys had come by the embassy to tell him his young cousins from Goalpur had come to visit. He set the table for the afternoon *fika* – he had learnt the Swedish concept "fika" involved any kind of tasty treat, just no warm food - thinking he might be able to sneak out at four.

Nazreen and Meena.What were they doing in Dhaka? Without Mokta? Babul was looking forward to showing them the city. Poor little dears, they had probably never even seen a high-rise before. He was going to take them to Shopper's Paradise, or maybe to Pink City. They were going to head down to the market so he could buy them *fuchka*, chickpea balls, or *shingarra*, tiny pierogi, and show people in Bada that he had beautiful, female cousins. The girls would marvel at the lights and the things for sale. Maybe he would buy them a shalwar kameez each.

So . . . eight coffee cups and the teapot for the ambassador. He wished he could have shown his little cousins around the embassy, but that was out of the question, of course. The Swedish embassy. Embassy, *dutabash* – even the word sounded important and fancy. Everyone back in the village knew he was an important man these days, someone who'd made it big in Dhaka. But no one from back home had come to visit yet.

Growing up in Goalpur, Babul and the girls' father had been cousins and close in status in the village. Landowning farmers with tiny plots of land. It had probably been implicitly understood that he would eventually marry one of the girls. He was eight, maybe ten years older than the eldest sister, Mokta, she would have been suitable. But since then, the two families' destinies had diverged. Small nudges upward and forward had helped Babul's family to climb the ladder of society, while seemingly equally minute obstacles had impeded the girls' family. It had started when Babul's father got a job at a new cement factory and the girls' father lost his day job at the burlap factory as it was first privatised and then shuttered. He'd been forced to cultivate his land himself. Babul's father, by contrast, had been able to lease his fields to tenant farmers, charging hefty rents, and his salary from the cement factory was substantial and reliable. Eventually, Babul's parents had built a house out of cement, with wide front steps, a small veranda and a tin roof.

Then there had been a bad flood. The girls' father had lost all his land to the ravenous river overnight. A lot of people in their village had been affected, but the Bhuia family had been hit the worst. They'd gone from being proud landowners with good prospects to landless, the lowest of the low.

Landless. Babul shuddered.

In order to raise the money to buy some rickshaws, the Bhuia family had taken on crippling debt and before long, the mother, Farida's, salary from teaching English was their only regular income. To make matters even worse, the couple's only son, Mostafar, who was much younger than the three girls, had been unable to learn how to walk. Babul had heard Farida had been forced to restrict her teaching to tutoring in the home. No one had talked about Babul marrying one of the girls anymore, since the family was clearly never going to be able to afford a proper dowry. When Mokta was finally married off, it was, from what Babul had been told, to a less than pleasant man.

But things had turned out well for Babul and even better since Reka's family had made him an offer. That had really made him. Reka wasn't just a girl he'd fancied in high school, she was also part of a family with members in Dhaka and important contacts in the world of the *bideshi*, the Westerners. Her family had put up a significant dowry which they had both agreed should be invested in a small flat in Badda, and Reka's parents had helped secure him the job at the embassy.

To Babul, life was milk and honey, and the longer he lived with Reka, the more he felt they belonged together. She was a career woman, he liked to say. She earned a respectable salary working as an aya for a Dutch family and was always saving and planning and making new contacts that might come in handy in the future. Babul also found her pretty and secretly admired the way she was able to be in charge without making him lose face. Reka had helped him see how he wanted to live his life, and he'd slowly come to share her wishes. They wanted to put off having children. They were only going to have one child. They wanted to go to Cox's Bazaar and see the ocean. And in their old age, they were both going to make Hajj, pilgrimage, to Mecca.

Babul loved his job at the embassy and had felt at home from his very first day. The cool air, the beautiful furniture. The kitchen with its running water and stainless-steel counter. The elegant, rich, Christian people. His title was Administrative Assistant, and it was his job to make sure there was paper in the copying machines, that everyone was served their morning coffee in their offices and that the afternoon coffee was ready at three. He was also often asked to run little errands for the staff and made it a point of pride to always look neat and presentable and to greet the embassy staff – especially the Swedes – with little bows and smiles. He'd had business cards printed up for himself with the Swedish embassy and SwedeAid logos on them after seeing that other people in the embassy had them. He'd given his title as "Administrative Assistant" in English, but as "Administrative Manager" on the Bengali side of the cards. He wasn't sure the actual administrative manager, Siv, would have been best pleased about that if she'd known, but he told himself not a lot of people in the market place knew how to read anyway. And the small, white cards did what they were supposed to. Wherever he went for his errands, in bazaars and markets, everyone now knew he was an important person at the Swedish Embassy. He enjoyed being treated as such.

On his visits to the village, he'd learnt that life was still hard for his three little cousins. He was told his own family had lent the girls' parents money and rice, and that weren't able to afford a tin roof for their simple hut.

Even so, they were nice girls, all three of them, Babul mused. Good girls, devout and pretty. Well, the two younger ones weren't in the same league as their stunning older sister Mokta, but still. Somehow, the family had managed to put even the youngest, Meena through high school, and their mother, herself an English teacher, had made sure their English was more than adequate.

Farida was in fact not from a poor family herself. For years, she'd been a highly respected teacher with a good job. She was known in the area for her knowledge about Bengali literature and history.

"Babul, why don't you tidy up here and make sure the guards get the leftover sponge cake."

Siv's urging snapped Babul, who was usually always one step ahead and rarely had to be told to do things, out of his reverie. He bowed, nodded and at four on the dot, he left the embassy for the day.

He felt eager to get home and see the girls. But the rain had made it impossible for the auto rickshaw to reach his home in Badda. He had to cover the last bit on foot, slipping and sliding in the mud. He could tell from afar that his little house had drawn his neighbours' interest. A handful of people were hanging on the window frame and crowding the doorway. He knew full well his visitors offered a welcome break in their everyday drudgery.

Badda was the closest to the diplomatic quarter of Dhaka's many slum areas and therefore supplied it with a constant stream of chefs, ayas, cleaners, kitchen boys, gardners, drivers, shoe shiners, lamp changers, dog sitters, coconut openers, movers, rickshaw *wallas*, refuse collectors, street sweepers, alcohol smugglers, masseurs, sex partners, car mechanics, plastic bag collectors and doormen. Around fifty thousand people lived in Badda, or maybe a hundred thousand. No one knew exactly. The residents were packed in tight, almost glued together like grains of salt in a shaker. They lived in homes that ranged from tarpaulin covered bamboo lean-tos to low, gloomy apartment barracks made of cement. Babul and his wife Reka lived in one such block of flats, together with Reka's elderly parents and her brother. Most rooms in Badda housed whole families, each consisting of at least three, often four or five generations in various constellations.

In Badda, there was no such thing as privacy. People ate, laughed, loved, quarrelled, had discussions, raised children, grieved and died together, and any experience or feeling affecting one individual was soon gleaned and enthusiastically discussed by the entire neighbourhood. They lived in complete intimacy, both physically and mentally and no one who ended up in Badda had any idea things could be different. Residents were like the legs of a millipede, notes in a symphony, necessary but not indispensable, and never really alone.

That was why Babul was not at all surprised at the curiosity his guests had stirred up in the neighbourhood, indeed, he was looking forward to showing off his pretty cousins.

It wasn't really a house, more like a ground-floor flat in one of the long, low cement buildings that lined the outskirts of Badda. The flat had two small, dark rooms and a small nook for cooking over open flame. Reka and Babul had one of the rooms all to themselves and her parents and younger brother lived in the other. The rooms were clean and tidy, the floor was made of cement and the structure of the house was sound, nothing like the slum shacks a stone's throw away, in central Badda. Around the corner there was a street with tea stands and little shops, yes, even a barber and a pharmacy, though they were no more than holes in the wall behind steel grates.

Babul and Reka had often lain awake at night, whispering about how lucky they were, about how merciful Allah had been to them. Both of them worked for foreigners, and they owned a home in one of Dhaka's suburbs. Could life get any better?

Babul quickened his step, shooing aside the children blocking his way, but he could tell before he even entered that something was wrong.

Nazreen jumped up from the bed where she'd been sitting.

"Babul, dear cousin, *assalumu alaykum*, thank you for receiving us in your home."

"*Nazreen-apa, wa alaykum assalam*, it's wonderful to see you. And Meena, you've grown so much, you're practically a lady."

"Babul, the girls have run away from home. Mokta was murdered last night. They're afraid to stay in Goalpur."

Reka put her arm protectively around Nazreen.

"Wait, what? What are you saying? Mokta's dead?"

Babul sank onto a stool. Everyone in the room held their breath.

Nazreen burst out crying and started filling him in. It was an effort for her not to sob and moan but she focused on speaking as clearly as possible. Meena stayed seated on the bed, staring at her bare feet.

Babul listened with horror. How terrible! Beautiful Mokta, dead. How were these girls going to get by? They had always been a trio, and Mokta their leader. So intimately entwined, so serene in their trinity. But how inappropriate of them to come here! And what was he supposed to do with them? What would their parents think? There wasn't really any room, and had they . . ."

"They brought money," whispered Reka, who had discreetly leaned down to him, as though reading his mind. She shot him a look and nodded discretely, as if to indicate what she thought about it all.

Babul looked around. Judging from his neighbours' curious faces in the glassless window and the doorway, the girls' fate had been discussed all afternoon. Everyone knew what had happened, and had been airing their views and opinions about what should be done. As the man and head of the house, however, Babul was the one who had to set the tone – was he going to welcome the girls, or show them the door? Reka's look had told him she wanted the girls to stay, at least for a while.

“How did you get to Dhaka? Who knows you’re here?”

Babul was playing for time because he didn’t really want the girls to stay. He’d really enjoyed not being so crowded, being alone with Reka in their room at night. Besides, he needed some indication as to what his family in Goalpur would think.

Nazreen told them about the bus, both to Dhaka and then out to Badda. She also told them about Mahmoda, and Babul had a good laugh at his great aunt’s resolute actions.

“She’s absolutely right, they’re a bit old-fashioned back in the village. Why do they keep their girls on such a short lead? But Dhaka is pretty tough, girls, you realise that, don’t you? You’re going to have to work.”

Meena looked up for the first time. The grave young woman had grown into her angular face, Babul mused. She was beautiful. Her eyes were crystal clear when they met his. How old was she now? Fifteen?

“We can work. You know that, Babul. Just give us a place to stay for a while and before you know it, we’ll be able to get by on our own. But you have to give us a chance to make it in Dhaka.”

Babul chuckled. The girl was so direct. He could see his neighbours watching out of the corner of his eye, waiting for his response. Silence suddenly fell. Someone took the opportunity to hand back a cooking pot they’d apparently borrowed. Another felt compelled to retrieve a chicken that had wandered in under their bed. Reka cleared her throat.

“But of course, girls. You have to stay!” Babul exclaimed, as though that had been a given from the start. “Little cousins, you will stay here with us, until we can find another solution. Reka, have the girls had dinner?”

The relief that followed was palpable. Nazreen laughed and Meena smiled. A neighbour spontaneously hauled in a large bed and squeezed it into a corner of the room, and people lounging in the doorway started discussing potential jobs for the girls.

“No construction, no, these are nice girls, and we’re not that desperate!”

“But the fruit monger on the corner, maybe?”

"Yes, and I can ask my nephew."

"Tomorrow, they could come with . . ."

"Allah is greater than Satan and the biggest demons," Reka's father mumbled. "He has sent you to us to show his mercy."

The room was suddenly seething with activity. The entire neighbourhood was invested in the girls' fate, and Nazreen had to tell and retell the story of how Faruk's sister had called her that morning while several women loudly lamented Mokta's fate.

When dinner was finished, and a mattress and linens put on the bed, Babul felt the anticipation of the afternoon returning. This was good. It felt positive, despite the underlying tragedy. He had to expand his network in Dhaka, and these young cousins could be a useful tool. Reka had always liked Nazreen, and Meena seemed to have a good head on her shoulders. Having them around could turn out to be a stroke of luck.

"Girls! What do you say we take a rickshaw down to Gulshan-2? The night is young! There are a million lights here in Dhaka. Have you seen the skyscrapers yet? And the beautiful houses? Girls, everything's going to be okay. Dhaka is kind to newcomers. Just look at me."

*

"*The Village* . . ." Sofia chuckled. "In a city of sixteen million people?"

"We obviously don't have sixteen million readers. But maybe five hundred. The five hundred that count. We're *The Village*, hence the name of the online magazine."

The woman who had introduced herself as Shannon made herself comfortable in Sofia's visitor's chair and scanned the room. Sofia hadn't settled in properly yet and hadn't left any personal clues about her office. *The Village* had been quick to get in touch.

"We print a paper version once a month, but the website's updated daily. You can't get by in Dhaka without checking *The Village* every day," Shannon had explained over the phone.

Shannon was maybe ten years older than Sofia, blonde and very personable. The sporty type, Sofia mused. A potential friend? She'd introduced herself as the wife of the Australian ambassador and the editor of the UK funded online magazine.

"I used to work for UNICEF," she said, as though keen to make sure Sofia knew she wasn't "just" an accompanying spouse. "When my contract ended, I was offered to head up *The Village*. It's important for all the different agencies here in Dhaka to keep track of each other, as part of the coordinating efforts outlined in the Paris agenda. Don't you think?"

"Yes, very innovative and anything that promotes coordination in Dhaka is a good thing in my book. Who's paying?"

"The Brits, of course. The Brits own Bangladesh, as you'll soon realise. So, how do you like Bangladesh? We've been in Dhaka for four years and the whole family loves it!"

"You have children?"

"Yes, they're in high school. And yours? Younger, aren't they? We're planning to stay until our oldest finishes his International Baccalaureate, which is to say another two years."

"We have two children. Noella and Teo. Noella is seven in December and Teo three around Easter."

Shannon turned out to be well-prepared. She already knew about the children. The embassy had apparently already sent her Sofia's CV and she'd done a thorough Google search.

"You seem to be doing everything right," she said, putting on a pair of reading glasses. "You have a background in law, speak several languages fluently and have solid experience from both Tanzania and Rwanda."

"And Geneva," Sofia pointed out.

"And Geneva," Shannon said. She consulted her notes and continued:

"You have guest lectured at IDS in Sussex and in Bradford, two prestigious institutions, and you're listed as a "discussant" and panellist at a series of international conferences. You've authored several papers that are published on various databases and seem to specialise in human rights and gender equality. Is that correct?"

Sofia flushed slightly. Shannon hadn't had to go digging, she could've just asked.

"Yes, human rights as a working method, primarily, the so-called human rights-based approach. I'm convinced we have to view people as possessors of rights rather than recipients of alms. And without an analysis of how societies create different conditions for men and women, we'll never reach our goals."

Shannon gave her an encouraging nod.

"Very true. There's gender apartheid here, completely absurd! In my younger days, I volunteered in South Africa, and I recognise the patterns. You have to push that in Dev-Com. My husband has given up his seat to the head of AusAid, who's a woman. Try to team up with her, her name's Susan."

Sofia made a note of that before Shannon, looking pleased, homed in on a detail in her notes.

" . . . and my good friend Malena from the Nordic Club helped me translate this: 'Chair of the Småtting Parents' Cooperative'. Something about your children's school, right? And 'Treasurer of the Vanten housing association. Something about a flat?"

Sofia laughed, impressed.

"Wow, you've really done your work. You'll have to let me know if there's anything inappropriate about me in cyberspace. I haven't studied my own search results this thoroughly."

"You have no reason to be anything but proud," Shannon assured her and turned the page in her notebook. "Speaking of which, Malena runs Dhaka's best workout sessions at the Nordic Club, as I'm sure you already know. *Friskis and Svettis*, Fresh and Sweaty, isn't that a hilarious name? Thursdays and Tuesdays on your tennis court. See you there?"

"I'm afraid my evenings belong to my family, unless it's something work-related. I'm afraid I'm more likely to see you in other contexts."

Sofia didn't want to come off as cold, but workouts at the gym were definitely not a priority. Shannon didn't seem to mind, she simply pressed on with the interview.

"Alright. Why Asia? After such a long time in Africa? And how do you like Bangladesh so far?"

"It's exciting," Sofia replied honestly. "For anyone interested in foreign aid, Bangladesh is classic territory. The rebuilding since independence from Pakistan in 1971. The famines in the seventies. The emergence of some of the world's most interesting grassroots organisations: Grameen, led by Nobel Prize laureate Dr Yunus, BRAC, Projica and Khadija Anam's Alor Desh, which we Swedes pride ourselves on having supported for years now."

She paused to let Shannon take notes. Then she continued, letting her hands underline her words:

"At the same time, the hopeless, or shall we say infertile, democracy, the feudal and inert qualities of the administration, the corruption, the challenge of making economic growth trickle down. And possibly an increasingly violent Islamification. We don't know much about that yet. But aside from that storm cloud, all development indicators are impressive. The birth rate has dropped dramatically, infant mortality is improving, the number of illiterate people is radically down. Only maternal mortality is refusing to budge."

"Exactly, exactly. Bangladesh is doing much better than Pakistan these days. Who would have thought that back in '71? So, how do you like the people? I just adore the Bengalis. Their wonderful kindness is the reason my family wants to stay on here year after year."

"Unfortunately, I haven't had the opportunity to get to know many Bangladeshi yet. Generally speaking, though, they're an impressive people. The universe keeps throwing them curveballs. Cyclones, floods, pollution scandals, corrupt government ministers, the lowest salaries in the world, and now most recently the question of how climate change is going to affect their living conditions. And yet, they always bounce back. A tenacious country."

Shannon nodded and took notes, then she looked up, fixed Sofia intently and squinted.

"But why foreign aid? Why slide about in the Bangladeshi mud when you could be cruising around Europe's hippest city, Stockholm, in a BMW? What drives you?"

Shannon's question came out of nowhere. Sofia was surprised. Normally, no one questioned her choice of profession. Not even her parents had asked her why. Why? Why did a person want to work with one thing and not another? Why had she decided to slog around Africa and Asia, when the money and the prestige were to be found back in Sweden? She paused, trying to find the truth.

"I think I want to . . . change the world," she chuckled and leaned forward. "Do something bigger than me. Make a difference. Does that sound presumptuous? I've always been less interested in money than in making my mark."

"I get that. And what does your husband have to say about it? What does he do, by the way?"

"His name's Janne. He's a teacher. History and social studies. This is his first foreign posting, and since our youngest is only two, he primarily looks after him."

" . . . and supports your interesting life?" Shannon added and Sofia couldn't tell if she was being sarcastic or not. She pretended to take the question seriously.

"He likes photography. He's also interested in doing something that . . . well, that's maybe bigger than him. Make this planet better."

Shannon took notes without commenting and Sofia keenly felt the absence of a nod or an mmm. Was she coming across as pretentious? In the end, she couldn't help herself.

"As a lawyer, I'm fascinated by the gap between the law and reality. International law is clear enough, but what are the obstacles to applying it? Here and elsewhere? We have the tools, why aren't we using them more efficiently?"

"I get that, I've asked myself those same questions. Don't be offended by my asking about your personal motivations. After five years in Dhaka, I feel I have to ask everyone who comes here and is interviewed by *The Village* – what drives you? Maybe I'm cynical, but I can't help but wonder. Do you really think you can make a difference? Is that what everyone working here is aiming for?"

Sofia pondered that for a moment and then held up her thumb and forefinger with a small gap between them.

"Yes, little by little. At best."

*

"Sha! Sha!" There, he had it. "Sha!" Moberg shaped his mouth just so and let a quick gust of air pass his lips. It was hard to differentiate between the palatal, retroflex and dental sibilants. He'd spent a lot of time working on a generalisation that would make sense to a Westerner.

"Sha!" he got to his feet and walked over to the window, looked out and pushed up onto his tiptoes while he focused on getting the pronunciation exactly right. "Sha!" *Sha*msundar, *Shri*mongol, *Sh*ilpi." Yes, he had it now. The differences were clear in the transliteration from Bangla, but there was always trouble as soon as the words were spoken. He frowned.

His musings were abruptly cut short when his phone vibrated on his desk and his work duties suddenly came flooding back. He found the phone under a list he should have sent out; the list of invitations to Sofia's welcome buffet. But hadn't he made an appointment to see Sofia now, at two?

"Hello?"

It was Vanja.

"Hi, you sound far away. Are you busy?"

Moberg had to admit he wasn't and Vanja told him her reason for calling.

“It seems Arthur’s done something bad. During my art lessons this morning, I was told Arthur and those Bangla brats Aziz and Karim had apparently hacked into the school computer.”

Vanja was upset and Moberg tried to soothe her.

“Oh dear.”

“Oh dear?” Is that all you have to say? This is our son! I want to know *everything* about it and what the accusations are and I’ve demanded a meeting with the headmaster tomorrow. You’ll have to clear your schedule and come with me.”

Moberg was unable to suppress a snort of displeasure. Both because Arthur had got himself involved in some nonsense and because he didn’t relish the prospect of being scolded by the headmaster on his son’s account. What’s more, there was an edge of hysteria in Vanja’s voice. He couldn’t quite stomach a meeting like that right now.

“Can’t you go on your own, Vanja? I’m supposed to be in a meeting with the Dutch all morning and I have to write a speech for Thursday. Do I really have to . . . ?”

Vanja launched into an agitated enumeration of the reasons why he had to come to the meeting. In the end, he realised he’d better go with her. He would simply have to cancel his meeting with the Dutch.

A minute after ending the call, the new foreign aid counsellor, Sofia, appeared in the doorway.

“Hi, Sofia, good. I was just . . .”

“Don’t worry about it. But I have a lot of things I want to go over.” Sofia was carrying an armful of binders and her hair was efficiently pulled back into a messy bun. “Anna-Lena reminded me the invitations to my welcome buffet have to be sent out today.”

“Yes, very good. The reception, yes. I’m sorry we haven’t been able to get on that yet. Things are busy here in Dhaka, as I’m sure you’ve noticed.”

Moberg picked up the invitation list from his desk and nodded toward the sofa. Sofia took a seat.

"We've pulled up our list of usual suspects, which is to say our like-minded colleagues at other embassies, as well as representatives for the organisations and consortia SwedeAid works with."

"Thank you," Sofia accepted the list and scanned the many UN abbreviations, reading them out under her breath. "UNINCEF, UNDP, WHO, WFP, UNHCR, UN Women – seems like you got all of them. And the World Bank and the IMF. And these must be the local ones, right? BRAC, Grameen, Projica, BRWA, Alor Desh, Manusher Jonno. The local branches of Save the Children and Oxfam, Action Aid . . . hm."

Sofia sounded like she was familiar with the cast list and had found a deviation from the norm.

"No UNFPA? Or UNAIDS?"

UNFPA should be on the list, I think. If not, we'll add them; it's possible my secretary Tulsi forgot. But UNAIDS aren't big here. I realise after working in Africa for so long you might . . ."

"No, that's right. I remember now, they work under UNDP." Sofia nodded. "But UNOPS, I thought they had big infrastructure investments?"

"Booted out. UNDP felt threatened. Don't ask me why. Sometimes, the members of the UN family behave like children."

Moberg sighed and Sofia read on. Moberg was well-aware Sofia needed a good introduction to Dhaka. It would save her time and help raise Sweden's profile. Not least because Moberg had realised he was loath to give up his seat on the foreign aid managers' forum, the powerful Dev-Com. He didn't quite know how to break that to Sofia. Judging from her most recent email, she assumed he would be nominating her without delay. Granted, most ambassadors did nominate the person in charge of foreign aid, but there was no rule to say you had to. Each country's seat was reserved for its Head of Mission and it was up to that person to decide who was best placed to use it.

Moberg had taken over after Sofia's predecessor abruptly packed up and went back home, and he had no desire to leave now. Several of his bridge buddies were in the group and observing the foreign aid work was interesting. There was a bit more action there. His monitoring of Bangladeshi politics had become slightly tedious after five years, to put it plainly, and no one back in Stockholm cared about his reports. They disappeared into a black hole and were never talked about again. Sometimes, he wondered if anyone in Stockholm even read them.

Besides, he was the dean this year, the longest-serving ambassador in Dhaka. That came with certain obligations. He just didn't know how to explain that to Sofia. She was sure to want the seat on Dev-Com so she could use it to spread her gender equality message.

Moberg studied Sofia, who was sitting at the very edge of the sofa, below the portrait of King Carl Gustaf and Queen Silvia. Her entire person seemed keen and raring to go, brimming with will power. She was intensely focused on her list and even her way of sitting looked energetic to Moberg. She'd lined up a number of binders on the table in front of her. Moberg could see they related to a selection of Sweden's various projects in Bangladesh.

The first binder was from the Police Reform Programme, which Sweden had passively co-funded for years as part of a consortium consisting of Britons and Americans and in which Sofia could likely get more actively involved. Several of Rickard's projects were in the row of binders, too, all of them focused on the water sector. None of them required urgent measures. The sector support given to the Water Ministry, which administered the foreign aid donors' investment in clean water and sanitation across the country, did have a reputation of pervasive corruption, but what could a small donor do? Moberg felt a shudder of anxiety, but pushed it down. The World Bank was responsible for keeping the books and twice a year produced a list of suggested improvements to how payments, which totalled about half a billion dollars, were made. Sweden was in the clear. Its share of the support was just four hundred million kronor over five years. Peanuts in this particular context.

A more urgent question was Sweden's support for Alor Desh. In that case, the allegations of corruption were most certainly Sweden's concern. Moberg had prepared a little presentation about their work for Sofia.

"Alor Desh. It means 'radiant land' in Bangla, *desh* means land and *alor* is the singular for light, lantern. Which immediately makes you think 'Whoa! Then Bangladesh, Bangla -*desh* must mean the land where Bangla is spoken', right?"

Sofia nodded slowly, not sure she was following. Moberg blushed and pressed on.

"Anyway. Maybe you've had a chance to look at the preliminary audit by Ernst & Young? Very unfortunate, I have to say."

"I know, I read it. I think I have a fairly firm grasp of Alor Desh, I have, for example, met Khadija Anam and can see that . . ."

But Moberg continued down his chosen path.

"The organisation is run by a certain Khadija Anam, and has over the years become one of the prides of SwedeAid, well, of Sweden as a whole, really. We helped start it, and we're in charge of management. It's a grassroots organisation that works exclusively in the so-called *char* region."

Moberg stood up and walked over to a map of Bangladesh on the wall. A pen was pressed into service as a pointer.

Sofia knew all about Alor Desh and was familiar with everything Moberg was telling her. She would have preferred to talk about their Bangladeshi employees, their land strategy or the work at Dev-Com. What were the local caseworkers, Aisha, Manik and old Zakia like? When was he going to nominate her to Dev-Com? Now that she'd finally managed to sit down with Moberg, she had a battery of questions. The foreign aid bit and Alor Desh were the things she was best-versed in.

"Yes, I've already been briefed by SwedeAid's natural resources department, since this is very topical right now, what with climate change and . . ."

"Briefly put, the enormous rivers Meghna, Padma – which is to say the Ganges – and Jamuna run here and here, through the country. They're called the three sisters. In fact, the whole country is one enormous delta. I seem to recall people claiming there are at least nine hundred well-defined rivers flowing through this green country."

Moberg rambled on, going off on long tangents about the names of various species of rice. Sofia listened politely but increasingly impatiently. Moberg's pen moved slowly through the central and southern parts of Bangladesh as he went on and on. Sofia nodded and tried to cut in.

"Have you visited . . . ?"

But Moberg was droning on relentlessly.

"Char can appear after a flood, or disappear back into the river. No one knows. It's a kind of temporary land, you might say. It seems people tend to start cultivating the land within a few years of a char area appearing, and that inevitably triggers huge fights about land rights. Khadija Anam's organisation helps landless farmers gain access to farmable plots to prevent the mafia or big landowners from appropriating it."

Moberg let his hand drop and stood staring at the map, mumbling, mostly to himself:

" . . . and the pressure on the smallest piece of dirt is enormous. The access to land, to soil, is life, you might say."

Sofia seized the moment.

"Interesting. Have you visited the char areas?"

"No, unfortunately not. As the ambassador, I always find it difficult to leave Dhaka." Moberg said apologetically and Sofia hurriedly spoke up again to keep the conversation from going off track.

"By the way, are you nominating me to Dev-Com this week? I see a number of people on the committee are invited to my reception."

"Yes, about that," Moberg cleared his throat and walked over to his desk. "I figured we'd break you in slowly. After all, this is your first managerial position. Since I'm the dean this year, I think I had better represent Sweden for now."

"But Dev-Com is a forum for foreign aid people, isn't it? I'm not sure I understand?"

"It goes without saying I will relay all decisions and information to you." Moberg gave her an encouraging smile. "Our secretary's exceedingly efficient and . . ."

"How am I supposed to work if I have no overview? I'm not sure I'm understanding you. Dean is an honorary title. Am I wrong in thinking it entails no executive responsibility?"

Moberg could feel Sofia's energy pushing at him. He inhaled quickly and pushed back.

"Being the dean means you have a lot of experience and know the country like the back of your hand. I'm convinced our colleagues at the other embassies appreciate it."

"Okay . . ." Sofia said slowly. "The thing is I have a number of plans that need broad agreement and I was going to work to raise Sweden's profile in the gender equality area. Without a seat on Dev-Com, I can't . . ."

Moberg inhaled again and pushed imperceptibly up onto his toes.

"I'm sure it will all work out. This is my decision."

Sofia broke off abruptly and looked thoughtful, but gathered up her binders and prepared to leave the room. Just then, it dawned on Moberg that Sofia might be able to solve a problem for him.

"Oh, and Sofia, since you're eager to raise Sweden's profile in the realm of gender equality work. I have something for you. I have a scheduling conflict tomorrow, Vanja called about something school-related with Arthur. But I have this meeting with the Dutch. Would you be able to sit in for me? It's about a major initiative by an organisation we work with, addressing violence against women with particular focus on dowries. I was going to have you take it over eventually anyway. Maybe you might as well start tomorrow?"

Back in her room, Sofia turned on the air conditioning and set down at her desk. Moberg's announcement that he was going to stay on Dev-Com had been a real blow. If Dev-Com was anything like its counterpart in Tanzania, this was bad news. She needed contacts and insight to be effective. It wouldn't do any good to complain to Stockholm, either, she'd sound ridiculous. The Ministry for Foreign Affairs and SwedeAid were bound to think a head of mission did what he thought was best, how was she supposed to challenge that? But maybe she was assuming the worst? Maybe Moberg meant well. Maybe he felt he could keep her informed while her active involvement was needed elsewhere? At least until she had settled in properly?

Scanning the list of people who had been invited to her welcome buffet, she kept an eye out for Khadija Anam's name in particular. And, lo and behold, there she was. Director and Founder, Alor Desh, Char Livelihoods and Rights Programme.

She'd already met several of the invitees in various contexts during her first weeks in Dhaka. Many of them had contacted her directly, eager to give a presentation of their organisation or project.

She made notes and drew arrows on the list between names and organisations SwedeAid worked with. She had to get an overview quickly and find a way to stay up to date without being on Dev-Com. She noted the Brits and Dutch seemed to be active in all the same areas as the Swedes. When she was done, there were a lot of circles around and arrows pointing to a woman called Antje van de Ven at the Royal Netherlands Embassy, RNE, and a man by the name of Peter Lewis at British DFID, the Department for International Development.

She had no problem remembering the western names on the list. But the Bengali names! How was she ever going to learn the names of government ministers, researchers, colleagues, teachers and organisations: Kulpana Sobhan, MD Alam Mouzzaman, Nirmol Khatun, Iauhudin Karim, Hafiza Nabi, Hossein Adabar, Ifthekhar Bakolia, Badirur, Rahman, Mabub Wazed, Saima Putukl. Names that didn't give her anything to remember them by, no associations to build on. They slipped out of her memory, like water off Gore-Tex. The only names she recognised were the ones with Arabic roots: Ali, Faruk, Mirjam, Fatima. She was deeply impressed by Moberg's ability to always pronounce everyone's name both elegantly and correctly. During their

Sunday meetings, he referred to ministers and colleagues using their full names, as though it were the easiest thing in the world.

She took out the folder Moberg had handed her as she was leaving, and suddenly felt a crackle of irritation. The whole reason she'd opted not to be a company lawyer, like her uncle and younger brother, but to use her law degree for something else instead, was her interest in human rights. And here it was. Women's human rights, the right to have one's life and choices treated with respect.

She flipped through the papers and was startled by some photographs that fell out. Burnt, charred women's bodies photographed in brutal detail. Deformed, lizard-like women's faces where a single eye was the only thing to suggest the picture was of a living person. Eyes without eyelids, wide-open mouths, patchy burns and faces whose features had been burnt off by acid. She read quietly:

> Across Bangladesh, acid attacks against girls and women resisting marriages proposed by family or interested suitors are becoming more common. The social dynamic around dowries seems to be the trigger for a previously unobserved pattern, in which the husband's family attacks the wife in retaliation for unpaid dowries. The Bangladeshi practice is different from many other cultures as it dictates that the woman's family pay a dowry to the intended husband. The symbolic significance is that the dowry is meant to offset the increased cost associated with accommodating the woman. Research on the subject, however, unanimously indicates that in the modern economy, dowries have come to play an increasingly central role in the consumption patterns of Bangladeshi families. Demands for ever greater dowries is a growing problem in both high and low income families with daughters. The price of a son-in-law can equal several years' salary for the girl's parents and is a common cause of severe indebtedness and the re-mortgaging of land every year. When a family is unable to pay a promised dowry, married

> women are pressured to commit suicide or become the victims of "accidents", to ensure that the husband's family can marry their son off again and thus receive an additional dowry from the family of his next wife. Acid attacks or threats of acid attacks occur in these contexts as well.

The pictures made Sofia feel nauseous. Young girls, faces that had been pretty and full of life. The devastation. What if someone was to attack Noella, she thought suddenly, irrationally, before shaking it off. No one was going to attack Noella.

She shuddered, gathered up the photographs and made a note in her diary of the meeting with the Bangladesh Women Legal Association and the Dutch in the morning. Her intellect commenced a Google-like search around the gender issue she had been so focused on when she first began working with human rights. Yes, whether in the private or the political sphere, it was always the same. Women's personal hardships were reflections of the bigger context, of politics and society. That was the way of it, both here and in Sweden. No one is an island. She was looking forward to the meeting. She was curious to find out how the Bangladeshi women's movement was faring, squeezed as it was between fundamentalists and garment factories.

6

The tiny black ant had discovered the compelling smell of sugar and was following it with every ounce of its survival instinct. The carbohydrates would allow it a few more hours of life, a few more hours. Across the floor, up onto the rug, the strange contour of the rug, up, up, up, wrong way, right way, there . . . suck, suck, wet the sugar, suck . . . live, suck, live.

Janne half-lay across the breakfast table, watching the tiny ant's journey across the vast tabletop. Ants always found the slightest trace of sweetness. Not least in this house, where the children were constantly leaving sticky, saccharine trails behind, which the ants gratefully followed. The tropical climate brought out an insect fauna worlds away from the one he was used to, a fauna they had to beat back with chemicals at regular intervals to keep nature from taking over their house.

It was half past ten. All morning, a violent rainfall had pounded against the roof of the house, making any outside endeavour impossible. It was the tail-end of the monsoon season and the rain came and went as though on a schedule. Suddenly, the sun had broken through the clouds and through the gold grate covering the living room window, Janne had noticed the water had already subsided. Having cowered in the lashing rain, the bushes in their garden were now cautiously turning their leaves and flowers back toward the sun.

He could go and play tennis now. Or he could go work out at the American school. Or head upstairs and read for a bit while he waited for Siv and the embassy driver to pick him up at one. He'd started on a book about Bangladeshi politics, but to be frank, it seemed to be a faux democracy. Two unhinged ladies, each the head of a thoroughly corrupt party, and apparently with some kind of bone to pick with each other. As far as he could make out, the leader of one party, Khaleda Zia, accused the opposition leader Sheikh Hasina's husband of having murdered her father. Or was it Hasina's father who had murdered Khaleda's husband? Either way, it felt like a medieval family feud camouflaged as democracy.

He decided to skip tennis and headed upstairs while the cook cleared away breakfast. His first week there, they'd set the table and cleared it themselves, but it had been surprisingly easy to get used to not doing it. And no one seemed happier about their newfound indolence than Hanif. He approached his domestic chores with great care and skill and it made him visibly nervous when they tried to get involved in any way. These days, neither Sofia nor Janne ever set foot in the kitchen.

Everything had started falling into place in the past few days and their everyday life was beginning to work out in a way that suited everyone. Janne had, after some hesitation, talked to the guards about their spitting. He had, eventually, recognised that Sofia had a point there. They'd looked surprised but had agreed to stop spitting where the children played. The house was almost cosy. A tailor sent over by Siv had quickly made curtains of the fabric they'd bought in Chandni Chowk and they had been hung. Today, Janne was accompanying Siv to pick up some furniture they'd ordered from a carpenter. Siv had been almost accommodating recently, allowing them to order anything they wanted from a tattered Ikea catalogue. They had selected some bookcases, a TV-table, a dining table and twelve chairs. Janne had also ordered a bespoke daybed, which was going to serve as Noella's bed and would be useful for overnight guests. The bed had a pull-out underneath because Janne and Sofia figured they would all be able to fit when they read to the children. Like in the big sofa they'd left behind in Sweden.

On Friday, the ambassador was hosting a welcome buffet for Sofia in the residence. Ninety people, mostly from other embassies, had been invited and Janne had accidentally seen a note Sofia had written to Siv. Something about how it might be nice if the invitations said "To welcome new Counsellor Ms Sofia Paulin and her husband Mr Janne Paulin to Dhaka". He was touched by Sofia's thoughtfulness and felt a pinch of satisfaction. It would have been odd if only Sofia's name had been on the invitations. Granted, the event was primarily for her. But still.

Janne thought about all the times he'd been the at the centre of things, as a headteacher, teacher or youth expert, and now, suddenly: that blank slate staring accusingly at him every morning. His life. He'd always figured he'd find himself in Bangladesh, do something different. The question was what.

Bjarne, the Dane, had already approached him, offering him a job as some kind of buyer or controller of garments, and a perky Norwegian man at the pool had asked if he wanted to write press releases in English for Telenor. Janne was more interested in finding out if he was still interested in photography. As a student, he'd been a member of the university's photography club, snapping some black-and-white shots and developing them himself. Then life had intervened. But maybe now? Just before leaving Sweden, he'd bought a monster camera, figuring he would start by just riding around in a rickshaw, taking pictures of things he came across.

He must've dozed off, because suddenly Hanif was standing in the doorway, announcing that Siv was there to pick him up. They were going to pick up the furniture from the carpenter and then potentially go and take care of the paperwork relating to their alcohol quotas.

Being a Muslim country, the alcohol restrictions in Bangladesh were very strict. Diplomats, a category to which Janne and Sofia belonged, were allowed a quarterly quota to enable representation, and were consequently a socially privileged group, compared to the representatives of private businesses or NGOs. Aside from the diplomats' private quotas, the only alcohol to be found was served in the many clubs sprinkled throughout the diplomatic zone: The Nordic Club, American Club, High Commission Club, Australian Club, German Club, Bagha Club, Japanese Club. There were about ten clubs in Gulshan and Baridhara and as a Westerner, you belonged to a club, took your family there, used the pool, played tennis and had a drink. But you were also welcome to visit other clubs for jazz nights and aerobics sessions.

"Boss, Madame Siv from the embassy is here."

Hanif had reached the front door and stood frozen in a bow as Siv swept past. She looked combative and pushed past Janne into the hallway.

"I really don't think it's appropriate for you to be using that shelf for your shoes." She pointed. "That's a nice shelf, it should be kept in your living room."

Janne had to check himself.

"I'm sorry, it's made of untreated lumber, what exactly makes it a nice shelf? I think it's just right for shoes."

"Fine, but you're not getting another nice shelf," Siv sneered and marched on into the living room.

"So, how many chairs did we order? Eight? Do you really need eight chairs? And the table, let's hope it's finished today."

"We ordered twelve chairs, and I hope we get twelve. According to Moberg, we have a right to that many, and if I know Sofia, we're going to . . ."

"Oh no!" Siv had turned her attention to the ceiling. "Who gave you permission to move the AC unit? This is outrageous . . ."

Janne and Sofia had noticed the air conditioner in the living room was constantly blasting the dining table, giving the whole family stiff necks. So they'd asked the caretakers to move the unit. It had taken twenty minutes and improved the climate in the room significantly.

"I think Mr Hossein and Sofia . . ."

"That's not up to Hossein. I want to see a written work order to approve this kind of relocation! I'm going to have to bring this up with headquarters."

Siv's neck had flushed with indignation and she shook her head as though what had happened was unforgivable.

"This is not how it works! I'm in charge of these decisions! Am I making myself clear?"

For a split-second, Janne lost his cool in the face of the unreasonableness of Siv's outburst, but in the end, he mumbled something about a "misunderstanding". He took a deep breath to stop himself from saying anything that would likely only provoke Siv further, and thought to himself that Siv was lucky he wasn't in a bad mood today. Then a confrontation would've been unavoidable.

"Should we get going?" he managed to say instead, in a relatively neutral tone.

Siv calmed down in the car and launched into a detailed account of her life in Bangladesh, delivered in a conciliatory voice. She leaned closer to him in the backseat.

"Well, let me tell you, you can't trust the guards. Never let them into your house! They'll see all the goodies and relay the information to their accomplices! And, let me tell you, these poor Bengalis, they're almost like children or dogs or something, pardon the analogy. You have to take charge, show them who's boss."

Janne said mmm and nodded, but was inwardly shocked. Were there no limits to what a Foreign Ministry employee could say? But Siv wasn't discouraged by his silence.

"As their manager, I do my best to be fair-minded, I really do. But I have to say I'm often disappointed. Though that being said, they're malnourished, the lot of them. You know, three, four generations of malnutrition, they don't get enough of those oils you need for proper brain development . . . what are they called again? Do you know which ones I mean? I read an article and it was spot on. It's not their fault! They just aren't as bright and far-seeing as we are. But there's nothing they can do about that, nothing at all."

The embassy car had got stuck in traffic and Siv leaned forward and tried to give the driver instructions on where to go, even though there was clearly a complete logjam. Janne stared at her tense back and flushed neck in fascination. For some reason, Siv aroused his curiosity. Exactly what was this woman's world view? He wanted to know more.

"So . . . Siv, how did you end up in Bangladesh?"

"I got involved with SwedeAid by accident, you might say. I'd worked with staff transfers at Skandia before, and took a three-month contract with SwedeAid's HR department to handle one of the waves of cutbacks in the nineties. It didn't take them long to see my value: I got the job done. And, well, the rest is history."

Siv broke off and hurled herself at the front seat, grabbing the steering wheel and shouting at the driver to blow his horn. Then she turned back to Janne, seemingly unperturbed.

"Bangladesh is my second foreign posting, I was in Guatemala before. And to be honest, my first choice would've been Vietnam or Cambodia this time, Asia Light. But I ended up in Bangladesh. And it's not so bad here," Siv said smugly. "Moberg and I understand each other and allow each other a lot of room. Imagine that, lots of freedom and a whole embassy to look after. It doesn't get better than this!"

Janne smiled wearily. Siv suddenly started talking in a baby voice.

"And I want you to settle in really nicely, really nicely, and just love it here, that's what I live for. I know I meddle too much sometimes, but it's only because I care!" She tilted her head to the side, pleadingly. "That's the way to look at it, Janne!"

She squeezed his arm and Janne realised he was supposed to act friendly and say he understood or reassure her some other way. Instead, he pressed on with his inquiries.

"So, about Bangladesh . . ."

"Pah, Bangladesh, Kenya, Nicaragua, I applied for jobs all over. I don't care which country I'm in, per se. I don't actually socialise with the Bangladeshi; I have, how can I put it, an international circle of friends. A lot of Americans and Australians, actually. And Canadians.

The car had reached a large gate and Siv leaned forward and directed their driver. A bowing guard let them through.

A jumble of furniture in various states of completion filled an unkempt courtyard garden on the other side of the gate. A young man in a loincloth approached them.

"Madame," he greeted Siv. "The furniture you ordered is ready. The table . . . here. And the coffee table, fairly large, are the measurements correct? And then this."

The man made a sweeping gesture toward a gigantic piece of furniture at the centre of the courtyard. It took Janne a few seconds to figure out what it was.

"Is that the sofa bed for Noella's room? But . . . ?"

He faltered. The sofa bed had been made with the pull-out extended, one high and one low bed next to each other. Just like in the catalogue. Except the pull-out couldn't be pushed back in. Janne walked around the thing, a smile slowly spreading across his face. Just as Siv was getting ready to lay into the carpenter, he stepped in.

"No, I like it! Talk about getting what you ask for. Down to the last detail. This is what I call service."

*

Bright red spit landed between Meena's feet. Even though the light was still faint so early in the morning, she could see the man's face was covered in a web of fine wrinkles. He must be at least fifty, she thought. An untidy turban covered his head and he had tied his *lungi* up between his legs and betel juice was swirling around his mouth, colouring his lips blood red. She did her best to appear both proper and eager to work. Reka's neighbour had said he hired anyone who turned up at five every morning, and, so, here she was.

"Try to get mangos, if there are any to be found. Mango prices are sky-high now at the end of the season. You can make a taka per melon, if you buy them for less than ten. Cauliflower is two taka if you buy more than fifteen for less than twenty." The man reeled off numbers while eyeing Meena steadily. "But I need the goods here before nine every morning. Only Allah can protect you if you don't bring me back a full load. I'll let you work this week, and we'll see if you're good enough."

He spat again and turned around. The conversation was over.

Meena nodded eagerly at his back. This was the start of a new life in Dhaka. She was going to show him, the Hindu fruit and vegetable monger they called Patel, and she was going to show Reka and Babul and everyone else that she could make a good living. If they would just give her chance to prove herself.

Just as northern Dhaka's many mosques turned on their loudspeakers with a crackle and began to recite the first prayer of the day, Meena pulled her *dupatta* tighter around her shoulders and jumped up onto the cargo bed of the rickety pickup truck. A boy a little bit older than her was already sitting there. The truck was driven by a man in his twenties, who called himself Miraj.

"He's Hindu," was the first thing Miraj shouted to them from the cab as the truck bounced out onto the road leading north to Uttara. "That's why he's so fucking stingy. Two taka at least, that's his standing price! He's cheating you!"

Meena had her hands full clutching the sides of the cargo bed but she glanced furtively at the boy to see if he'd heard the driver's comment. He had, but he just shook his head. He sat in silence for a long time, then he suddenly opened his mouth.

"Never mind him," he said and Meena started. The voice didn't seem to belong to him, an almost full-grown man. It was high and reedy and ended in a croaking bird sound. He noticed her reaction but carried on talking in a voice that hissed and squeaked by turns.

"Just follow my lead, you'll make twenty-thirty taka before lunch. It's okay. I'm Rifat, by the way. But everyone calls me Bird Boy."

The truck reached a terrifying speed long before they got to the villages in the Tongi area. The many half-finished high-rises and workshops around Badda were replaced by the large display windows and wide staircases of the new shopping centre in the middle-class suburb of Uttara. Meena marvelled at the number of shops Dhaka seemed to have, and the strange machines they seemed to sell. What were they? And where did they come from? Who was going to buy all those things?

She curled up in the cargo bed, wishing someone from home could see her now. Amma . . . or Mokta. The thought of Mokta slammed into her stomach like an axe, almost knocking the air out of her. It was her first day at a real job. Would they be proud? Or dismayed? Probably dismayed, she realised sadly. Dismayed she had to work unaccompanied, side by side with men.

Once they had left Uttara, small workshops lined the road and early risers were gathering around broken rickshaws, half-finished furniture, half-stuffed mattresses and stands selling fruits and vegetables. Women carrying water buckets on their heads and children looking for a handful of sticks for their morning fire could be seen hurrying down the alleyways. Thirty minutes later, they reached the outer edge of the city and Meena realised she was surrounded by the same landscape she'd known all her life. Green, sweeping fields, waterlogged rice paddies and between them narrow paths or roads on which people, animals or vehicles balanced precariously. And always the feeling of a river, of water very nearby. That there was a river nearby, pulsating just around the corner, made Meena feel safe.

The sun had come up quickly. It was hard to believe she'd felt chilly earlier that morning. It was going to be a sweltering day.

The truck's first stop was next to a gently sloping riverbank, along which a row of boats were moored. Every boat was filled to the brim with cucumbers, watermelons and cantaloupes, apples and clutches of lychee. Commerce was already in full swing. Rifat started screeching before he could even get down from the truck. His bird-like cries left no one in any doubt which truck had just pulled up.

"Ten melons for fifty taka, we'll give you fifty taka for ten."

"Seventy-five," someone called from a boat.

"Seventy," from another.

The boy hesitated as several more trucks pulled up behind them.

"Then we'll take twenty for sixty."

Meena did a quick mental calculation. Three taka a melon, that was good, right? Though, were they good melons? Did it matter? While the boy shouted out his bids, Meena slipped off the truck and walked over to one of the boats. She asked to see some of the melons, remembering what the fruit monger at home had told her. If you saw a light green circle at the top of the watermelon, it meant the fruit had been dipped in a magical potion to make it look ripe, but on the inside, it was in fact white and unripe. She passed unseen from boat to boat, noting that the one at the far left had the best, sweetest-smelling melons.

"Rifat . . ." she said, but the boy was already buying melons with green tops for seventy taka.

She walked over to the left boat and was about to name her price, seventy taka for fifteen, when a burly man suddenly shooed her away.

"Who are you? Did you pay customs? I'm Khaled, I'm the boss here. I work for the government, The Government of Bangladesh. Who gave you permission to buy melons here?"

Rifat dropped everything he was doing and came running.

"Boss, she's with me. She's working for Patel, too."

"Ah, you should've said. Who the fuck isn't working for Patel these days? Ha ha! I'm Patel's man in the field, always at your service. Rifat, bloody hell, you have to get he price down, Patel's going to murder us both. I can only keep the other merchants out for another thirty minutes."

"It's not easy, they know the others are coming. Meena – was that your name? – what price did you get? I saw you talking to the smallest boat."

Meena quickly got over being addressed directly and reeled off the price and information she had. Khaled listened and Rifat looked relieved.

"That's right," the man nodded. "Patel's been saying people have been dissatisfied with the fruit recently. People have started complaining about unripe fruit or fruit that's rotten on the inside but pretty on the outside. You say you can spot that kind of thing? Then we'll go with your boat."

Three hours later, the little group had visited five different vegetable markets and bought a mountain of melons and a few stems of banana at a good price. Rifat was in a great mood when the truck turned off toward Badda.

"Now Amma and I can buy rice today, too," he laughed.

When they got back to Badda, Patel and one of his sons were surrounded by several small trucks and a number of rickshaws, which they were dispatching in different directions. Patel greeted them with a grim look on his face.

"How the hell can you take this long from Tongi! Where have you been? This fruit would've been in Mirpur by now you weren't so lazy!"

It was almost ten. Ideally, he would have wanted the fruit to have been sold already, or at least on its way to one of the fruit stands he ran.

Patel was an important man in Badda. He was one of the Hindus who had come to stay in Bangladesh, when many of their coreligionists chose to leave the country for good. With a brilliant head for business and stellar contacts, he'd risen to a position that made it difficult for anyone to discriminate against him, even though there were doubtless people in Badda who would have loved to see him leave Bangladesh and reunite with "his brothers in India". Every morning at four o'clock, he got up and set to work. Fruit, vegetables, fish, perishable goods that could be brought in quickly from the surrounding villages north of Dhaka, distributed to the central market places and sold during the day. There was nothing he wouldn't consider selling. Throughout the day, a network of local associates kept him up-to-date on the going rates for things via mobile phone so Patel always knew about the slightest market fluctuation. That's why he eventually listened with appreciation to the deals Rifat and Meena had made in the early morning.

"And she's right about the ripe and unripe fruit," he mumbled.

During the monsoon, too many fruits had had to be thrown away. The merchants had grown irritable when they were harangued by angry customers. And he couldn't afford that. Unhappy merchants could quickly put him out of business.

He gave Meena thirty taka, spat out another bright red squirt of betel residue and announced curtly:

"Tomorrow. Same time. But the devil help you if you're late."

*

The Swedish ambassador and his wife were hosting the reception. Every part of the residence's garden was decorated with teeny tiny lights and large flower arrangements greeted the guests in the hallway. Janne had never seen anything like it, stepping through the front doors made him feel like a film star. Vanja looked radiantly beautiful, dressed in a dark blue sari sprinkled with sequins.

"You both look so lovely. Janne, a panjabi, very handsome! I think embroidery looks so masculine on a man, don't you, Sofia?"

Vanja glanced appreciatively at Janne, who was wearing his first ever panjabi, an embroidered, shin-length shirt. Looking past Vanja, he noted with relief that almost all the Western men were also wearing the Muslim garment, just like Sofia had assured him they would. Otherwise, he would have felt a bit over the top.

"You have to say hello to Heidi, my friend who's married to EU Commissioner Rickardsen."

Vanja led Janne and Sofia over to a couple standing in a corner, relaying information under her breath along the way.

"So, Heidi's a professional yodeller with the Vienna Concert Hall and just married Rickardsen whom we all thought was gay until he turned up with her. And she's lovely! We're hoping she'll give a performance soon."

"Professional what?" Janne had time to whisper back, before they reached the couple.

"My new EU colleague, delighted. Welcome to Dhaka!" Rickardsen greeted Sofia. "When did you arrive? Have you had time to familiarise yourself with the strategic plan we drew up last spring? Probably not, but let me give you a briefing before Wednesday's meeting, which I'm assuming you'll be attending."

The EU bigwig focused exclusively on Sofia, leaving Janne and his new spouse out in the cold, casting about for a topic of conversation.

"Right, so you're new to Dhaka, too? I thought Vanja mentioned you used to work at the Vienna . . ."

"Yes, that's right. I'm a yodeller at the Vienna Concert Hall."

"Yodeller, so we're talking about yodelling, I mean, some kind of . . ."

The woman smiled. This wasn't the first time she'd had to explain what she did for a living, that much was clear. She leaned in closer and emitted a rolling, low yodelling note.

" . . . like that! We like that kind of thing in Austria, you know, and you might say I'm the head of the nation's premier yodellers. Or, I *was*, until I met that one, Mr Rickardsen," she nudged Rickardsen affectionately with her elbow. "My new identity is to be a size 10 for H&M."

"I'm not sure I follow?" Janne looked at the woman who spread her arms.

"Can't you tell I'm a perfect size 10?" She did a spin. "H&M in Dhaka uses me as a test person for their size 10. The local women tend to be smaller, so someone has to step up. A new career, in other words." She laughed and winked. "And you, what did you do before you came to Dhaka. Not just a 'plus one', I hope?"

Janne laughed and gave a brief account of his professional life. He wouldn't have minded spending more time with the Austrian woman, but Sofia had put her arm through his and was ushering him toward other guests.

"You mustn't get stuck, you know. The whole point is to mingle . . ."

A lot of the guests came up to Sofia to congratulate her on a speech she'd given earlier in the week and Janne realised Sofia had, as usual, already carved out a bit of a platform for herself. Sofia had come home after work one day, telling him something about how what she'd thought was a normal planning meeting had in fact been a big seminar. Moberg had been scheduled to give a speech about women's rights and the scourge of honour-related acid attacks against women, but had forgotten all about it. Due to a series of misunderstandings, Sofia had suddenly, with five minutes' notice, been forced to improvise a speech about acid attacks. This was what people were congratulating her on.

"Your well-informed wife reduced us all to tears," said the Canadian foreign aid counsellor, who was a relatively young but corpulent man with a side parting.

"Yes, what website did you crib that speech off, Sofia," joked a woman who had introduced herself as a health expert working for the British. "Very impressive! And I think your suggestion was good, some form of cross-sector thinking about violence against women is required to affect real change. We have to stop the attacks on innocent women. A holistic strategy rather than isolated interventions. Maybe a conference?"

Janne suddenly spotted a familiar face in a corner. Bjarne, the Dane, was talking to Moberg. Janne walked up to them.

"Nice party."

"Well, the snacks are good, at least," Bjarne said, holding a piece of Swedish rye bread with blue cheese up for Janne to see. "Imported by the Lady Ambassador herself in her handbag. Special delivery by Thai Air. Bloody fancy." The bread disappeared into his mouth and he smacked his lips loudly.

"How's life as an accompanying spouse treating you, Janne? What the fuck, Moberg, what the hell kind of term is that – accompanying spouse?" He pronounced it in pretend-Swedish, nudging the Swedish ambassador somewhat disrespectfully in the ribs with his elbow. "Is that the best the Swedish Academy could come up with? Don't you have some kind of consultant who could take a swing at finding a better word?"

Moberg chuckled awkwardly, apparently speechless, which Janne noted seemed like par for the course for him.

"I don't mind being an accompanying spouse. So long as I'm not described as 'plus Madame', like I saw on one of Sofia's invitations. 'Counsellor Sofia Paulin plus Madame' . . . that's tough to swallow, I won't lie."

Bjarne let out a hearty laugh and slapped Janne's back.

"Bloody hell, Madame Janne, that one, *that one* is going to haunt you."

Moberg laughed in a slightly forced way, but then his eyes started darting this way and that. It was time for a speech and some welcoming words to Sofia. He cleared his throat.

"Ladies and gentlemen," he began. He had to tap his glass three times to get everyone's attention. Eventually, people stopped talking and turned their attention to the Swedish ambassador.

"It's not every day an embassy gets the chance to welcome a colleague as eminently suited to and qualified for her role as Ms Sofia Paulin. Sofia is a lawyer who specialises in human rights and despite her young age, she has worked for both OHCHR, the UNs office for human rights in Geneva, and the Swedish embassy in Tanzania. We hope she will be able to contribute to raising Sweden's human rights profile here in Bangladesh, where we've spent almost twenty years working with women's and children's issues. Welcome to Dhaka, Sofia, I hope you'll like it here despite all the floods and catastrophes!"

He wrapped up by assuring her Dhaka wasn't as terrible as rumour had it, and by saying again that he hoped she would like her new home. It was a very flat speech, the phrases lined up like train cars. Even so, Janne could tell Sofia was pleased. The speech had done what it was supposed to.

Moberg did, however, forget to so much as mention Janne, which Janne noted with a wry smile. As did Vanja, who stood next to him, gesticulating and pointing to Janne in an attempt to make Moberg realise his faux pas.

"Oh, don't worry about it, this is Sofia's night," Janne said, but before he realised what was happening, Vanja was climbing onto a chair. He noted she was swaying precariously.

"Ladies and gentlemen, that was only half the truth. Let me also welcome Janne to Dhaka. Janne who is to Sofia what rice is to daal or the bun to the burger or however you choose to look at it. Perhaps simply the other leg of the Paulin family? And it takes two legs to walk, I think we can all agree on that? Janne has for many years been one of Stockholm's most popular and celebrated headteachers, I have that from a reliable source. But out of love for his family and his wife, he has decided to take up residence here in Dhaka for a few years. Janne, I hope you will come to love Bangladesh and its wonderful people as much as I do and find your own path through this jungle. What I mean is, some of us are grownups and don't need guidance from headquarters . . . A lot of us have the privilege of exploring this city full-time and I want to tell you what I've told a lot of newly-arrived spouses – it's easy to lose your mind in Bengal. Cheers!"

Vanja's speech was met with laughter and applause and Janne realised her spontaneous initiative warmed his heart. After the speech, a number of people came up to him to talk about education, asking him his opinion on the quality of teaching at the American International School. He smiled inwardly at the social status of the teaching profession, at least in a context where people had school-aged children. And these days, they usually did. He remembered the years between twenty and thirty-five, when all his friends who worked in media or in the film and music industries almost seemed to take exception to the fact that he was nothing but a regular, boring, high school teacher. A few years later, his experiences and opinions were the ones that carried more weight. Everyone wanted to talk education with him and discuss the problems they were having with their children and their schools. Apparently, that was no less the case in Dhaka. Over the course of the evening, Janne also had two invitations to play tennis the following week and a charismatic woman who was head of the Asian Development Bank pushed him into a corner and interrogated him about his life. She felt very strongly he should start working as a consultant in the education sector.

"Call me any time, Janne," she'd told him, handing him a business card.

Out of the corner of his eye, Janne watched Sofia doing the rounds, seemingly talking to everyone. She was good at that. Didn't get bogged down in deep conversation, just hop, hop, hop, like a goat seeking out new tufts of grass. When he saw her like this, like tonight, he could feel how obsessed he still was with her. The way she pinched her ear when she was thinking, the way she focused on people, her lucid intelligence and determination. Even her rough edges. They interested him, had always attracted him in a way other women's personalities eventually weren't able to. His previous relationships had always petered out because he'd lost interest, grown bored and felt everything was too predictable. But life with Sofia was a challenge. A challenge he'd come terrifyingly close to failing. If anyone had acted predictably, it was him.

And now, in her element. Her small, perky breasts, hidden under a brightly coloured scarf. His stomach flipped when he saw her like this, in full bloom. Early on in their relationship, his older brother Mikael had once pointed out that Sofia wasn't as pretty as his previous girlfriends. And someone had called her "unconventionally attractive". Janne didn't know what they were getting at. He could still only see the attractive.

Janne wasn't as efficient in his socialising as Sofia. He preferred to linger with people he liked, didn't mind nibbling on the same tuft of grass all night. It was more rewarding. Or at least the reward was different, he mused.

When it was time to leave, he found Sofia deep in conversation with an elegant woman in a sari. It was only when the woman turned to Janne that he realised her left cheek had burn scars.

"Janne, let me introduce you. This is Khadija Anam, the woman who works in the char area. You know, the delta I've been telling you about."

Sofia turned to the woman and put her arm around Janne's waist.

"This is Janne, my husband. He's not fully acquainted with the world of foreign aid."

"All the better," Khadija laughed. "Then maybe it's safe to assume you're normal?"

She raised her glass of orange Fanta encouragingly to Janne. A signal that the person was a practicing Muslim, Janne was given to understand.

"Sometimes, I think all the expert opinions render us unable to think beyond simple fixes. Very few people in the foreign aid sphere have the ability or the mandate to approach things holistically."

The woman spoke perfect British English and Janne approved of her comment. It opened things up nicely and seemed to be about something he understood. He followed up on it.

"Seems to me every last person here in Dhaka's an expert. If not on children's issues or sexual health, then on food hygiene or irrigation. Expert or advisor, apparently that's the name of the game."

"And yet very, very few people work with what actually makes a difference. I mean for the poor people."

"Tell me more."

"Well, listen, to put it simply. Astonishingly few experts spend any time listening to what the poor have to say. They're the real experts, no? Experts on living in poverty."

Janne thought Sofia seemed quiet on the ride home.

"What did you think of the attendance? Did anyone you expected not show up?"

"On the contrary, it was a great turnout."

"Are you angry?"

"Angry, no, why? A bit tired, maybe."

Janne was silent for a while, watching rickshaw drivers settling in for the night on top of their bikes through the car window. The jumble of rickshaws you'd at first glance assume were just parked willy-nilly on street corners, were in fact their drivers' beds for the night. For what had to be the hundredth time, Janne wondered how they did it. Sleeping with your back against a four-inch backrest and your feet on the handlebar looked insanely uncomfortable. And yet, that's how they recovered after fourteen hours of pedalling. Sofia was quiet, too, staring out at the traffic, her head turned away from him.

"How did you like the furniture?" Janne tried again.

"The furniture?" Sofia was miles away.

"Noella's bed and the dining table?"

"Oh, right. No, that table won't do. You did realise that, right? We can't have legs like that if we're hosting events. You're going to have to return it."

"What? Return it? Are you kidding me?"

Janne stared doubtfully at Sofia, taken aback by her reaction. The table the carpenter had copied from a Norrgavel catalogue hadn't looked exactly like they'd expected. The legs had grown lion's paws and sprouted leaves, which Janne had let pass with a wry smile. She turned to face him.

"No, I'm not kidding. The table's going back. It's embarrassing. Ugly and embarrassing, completely tacky. Lion's paws, Janne! They've carved leaves on the legs. We wanted clean Scandinavian lines. Return it."

The conversation died again. Janne realised he didn't have the energy to confront Sofia's unreasonableness just now. Sometimes she was like that. All rigid and devoid of humour. When they were brushing their teeth a few minutes later, side by side in their enormous bathroom, Janne made one last attempt.

"I can tell you're pissed off, Sofia. Why can't you just tell me what's wrong?"

"Tired, not angry."

Sofia spat into the sink, put her toothbrush back and took her contacts out with her mouth open.

"You're not upset about that thing with Vanja, are you? Because she gave a speech about me?"

Sofia made no reply.

"Come on, seriously? Is that it? That I stole half a second of your limelight? Sofia!"

"That's not how I see it, Janne. I'm happy to give you all the space you want, but I actually thought it was pretty vulgar. Yes, I thought it was tasteless."

"You're kidding?! It was a lovely speech. Everyone laughed."

"Yes, because it makes everyone really uncomfortable that the accompanying spouse is a man. It's so predictable. If I'd been the spouse, no one would have given a speech about me."

"But there was a speech for you, and one for me. Sofia, come on!"

"Yes, and mine was short and dull and yours was long and spiritual, and delivered by yet another radiantly beautiful woman who likes Janne. Big shock. All eyes on Janne. As usual. I just want to know . . . how do you do it?"

Janne stared at his wife in the mirror. He'd frozen mid-movement, his mouth full of toothpaste. Suddenly, he imagined what a text from Mikael in Jönköping might say. "How's that hair shirt treating you, Janne?" Was it about that again, about his betrayal?

Sofia bent down to wash her face and Janne broke in.

"Sofia. Hello?! I can't believe this! Tell me you're not serious?"

Janne searched her face for little twitches or a twinkle that might reveal that the whole thing was a joke Sofia had taken just a bit too far. That she was about to launch into a pretend-serious, deadpan harangue and then giggle. But nothing.

"You're . . . completely unbelievable! Sofia, snap out of it! I'm here too, you know. We're a family, surely there's room for all of us? Vanja's right! Two legs . . ."

"The timing, Janne. I still think it was extremely poor timing. We don't know people well enough yet, and Vanja's a bit . . . well . . . am I right in thinking she was drunk? But sure, it's not your fault, it really isn't. But since you're asking why I'm angry . . ."

"No, we don't know people. Exactly! And you don't seem to want anyone to know me as anything other than your appendix. Are you going to shut me out the entire time we're here? Is that the deal? And what do you mean about Vanja being a bit . . . what?! She's a delight – a real-life person among all the self-important diplomats."

"No, Janne. You're allowed to shine, too. That's important to me! That you find something for you. But there's a time and a place for everything, and this was kind of . . ."

" . . . *your* night. My god. You're being completely absurd. Goodnight!"

Janne spat angrily into the sink and went to bed. Sofia joined him a minute later. They lay in silence with their backs to each other. Janne heard the rattling of Sofia putting her bite plate in her mouth. For a fraction of a second, his anger subsided and he felt sorry for his wife instead.

7

Farida dried her hands on her sari and hoisted the water bucket up onto her hip. Her back ached from carrying the little boy around. She looked up at the trees, where a troop of monkeys were chattering, then her eyes were drawn to the fruit she'd just put down on the veranda. Had they already got to her bananas? Mostafar was lying on a blanket on the veranda to keep the monkeys away, but the monkeys were sly. They knew he wouldn't chase them away.

Her breathing had eased slightly since the *chollisa*, Mokta's memorial ceremony. At first, she'd been unable to breathe, then she'd been unable to sleep, and finally, she'd been unable to talk. First Mokta, then the little ones. Farida could feel that pain in her chest again, feel her breathing getting laboured. Her three beautiful daughters, her pride and joy. Life had suddenly been upended, again. First the river had swallowed their field and now this. Allah was certainly testing them. Now she had only the boy. Allah be praised for making her so busy she didn't have time to think.

Her husband had closed himself off. To him, all three girls were dead. Whenever he wasn't pulling his rickshaw, he sat outside the mosque with his brother Mullah Lutfar, asking for forgiveness for the shame that had destroyed his family. He hadn't blamed her openly, but the accusation hung between them, unspoken. She'd failed to raise his daughters right.

It was going to have to be *shalon*, rice powder and salt, for dinner again. Some sweet potatoes and a bit of cabbage. Farida moved slowly across the yard, trying to look dignified, acutely aware of the eyes watching her. Farida had always attracted attention, but it was more important than ever now not to let their detractors be right. With her tall beauty and calm dignity, she had probably always irked the other villagers. Because she looked the way she did, because she spoke English. Because she got a job as a teacher. Because she worked. Of course Allah had punished her eventually. The Evil Eye had done its job.

Her parents had married her off in a panic when she was about fourteen, knowing a girl as beautiful as her was bound to attract the Evil Eye. By then, young men had started acting menacingly and making demands and suggestions, even though her parents had done their best to keep her indoors as much as possible. In the end, the promise once made to her cousin Nurul had been fulfilled in haste. A big dowry in exchange for a guarantee that she would be allowed to carry on studying. And Nurul had always been a good man, considerably older than her but a kind person who didn't seem bothered by her beauty. He had let her become a woman before he came to her bed. But he had expected a son, not three girls.

"*Shonamoni*," she spoke gently to the boy while she prepared dinner out on the veranda. When her husband was out of earshot, she could call him shonamoni, darling, without being told off. You weren't supposed to call boys that, it could make them soft.

"Shonamoni, what do you think my girls are doing now?"

The boy didn't respond, but he looked up at her. He drooled and waved his arms about. She reached out and stroked his shaved head. He probably missed Meena and Nazreen.

"Do you think Meena laughs sometimes? Do you think she will keep doing maths?" The thought of Meena, her youngest daughter, Farida was overcome with guilt. Little bony, scrawny Meena, who wasn't like anyone else in the village. Her daughter, who never laughed and rarely smiled but who was always alert and noticed everything. Meena had always been her own person, had always had a unique way of sitting still, intently observing and scratching her arms while pondering things. Then she acted. It was almost eerie how Meena seemed to think events into being before they came to pass, and when everyone else caught on, Meena had already been there, already put things in order, arranged things to make sure everything turned out for the best.

Like the micro credits. It was Meena who had figured out the family's many micro credits had become unsustainable and who had, chewing on a pencil, calculated how much money they needed to make each month. Then she'd negotiated a payment plan with Farida's women's group. And it was Meena who had made sure the deep new well had been drilled right in front of Nurul and Farida's house so they could fetch water without having to leave their little brother unsupervised. When the maps were rolled out and the men with the manual drill arrived in the village, Meena had with little nudges and questions and observations managed to make them think that was the best spot. Now, Farida had a full view of both the boy and the women of the village, and didn't have to go very far for water.

"Even demons are powerless against that girl. She's like the part of me I've hidden away," Farida mumbled to the boy. Guilt stabbed Farida in the gut when she thought about the fact that Meena had also been the one to warn them about Faruk. Meena had said Rahima beat Faruk's younger brothers and that they were a bad family. But who would listen to a girl? And a younger sister, to boot. Farida hadn't intervened when Nurul beat Meena for not blessing her sister's marriage by putting henna on her forehead.

She thought about all the times Meena and her father Nurul had fought. When Meena refused to come out of the mango tree. She'd been five at the time. When she gave herself that bizarre haircut. She'd been eleven. No one in the village had hair like Meena, short on the sides and with a fringe covering her forehead. Who looked like that, except boys and crazy *baul* singers? In the village, girls took pride in their long hair. Nazreen and Mokta had spent hours combing their blueish-black manes, treating them with oils and herbs and putting them up in heavy buns at the napes of their necks. Meena had cut hers off.

Nazreen loved her little sister, but they weren't the slightest bit alike, as Farida was well aware. Did Nazreen understand Meena at all, now that it was just the two of them? Worry slithered through Farida, like a slow snake through grass. Alone in Dhaka, Mahmoda had told them. Alone on the bus to Dhaka. She chased the snake away and turned back to her son. He was getting hungry.

"Meena is like chili and Nazreen like coriander," Farida mused out loud to her son, thinking warmly of Nazreen. Happy, pliant Nazreen who was friends with all the world. Competent, proper and light. Like a woman ought to be, always obedient, always unobtrusive. Farida picked up the boy and got ready to go fetch Nurul from the steps of the mosque. Dinner was ready.

The thought of her girls in the big city secretly delighted her. They had run away. Who would have thought it?

She smiled.

*

Nazreen woke up when Meena got out of bed in the dark, washed her face and disappeared off to her job at the fruit market. She hoped her sister had at least grabbed a chapati and some cabbage for breakfast, but she couldn't be sure. Meena seemed to have made an art of making herself inconspicuous at Reka and Babul's. Nazreen stayed in bed a while longer, enjoying the warmth her sister had left behind, listening to the sounds of the early morning. It was still cool. The alley was still deserted.

On the other side of the wall, she heard someone clear their throat all the way from the bottom of their lungs and then spit into the open sewer. Shortly thereafter, she heard the distinctive sound of a urine stream drilling into the water. Water buckets clattered, a cat meowed and early rickshaws rattled. But the first call to prayer hadn't taken place yet. She could stay a while longer.

Nazreen allowed her thoughts free rein for a short, short while every morning. Like when a woman adjusts her burqa and you catch a glimpse of her face behind it. Then she shut them down again and refrained from thinking all day and all night. Instead, she made sure she was busy. She did chores around the house, talked, looked for work, helped out, lifted, poured, emptied, walked up and down the alleyway. She only ever let her thoughts out in the early morning. Thoughts of Goalpur, her mother and Mokta.

She could picture the village as vividly as if she were there. The fields that would be flooded this time of year, her friends and relatives crouching in the water, planting rice. The joy and beauty of a newly-planted rice paddy, the pale green of the outermost tips of the rice plants. The same colour as Mokta's hair tie, which Nazreen still wore around her wrist. The children dragging goats around, the skinny cows, and up by the road, the tea stands and the little shops. The smell of garlic being fried, the coriander being ground and the pakora bobbing in oil over the open flames. Mother, what was she doing right now? And Mokta . . . but at that point, Nazreen always got a knot in her stomach.

She pushed the images away and let the present flow into her instead.

The days she'd spent at Babul and Reka's had blended together, melting into an everyday life that was fairly enjoyable. Nazreen and Meena had been embraced by the neighbourhood without much fuss and Babul and Reka had generously made room for them in their home.

One morning, they had all been woken up by a loud knock on the front door and a voice shouting all residents had to come out into the street immediately. Babul had whisperingly told them it was Mamod, the local gang leader who worked for a *mustaan*, a slum bigwig. Mamod was a large man, dressed in jeans and a white button-down. Nazreen had noted a gold chain hanging down his exposed chest. He'd brought a band of smoking, unsmiling young men with him. One of them had been tapping a nightstick against his calf. Nazreen and Meena had been terrified, but after a short negotiation, Babul had managed to get

Mamod to accept their presence in the neighbourhood, in exchange for a small monthly payment.

"You need our protection," Mamod had told the girls. "No one can get by here without our protection. If anyone causes you trouble, you come to me."

He'd wanted the girls' mobile phone numbers and had asked how old they were. He'd said he might have work for them, but hadn't said what kind. Then he'd disappeared with the rest of his posse.

"They just want to know what's going on," Babul explained, his voice tinged with worry. "It's good that we're open about you being here, it's very good. And on that note, maybe we should go to the mosque and let the imam know you're staying with us. Go with Reka on Friday, after prayers."

But aside from that, no one had objected to them staying with Babul and Reka, and their hosts hadn't said anything about them finding somewhere else to live, either. Quite the opposite, it seemed to Nazreen. Reka and Babul seemed pleased the girls paid them a little something each month for room and board.

Meena had been lucky. Patel, an important fruit merchant in Badda, had taken her under his wing. Her salary was meagre, but she was guaranteed work every day so long as she showed up on time. It wasn't really proper or common for a young girl to work alone among men, but Meena seemed so doggedly determined that Nazreen let her be. And what choice did they have, anyway? Starting out, it was all about making enough taka, so they wouldn't have to use the money in the plastic box.

As far as Nazreen could make out, Meena either went around the villages north of the city in a pickup truck buying fruit, or she sold that same fruit from a cargo rickshaw in the local marketplaces. She didn't like to talk about her work, but every night, she put a crumpled note in their plastic box. Nazreen would have liked to sit down and talk to her sister, but Meena was always on the go and when she did have some free time, she made sure to make herself scarce.

Nazreen had worked, too, a day here, a day there. But she hadn't found a permanent job yet, so far, it had all been one-offs. Reka, as it turned out, had a remarkable network and had shown herself to be a true friend, she assured Nazreen she would get a job before she knew it. She often came home with leads on potential jobs in the bideshi world, the world of the foreigners in Gulshan and Baridhara.

"With English as good as yours, you'll get a job. No problem," she told Nazreen. "And garments, maybe you should try finding a job making clothes in one of the big factories in Ashulia. It's tough, and not particularly well-paid, but it's steady. And some factories let the girls go to school."

But today, it was the Radisson Hotel that was looking for people. Nazreen was going to head over with a girl from the neighbourhood, Dipita. The notion of working in the luxury hotel gave her the energy boost she needed to get out of her soft bed. She folded her bedding up and bagged it, so the bed could be used as a table or bench during the day, and took out her freshly-ironed shalwar kameez. The shalwar was new and had cost a pretty penny, but it elevated her a step or two above the regular slum women with their thin, motley, unmatched outfits. Babul had nodded approvingly when she put it on.

She had noticed Babul was concerned about the family's appearance, and that he'd adopted some habits his neighbours sniggered at. He'd brought home teacups and saucers from work and smugly shown off their gold rim. The people he worked with were apparently going to throw them away, but at the last moment, they'd decided to give them to Babul instead. Now they held pride of place in the house's only cupboard, a battered glass cabinet.

He would fuss over his three white shirts for hours and spent a long time in front of the mirror in the morning, combing his hair into a perfect wave. He talked about how Reka and he might convert to Christianity. He was clearly impressed by the fancy Christian people at his office, Nazreen mused. And he'd been spotted eating with a fork. Nazreen smiled. If a new shalwar could land her a job, and make Babul happy, it was well worth the expense.

A couple of bouncy toddlers and the meowing of a cat announced Dipita had arrived to pick up Nazreen. A smell of sweet perfume accompanied the young woman, whom Reka had described as "a tough one". Born and raised in Tangaj by a mother who made a "dubious" living, as Reka put it. Reka had, however, judged that Dipita might be the way in Nazreen needed in Dhaka.

"*Kemon acho. Khub bhalo?* I'm Dipita. Are you ready? I thought we might share a rickshaw?"

"Bhaloi, Dipita. My name is Nazreen. Absolutely, sounds great. We'll share."

The girls rattled off in their rickshaw, away from the muddy alleyways of Badda, joining the busy main roads leading north.

The Radisson Hotel was located just outside the diplomatic zone, halfway to Dhaka's international airport. During their journey, Nazreen was given a brief lesson on how to survive and make your way in Dhaka.

"The bideshi world, the westerners, that's where the money is," Dipita explained. "Working for rich Bengalis is awful, avoid that. You make a tenth of what the bideshi families pay, and they make you work every day except Eid. The westerners give you a lot of time off, sometimes two days a week. It's nuts."

Dipita pulled out a lipstick and tried to paint her lips, parrying the jerky movements of the rickshaw. She studied her work in a small mirror. Then she offered Nazreen the lipstick, but Nazreen declined.

"I'm really an actress. Or I'm going to be," Dipita confided. "This hotel stuff is just a way to make money until my real career takes off. I'm planning to do Bollywood first and then Hollywood. They love Bengalis in Hollywood."

Dipita slipped the little mirror into her handbag and proceeded to scrutinise Nazreen's shalwar kameez.

"Where'd you buy it? It's nice. If we don't get hired today, I can go shopping with you. There's an incredible mall down in Mohakahli."

"Do you think we have a chance at the job?"

"Maybe, but we're probably going to have pay *baksheesh*. Did you bring money? And papers? I have forged papers saying I attended an English Medium School. They come in really handy! I got a job as an *ayah* for an American family and it took them a year to realise I didn't know any English."

Dipita laughed, but Nazreen looked quizzical.

"Well, what? If they don't get that their kids speak Bangla better than English, you have to wonder what kind of parents they are. No? But the gifts they gave me were amazing! They gave me something called a Christmas present, a camera! Can you imagine? It was worth six months' salary!"

"What do you mean, forged papers? I speak English, but I don't have any papers to prove it. No, actually, I have an essay I wrote."

"Little Nazreen," Dipita shot her a pitying look. "Poor little country girl. You have so much to learn. All the papers you need are for sale in Gulshan Market. Go buy some. And if you already speak English, then what's to stop you from claiming you went to college? Say you did, Notre Dame College, that's where all the rich Bengalis send their brats. You can buy a diploma at the market."

The rickshaw driver's back was wet with perspiration, and the last incline up to the hotel was slow. Nazreen suggested they walk and jumped off. Dipita's face was expressionless and she stayed in the rickshaw and continued to dispense advice.

"It would be good if you'd consider becoming a Christian. Do you know what a Christian is?"

The question made Nazreen feel ignorant again. Babul had talked about becoming a Christian, too. She tried to remember what she'd heard.

"It's some kind of . . . cult, right? Jews and Christians . . . it's like the Americans, no? And Israel?"

"Yeah, you could say that. A lot of westerners belong to that cult. Like Obama, do you know who that is? Bush? It's kind of like being a

Muslim, except they have a pope. An old man with a hat His name's Jesus. And he lives on a cross. I can introduce you to some Christians, if you want. They're alright, not filthy and nasty like Hindus. Because Hindus don't have a book. The Christians have a book."

Nazreen listened attentively. Any information that might make life in Dhaka easier was a good thing, Reka had impressed her. And this about the book and the man on the cross sounded vaguely familiar.

Outside the main entrance to the Radisson, they were brusquely pointed to a small backdoor. Nazreen's new-found friend snorted in derision and said something vulgar to the guards. Nazreen blushed. When they got inside, they were taken to a room where fifty young women had already gathered. The room was hot and didn't have air conditioning. A few tired ceiling fans spun sluggishly round and round, utterly unable to provide any relief. Nazreen realised it would be a long wait.

Dipita knew several of the jobseekers and quickly picked up the gossip floating around. Apparently, the newly-opened hotel was looking for all kinds of staff. Waitresses, chefs, cleaners, receptionists, guards. People with previous experience in the hotel industry had been interviewed during the previous three days and now they were giving anyone willing to work a chance. By lunchtime, it wasn't just the room that was packed, the whole parking lot behind the hotel was teeming with people, too. Most were young men and women, waving certificates and transcripts. As far as Nazreen could make out, her only merit was that her English was relatively okay. Better than Dipita's, at least. But Dipita was nice. She'd brought a pair of glasses she said Nazreen could borrow.

"Glasses make you look reliable and educated. Put them on. And speak English as soon as you get in there, just talk, talk, talk. The people interviewing you probably won't be as good as you."

Nazreen listened and learnt. The glasses were exciting. It suddenly occurred to Nazreen that it was a bit odd for Dipita to be looking for a job here, at a hotel.

"Why don't you stay in the bideshi world? Since you say can earn a lot more there? And surely it's a lot easier if you've already worked as an ayah?"

Dipita chuckled and seemed to contemplate Nazreen for a few moments.

"You're not as dumb as you look, Nazreen. You're right, *ayahs* make more money than hotel girls. But . . . hotel girls with the right contacts make more than anyone else. I'll tell you more about that later. Let's just both try to get hired, and then I'll let you in on how we're going to get really, really rich so we can get out of here. Far, far away."

*

Sofia carefully closed the Bob the Builder book and signalled to Noella that Teo had fallen asleep. The boy's dummy was still bobbing up and down in his mouth, but given as how Teo was a deep sleeper, she figured it was worth trying to move him.

"Shh, mummy has to put Teo in his own bed, but you stay here, Noella, I'll be right back."

Sofia picked the boy up and walked through the over-sized hallway to the boy's room. Oh well, one night out of . . . how many? Five? Ten? She didn't get home in time to put the children to bed often enough, she knew that, but sometimes she managed. Like today. It was only seven and she would have time to play with Noella a bit before bedtime. Give her some quality time. Janne was at the club playing tennis and wouldn't be back for a while.

Noella was thrilled at the prospect of having her mother to herself and flitted, rosy-cheeked, between the doll's house, the tiny trampoline and her bed.

"Mummy, we're going to be teachers! I'm a teacher and you're . . . the person who goes to school."

"You mean the student."

Sofia was careful to use the proper words when she played with the children, since they had very limited exposure to Swedish these days.

"Right. Sit down. You're going to do homework now, and I'm going to come over and tell you what to write. I'm in charge."

"Okay, what do you want me to write?"

Improvising long, meandering sentences full of monsters and princesses, the over-excited teacher was soon so worked up she was jumping up and down on her bed, shouting out words.

"Now write that they hid in the cave, write that! C-a-v-e."

Sofia got into the game and before she knew it, she'd built a roof for the school and pulled a bin and a rug in from the study.

At least she's a happy sort, my daughter, Sofia mused. I may not be here all the time, but she has her dad and her little brother. Children in Sweden go to day care at six every morning.

The game grew wilder and wilder until Sofia had to take the mattress off the bed to protect herself from monsters.

At that exact moment, Janne appeared in the doorway.

"Right, it's playtime, I see," he said unenthusiastically. "Sofia, it's nine o'clock and Noella's bedtime is eight."

"I know, but just this once . . ."

"What, because mummy has time to play? When mummy's here there are no rules?"

Janne looked both belligerent and tired. Sofia tried to calm Noella down.

"It's time to turn in now, isn't it, Noella?"

Sofia managed to get the girl to bed and read a chapter of Pettson. Noella fell asleep with her arm around her mother's waist. She lingered for a minute next to her daughter, stroking her sweaty forehead, enjoying the nutty smell of warm child's skin. Why didn't she spend more time with her daughter? Playing wasn't too bad, so long as you threw yourself into it. Noella was so big already, so tall, with stretched-out, almost grotesque legs, and hadn't her face lost some of its childish roundness?

With a pang of guilt, Sofia recalled sitting outside in the car the other night, waiting for Janne to put the children to bed. She'd waited until the light went out in Noella's room before sneaking in, too tired to deal with the bedtime mayhem.

Ever since the welcome reception, there had been tension between her and Janne. Their conversations kept morphing into pinball games. Spiteful words bounced rapidly back and forth, then the ball disappeared into a black hole.

She probably owed Janne an apology, she could accept that. But there was something about the way Janne always ended up the centre of attention that riled her. Couldn't he take a backseat, just for now, just this once? It was her turn, he owed her that. Janne's gentleness only made her more rigid because she found his lack of structure disconcerting. He was an amazing man and she often enjoyed his charisma and boundless warmth, but right now she wished he could content himself with keeping a low profile. The black, black shame at how he'd treated her when she'd needed him the most was like a thorn in her soul. The time after Teo's birth, which should have been the best days of their lives. Sofia sniffed Noella and closed her eyes. She had to push that down now because they'd promised each other they'd try.

Sometimes, Sofia wondered if it was true, what Janne sometimes accused her of. That she was a workaholic. It was as though she had two modes; she either had her family switched on or off. Sometimes, she wondered if it was healthy to be as good at compartmentalising as she was.

"Hello, we exist! You know, your family? Remember us?" he would text or exclaim from time to time, and maybe he was right.

When she was working and on a roll, it was as though everything else ceased to exist. She felt good, she felt mindful and one hundred percent focused on the tasks at hand. It was the complete opposite of family life. At home, she lost her edge. Everything became nebulous and skew-whiff. Decisions had to be collectively mulled and discussed endlessly, and nothing ever came out the way she'd planned. Noella sulked or Teo screamed and tried to escape. Janne didn't want the same thing as her, and no one seemed to know where they were going. She loved the children deeply and purely, but sometimes she didn't know if she was really cut out to be a wife and mother. Janne was somehow much more suited to handle the children and the family things, she mused. He was always a bit nebulous and messy anyway and didn't seem bothered by the constant chaos. Truth be told, she felt relieved every Sunday morning when the embassy re-opened, the same way she'd felt relieved every Monday morning in Sweden, going back to work. It was the feeling of direction, the semblance of structure. It was logging into her computer and having time to think.

But now she had to get back on Janne's good side, or at least get them back on speaking terms. She reluctantly left Noella's warm bed and found Janne slumped in front of the BBC. His big body was sprawled across the Ikea sofa and he'd left his tennis racquet and trainers sitting on the floor. The sweat in his blonde hair was drying in the chill of the air conditioner and there was an angry red blemish on his neck.

"Did she fall asleep?" Janne's voice was gentler than she'd thought it would be.

"She did. I'm sorry I got swept up in our game. But she's so lovely . . . I couldn't help it."

"This is when I'm supposed to say 'so come home early more often, then', but I'm *not* going to. Tennis went great, I beat Bjarne six-three, six-one, four-six. Are you tired?"

Janne's thoughtfulness shone through and Sofia sensed she wasn't going to have to defend herself.

"Yeah, pretty tired. Actually . . . exhausted. All the time. And, Janne, I . . . miss you. Us. I'm sorry. The party went completely wrong. I should've . . ."

Janne held his hand out to her.

"Come here, you stupid old goat. I'm here. We're here. Do you have to be such a good girl all the time? That job seems to be sucking you dry."

"It'll probably get easier," Sofia mumbled and draped herself like a blanket across Janne. He kissed her hair and let his hands slip in under her top to stroke her naked back. She felt a gentle wave of warmth surging through her and breathed in the smell of man, of testosterone, wafting from Janne. And through the exhaustion, she was surprised to feel her body responding.

"Get this burqa off," Janne mumbled, unhooking her bra. "Get it all off. What do you even look like these days under all the weird layers of cloth?"

"The guards, Janne. They can see everything." Sofia giggled. "And here, on the counsellor's sofa? What would Siv say?"

Janne jumped up and pulled the curtains. He noticed one of the guards lighting a cigarette. A glowing pinprick in the night.

They pulled off their clothes, tennis shorts and shalwar kameez, and kissed, giggling, like in the olden days. Sofia realised she'd missed Janne's body, his big, solid man's body, and crossed her ankles behind his back. She curled up, making herself small, smaller than she was, in his embrace. As though she needed consoling.

Afterwards, they lay in each other's arms and Sofia tried to explain why she had reacted the way she had the night of the party.

"I was being stupid, I know. I'm sorry. I'm just . . . well, tense. Wound up. And it really wasn't your fault. That you ended up the centre of attention, I mean."

Janne pushed a few stray strands of hair out of Sofia's face.

"But . . . was I really the centre of attention?"

"Yes, you were! At least if you follow the unwritten rules of diplomacy. And Vanja should've known that. It was my night, you know, but because of her speech, the focus switched to you. A man! Hallelujah, order has been restored!"

Sofia knew there was an ounce of truth in what she was saying, but that the other ounces were significant, too. Vanja was, for instance, a more gifted public speaker than her husband, and Janne always attracted attention and approval, especially from women, wherever he went. Whether it was protocol or not.

That line of argument touched on Janne's guilt. His masculine appeal. The fact that he had recently demonstrated that he could if he wanted to. Consequently, he carefully avoided going down that route, relieved to find another, less fraught, angle.

"I reckon you're right about that, actually. A grown man without a job, that's scary! I've noticed everyone panicking about the fact that I'm not working. Apparently, I'm upsetting the natural order of things. And none of the other housewives are particularly welcoming, to put it mildly."

Sofia distractedly marched her fingers around his chest and didn't comment on his observation. She'd already hopped on to the next thing.

"Seriously, Janne, I really don't know if I'm any good at this job."

"What do you mean? You're always the best, you know that."

She smiled.

"I actually have a lot to learn and read up on. It's all about getting value for money, but it takes longer to report on results than to achieve them. Do you know the difference between outcome and output and impact? It's nuts. I don't feel like I'm really . . . getting it."

"What about Moberg? Can't he help?"

"Sure, maybe. But he's evasive, somehow. He should have nominated me to Dev-Com, for example. Then I would have had insight and overview and been able to assess and prioritise things. Everyone expects me to be on there, but . . ."

Janne broke in.

"I'm sorry, Dev-Com? You're bandying all these abbreviations about, they're not easy for a layperson to remember."

"I'm sorry. Dev-Com stands for Development Committee, it's the power centre of the foreign aid community here in Dhaka. And since I'm in charge of foreign aid, I should be representing Sweden. But Moberg says he doesn't mind staying on. Just like that."

Janne listened and stroked Sofia's forehead.

"Give him some time. Maybe he's not used to dealing with people like you who are like forces of nature. Maybe he's intimidated by your energy and impact?"

Sofia snuggled deeper into his embrace.

"I don't know what the problem is. He's behaving like I'm invading his little kingdom. And he's right, I kind of am."

"What do you mean? Isn't that your job? To distribute Sweden's foreign aid and make sure there is a clearer focus on human rights and gender equality?"

Sofia looked her husband in the eyes for a moment.

"Yes, that's my formal job description. But I'm not sure that's what Moberg *wants* my job description to be. Those are the Swedish government's priorities, not his. He might be more interested in maintaining the status quo . . ."

Janne silenced her with a kiss.

"But an embassy is a government agency, right? You're both civil servants, tasked with, what is it you call it . . . *implementing* policy. As a democracy, we've elected a government that prioritises human rights and women's . . ."

"You're being naïve, Janne. Do you really think that just because I've climbed a few rungs on the ladder and have a formal mission, I automatically have the support of my superiors? Bureaucracies are full of individuals whose agendas are radically different from the government's!"

"Yes, I'm probably naïve about that. I am. As an historian, I have to say I believe in democracy and in a bureaucracy that serves the will of the people. I'm sorry if that's blue-eyed. What? You should be working toward the same goal, he should be making your job easier . . ."

" . . . or at least reply to my emails. And nominate me to Dev-Com. It's absurd, our offices are fifteen feet apart and I never get a chance to talk to him! No one seems to know where he is during the day. He sneaks out for pointless lunches and meetings without saying where he's going or when he'll be back," Sofia sounded annoyed. "I feel like everyone's waiting for him to make decisions, or take charge. Everything just ends up in the air. Should I step in and call the shots? Everything's so vague, I should . . ."

"So many shoulds. Do what *you* want to do and what you feel is important instead. Fuck him! You came here because you wanted to do something meaningful, right? And he's going back to Sweden soon, isn't he? Can't you complain to Stockholm?"

"Stockholm doesn't care about Bangladesh. Plus, if you complain to them, you get labelled a "difficult" embassy, they only want good news."

"And you don't want to be a difficult person at a difficult embassy? Do you? But maybe you have to be difficult sometimes to get something done?"

The room was getting chilly so Janne stood up to turn off the air conditioner and gather up their scattered clothing. He threw her a shawl.

"Huh, Miss Diplomat? Maybe you have to be prepared to rub people the wrong way to get somewhere? Since when is gender equality unproblematic? Maybe the struggle just looks different in different eras?"

Sofia lingered on the sofa. It was nice to finally have time to talk to Janne.

"Even if that's true, I don't want to rub people the wrong way right off the bat. My first priority is to figure out what being a manager is all about. Holding everything together, how did you do it when you were a deputy head? Everyone here is just fighting for their particular issue, whether that's women's rights, the environment, health, education, human rights or building roads. All the experts and advisors are convinced their area is the one that truly matters. Who's looking at the whole?"

"That sounds like the world of education. Maths teachers feel their subject is the most important, Swedish teachers consider their work the foundation of everything else and history teachers claim that without their subject, nothing can be understood. P.E. teachers try to broaden their mandate to include diet and lifestyle, and music teachers are never happy. And in a weird way, it's always more about ego than the issues per se."

Janne knew Sofia had heard all that before, so he switched to teasing her instead:

"Poor Sofia, how is she going to fix everything? How many millions of poor people do you have to save? Is it sixty million who live on less than a dollar a day? That's how poverty's defined, right? Listen, I saw a few of them outside the club tonight. What is it you do at work all day, eh?"

Sofia giggled and pulled on her kameez.

"You want to know what I do at work? Alright, great, let's go visit Alor Desh in Barikhali. That handsome woman Khadija Anam, remember her from the reception? It's her organisation and it's being investigated for corruption. We can head out there ourselves and try to figure out just how corrupt they are."

*

Meena stared at the sandals for a long time. Red, green, brown, black. Some were patterned, others a solid colour. The man squatting on the pavement had a mountain of them in front of him and seemed uninterested in lowering his asking price. Seventy taka, he'd told her. Seventy taka for adults, fifty for children. Buying three of each, Meena did a quick mental calculation, would cost three hundred and sixty taka. She made a note of the number and hurried back to Rifat and the waiting truck. Miraj had already started the engine and was shouting at her.

"Fucking bitch, is not being late too much to ask?"

She'd grown used to Miraj's foul mouth and Rifat gave her a kind look and rolled his eyes, as though he wanted her not to take offence. They sat in silence in the cargo bed, watching the city wake up. She felt a silent kinship with the scrawny man-boy, so much like one of her cousins back home. Meena thought about how people used to tie goat kids together, back in the village, to keep them from wandering off too far. That's how she felt about Rifat. They were two kids who roamed the markets together, making purchases for Patel, who was more than happy with their exploits. Sometimes, Rifat pulled one way and she had to keep up, other times, she set their course. They stuck together, both slightly surprised and perhaps reluctant, but ultimately loyal. Rifat knew Dhaka like the back of his hand, knew where all the markets were and what they sold on what days of the month. He knew the tricks to getting a good price and avoid being cheated. Knew the shortcuts the rickshaws used and which areas and gangs might put them at risk of being robbed. But Meena could count, quickly and accurately, and had the ability to foresee how a deal would come out several transactions down the line. She often mulled things over in silence before suddenly making a suggestion that changed everything for the better. She was also a quick learner and seemed to be able to work non-stop. Rifat admired the serious sister he'd suddenly been saddled with and was surprised anew every day at the way her mind worked and what she saw. Even though she was just a regular country girl, barely older than him, she was unlike any girl he'd ever known. Not that he'd known many, but Meena was smarter. Definitely smarter than his mother, and she paid attention to things the other women and girls in his neighbourhood didn't. Meena's sharp mind and Rifat's experience of the metropolis' alleyways and markets made them unbeatable.

Even Patel had begun to notice how much more profitable it was to send Meena and Rifat on assignments than to rely on his usual suspects and had discussed with his sons if it might not be worth sending Meena and Rifat down to Kawran Bazaar at midnight. It was when the big fruit lorries from India arrived at Kawran Bazaar that the really profitable deals could be made.

But despite the money she made and the appreciative grunts her work sometimes drew from Patel, Meena's stomach often ached with hunger. She was determined not to eat the money she earned, every paisa was going into the plastic box. That was where her dream of a new life lived, every taka in the box would contribute to showing her Amma, Abba, everyone back home, Hanif, Reka – yes, everyone – that the girls had been right to leave the village. In her head, Meena had a secret goal of fifty thousand taka, fifty thousand taka, ten times more than Nasty Ali had demanded of her father in exchange for marrying

Nazreen. What exactly was going to happen once she'd accumulated fifty thousand taka was unclear, but she was obsessed with the idea of having access to that kind of money, together with Nazreen. It would be enough for two solid dowries and a small shop back in the village. Maybe their future husbands would let them run a shop together? A shop selling goods from Dhaka?

This was why Meena had been shocked to discover that Nazreen had taken four hundred taka from the box to buy herself a new shalwar kameez. She'd been so upset by this betrayal she'd been unable to sleep and had felt compelled to wake Nazreen up in the middle of the night.

"How could you?"

"What?" Nazreen had asked drowsily.

"The money. How could you just . . ."

"But Meena, we never have a chance to talk. You're always out doing things for Patel. I had to buy a new shalwar kameez. I've been hired by the new hotel by the airport, the Radisson Hotel, you know, that big, new one. They're going to let me work there for a month to see if I'm good enough. I definitely wouldn't have got that job if I'd shown up in a tattered cotton shalwar."

Meena calmed down. Nazreen was right, there was a big difference between the shalwar kameezzes the poorest women wore and the ones worn by those with slightly more money. And it was the ever so slightly richer, or less poor, women who got jobs.

The girls started whispering in the night about how much money Nazreen might make, and Meena told her sister about learning how to negotiate, haggle and purchase from Patel and his loosely assembled gang.

"Nazreen, Patel is a master of the difference. The difference is what matters. I can see that now. The difference between what you buy and what you sell. You have to make that as big as possible. Do you see?"

Meena felt she'd realised something pivotal and wanted to share the experience with her sister. She tried to make her see what she saw, that you could push the price down when you were buying and up when you were selling. To maximise the difference. Nazreen laughed and stroked her hair gently.

"Silly girl. Yes, I get it. And if the difference is big enough, we can buy things with it. High-heeled sandals, maybe. I would love to try walking in heels."

"We're not buying things for ourselves! Are you out of your mind? We're going to buy more things to sell on in the same way, with a bigger difference. That's how it works, Nazreen, that's what we have to do."

And lying there in the dark, with her face inches away from her big sister's, she told Nazreen about the pickup driver Miraj and his insults.

"They flow out of his mouth like black tar," Meena tried to explain, feeling fear crash over her like a wave. "He says I'm the child of a whore, that Allah hates people who don't keep purdah, that I'm going to burn in hell and that all of God's demons . . ."

"Stop! What an idiot! Meena, it sounds like the mullah back home, you know. There's always people like that. Can't you just ignore him? Just tune him out like . . . well, like you do with the muezzins when they call to prayer. Just let them do what they do."

She giggled, but Meena looked unhappy. What if Miraj was right? Nazreen had always had a casual relationship with religion, with life in general, in fact. Meena took the talk about Allah much more seriously. Because Miraj was right. It was true. She had been a bad girl since they came to Dhaka. She often moved about alone among strangers, didn't wash as often as the Quran dictated and didn't cover her body as carefully as she should.

Bouncing around in the cargo bed at dawn, she thought about all the things Miraj spewed at her, and Nazreen's voice in the night wasn't quite enough to reassure her. She was told worse and worse things: that she might as well prostitute herself as work the way she did, that she was Patel's little whore and that her and Rifat's offspring would be deformed devils. There seemed to be no end to it. He even twitched and gave her repulsed looks if she accidentally touched him while they handled the fruit and fish.

He also threatened to beat up both Rifat and Meena if they told anyone he took long detours to hand out fliers during their outings. The fliers were about secret meetings of the banned political party Hizb-al-Islami-Bangladesh, which Miraj was constantly claiming would overthrow the government and take over the country.

"And then dogs like Patel and his Hindu rabble will be kicked out of this country for good. And you, you filth, will learn not to sashay around, with your face on display like a whore. Then we'll have some order in this country. A lot of us are tired of the moral decay, you hear me, a lot of people!!"

He went on and on about how the Bangladeshi people had been cheated since independence, about how the Americans and Indians were secretly in charge of everything and how there was only one God who could save them and that was Allah.

On this particular morning, however, Miraj lapsed into silence after greeting them, leaving Meena and Rifat to work in peace. In the very first village they stopped, they bought twenty large cauliflowers for next to nothing, got a good price on sixty-five pounds of red onions and refused to accept their regular farmer's rotten garlic. Meena was uncompromising when it came to quality, ever since she'd found herself in the middle of the Mogh Bazaar in central Dhaka with a load of half-rotten melons she couldn't sell.

"What about the tomatoes, then? We usually buy tomatoes from that farmer," suggested Rifat, who was chatting to a wizened old man with a pile of tomatoes in front of him on a burlap sack. But Meena barely looked at the tomatoes.

"They're too small, and too lumpy. People want the big, red tomatoes from India. Granted, they have no flavour, but still . . ."

The farmer sitting in front of Rifat tried to persuade them. A hundred and fifty taka for eleven pounds, it was next to nothing.

"But if we can't sell them, they'll rot in a few days. Then that's a hundred and fifty taka wasted. We're going with the Indian ones."

"A hundred taka." The farmer whimpered his offer and Rifat shot Meena a pleading look.

"Eighty taka. Okay. But you know we'll be the ones paying if we can't sell them, Rifat."

Rifat nodded and the deal was struck. The farmer quickly counted his money and Meena saw a tear in the dried-up corner of his eye. He wasn't going to start crying, was he? Or worse, beg? Just as he was about to turn and walk away, Meena had an idea.

"Baba, wait! We'll be stopping here again in two days. Before then, you should ask everyone in your village if they want sandals. Like these ones."

She held up her foot, showing him her sandals.

"I charge a hundred a pair for grownups and eighty for kids. Thik ache? If you can find people who want to buy sandals, I can bring them here and we can split the profit. Ten for you, twenty for me?"

Profit margins and taka. The farmer was quick to catch on and nodded, his face breaking into a toothless but alert smile. A small profit. Money. Food. He held up two trembling, dry fingers.

"In two days. Here, by the road. I'll be here. By Allah, I'll be here."

Rifat looked at her quizzically, and she realised she was sweating. This could be dangerous. If Patel found out, he'd be furious.

"Rifat, not a word to Patel or Miraj. This is our business, okay? But out here in the villages, they don't have the things they sell in Dhaka, and we're always going back and forth like crazy roosters. Why not do business? Our own side business? We would have paid a hundred and twenty for sandals like these back in Rajigonj."

Meena watched as Rifat's surprise turned into delight. Her goat-friend was pulling in the same direction she was, she thought to herself, with relief.

8

"Water, mosquito nets, crackers, paracetamol. You didn't forget to pack your favourite pillow, did you? Rural Bangladesh isn't exactly the land of down pillows. And earplugs, you remembered earplugs, right? The crickets are deafening. And the roosters start up really early. And a spare tyre . . ."

Charlotta leaned into the boot of the Pajero, doing one last check. She'd been dispatched from Alor Desh's headquarters, where she lived, to accompany Janne. Sofia had at the last moment been forced to cancel their field trip yet again. Now she came out the large, carved wood front door, wrapped in Janne's dressing gown.

"You're going to tell the driver to be careful, aren't you? No crazy overtaking. And you're back on Thursday? Did you pack a phone charger, Janne?"

Janne nodded and Charlotta answered.

"Absolutely, we'll drive carefully. Traffic normally isn't too bad in the next hour or so, it's still prayer time. We'll get to Lalpara by ten and have breakfast with Siraj there."

"Oh, I wish I could come. You're going to have to tell me everything when you get back, Janne! And take lots of pictures!"

Janne climbed into the car and threw Sofia a kiss. He felt impatient like a child and didn't want a drawn-out goodbye. There had already been so many discussions about when and if Sofia would be able to go. First, a delegation from Sweden had suddenly showed up, so they had cancelled their trip. The next time, there had been a conference in Bangkok and now, when Alor Desh had invited them a third time, the Brits had suddenly called, asking her to be the keynote speaker at a UNICEF conference about the scourge of child marriage. Sofia hadn't wanted to turn them down. In the end, Janne had become annoyed and suggested he go with Charlotta, the punk girl who had introduced herself at the club, since Sofia didn't seem able to prioritise a field visit right now. And the invitation had actually been addressed to him as well.

Twenty minutes later, they had left inner-city Dhaka behind and were crossing a rickety bridge spanning the Buriganga River. Brightly-coloured lorries with roses and tigers painted on their sides were jostling to get out of the city. They'd probably unloaded their cargo in Dhaka overnight and were heading back out to the villages, fields and markets outside the city to restock. What an enormous supply system these lorries must be a part of, Janne mused. Like the enormous lungs of the city, in and out, in and out. In with vegetables, fish and fruit every night and out again a few hours later, empty.

Charlotta was asleep next to him so Janne could study his travel companion at his leisure. Her blueish-black hair was standing straight up and her head rested on her silver ringed hands on a pillow in a corner of the backseat. Her mouth was half open and a small rivulet of saliva was trickling down her hand. Her T-shirt with the Ethiopian flag and the words "One Love" on it had slid up, revealing that the tattoo Janne had noticed on her arm wasn't her only one; sunbeams writhed like snakes around her belly button. In her belly button was a small silver ring, pressed into white, fleshy womanhood. She really was a bit chubby, Charlotta, almost puppy-like, Janne thought to himself. How old could she be? No older than thirty? He made a mental note to ask when she woke up.

Janne was fascinated by tattoos. Neither he nor Sofia had any, and he felt like the tattoo ship had sailed. But he liked them, a lot of the students at Lindebergska had tattoos. More than once, he'd toyed with the thought of getting a band around his lower arm, but Sofia had just sneered and asked why. So he'd never got around to it.

Charlotta worked as a volunteer for Alor Desh, an NGO with virtual cult status in Bangladesh, Janne had been given to understand. Partly, because it was active in the mythical, inaccessible char area, partly because the organisation was structured in a way that made foreign aid people's eyes light up. Rights-based, poverty oriented. Small groups of landless, destitute women and men joining forces to put pressure on local authorities to grant them the resources needed to live in the delta. The organisation had also, apparently, come up with a ground-breaking, innovative way of creating so-called livelihoods, means of making a living, for people in the delta. They built their houses on stilts, for example, to keep them safe from the frequent flooding, and experimented with various crops that could grow in water.

"When there's talk about people doomed to drown when the rivers flowing down from the Himalayas grow bigger, and climate change raises the water level, these are the people they're referring to," Charlotta had explained to him before she fell asleep. "They're, like, the world's most . . . vulnerable. We owe them, kind of. They're the ones paying the price for our overconsumption and lifestyle."

Janne looked out the window. He couldn't say the landscape was pretty. It wasn't. It was flat and featureless as far as the eye could see. Rice paddies stretched out on either side of the poorly paved road. The monotony was broken only by enormous, derelict billboards, where laughing women's faces in extreme closeup created a grotesque contrast with the emaciated rice farmers working in the water underneath. Janne glimpsed houses sheltered in dusty groves scattered between the paddies. Every once in a while, especially at first, rickety chimneys loomed up over the plain, like moth-eaten hackles. After a while, Janne realised these were the brick factories he'd heard about. The business of making and crushing bricks had employed Bangladeshis since time immemorial. Because the country was one big delta, stone was scarce. Instead, bricks were what the Bengali turned to for building all the roads, buildings and other structures that popped up in the wake of economic growth.

After a week of semi-convalescence, Janne's stomach was still upset and he prayed it wouldn't act up out in the villages. His hurried breakfast was causing significant gurgling now. He felt relieved Dr Hassan's test had so definitively ruled out dysentery. And salmonella. And giardia. And shigella. He'd looked up all those diseases in his *Guide to Tropical Medicine* and realised there were a number of reasons to worry about what you ate in Dhaka. Worms being one. Not to mention another terrifying parasite he'd forgotten the name of, which could lurk in a person's colon for years. But Dr Hassan had found none of these things in his laboratory. He'd just told Janne to stay hydrated and buck up.

About an hour later, Charlotta roused herself and stretched. She glanced out the window and announced it was time for a bathroom break.

"There's one single place to stop where the toilets are acceptable, so make the most of it."

When the car pulled into the small petrol station-cum-café, they were immediately surrounded by people. No one begged, everyone just stared with uninhibited curiosity. Charlotta reeled off some phrases in Bangla. When they got back after doing their business, around twenty people had gathered around their car, all pressing their noses up against the windows of the Jeep. They had to push their way to the vehicle and Janne couldn't help laughing.

"Isn't it nuts?" Charlotta shook her head. "It's like we're big-screen TVs or something. We can pretend we're Posh and Becks." She smiled and ruffled a little boy's hair. "I don't think I'll ever get used to it. But it's better out in the villages. Out there, people take one good look and then leave you alone."

Once they were back in the car, Charlotta had shaken off the last remnants of sleep and set to work telling Janne what to expect in the village.

"We're going to be staying on the island where the Alor Desh headquarters are located, and where I have my humble abode," she explained. "It's a bit primitive, but you'll be fine. You'll be staying in our guesthouse, but I reckon you'll be having your meals with Siraj, who's Khadija's right hand and head of operations. The villagers are amazing."

"Is Khadija Anam going to be there? I met her at Sofia's reception, but I figured she spends most of her time in Dhaka?"

Janne remembered the handsome, sari-clad woman with curiosity.

"She definitely will be, she spends as much time as she can in the field. And aren't you some kind of VIP? She's amazing, and I mean to-the-core amazing! Her family was murdered by the Pakistani army in 1971, when she was just twelve years old. A fifty-year-old relative offered to marry her, but after the wedding night, she ran away and was picked up by a British diplomat who took her under her wing. She was given an education and a life in England."

"I noticed her perfect Queen's English. But the burn?"

"She never talks about it. And I've never asked. But she's cool. She could have lived a global jet setting life, or stayed in the UK as an academic. Instead, she's here, building one of the most powerful NGOs in Asia. Respect." Charlotta put her hand on her heart and bowed slightly. "If there's one person in Bangladesh who deserves the peace prize, it's Khadija Anam, not that banker, Dr Yunus. Isn't it interesting? He invents microcredits, which have been a disaster for a lot of poor people and mostly end up benefitting the banks, which charge forty-fifty percent interest. But him they give a Nobel Prize. Meanwhile, Khadija Anam – same generation, similar background, but a woman – realises that poor people need to *save* first and *spend* later. She doesn't fuel the lending bubble, she advocates responsible micro saving. There are no banks cheering her on, no Nobel Committees lining up to meet with her. There you have it – male and female. And who's right?"

Charlotta looked out the window.

"I thought microcredits were designed with poor women in mind," Janne said tentatively, but that instantly drew Charlotta's ire.

"PR, nothing but PR. Yunus is a PR man, not a poverty expert. Poor women are pitted against each other in the villages as they try to find the money to cover preposterous interest payments. Bear in mind that the interest rates for some microcredit programmes are over fifty percent! It's no different or better than the usurers of old. Only more efficient. A capitalist's wet dream – to turn even people who have nothing into consumers and borrowers."

Janne was going to open his mouth and argue, say something about how the access to credit was absolutely necessary to enable an economy to transition from agrarian bartering to capitalist mercantilism. But he didn't want to come across as a hectoring high school teacher, so he let Charlotta have the last word.

Their driver suddenly turned off the road without slowing and roared through the terrain. Janne saw water glittering ahead. A small motorboat was waiting for them, moored to a riverbank. Their luggage was transferred and Janne crawled in under a hemp fibre canopy on deck, meant to keep the sun out.

Once they were safely on board, Janne and Charlotta leaned against their backpacks and took out their water bottles. Janne poured half of his over his head to cool down. Outside the air-conditioned car, the day was sweltering.

Charlotta started to expound eagerly on the villages of the char area.

"We're heading into the dry period now, so we're going to have to take motorcycles across the sand to get to Khadija's village. In the summer, I could get pretty much all the way by boat." She made a sweeping gesture at the horizon. "Every inch the water rises makes an enormous difference here. The richest people live at the highest points, as you might imagine. Well, I mean, the richest people don't live around here at all. But there are hierarchies and levels here, too, and the weakest drown first."

"What happens to the people who live on islands that are submerged? I mean, for real. Practically?" Janne looked around, puzzled.

The landscape surrounding them looked a bit like Stockholm's archipelago, except sandy rather than rocky, with some larger chunks of land and countless tiny skerries. The little islets seemed to consist primarily of sand and mud, and even the smallest ones had at least a few huts or sheds clinging to it.

"There was flooding in the summer, as usual, but thankfully no cyclones this year. While the rain was pouring down, people grabbed their children and their only cow or goat and got into boats. Then they crowded onto whatever patches of land remained. Unbelievable. And then you wait. Some retreated to their roofs as soon as the water went down, and then they sat there for days, waiting to salvage their belongings."

Janne peeked out from under the canopy and tried to picture it. Even more water. Even fewer islands. Charlotta pointed.

"Now each village looks like an island. Look, there – three houses and maybe twenty people on that one. And there – an old man and a cow on that island. And when the water subsides fully, all of this is just green, rolling hills. Hills between rice paddies."

"And they live off the sale of that rice all year?"

"Yes, but that's the complicated part, and that's where Alor Desh comes into it. According to some ancient law, landless farmers have a right to cultivate the char land for their immediate subsistence, since no one can own land that, geographically speaking, doesn't really exist. That keeps millions of landless people alive. The problem is that in recent years, land has become increasingly valuable in Asia. Big landowners want to appropriate the extremely fertile char delta to grow their crops."

"So, land grabbing," Janne put in.

"Exactly. In brief, you might say the people here are under threat from both climate change, which will in the long-term make the land literally disappear, and from mustaans, the local mafia, who bully them and drive them from their land so the big companies can roll in with their pineapple or tobacco growing. Well, and then there's the mullahs . . ." Charlotta shook her head again and let out a dry laugh. "My theory is that this area's being radicalised. Money from the Middle East, new madrassas and mosques being built. What's happening in Afghanistan, Iraq, New York and Karachi is linked to, well, Khadija Anam's Alor Desh."

"And that's not a good thing, in your opinion? I mean, freedom of religion is a human right, no? And this is a Muslim country. Bangladesh came into being as East Pakistan to separate Hindus and Muslims, right . . . ?"

Janne posed the question tentatively, well aware he was treading on thin ice. But foreign aid people always irked him slightly because there were so many things you weren't supposed to ask about. You were never allowed to question their mission. Sofia was extremely sensitive to any questions about the existential purpose of foreign aid.

And, as expected, Charlotta, who had been lounging against her backpack, suddenly sat up straight. She clearly needed her hands and arms free to gesticulate.

"Sure, if you think it's okay for whatever quantum of freedom these women have gained to be taken away again, then it might not be a big deal. If you want the kids to learn to recite the Quran by heart in Arabic instead of how to read and write, I guess it's alright."

"Well, I just meant . . ."

"Or that they start stoning infidels and ban girls from attending school. Is that the kind of religious practice you want to get behind? I think the creeping Talibanization in this wonderful country is tragic and horrifying. The women don't want it! They're *not* like in Pakistan, they're *not* like in the Gulf. They're Bengalis first and Muslim second."

"That's not exactly what I meant. I was just saying it's a difficult balance to strike. Isn't it? Between a people's own religion and our Western equality agenda. Aren't you asking them to . . . square circles?"

Janne smiled to divert from Charlotta's gravity. She went along, laughed and leaned back.

"Square circles, my ass. You'll see how Khadija works, she tries to find progressive mullahs to work with. Mullahs who aren't violent, or fundamentalists. They exist! Lots of them!"

She broke off and heaved a sigh.

"But sure. I guess it's not like the gender studies department back home, exactly. But if you think you've reached the end of the world, I just want to tell you you're wrong. This is where it's happening. In real life. What you read about in the papers back in Stockholm is actually taking place here."

Janne nodded with a wry smile and kept prodding her.

"I guess, but they didn't reckon with Charlotta from . . . I'm sorry, where are you from?"

"Norrköping."

"Right, so they didn't reckon with Charlotta from Norrköping. Did they?"

Charlotta laughed and raised one finger.

"Exactly. Now that *I'm* finally here, things are going to be different!"

Janne liked Charlotta's ability to shift quickly from joking to being serious and back again, and to poke fun at herself, like Sofia had used to once upon a time. Sofia, right. He'd promised Sofia to take a lot of pictures in the delta, to compensate for the fact that she couldn't come with him.

"Are we almost there? Is there time for me to take a few pictures?" Janne tugged on his backpack. Charlotta leaned closer to the young man steering the boat and said something in Bangla.

"He's guessing ten minutes. By all means, get your camera out, or better yet, give it to me so I can take a picture of you. Janne from . . . well, where are you from?"

"Jönköping."

Charlotta took the camera from him, focused on Janne and mimicked a typical Stockholm reporter.

"So, Janne from Jönköping. Father of two, trying to escape the expat bubble. Out in the real world. In Bangladesh."

Janne took the camera back, turned it on Charlotta and continued in the same tone.

"A young woman. Vegan. Animal rights activist. Punk rocker. Where is she going? From Norrköping to Dhaka. How unfair can the world be? Follow Charlotta's struggle for a better tomorrow."

"I'm not an animal rights activist." Charlotta giggled and leaned back against her backpack. "And I'm not as young as you think either."

*

Nazreen could tell from a mile away that Babul's round full-moon face was shinier than usual as he came bumbling down the alleyway. He was also merrier than usual. A few young men she recognised from the neighbourhood were propping him up as he stumbled and kicked at a dog that got too close. When he approached the doorway, where Nazreen was standing, a number of small children seized the opportunity to slink in, hoping for a spectacle. Reka raised her eyebrows when she saw the state of her husband and Nazreen sat down on the bed, not sure what to do.

"Happy birthday to Babul, happy birthday to Babul, happy birthday to Babuuuuuul," Babul bellowed, giggling uncontrollably. "Look, look, Reka, my wife, here's a man, your own husband, who's just turned thirty. Look."

Babul swayed and held up a card. It said "Happy Birthday", in sparkling letters and an explosion of flowers seemed to be growing out of something that must be a gigantic birthday cake.

"Birthday," Reka said, sounding annoyed. "You don't have a birthday. That's the stupidest thing I've ever heard."

"I don't? Yes, starting today, I do, on . . . well, on this very day. The ambassador has signed a document to that effect. So there!"

He waved the card around as the room filled with curious neighbours and children. Lame old Iftekhar came hopping in on his crutches, mumbling his *ashadu an laa illah ill-Allah*, there's no God but Allah, and sat down curiously on the bed. Reka and Nazreen snatched the card from Babul.

"Indeed, and then they served a kind of beer, I think it was. Champagne. Not only to celebrate me, I mean, but *also* to celebrate me. That's what the ambassador said. This is *also* to celebrate . . . that's what he said!"

Nazreen studied the card. She could read English letters and sounded her way through the strange names. Karl-Otto Moberg, Sofia Paulin, Rickard Roftlin, Siv Andersson. Such strange names. How could people be called things like that?

"Are these Christian names?" she asked Babul and he nodded.

"Christian names and Christian people. That's the ticket! Jesus Christ, Happy Christmas and Happy Birthday!" Babul belched loudly and patted his stomach smugly. "My Christian friends, let's see . . . Karl-Otto, how do you do? Karl-Otto, my best friend! And Sofia Paulin, do you want to marry me? Reka, let's become Christians!"

He laughed delightedly and Nazreen noted that several of the assembled neighbours were watching them with a mix of envy and consternation.

Reka broke in:

"As if you know when your birthday is! What birthday? Since when do regular people have birthdays? Nonsense!"

She sounded annoyed.

"No, exactly, my darling wife. And that's why it's today. Happy Birthday! When you work at an embassy, you have to have a birthday, otherwise you can't have a job. And so someone put down 11 November. Four of us at the embassy have the same birthday, 11 November. So today, they celebrated us!"

The card was passed around the room and everyone wanted to touch the strange sparkly patches on the front. Old Iftekhar mumbled something about "Christian devilry" and recited a long harangue from the Quran while he squinted at the card.

Nazreen felt contentment spreading through her. If only Meena had been here! As usual, she was out working for Patel and wasn't expected back until after dark. This life of theirs in Dhaka was turning out well, she felt. The bideshi world that was suddenly all around them seemed full of promise. With her new job at the Radisson, she felt closer to Reka and Babul. She worked with bideshis, too. That strange otherness she'd seen from afar all her life was suddenly part of her.

At least that's how she'd felt that morning, when she shared a rickshaw with Dipita on her first day as a breakfast hostess at the Radisson Hotel. She could barely believe that she, Nazreen Bhuia, was going to work in such a beautiful, clean, cool place. Her English had been considerably better than her interviewer's, so despite a slightly too modest baksheesh, she'd been given a chance.

In the staff room, she'd quickly changed out of her fancy shalwar kameez into some kind of uniform, and at five on the dot, she'd helped the chefs carry out the large platters of fruit and freshly-baked rolls. A big group was coming in from London soon, she'd been told. She was supposed to greet them in English and make sure their every wish was fulfilled.

"Whatever they want, you make it happen, understand?" the restaurant manager had roared at her and the six other breakfast hostesses. "You have a month to impress me. If you don't, you're out."

The guests had started arriving around half past five. Their first stop had been reception, where they were greeted by Dipita and some other girls. Then, after leaving their enormous, beautiful bags with the staff, they'd filed into the dining room to crowd around the breakfast buffet. Nazreen had never seen so much and such wondrous food, but the guests didn't seem particularly pleased, she noticed. They picked at the platters and left a lot of food on their plates. Maybe they missed the chapatis and daal? No matter how hard she looked, she couldn't find any chapati or daal on the buffet table, nor any fried cabbage. What she did spot was three different bowls full of eggs; one bowl for hard-boiled, one for soft-boiled and one for medium-boiled. One of the chefs was manning an omelette station, and she recognised both the yellow mango and the orange papaya on the table. But she had never known fruit could be cut like that, like flowers. What a splendid idea!

All morning, she'd stood in a corner of the dining room, ready to dart forward and clear plates whenever guests seemed done. One time, she had apparently jumped the gun and a plump little old lady with blue hair had chased after her and reclaimed her plate with a whine of displeasure. Nazreen could tell she spoke English but was too focused on her hair to hear what she was saying. It was blue! And the lady's English, it was a different kind of English than the one she was used to hearing from her Amma and in school, and she was suddenly struck by an alarming notion. Were there several different types of English? She had to ask Babul.

But right now, Babul was still too excited about his birthday card, and Reka whispered he'd probably had one too many of those beers. Old Iftekhar shook his head, glared with his one eye and muttered something about a den of iniquity. But he readily accepted an invitation to stay for dinner. Plates were brought out and placed around the high bed. Just as the evening prayer echoing out from the nearby Badda Mosque drew to a close, Meena slipped in.

Nazreen watched her sister and could tell she was happy. Meena discreetly passed the corner where they'd hidden their plastic box, opened it and slipped some crumpled notes into it. "How much," Nazreen asked when her sister sat down on the floor next to her to eat.

"Two hundred and eighty taka, two hundred from the sandals since the day before yesterday. The rest from Patel."

Nazreen was taken aback. That was a lot of money. Meena had apparently hit upon an idea that actually generated income. And if she landed the job at the Radisson, she would take home at least two thousand taka a month. And then all the other side jobs. Maybe it wouldn't take very long to put together a respectable dowry? If that was even what they were doing?

Lately, Nazreen had started thinking she might be one of those modern girls, not a village girl. Maybe she should stay here in Dhaka, find a man of her own choosing? The thoughts she gave free rein in the early mornings had changed recently. She thought less and less about the village and the river that flowed slowly past it. And she dreamt more and more often of Pink City's fancy shalwar kameezzes, and she would love to buy the kind of handbag Dipita had.

She often had an urge to tell Mokta about everything she saw and experienced. In her mind, she often pictured her back in the village. It would take reality a few seconds to catch up with her and stab her in the stomach. Mokta. Big sister. Why aren't you here with us?

After dinner, the girls tidied up and gave Reka and Babul some privacy. Nazreen motioned to Meena to join her outside. They'd found a corner next to an abandoned water pump where they could sometimes talk in private.

"Two hundred and eighty taka, and that's after paying for things. The difference? That's amazing!"

"If you add up all the differences, it's two hundred and eighty. But it could be more, so much more."

Meena nodded pensively and Nazreen clapped her hands, unable to hide her delight. Meena continued.

"I'm going to buy even more sandals, and a few buckets, too. I've put a thousand taka aside for that, and I have seven old men in five villages selling the goods for me. But there could be more. Easily."

Meena's eagerness was unmistakeable.

"If they just sell five pairs each, hold on . . . seven hundred taka each round. And we pass each village once a week . . ."

"What old men are talking about? Why are they working for you?"

"There's old men like the ones by the crossroads back home in every village. You know, like Hanif's grandad, grandad's cousin Mustafa. You know, old men who can't work anymore, who just sit around and talk and sometimes even beg. You know."

Nazreen did know the kind of man Meena was referring to. Elderly men were a common sight in any village. Everyone felt they'd outlived their usefulness. They couldn't help out around the house like their elderly wives, and were unable to move very far. There was something desperate about them.

"When I offer them money for just sitting on a street corner, selling my wares, they're thrilled. Since they're sitting there anyway. And their children and grandchildren are thrilled, too," Meena told her. "Their families don't have to support them, instead, they can contribute a little. And when they die, there's always more old men. I have lots of people asking to work for me."

Meena's matter-of-fact description of her business plan impressed Nazreen. Clearly, her sister knew what she was doing, as usual, and the growing pile of money in their plastic box made her feel safe.

Before they moved to Dhaka, Meena had been the member of their family whose mind worked differently from the others'. She'd bought a broken rickshaw for next to nothing and since then, their father had been able to use spare parts from that for years. Meena thought backwards and forwards, in and out, up and down, while everyone else focused on one thing at a time. But she was very hard on herself, Meena. Nazreen wanted to see her smile more. She put her arm around her little sister.

"Oh, Meena, why don't you buy yourself a pretty shalwar, or a new shawl! Let's go over to Pink City on Friday afternoon, just you and me?"

"Absolutely not."

"You'd look so pretty, Meena. You have to take time off sometime, come with me and Dipita. We have some money to spend now."

"You're not getting it. How many times do I have to explain this to you . . ."

Meena's face darkened, she crossed her arms firmly and heaved a short, angry sigh. Nazreen waited her sister out. It was best to let Meena explain what she meant in her own time, without pushing, Nazreen was well aware of that. At length, Meena spoke. The words came out in staccato bursts.

"If you waste the money, it can't be turned into more money. You need money to create more difference. It's the only way. I would never, ever buy an expensive shalwar. Why? Because it won't make me rich! The money should be used to buy something you can sell for a bigger profit. It's the difference, that's what matters. The difference! A lot of tiny differences, like with the bracelets, or a big one, like with the jackfruit."

Meena's determined, square face was ablaze in the gloom, and she pressed on gravely:

"We came here to earn our own dowries. Have you forgotten about that? And to make money to give Amma and Abba? I'm staying here until that's done, then I'm going back home. I want to find a nice man who's not too old and who will let me run a small shop. That's all. Twenty thousand taka for me, twenty thousand taka for you. And ten thousand for Amma and Abba. Fifty thousand. Then we're going home."

Nazreen listened in silence, not bothering to argue with her sister. But it felt odd to realise she and Meena no longer shared a vision. She leaned her head against Meena's. Or feelings. Since they left the village, it was like Meena had grown new parts. Or was it Nazreen who had changed? They sat there without speaking for a while with their heads together. Meena kept her arms crossed.

"Also, I talked to Great Aunt Mahmoda." Meena raised her chin, looking combative.

"What? You talked to Mahmoda? Without telling me? I thought we were going to wait until Eid!" Nazreen felt sheepish. Maybe she should have called. But she thought they'd agreed to lay low for a while. "How are Amma and Abba?"

"Mahmoda says Abba doesn't even want our names mentioned, but Amma probably understands. She says the only way to make Abba see that girls can be useful is to send money. If we ever want to return, we have to stop the mosque committee from issuing a fatwa."

"Then let's send money," Nazreen said.

"I found out how to do it via mobile phone," Meena explained eagerly. "You can send a hundred or a hundred and fifty taka in one go. With Flexi-load. They give you a code and whoever's receiving the money gets cash when they show the code. Mahmoda can accept the money and take a rickshaw to the village."

"Did she say anything about Mokta? Did they have a chollisha?"

Nazreen's question effectively stopped Meena's intense rush of words. The sisters hadn't discussed Mokta in a long time and her name made them both feel dull and heavy. Their sister was suddenly there with them. Meena lowered her voice and answered Nazreen's question.

"There was a chollisha in the village. Everyone came. A lot of people cried. Abba's apparently inconsolable. Mokta's the only one whose name can be spoken at home now. At least that's what Mahmoda says."

Meena trailed off and the girls took each other's hands. Nazreen dried Meena's tears and Meena whispered:

"It's so strange, Nazreen. Mokta's dead, but we're alive. We're alive, but we're dead. To Abba, at least."

Mokta's presence was intense in the dark alley. Her slender figure standing next to her sisters. A tender caress across Meena's forehead, hands that cupped Nazreen's cheeks for a moment. Meena turned her face up toward the night sky in an attempt to quell her tears, or at least slow them. Nazreen just closed her eyes and slowly shook her head. The grief they shared was rage, helplessness.

Nazreen was the one to break the silence by heaving a quick sigh and asking in a completely different tone.

"Do we have money to send?"

The Mokta moment had passed.

"I've already sent five hundred taka, and if you can refrain from using all our money to buy clothes . . ." Meena was still upset.

"We can't walk around in our old shalwar kameezzes if we want to work for bideshis. I have to look good!"

"But if you let me do business, there will be more money. I thought you understood." Meena glowered at her sister from under her dark fringe.

"I understand, Meena, I understand. Pray to Allah that I get to keep my job at the Radisson. You'll see, we'll make enough for both Amma and Abba and ourselves. We should pray to Allah to protect us and perform *namaz* for your business. We'll pray namaz with Reka on Friday."

Nazreen put her arms around her sister's neck, stroked her head and mumbled into her hair.

"Meena-jaan. You're so good, always so good. But there's two of us, I want it to still be the two of us, since it can't be the three of us anymore."

9

The boat moored by a sandbank and when Janne crawled out from under the makeshift canopy, he was blinded by the glaring light. They had arrived at an island that was almost completely submerged in water, but which nevertheless appeared to be the most substantial piece of land in the vicinity. The island consisted of white sand, which reflected the sharp sunlight. He wished he'd brought sunglasses. A few hundred yards from the water's edge, he spotted a cluster of huts encircling a handful of ragged-looking palm trees.

The boy who had piloted the boat tossed their backpacks ashore and three young men on motorcycles greeted Charlotta.

"Hop on," Charlotta said. "The houses are still a way off. This is how you get to places when the water recedes."

On their way to the cluster of buildings, they were met by a gaggle of children, screaming and hollering with delight. The motorcycles slowed down and the children hurled themselves at the vehicles, somehow finding ways to hold on. One small boy clambered onto Janne's back and another clung to his right arm. He, for his part, had his hands full holding onto his driver. The motorcycled lurched this way and that in the sand, but no one seemed particularly concerned. Janne thought to himself this clearly wasn't the first time they'd done this.

Once they reached the village, Charlotta was received like a beloved family member by the children. They shouted "*apa, apa*" to her, and between hugs and hair ruffling, she managed to explain that "apa" means "sister".

"I'm 'apa' and before you know it, you'll be 'bhai', brother. Just go with it, Janne!"

The children were lugging around a couple of scrawny puppies and soon tried to make Janne hold one of them. A group that Janne surmised was the official welcoming committee were waiting behind the children. He recognised Khadija Anam. Two girls in identical saris holding flower garlands were standing in front of her.

Janne had to give the puppy back to greet Khadija. He bent down so one of the girls could place a fragrant garland around his neck.

"Welcome to our home!" the girls giggled in halting English. Janne was moved.

"My goodness, this is a reception fit for a king!"

"It's how we do it in Bangladesh," Khadija said. "Strangers are always honoured guests here."

Khadija was dressed in a plain sari which she pulled tighter around her to move through the loose sand as she led them toward the houses. A couple of boys ran up to Charlotta, who explained that a woman who had just given birth to a daughter was insisting she go speak with her. Janne was left alone with Khadija.

The Alor Desh headquarters turned out to consist of a few low concrete buildings forming a square. One of the wings was a school, another a simple garment workshop and a third was a dormitory in which Janne gathered he would be staying. "Guesthouse" was written on the wall of that building. Someone had already brought his backpack up and placed it on a bed.

In the courtyard between the buildings, a few teenagers were playing badminton while chickens scratched for food. The regular village began directly behind the buildings and Khadija showed Janne around with palpable pride.

"This patch of land has been here for more than ten years and our headquarters were built five years ago. We've made sure almost all the houses have tin roofs, and that the villagers have a steady supply of food and money. No one in our villages starves anymore."

Janne thought it looked like a quaint village, with small clay or concrete houses that all looked well-kept and tidy. Even though he'd never been to a third-world village before, a lot of things looked familiar: the cooking pots drying in the sun, the naked children in the doorways, the rice spread out to dry on the ground in front of the houses. Cows and goats were sheltering in the shade under the trees and women were squatting outside their homes, working with their hands. The ground was clean and newly-swept, almost like sculpted clay. The women seemed to have gathered around a water pump, and outside a white building that had to be the local mosque, Janne spotted a pile of shoes suggesting the men had gathered for prayers.

Unlike in Dhaka, no one moved quickly. Khadija herself seemed unrushed, chatting and joking with everyone she met. Janne seized the chance to practice his very limited Bangla and his attempts caused much merriment among the villagers.

"My wife is named Sofia. We have a boy and a girl. Good children, a small boy, *chotto chelle*, and a big girl. Sweden is my country. It's cold in Sweden."

The words were repeated and scrutinised by the curious villagers, who seemed to hold them up to the light like gemstones. They turned each shard of information over and over.

"The little boy. How big? Like this? Is he in school? And Sweden, is that a good country? And your wife, is she a good wife?"

Khadija did her best to interpret and explain. Janne found everyone's kindness and curiosity charming. A young man who had decent English offered Janne an analysis of why the villagers were so interested in him. With a wide, winsome smile, he announced:

"You see, in your country you mind your own business, but in Bangladesh, we like to mind everyone else's business."

Janne nodded his amused agreement. The young man's friend, who was leaning on him in a way Janne had noticed young Bangladeshi men seemed prone to do, felt encouraged to test out a textbook phrase or two.

"What is a young chap like yourself doing, strolling around on a nice day like this? It's raining cats and dogs."

The young men held a brief whispered conference and then made Janne a suggestion. The gist of it was that they should start an import-export business together immediately and that Janne should invite them to Sweden for this purpose. He should feel free to sort out visas and tickets, too. Both boys beamed like suns at their proposal.

After spending some time trying to persuade him, the young men realised Janne was reluctant to take them up on their offer and ended the negotiation with a few heartfelt high-fives with Janne. Then they walked off hand in hand toward a small stand made of four bamboo sticks and a tarpaulin. Khadija smiled after them.

"Well, you can't blame them for trying, can you?"

Khadija suddenly turned in between two low buildings and walked up to a cylindrical clay formation sitting on a raised cement platform.

"Guess!" she said, putting a hand on the dried clay. Janne shook his head, confounded.

"A flood-proof stove. Inside, there's dry fuel, rice, dried fish and matches. When the flood comes, the villagers break the wall and then can cook here for a few days until the water subsides."

Janne studied the small clay bunker with interest. Khadija pointed at some ducks waddling around the courtyard. A girl of about seven with missing front teeth and close-cropped hair was watching them talk intently.

"The ducks swim while the chickens drown," Khadija explained while she reached out and took the girl's hand. "We try to persuade the villagers to go for ducks and plants that float. There's no knowing how long the floods will last in the future, or if it's going to be possible to live here at all." Khadija looked at the girl and swung her arm back and forth. "And this little one, Tinto, is the village hero."

She said something in Bangla to the girl, who pulled herself up straighter.

"She swam by herself, with a water bottle in one hand and a bag of rice in her mouth to rescue her old grandmother who had ended up cut off on her roof last summer. Everyone was in such a rush to save the animals and the youngest children that they completely forgot about the old widow."

The girl giggled and hid behind Khadija when Janne tried to make contact. He squatted down and tried again, but then turned to Khadija.

"From what I gather, your work has had a big impact, but it has also made you powerful enemies?"

"So Charlotta told you? Yes, you could say we have powerful enemies. More powerful than your wife and other donors understand, perhaps. But I don't want to bring you down. Make sure you get to know us now that you've come, and you're welcome to take pictures, so long as the villagers give their consent. I'll go over the more unfortunate issues with your wife, the counsellor, when I get a chance."

"So what do you think? Are the auditors going to clear you?" Janne had to ask. Khadija froze mid-step and slowly turned to him.

"Clear us? Of course not. When four accountants from Ernst & Young scrutinise every last payment and every last invoice in a programme reaching a hundred and fifty thousand poor people in one of the world's poorest countries, it goes without saying they're going to find corruption. This is Bangladesh. Why would our organisation be the one that's cleared?"

Janne and Charlotta ate lunch, which to Janne's horror consisted of a fishtail sticking out of a mountain of rice, sitting on the floor of Siraj's house. With an embarrassed smile, Siraj explained that the household's only fork had gone astray.

"You're going to have to eat like we do," he said and Charlotta stage whispered in Swedish:

"Go on, professor, you're going to have to munch down your fishtail with your hands. And don't forget – use your right hand for food!"

While they ate, Siraj's young daughter stood in the doorway, watching them. She was naked, apart from a piece of string around her waist and a small leather pouch around her neck. Her hair was shaved and there was a painted black dot on her forehead. She suddenly threw herself into her father's arms and bit him.

"Tomelilla, stop! That's enough!"

Siraj laughed and grabbed his daughter.

"She's always biting people," he mumbled. "My wife and I don't know how to make her stop."

Janne nodded and had to ask.

"Her name is Tomelilla?"

Siraj nodded and Charlotta gigglingly explained:

"There's a steady flow of volunteers from a college in Tomelilla. So Siraj and his wife thought it was a nice name, Tomelilla. And it is. Actually sounds like a lot of other Bengali names."

Janne nodded, turned to Tomelilla and stuck a finger in his mouth. He inflated his cheek and made a popping sound with his finger. Tomelilla laughed.

"My son, Teo, is a biter, too. How old is Tomelilla? A year and a half?"

"Yes, almost two. She started biting a few months ago, but only when she was angry. Now she's biting all the time, we're all full of teeth marks."

"They say it's because they can't express themselves verbally," Janne said. "What do you think about that? Teo has been slow to speak. Does Tomelilla talk?"

The men launched into a conversation about childrearing and Janne felt a growing sympathy for Siraj. The man had strange, light-brown eyes, which his daughter had inherited, and turned out to be deeply involved in the raising of his child. A young woman was listening from a dark corner.

"Fatima became my wife three years ago. Our families decided it was a good idea. She is a good wife and as distraught as I am about Tomelilla's mischief," Siraj said.

The young woman suddenly came up to them and awkwardly placed a photo album in Janne's lap. She pointed to both Charlotta and Janne and then the photo album, smiling gently.

"Ah, our wedding album. Would you like to have a look? Fatima is very proud of our wedding."

It was a large plastic album with gold trim. Every page was gold-framed and full of pictures of serious-looking, dressed-up relatives in various constellations. Fatima and Siraj were standing next to each other in several pictures, like stiff mannequins, two feet apart. Janne didn't quite know what to say, but Charlotta understood.

"How lovely, bhalo. You look so beautiful, Fatima. And such expensive clothes. And how many guests did you have? How many dishes did you serve?"

Siraj and Fatima talked over each other in their eagerness to answer. Fatima flushed and withdrew when her husband spoke, but then mustered the courage to speak. Adding things and pointing. Charlotta translated.

"That relative there. I see, he's a doctor, imagine that. Your uncle? And that aunt died of a terrible cancer. I'm so sorry. And your second cousins are having trouble conceiving, poor things. They've gone to see a *kobiraj*, a witch doctor? That's good."

Janne had to ask how old Siraj was. By his estimation, Fatima was still in her teens. Siraj laughed.

"How old I am? How old do you want me to be? I might be thirty-five, or maybe thirty-eight. Does it matter? Fatima is seventeen now, that I know."

That evening, Janne had said goodnight early and retreated to his room, where the furniture consisted of beds with rock-hard cotton mattresses. Mosquito nets with a pattern of red roses shrouded each bed. Janne had tested all the beds in an attempt to find one with a bit of give, but they were all rock-hard and unyielding. Charlotta had told him one of the volunteers who preceded her had been so fed up with the mattresses, she'd dragged out a double bed with springs.

"Seriously, you can sleep in my house if you want. A few days on those torture implements and you'll feel battered."

Janne had thanked her for the thoughtful offer, but declined. He wanted to be able to answer honestly if Sofia asked where he'd slept. No complications.

The room smelled strongly of moth balls and mould and a single lightbulb flickered overhead. The night outside was pitch black; no one in the village had electricity. The pulsating song of the crickets made him linger by the open shutters for a minute. The sound of dry husks and wings. The moonlight was reflected in hundreds of tiny silver shards outside. From the village pond, from the shiny palm leaves, from the corrugated metal roofs. Somewhere, two dogs started fighting. A feeling of intense presence filled him. He wanted to share this with Sofia.

A faint tap on the door snapped him out of his reverie. The door opened and Charlotta popped her head in. She was holding a bottle of wine in one hand a toothbrush cup in the other.

"Nightcap? Come on, let's go sit outside. Turn out the light."

Janne found a reasonably clean glass that he rinsed with water from a bottle before following Charlotta outside. Around the corner, facing a stand of parched bamboo, were two stools and a rickety table with a candle on it. Charlotta poured them both wine and lit the candle and a cigarette.

"A *bidi*, it's what the locals smoke," she explained and took a deep drag. "I take what I can get."

"Won't the villagers be upset if they see us drinking wine? Given as how they're Muslim?" Janne asked, sipping his toothbrush cup. For a brief moment, he considered grabbing a cigarette, too, but he decided to refrain.

"No one can see us back here. And people aren't all that orthodox, really, plus they know we're not Muslim. Some are of a more fundamentalist bent and want to push the Quran on everyone else, but most people out here believe all kinds of things. Allah is just one of their gods," Charlotta explained, pulling hard on her cigarette again before adding: "Besides, they already think we're weird. I mean, we don't exactly blend in, do we? Look, fireflies!"

Her attention had turned to the darkness beyond the pool of light from their candle and Janne realised the night was full of hovering points of luminescence.

"Cool, right?"

Janne nodded. Noella would've loved this.

He enjoyed Charlotta's unaffected passion and idealism. It was unusual to hear young people talk about politics and social injustice with the kind of searing anger Charlotta exhibited. As a teacher, he'd often been appalled by how self-absorbed his students were, how mesmerised by their own reflections and little worlds.

Charlotta started talking about her work in the villages and about the choices people there had to make:

"Some of these women are so clearly smart and driven, it makes you want to cry that they don't have access to education," she said quietly. "Sometimes, I can't help but think that I'm sitting here with my mediocre intelligence and stellar education, looking at geniuses like Marie Curie or Hillary Clinton. Except they're dressed in rags, have no teeth and can't read. They have no options whatsoever. If they want to avoid being stoned or shunned, there's only one path open to them: get married, obey your husband, bear children, support them, die."

Silence fell. Charlotta picked tobacco flakes out of her mouth. Janne watched the fireflies dance and thought about what Charlotta had just said. The limitations intrinsic to poverty. Charlotta continued:

"They're born into poverty and will never be able to live up to their potential. Mozart might be living in this village right now. Or Frida Kahlo. But instead, they'll take out a two-thousand-taka loan to buy a goat." She sighed and had a few sips of wine. "They're ground down, these strong, beautiful women. You know the woman who wanted to see me when we first arrived?"

Janne recalled that Charlotta had been dragged away by the villagers.

"It's a woman I know well, about my age. When she was fourteen, she was married off to a good-for-nothing who has got it into her head that she mustn't use birth control. In order to get the pill, she needs her husband to sign the prescription, and since he refuses, she's now the mother of eight. And note that it has to be the woman's *husband*, unmarried women are not allowed the pill. When there were complications during her last delivery and there was talk of a caesarean, the doctors needed her husband's signature to do the surgery. So the bastard divorces her, right then and there, so he won't have to pay! Well aware that she might die, or be left alone with enormous debts and eight children to feed. Apparently, he went straight to his mistress in town and started spouting all kinds of Western nonsense about "not loving her anymore". As if love ever had anything to do with it. And now she's the humiliated one. A single mother of eight, ostracised, and she would've had a gigantic debt if Alor Desh hadn't paid it for her."

Visibly agitated, Charlotta downed the rest of her wine and topped up both her own and Janne's glass.

"I don't want to sound too academic, but in the collision between traditional village life and modernity, gender norms break down and women lose out twice over. Do you see what I mean? Alor Desh helped her with the debt, but now the woman wants to drag her husband before the *shalish*, the local court, and she wants me to testify."

"Isn't that a good thing?" Janne asked.

"Sure but going to the shalish is a very risky proposition. If the wrong old men are on it, the judgment will be deeply misogynistic. Last summer, a fourteen-year-old girl was whipped to death in the northern part of Bangladesh after being sentenced to lashing by the shalish. She'd been raped, but the shalish felt she'd seduced the man. Here in Lalpara, Alor Desh has managed to fill half the seats on the salish with women, so hopefully they might see things differently. But there's no guarantee . . ."

Janne shuddered in the warm night and wanted to know more. Clearly, the bucolic idyll of these villages concealed a very dark underbelly. Charlotta lit another cigarette.

"It sounds very – and I apologise if this comes off as pretentious – meaningful. Your work, I mean," Janne said slowly. "These women, how can they be empowered? Without making the men feel threatened?"

"Locally by working to do good, in the shalish and the mosques. And nationally through lobbying groups and networks. Well, the kind of thing your wife does. There are people in this country who really do want to move out of the Middle Ages and build an equal society. And the key to that is to make sure the next generation of girls have access to education and good food to make them strong and healthy."

"And aren't discriminated against?"

"Discriminated against," Charlotta repeated the words slowly, chuckled and put her cigarette out. "What an incredibly Western thing to say. No, they shouldn't be *discriminated against*. Should they? I think I see it more as . . ."

Just then, Janne's phone went off. He saw it was Sofia calling and turned his back to Charlotta to answer.

"Finally, decent reception. Can you hear me?" Sofia's voice sounded tinny in the night. "How are you doing? How's village life?"

Janne gazed into the gloom, letting his eyes rest on a cow dozing under a reed roof. The crickets made it difficult to make out Sofia's words.

"Good, thanks. It's amazing out here. Completely different from Dhaka, we have to bring the children sometime. There are fireflies and . . ."

"Janne, we have to decide if we're going to the Glitter Ball. And if we're going, the question is whether we should sit with the British or the Australians. And I was told Bjarne's apparently expecting us to sit with him? Did you agree to that?"

"What's the Glitter Ball?" Janne had a faint memory of someone mentioning the "party of all parties". "Is it something we have to attend?"

"No, it's not! Let's boycott the Glitter Ball!" Charlotta hollered from the little table when she realised what they were talking about. Janne looked over at her. She was making a time-out sign with her hands and shaking her head frantically.

"From what I hear, it's an important social event," Sofia said. "Everyone's in themed costumes and the tables compete. It's supposedly the party of the year. Important for networking with different embassies . . ."

Janne said nothing for a while, giving Sofia time to explain. She had browsed through *The Village*'s picture archive and seen pictures from last year. It had looked like fun. Janne's eyes rested on the drowsy cow and a firefly alighted on his stretched-out hand. Then he felt the decision touch down inside him with a thud.

"No, let's skip it, Sofia. Seriously. I have absolutely no desire to go."

"Next year, maybe?" Sofia seemed to want to.

"Sure, maybe next year. We'll see."

They ended the call and Charlotta celebrated over by the table. Janne went back to his stool. He tried to pick up where they'd left off, but Charlotta cut him short.

"Do you know what the Australians and Yanks did at last year's Glitter Ball? Just so you know what you're passing up? A "wet burqa" competition. Ambassadors and foreign aid counsellors were jumping around wearing wet burqas. Bjarne and his lot came third." She laughed resignedly and shook her head. Janne made a face like he'd just eaten a lemon.

"Wow, that's outrageous."

"Yep, seriously politically incorrect on so many levels. I'm telling you, ex-pat life is bizarre. A bizarre context that everyone just seems to accept. In order to cope. The distillation of every injustice in the world. It's never over in a Land Rover, or whatever it is Bjarne likes to say."

*

If only Beppin had been woken up by the crickets. Woken up as he was sitting in the dark in his guard hut of corrugated metal. Or, if he had been as hungry as he usually was and therefore unable to doze off, he would have been able to keep his job guarding the residence of embassy employee Sofia Paulin and her husband Janne. But on this particular night, the emaciated father of five, husband of Alama Begum, both from the village of Noakganj, had eaten a substantial meal. He'd been invited to share the leftovers of Mohammed the rickshaw driver's daughter's wedding dinner – a juicy mutton biryani, a large portion of rice, as tall as a tussock of grass – and for once, Beppin came to work at the house with the Swedish Embassy brass plaque on its gate feeling full. Full and bloated and sleepy. He did his usual lap around the house, exchanged a few words with the other guards and traded some gossip about the Swedish family that lived in the house. Yes, Boss was away. But Madame and the children were asleep. The chef had gone home and the day-shift guards were about to leave, too. Beppin was set to watch over the house until the second morning prayer.

Or, if only the batteries in Siv's flashlight had run out. Or, if Siv had parked her car by the gate instead of down the street. That would have roused Beppin. It definitely would have. Or, if the gate hadn't been greased the day before, so it would have emitted its usual grating whine, waking him up. Or, if the thought of the Rules That Must Be Followed hadn't taken root in the mind of the Swedish Embassy's Administrative Manager Siv's mind on this of all nights.

He would have needed just one minute, one measly minute, to get his bearings. If the heat hadn't been so stiflingly heavy and his fullness so intoxicating. If the chair had been less comfortable or the guard hut less secluded. There were a lot of little things that went wrong that night and didn't give Beppin sixty seconds to open his eyes, straighten up, get to his feet, salute Siv and reach the gate in time.

Instead, Beppin woke up with someone shouting in his ear, shining a flashlight in his face. He fell off the chair, hit his head on the corrugated metal and felt someone kick him in the ribs. Someone ripped off his uniform cap and then he was pushed off the property, expelled from his workplace. Shoved into the ditch outside the wall surrounding the house as the iron gate slammed shut behind him.

*

Carlos Portillo, Carlos Portillo. The name sounded very familiar. Arthur was to apologise to a Carlos Portillo for his online bullying, stated the "action plan" sent out by the psychologist to bring the Arthur affair to a close. Moberg frowned.

"Vanja, this Carlos," he called to his wife, who was upstairs. "The name sounds so familiar somehow . . ."

"Portillo. Isn't he Alberto Portillo's son, you know, the head of UNDP? Maria-Luisa and Alberto. Tall, dark, both of them. She's in my book club."

Goddamn it! Moberg gasped. Oh dear, this wasn't good. Alberto Portillo was one of the central players in Dhaka's diplomatic corps, a beefy Spaniard who rarely if ever avoided a conflict about anything relating to the UN sphere. Moberg had instinctively done his best to steer clear of him, but he knew he was due to meet with him next week to discuss a plan to harmonise efforts that the like-minded group, a collection of embassies operating according to a set of shared values, had outlined. It would be a blow to Sweden if the group's proposal wasn't accepted by UNDP.

"Vanja . . . For God's sake . . ."

Moberg climbed the marble staircase in a few long strides and found his wife on one of the residence's many terraces. She was tending to a plant, humming to herself.

"What are we going to do about Arthur? Do you realise it's Alberto Portillo's son he's been harassing, or whatever it's called on the internet? I have a meeting with Portillo next week."

"Is that right, Mr Ambassador? So, what are you going to do about it?"

Vanja didn't look up from her plant, simply kept pinching off withered leaves, then carefully scraped something off the trunk.

"This is incredibly embarrassing, Vanja. Should we write to the Portillos, as Arthur's parents? Do you know his wife? Couldn't you maybe . . . or maybe I should . . . oh my goodness, I just hope the Portillos aren't invited to the Canadian ministerial meeting on Thursday."

Moberg was thinking out loud and didn't realise his wife had stiffened.

"Karl-Otto. To be honest, you sound more concerned about your relationship with this Portillo than about your own son. This isn't embarrassing, this is a tragedy! Arthur is walking around with a daddy-shaped hole in his soul, screaming out for yang, and all you care about is what some brusque Spaniard's going to think!"

"Vanja, a daddy-shaped hole, I don't know . . ."

Moberg tried to placate his wife, but then he realised he had, as was so often the case, failed to see things from her perspective. Vanja was on the war path.

"You're coming to the full-moon meeting next week. Arthur has already promised to attend, and it's suddenly very clear to me just how important it is that you're there, too, to help him through this. He has to be given a chance to balance his chakras, and your presence is crucial! You *are* yang!"

"No, Vanja, not that. That's where I draw the line. I'll talk to Arthur, I will. Spend more time with him. But it's not easy, he wants nothing to do with me. Bloody hell!"

"It's not mumbo-jumbo, Karl-Otto! Don't be so closed-off. Steve and Iris run full-moon meetings on their roof every month and they're always packed! Last month, the American ambassador's private secretary was there, and the wife of the head of Ericsson never misses a meeting. No one is going to think anything of the Swedish ambassador turning up in a private capacity!"

Moberg sighed inwardly and thought to himself that more than one eyebrow would have been raised at the Ministry of Foreign Affairs if it got out that Sweden's ambassador to Bangladesh attended shamanistic full-moon parties. He had to deflect Vanja's attention right now.

"I forgot to mention I booked a trip to Nepal for me and Arthur. Well, maybe not actually booked yet, but I've looked around online. I figured we need to work on our relationship, climb some mountains together."

Moberg had no idea where that came from. The last thing he could see himself doing, with or without Arthur, was climbing the Himalayas. But Vanja lit up and dropped the full-moon train of thought entirely. The misdirection had worked.

"Darling! Really? That's so beautiful and wise of you! That's exactly, *exactly*, how we have to approach this. When were you thinking of going? And where?"

She let go of the plant and wrapped her arms around him. Before he could answer, she was whispering with her lips against his neck.

"You know you're my healer, don't you, Karl-Otto? You don't know it, but you're a great healer."

When Moberg arrived at the embassy the next morning, he felt miserable. Anna-Lena had been trying to arrange a meeting with him for a while and he knew she'd eventually proceeded to schedule one through his secretary for ten o'clock. Over the course of the previous week, he'd noticed her circling him impatiently as soon as he entered the embassy. He had avoided opening any email from her with the subject header "when you have a minute" or "urgent meeting". He'd mumbled something about taking any foreign-aid related questions to Sofia before making himself unavailable. Sofia had sent him countless emails, too, and now he spotted a dossier on his chair, which she must have put there the night before. A yellow post-it beamed up at him with the word "Urgent". He put it in his in-tray and ruefully walked over to the door to let Anna-Lena in.

When Anna-Lena left his office thirty minutes later, she'd got what she wanted. She had made him promise to grant visas to a theatre group from Chittagong who wanted to go to Borås for a theatre fair.

"It's about cultural exchange, Moberg. How are we supposed to have an exchange with Bangladesh if they're never let into Sweden?" she'd argued. "It's about building bridges of trust."

Erik, who was in charge of consular matters, had firmly advised against it, claiming there were bound to be defections. Moberg sighed. He had a point there. But Anna-Lena was so adamant he eventually felt obliged to step in and grant the visas. At least that would keep her off his back for a while.

Moberg sighed again and picked up the form he had to fill out to be reimbursed for the outlays for Sofia's welcome reception. Tent rental, lights, staff, wine and food. Moberg skimmed the posts. Ninety people had been invited. He hesitated for a split second, then added a one before the post "number of guests". One hundred and ninety people. It could have been a hundred and ninety. The Ministry of Foreign Affairs never compensated him for all the overtime he put in on evenings and weekends, so it was only fair. One hundred and ninety people, good, that would give them some extra funds and Siv, who had to countersign, was discreet. They knew where they stood.

That being taken care of, Moberg could no longer avoid the folder Sofia had left for him. He soon realised it contained printouts of every email she had sent him and he had ignored. This way, he couldn't avoid them, true, but her approach was openly impatient. Undiplomatic, Moberg mused. He wasn't used to that. Not used to the kind of willpower Sofia radiated. At the Ministry of Foreign Affairs, politicians inevitably wanted things done, but in the field, it was usually easy enough to hide from all of that. Initiatives rarely came from inside the diplomatic corps. But apparently, foreign aid people were different.

He read. A big women's conference. All the smaller donors in the like-minded group were teaming up with UN Women, inviting the Justice Department and the police to a discussion about violence against women and girls. Moberg read. Sweden would host and make it a high-level event by guaranteeing the attendance of at least one Swedish government minister. The funding to be jointly provided by all donors and local staff recruited to plan the event. The goal being to present an action plan to educate police officers and prosecutors through local courts about how to interview women, formulate charges and make cases against perpetrators. The document made clear these were often the women's relatives or spouses.

The plan was ambitious and eminently feasible. Impressive, actually. Sofia must have given it a lot of thought. It was a good idea. It would raise Sweden's profile while also laying the groundwork for future change, at a low cost. Smart. And yet, Moberg's only feeling upon reading Sofia's enthusiastic proposal, was weariness.

"Work. Lots of work," he muttered to himself. And also, women's issues. Something about women's issues made Moberg uncomfortable, almost embarrassed. Was he, as the host, supposed to stand there at a big international conference and talk about women? When there were so many other problems in this country? No thank you. That was on Sofia. All on Sofia. He wasn't going to stop her – couldn't, really – but he wasn't going to help her either.

When she popped her head in a while later, asking if he'd had a chance to look over her proposal, he voiced a number of concerns.

"At the start, you write the police's capacity to handle violence against women is "limited". Could we maybe make it "unsatisfactory" instead? And I suggest you use dashes instead of bullet points. Here. And here."

Moberg indicated the instances on the paper and Sofia agreed readily, but wanted more feedback.

"What about the contents? Do you have any thoughts about the content?"

"Well, this habit of writing 'women and men/girls and boys', I know it's how you foreign aid people like it, but is it really necessary? Can't you write 'people' instead? A sentence like this one:" He took a deep breath and read aloud. "' . . . despite the lack of opportunities in the rural areas, pressure mounts on women and men/girls and boys to sustain . . . ' Couldn't you just as well say ' . . . pressure mounts on *people* to sustain . . ."

"*People* tends to denote men. Women and girls are omitted." Sofia replied automatically, a hint of resignation in her voice. These formulations had been agreed on as a standard for international conferences on gender equality, they weren't her invention. She could see the point in using them, but at the same time they were often a source of mirth among the men and tended to distract from the real questions. She asked again:

"But the proposal as a whole, the plan for the conference? The strategy, the substance, do you have anything to add?"

"Not really, but let me think about it. I'll hold onto the folder."

Moberg checked his watch and realised it was time for lunch. The Egyptian ambassador was hosting a welcome lunch for his new attaché at one and an embassy car would arrive shortly to pick him up. Before he could make it out of the building, however, Siv pounced on him with a triumphant smile on her face.

"I caught one of them red-handed!"

"Pardon?" Moberg had no idea what she was talking about.

"The guards. Sofia's night watchman. I did an inspection last night. And he was asleep. Asleep in the middle of his shift." Siv held out a flashlight. "I went around all the houses last night around four to check up on them. Obviously, it's part of my duties to make sure the rules are being followed. And then . . . there! At Sofia's house! A sleeping guard!"

Siv laughed smugly.

"Oh dear." Moberg didn't know what to say.

"It goes without saying I fired him on the spot. We can't have snoozing night watchmen. Can we?"

No, of course not," Moberg was about to leave to get into the car waiting for him, but sensed Siv was expecting more. He added hesitantly. "Good thing, then. Good thing you caught him, red-handed, I mean. Well done."

*

Meena pulled her goods out from the bin under the bed, moving silently so as not to wake Nazreen. She wrapped hemp string around the last pair of sandals and carefully placed it in her sack. There, yes, forty-nine pairs. Seven pairs for each of her seven old men. And the bracelets, twenty pairs of glass bracelets each and five red buckets. She took out the plastic box wedged between a broken dresser and the wall, opened it and looked at the money inside. She had counted it last night, but just wanted one more look. The sight made her giddy. She wet her lips. So much money.

Slowly breaking off a banana from a bunch Nazreen had left out, she counted silently in her head. If everything sold, that would give her a tidy little profit of . . . one thousand two hundred taka. Four hundred and fifty was going to the farmers, which left seven hundred and fifty for her. And then half of that she had to give to Rifat, and maybe a hundred to Miraj to keep him quiet. On the other hand, Miraj was so busy with his leaflets and his Caliphate, he didn't seem to notice their side hustle.

"Allah is unhappy. Allah wants to see a Caliphate in Bangladesh. The infidel dogs must die. All Muslims will be united in the great brotherhood."

Meena giggled inwardly. So stupid. What made him think Allah was angry and wanted to kill people? Surely Allah had his hands full helping people and listening to everyone's prayers? If Miraj had been a bit savvier, he could have done business too, as he drove around Dhaka. He spent all day in that truck. Instead of going to mosques, he should be thinking about his young wife and the baby that was on its way. Meena shook her head, annoyed at the thought of Miraj, and heaved the sack onto her back. She left the house unnoticed.

Half an hour later, she'd reached the intersection where Miraj picked them up. It was half past four in the morning so the truck should be here already. She spotted Rifat running toward her through the early-morning mist and waved to him. Against her will, her heart leaped when she saw him. Was it because he looked so much like her cousin? As usual, he started goofing around, walking with a limp and hopping like a monkey and just before he reached Meena, he pressed his hand against his heart.

"Meena. One time. Come with me to the cinema just one time."

Meena shook her head.

"That's the stupidest thing I've ever heard. Cinema. What for?"

They didn't have to wait long for Miraj. He pulled up next to them so recklessly they had to jump out of the way. He seemed angrier than usual and was shouting abuse so loudly all the early risers around them could hear.

"Get in already, you fucking morons. Or are you too busy sucking face? I hope you charge enough, Meena, eh? Fucking whore."

Meena gritted her teeth, determined to not even let on that she'd heard Miraj's insults, let alone taken offence. But sometimes she wondered if that didn't just egg him on more. Rifat had whispered to her that she should look sad and talk back. Maybe even cry. That's what he was after, Miraj. Today especially, it was obvious her silence and pride provoked him. When they stopped at the first marketplace of the day, about an hour outside Dhaka, he didn't immediately disappear into the nearby mosque and leave Rifat and Meena to get on with work. No, he slowly circled the cargo bed where they were huddled and then gave Meena a shove.

"Give me your dupatta! Come on, let go!"

Meena clung to her shawl, not understanding what he was trying to do. Rifat tried to divert Miraj's attention.

"We have to buy tomatoes before . . ."

"Give it to me! I want to see your breasts. Do you have any breasts? Does your little whore have breasts, Rifat? Well, well, there they are. And how much do you charge for a squeeze?"

Meena had never experienced anything like it, she felt herself go rigid and wanted to sink through the floor. Her face burned with shame. Miraj had taken her dupatta and was waving it in front of her. She tried to cover herself with her arms.

"Put your arms down, whore! I said show me your breasts! Or do you want me to go get some mates to help you?! Huh? Huh?"

He shook the dupatta in Meena's face and grabbed her shoulder. Meena flew up and jumped down next to the truck, ready to run. Just then, an old man in white Panjabi and *topi* walked by. He turned to Miraj and called him over.

"*Bhai*, what are you shouting about? Why is the girl looking frightened?"

"*Assalamu alaykum*, Mullah. We were just joking around."

He threw Meena her dupatta and turned to the mullah.

"I was just telling my sister here that she has to put her shawl over her head when we're near the mosque."

"That's fine, little brother. You have to make sure you take good care of your sister when she rides the truck. You wouldn't let anyone hurt such a young girl, would you?"

"She had dropped her dupatta and I wanted her to cover herself. Surely you can understand that, Mullah? There are so many evil eyes that could hurt her."

The old mullah looked from Miraj to Meena, then gave Meena a warm smile. He nodded and disappeared in the direction of the mosque.

Meena's whole body shook. She wrapped her dupatta tightly, tightly, around her. Miraj slouched off without a word. Rifat had started to negotiate with the farmers and left her alone. She slowly pulled her sack of sandals off the cargo bed and went to find the old man who worked for her. He lit up when he saw her and launched into an enthusiastic account of how business was booming. He pushed a wad of crumpled taka notes into her hands.

Normally, Meena would have been all ears, but today she listened half-heartedly and eventually just handed the man another seven pairs of sandals of various sizes.

"In a week, see you. Thanks."

Back in the cargo bed, Meena curled up and had to keep swallowing hard not to cry. One hand clutching the balled-up end of her dupatta. How was she supposed to work with Miraj now? Could she let Patel know she was scared? Would anyone care? Had Miraj's insinuations tainted her forever? If she told anyone what had happened, it would immediately tarnish her as well. Modest girls, honourable girls, didn't tempt men. She longed for Mokta so badly it hurt. What would Mokta have done?

Rifat sat by her side in silence, staring into space. He gently placed an apple he was holding in her lap.

"For you, Meena. Eat."

When he spoke softly, his voice was little more than a hiss. After a while, he glanced at her and said:

"Close your eyes."

"What?" Meena didn't understand.

"Close your eyes, shut them, and just do exactly as I tell you. Do you trust me?"

Meena felt it was poor timing, but she didn't want to disappoint Rifat. She put the apple down, closed her eyes and felt his hand in hers.

"Stand up, good. And then turn around so you're facing the direction of travel."

The truck was hurtling down the relatively straight road between Tongi and Mymensingh. Miraj drove fast. The wind whipped Meena's face, but she kept her eyes closed like she'd promised.

"Put one foot up here, and then the other."

Rifat placed her foot on the horizontal slats running along the front of the cargo bed. One foot, then the other.

"And the next one. You won't fall, trust me."

Meena felt Rifat's body close to hers, just behind her. He had climbed up the slats, too, and was standing with his feet spread wide, cradling her from behind.

"A bit higher, one more step. And now . . . let go with your hands and spread your arms."

Meena giggled and almost lost her balance, but did as she was told. Now she was perched like a bird, like an airplane above the cab of the truck.

"Now. Open your eyes!"

Meena opened her eyes and gasped in wonder. It felt like she and Rifat were soaring above the landscape. The truck underneath them had vanished. Meena felt a joy, a freedom that made the events of the morning fade away.

Rifat laughed loudly too, gently pressing himself against her.

"We're flying, we're flying," he laughed. "Spread your arms, let's get out of here!"

Meena laughed loudly at him. What a loon!

"Meena," he whispered in her ear, his lips ever so close to keep the wind from snatching his words away. "I would never . . . I mean . . . I would never speak to you like that. If you were mine, I mean. Or not mine, but, look, I would always be kind to you if you trusted me. I think I've fallen in love with you, Meena."

Meena pretended not to hear, just stood there on the edge of the cargo bed with her arms thrown wide. The car pulled over by the side of the road and Meena and Rifat jumped back down. Before the car came to a full stop, Rifat whispered:

"I saw it in a film, Meena. In a film about a boat. If you wanted, maybe we could . . ."

Miraj came around to the back and shouted something at them. Meena could tell from the look in his eyes he hadn't forgotten where they'd left off before. But it was late. Meena and Rifat would have to hurry if they wanted to fill Patel's truck with vegetables and make it back before ten. He tossed them a few burlap sacks and disappeared into a nearby building.

The routine of their work had a soothing effect on Meena. She managed to keep the events of the morning at arm's length. But her brain was working feverishly. The two men who had approached her in such different ways, how was she supposed to handle them? Were they a threat or an opportunity?"

As a child, Meena had once found a toy kaleidoscope full of brightly coloured pieces of glass and mirrors that reflected the position of the glass in star-shaped patterns. If you looked toward the light, you could see wondrously beautiful formations that changed with just a shake or a small movement. She had stared into the kaleidoscope for a long time, noting how the same pieces of glass could have different effects on the whole, depending on where they ended up. She hadn't been allowed to keep the kaleidoscope for long though. Soon, one of her younger cousins had run off with it and thrown it in the pond, but the feeling it had given her had lingered. Like now. Miraj's threats and Rifat's admiration were new pieces of glass that changed the overall picture. A new pattern was taking shape.

Once the fruit and vegetables had been delivered to Patel and his staff had shifted everything onto about twenty rickshaws, Meena withdrew to have a drink of water. She told Rifat to come with her. They could choose to work another shift at this point; the fruit had to be transported to the marketplaces, from Kawran Bazaar in central Dhaka, to Mogh Bazaar, Badda Bazaar and all the smaller peddlers in between. But Meena had noticed the payment they received for their hard work was too low.

"Rifat, listen. If we only do the early-morning shifts for Patel, we get money from him and it's a way to distribute our own goods. But during the day, we should work for ourselves. We'd make more."

Rifat was all ears. Since going into business with Meena, he was making more money than ever before. And without realising it, he'd fallen head over heels for the strange girl with the fringe. He was prepared to try anything she proposed. She'd taught him to write on her phone and talked to him in a way his older brothers and mother had never done.

"When we go out to the villages for Patel, we'll run our own side hustle, right? But I think the old men we've found could sell other things, too. More things. Maybe things where the difference is bigger."

"The difference?" Rifat asked.

"Look, I think we should go down to the factories around New Market and buy things there, or maybe even directly from the docks. I heard about toothbrushes, you know, the white plastic kind that comes in from China. They cost two taka. I think we could sell them for at least ten in the villages. That means a big difference. What do you reckon?"

Rifat nodded, and Meena felt relieved. She knew she could trust Rifat. She could use his dedicated admiration and loyalty for her own benefit. But it was anyone's guess how long Miraj would leave her alone. She needed to build her own business as quickly as possible.

*

"What do the by-laws say?" Janne tried to talk over the loud Danish woman. "Can't we try to find a compromise?"

"I'm just saying I've had enough, I can't bear having this shit pushed on me day and night. The Nordic Club has to be a refuge for us Scandinavians. How else are we supposed to be able to cope here?"

"I agree." A Norwegian man who'd had his finger in the air for quite a while had grown tired of waiting his turn and broke in. "I would rather see Norwegian artists on the walls, or, well, Nordic ones. We need to remember who we are and protect our cultural identity. For the children's sake."

Janne realised he'd walked into a trap. Bjarne had asked if he would mind chairing one of the Nordic Club's quarterly meetings and since the agenda had listed items Janne had thought would be quickly worked through, he'd acquiesced. But the Nordic Club's small cafeteria had quickly filled up with Scandinavians who didn't seem able to agree about anything. Janne was sweating profusely. It had taken hours to settle the matters of the massage fees at the rooftop spa, the restaurant's menu, the possibility of using the tennis court to play floorball, the new salary of the in-house chef and the purchase of a new espresso machine- by now, the mood was dismal. The club had about one hundred and fifty members and forty or so had turned up to the meeting, mostly to guard their own interests. The tennis. The menu. The library. The children's activities. The guest lists. The alcohol.

The one time they'd all agreed had been when Siv from the Swedish Embassy had suggested a childfree day in the pool area every weekend. Siv had been voted down under loud protest and had stormed out of the meeting, her neck red and blotchy.

Now, the discussion of a matter raised by Charlotta from Alor Desh about the Nordic Club's cultural policy was reaching fever pitch.

Janne gave the floor back to Charlotta.

"As I argue in my motion, we're in a country full of exciting artists and a dynamic gallery scene. Zebha is one of Bangladesh's most prominent young artists and we should be grateful if she wanted to exhibit . . ."

"Then anyone who *wants to* can visit the galleries where her work is shown." An angry young Danish man was leaning against a doorpost. Janne recognised him as one of the many IT technicians running Danish projects in Dhaka.

"The galleries in Dhanmondi have inconvenient opening hours. And besides, we all know what traffic's like downtown. I agree with Charlotta, we have to be open to the culture of our host country. The richness it offers . . ." Sofia's colleague Anna-Lena rushed to Charlotta's defence.

"Host country?" The Dane snorted derisively. "I'm sorry, but I'm here to do a job. I don't feel anyone's hosting me, and I have zero inclination to learn more about Bangladeshi culture. The less, the better, actually."

"Can we all please stick to English? Honestly, you guys, my Scandinavian is terrible." A tall Finnish woman had tried to make herself heard several times. Since the few Finnish speakers at the club always complained about the awkward pan-Scandinavian usually resorted to in a Nordic context, no one paid her any attention. Janne shot her a smile but ignored her request. Bjarne broke in, saying the host country was whoever was paying.

The Norwegian man cleared his throat again. He was holding a child and tried to speak Scandinavian clearly, with a glance at the Finnish woman.

"I think it's important to emphasise Nordic holidays like Constitution Day and Lucia and such, over the Bangla New Year and Eid. Our children have to be allowed to feel they belong to a culture with traditions."

"Maybe we could have both? Some Bengali things and some Scandinavian?" Janne was trying to find a compromise. "Maybe a rolling schedule? Or themes?"

"So far, there's been too much Bangla, that's for sure." The angry Danish lady spoke up again. "As a purchaser of china I work really hard out in the factories. I need a break when I'm here. I want to eat Danish food, watch Danish films and relax in my free time."

"Then why don't you go back to Denmark?" Charlotta glared at her. "Where's the curiosity? Is no one interested in the country we're in?"

"There, there now," Bjarne took over before Janne could intervene. "I find it hard to believe the Yanks over on Road 14 are having these kinds of discussions. They're not shy about it. They serve burgers and root beer all day long and their Halloween parties are the best in Dhaka. Why are we making things so difficult for ourselves?"

"But the American club is awful. It's a reservation. Surely that's not what we want the Nordic Club to be like?" A Norwegian woman cut in, drawing agreement from several parts of the room. "Once those gates close, it's like you're in Illinois, or Texas. They walk around in cowboy hats, have you seen them? Even as a Norwegian, I feel unwelcome."

Janne tried to wrap things up, banging his gavel.

"Should we move on to a vote? What are the options?"

Bjarne interrupted again. Two long, furry arms shot up into the air and he announced his solution.

"I have a concrete suggestion. I will donate two hundred thousand Danish kronor to a culture fund for the club. Over the next two years, we can bring Danish, or maybe Scandinavian artists, singers, poets, or whatever culture people you want out here. On me. There, everyone's happy. So, case closed."

Cheering immediately broke out and more than a few people slapped Bjarne on the back. H&M and Telenor employees said they would see if their companies might want to contribute to the culture fund as well. Bjarne's wife clung to him and he gave the Danish IT technician a thumbs up. Janne tried to regain control of the meeting, but eventually had to give up. Chairs were pushed back and people dispersed into the pool area. Janne felt unsure if he'd done an acceptable job. Afterwards, Charlotta came up to him and lodged a protest.

"That wasn't a decision. It was a coup."

10

Sofia closed the door behind her and turned on the air conditioning. A whiff of mould spread through the room and a lizard skittered across the ceiling. She had just missed Moberg. Again. He was supposed to have been back from a brunch at the Radisson with a delegation from a Swedish company looking to enter the Bangladeshi market, but had slipped straight back out for a lunch with the Canadians. She really needed to discuss both Alor Desh and the conference with him.

Her irritation with Moberg was growing but she tried to break it up into little justifications and excuses. She was sure he meant well. He must be busy, being dean and all. Also, he seemed to have a rough situation at home. Arthur was a teenager and Vanja seemed high-maintenance. She had opinions on virtually everything and probably pestered him constantly.

Sofia hadn't been on the job for a week when Vanja stopped in to give her a lecture on male and female leadership that would have warmed the heart of every proponent of difference feminism back in Sweden.

"You make sure you embrace a feminine management style, Sofia. Don't copy the power plays and domination techniques men use. The most important task for a female manager is to make people feel good. When people feel good, they do good. Wouldn't you agree? Search your soul for how you want people to feel, then follow that feeling," she'd said, handing Sofia a book: *Leading with the Help of Your Inner Goddess.*

"I'm going to tell Karl-Otto to support you and help you blossom. Girl power, am I right?"

She'd made a fist and winked as if in secret understanding. Every time they saw each other at the club after that, she raised her fist in the air and whispered conspiratorially: "Girl power!"

So far, however, helping her blossom had not been a priority of Moberg's, not that Sofia could make out, anyway. He may not be her superior, exactly, but Sofia needed a functional ambassador to do her job. Going to interminable lunches and receptions at other embassies, when his presence and decisions were needed, was an incomprehensible way of going about things, to Sofia's mind. For the Ministry of Foreign Affairs, who were so obsessed with getting a good return on their foreign aid investment, did anything concrete ever really come of their incessant lunches? And all the information from Dev-Com he'd promised to relay to her, getting any of it was like pulling teeth. She had the distinct feeling he had no intention of giving her any girl power.

She missed Katta's thoughtful, strategic work advice badly. Katta, who was both colleague and friend and who had just assumed the position of head of SwedeAid's rights team in Stockholm. She'd told Sofia over instant messenger to build alliances with other donors and circumvent Moberg. Consequently, Sofia prepared to go on an afternoon field trip with Antje van den Ven from the Dutch foreign aid office with a specific goal in mind. She was going to build alliances.

Antje was one of the women her own age Sofia had taken an instant liking to. At a large donor conference, Antje had brought up the fact that all donors in Dhaka spoke urgently of the need to improve women's situation in Bangladesh. But that very little was ever done. After some humming and hawing from various ambassadors and foreign aid counsellors, and several attempts to move on to the next item on the agenda, Antje had got to her point.

"Words, words, words, nothing tangible. I thought all the strategies and plans outlining how much we're doing for the women of Bangladesh had something to do with reality. But all I hear is words. When are we going to act?"

Walk the talk, she had urged the people in the room. Since then, Sofia had gone to see the large Dutch woman to suggest they go on a field trip together. Antje had agreed and said Sofia should get to know the garment industry, being new at the embassy and all, and said she herself felt constantly guilty about "not doing anything" about the conditions of the garment workers.

"And you're Swedish, too," she'd added. When Sofia looked nonplussed, she'd expanded on her statement:

"The girls in the factories H&M buy from can't live off their salaries, you do know that, right? About thirty Euros a month. They're malnourished, often ill and work far too many hours a day. At the same time, of course, H&M turned a two-billion-Euro profit last year. Delightful, no? And they paid six hundred Euros in taxes here in Bangladesh."

That had made Sofia feel uncomfortable. Being Swedish was almost always a good thing in international contexts. Was she suddenly going to be associated with the low salaries paid by H&M?

Eventually, they'd come across an invitation in the online magazine *The Village*, in which representatives of the garment industry invited foreign diplomats. Probably little more than a PR demonstration, but they were going.

The jeep rolled out of the diplomatic zone, toward Savar and Ashulia, industrial areas in which state-of-the-art garment factories had been built during the nineties to compete for lucrative garment contracts with China, Turkey, Cambodia and Vietnam.

After making themselves comfortable in the backseat, Sofia commented on Antje's contribution to the donor conference, saying she'd been brave to ask questions about their gender equality work, and that the mood among the men had been almost comically awkward. Antje gazed out the window, where an overloaded bus was on the verge of toppling over onto their jeep.

"I don't think of myself as particularly brave, but sure, it makes you a party-pooper when you point out the discrepancy between theory and practice. Every single directive published by my government states that we should actively be working to empower women in Bangladesh. Preferably in joint efforts with other donors. So I have to ask – where are those joint efforts? I don't see any."

Sofia smiled and thought, fine, brave might not be Antje's preferred descriptor, but maybe that was exactly what she was. Obedient bureaucrats who did their governments' bidding were worth their weight in gold in an environment where panjandrums usually did whatever they pleased. The further you got from the foreign ministries, the less government policies mattered.

Antje might just be the partner she needed to launch her idea of a big international women's conference next year.

"It sounds interesting," Antje said a while later when Sofia had outlined her idea. "At least I would be doing something for gender equality in this country, even if all our male colleagues choose to pass. Would you mind sending me a draft proposal?"

Then Antje moved onto discussing bachelors that hung around the Nordic Club. She made no secret of the fact that she was looking to hook up.

"Dhaka's a desert, just a bunch of families with children," she'd sighed the first time Sofia met her at a dinner. "What am I supposed to do? I check the CVs of every consultant before hiring people for our office. Single? Perfect, your profile is exactly what we're looking for! Welcome to Bangladesh, feel free to stay longer. Antje will be your guide and friend!"

She let out a raucous laugh, spread her arms wide and kissed the air with her red lips, looking almost mischievous. "What? Just because I'm a woman doesn't mean I don't have needs."

Then she told Sofia about last year's romance.

"I had a torrid affair with Torgil, a wonderful Norwegian man from Telenor. It ended in the spring. We got a few months together," she laughed and twirled her hair at the memory. "Then, back to his wife and children in Oslo. But now my spies are telling me there's a single Dane at the Nordic. Apparently, he works with IT and likes to party." She snapped her fingers and shook her shoulders rhythmically, as if she were dancing.

"Jens something-or-other. Promise you'll introduce me?"

The car turned in behind a tall wall and parked under an enormous sign that said Hollywood Garments Inc. The factory was one of a thousand garment factories of varying quality, which powered Bangladesh's economic growth and employed more than three million women. Hundreds of thousands of girls commuted to them every morning from Dhaka's slums in busload after busload. Sofia had seen them pass through Baridhara at dawn.

Now the women were filing into the factories in drowsy herds. Sofia and Antje watched their zombie-like, silent queueing by the doors. They wore mismatched, cheap shalwar kameezzes and worried constantly about the factory owner withholding their salaries. At least that's what Antje was telling Sofia. Once the doors closed, the girls sometimes worked fourteen or fifteen hours straight.

Sofia and Antje were received by the factory owner himself, a tall Bangladeshi man with an American accent called Ben. He was remarkably handsome in a cool, white shirt and Western blazer, one of the sons of the owner of the Barkat Group, a prominent company in a number of different industries in Bangladesh.

"Proper Bangladeshi business elite. Obscenely wealthy. Zamindars, old landowner family," Antje whispered when Ben apologised and took a call on his mobile.

His elegant office was located in a building behind the factory facilities. Ben proudly told them about the factory, which he described as state of the art. Two thousand girls, six floors, a production pace to rival many factories in Cambodia and Vietnam. Modern machines, bright rooms. A water treatment plant in the back and hazard suits for the employees working with dyes.

Ben explained that when garments left the factory, they were taken in lorries to the docks in Chittagong in southern Bangladesh in the form of trousers, T-shirts, sheets, towels, skirts and dresses. The factory specialised in jeans and single-weave. Sewn-on tags showed who had placed the order. Gap, H&M, Tesco, George, Levi's, Lindex, KappAhl, Zara, Walmart, Marks & Spencer. From Chittagong, the garments had six weeks to get on the shelves in European shops, if it took longer, countries like Turkey and India became a more attractive alternative for purchasers.

"We factory owners have heeded the demands from the consumers in the West to provide decent working conditions," Ben said, handing them a brochure. "We take CSR –corporate social responsibility – very seriously here. We are working on all aspects of sustainability: the environment and social and economic factors."

He spoke the lingo, Sofia noted. Buzzwords like "socially responsible development", "sustainable development" and "human rights" were liberally sprinkled throughout his presentation.

The field trip was part of a garments industry charm offensive, aimed at foreign diplomats. Having been accused for years of being ruthless profiteers, Bangladesh's organised garment producers were now trying to improve their image and show that they were compliant with all current laws and paying their workers minimum wage. In the nineties, they had officially abolished child labour, now they were eager to appear to be responsible employers.

"Aside from decent working conditions, I assume salaries must be pivotal in the relationship between companies and their employees," Sofia said. "What do you pay your girls? Can they live off their salaries?"

Ben replied curtly that the factory complied with the country's minimum wage regulations and that the factory also offered both a health clinic and subsidised lunches. Clearly eager to show them around the facilities, he then brought the conversation to an end, stood up and led his guests over to the factory.

An industrial lift brought them up to one of the factory's production floors. Hundreds of women were seated in long rows, bent over modern sewing machines. Next to each seamstress was a mountain of perfectly cut fabric. They all seemed to repeat the same production step over and over. When they were done with one pile of fabric, the half-finished garments were picked up and a new mountain of fabric was supplied. Sofia spotted large rolls of cloth at the far end of the room. Between the rows of sewing machines were racks on which the finished garments hung. From cloth to clothes in one room, she noted.

The rows of hunched backs went on almost as far as the eye could see and Sofia wondered if this might not be the largest room she'd ever been in. It was loud and the air was dry and full of dust. Ben offered them surgical masks and ear protectors. Some of the women wore them too.

Antje brought the conversation back to Sofia's question. She had to raise her voice to make herself heard over the humming of the machines.

"Minimum wage. I see, so, three thousand taka?"

Ben replied vaguely that it depended on each seamstress' individual work description and what level of skill was required.

"Is H&M one of your clients?" Sofia asked, Ben nodded.

"H&M, KappAhl, Lindex, I think those are the Swedish ones. Zara's not Swedish, right? They all buy from us. We follow their CSR policies to the letter. Would you like to have a look at our logs of working hours and payments?"

Antje turned to Sofia.

"The minimum wage was just raised. It used to be one thousand six hundred taka a month, or, in other words, about fifteen Euro. The world's cheapest workforce. But not everyone pays minimum wage. In some rural factories, the women barely make nine-hundred taka a month . . ."

" . . . and some make much more," Ben added quickly. "You're forgetting that not all garment workers earn the same. More experienced seamstresses can easily make between forty and sixty Euros a month. Easily. And that doesn't even include overtime, which will add at least another ten Euros. A month."

He looked pleased with himself as he scanned the rows of seamstresses. Antje and Sofia started walking, leaving Ben behind. Antje rolled her eyes and told Sofia under her breath:

"The thing is the government sets the minimum wage and they don't give a crap about poor people. It's not their children working in the factories. They want to keep the minimum wage as low as possible to attract companies and compete with China and Cambodia. Low technical skill so they can hire people off the street and low wages-that's their business plan."

"And since the minimum wage requirement is met, suppliers and producers feel they've done their bit," Sofia added. "Why pay more than you have to?"

"Exactly. Neither the government nor the garment companies have any interest in advocating for these girls. That's up to us Western consumers."

Sofia looked down at the girls' hands, watched their quick movements. Several of them were using their own dupattas to cover their mouths. It didn't take her long to notice a pattern. The women were sitting down, working the machines and the men walked around, apparently supervising the women's work. Once or twice, she saw a woman get up to ask a man a question and receive either a nod or a shake of the head in reply. What were they asking about? She wished she could have talked privately to a few of the girls. That she could have sat down and just talked to them. Three thousand taka, what did that buy them? How much did a pound of rice cost?

They passed through several equally hangar-like rooms. They were free to go wherever they wanted in the factory. Ben was busy on the phone. On one floor, there was a door with a sign that read DESTRUCTION DEPARTMENT. Inside, rows of familiar brand-name jeans were stretched out on frames and young girls were scraping and untacking seams with razors to give the trousers a frayed, worn appearance. Girls were sitting on the floor, going at the jeans with sandpaper. They shot the visitors jaded looks. Sofia realised she'd never given any thought to how fashion jeans got their rips, or how Noella's little denim skirt got its colourful applique butterflies and flowers. Now, she was looking at it. It was the nimble fingers of impoverished young girls that untacked and cut, lined up and stretched.

Antje seemed to have had the same epiphany.

"Oh my god, I own those jeans! Got them at Zara in Amsterdam last summer."

Ben had stopped talking on his phone and caught up with them. He noticed their observations and launched into a PR harangue:

We give the girls a chance to become independent, to make something of themselves. You have to bear in mind that these are girls whose mothers likely never even left their home, and now look at them! Free and with their own money in their pockets."

Sofia and Antje resumed their tour and Sofia reluctantly realised she was impressed. She had actually never been to this kind of factory in Sweden, were they so different?

"Isn't this kind of okay? I mean, apart from the salaries?" she asked Antje, who nodded thoughtfully.

"It's hard to get too worked up. It does *look* okay."

On the way back, Sofia suddenly had an idea. She pulled out her wallet and flipped through her many business cards. There! Bjarne Jensen, CEO Copenhagen Garment Inc., Gulshan, Plaza 34:2.

"Look! This garment factory's probably a lot less flashy. And it was started with Danish foreign aid money. How would you feel about making a . . . spontaneous visit? What do you reckon? Next week?"

*

The computer was working hard. The pictures uploading from the camera flashed past on the screen. Janne could pull up the pictures from his Alor Desh visit with a few clicks. He'd already studied most of them carefully on the camera screen, and many had already been ruthlessly culled.

Suddenly, he missed the suspense and anticipation he'd associated with photography as a young man. When as the chair of his school's photography club he'd retreated to a darkroom in the basement to develop a few rolls of film. Back then, the pictures had gradually faded into view before his eyes, slowly surfacing through the chemical solutions, giving him the feeling he was looking at something brand new. An experience. Now, all his pictures were always just a click away.

He'd had a certain amount of talent, he really had, but then other interests had taken over and he'd packed away his old Nikon in a box in the family's summer house.

The pictures from Alor Desh were colourful: saffron yellow, bright red and deep blue. Children holding goats, women cooking over open flame, Siraj laughing with the sun in his eyes, Charlotta sitting on the floor with a spinster. The bride who had walked past, accompanied by a group of people led by a man playing the trumpet, the baul singer with his long hair and strange instrument. And then a few still lifes he'd snapped as he walked around alone during his last afternoon in the village. The cooking vessels drying in the sun, a chicken on a reed roof, shoes lined up outside a house, bright red chili peppers drying in the sun. Long rows of rods made of dried cow manure leaning against the wall of a house. The light was long, heavy and warm, except in the pictures taken by the water's edge. The dazzlingly white sand had made it necessary to close the aperture and all the portraits taken by the water came out as dark, featureless smudges.

Even so, Janne felt a bit morose after browsing through the photographs. He didn't quite recognise the scenes in them. There was something vulture-like, something predatory about cameras, he brooded. They always homed in on the spectacular, the extremes. The sharpest colours, the happiest children, the most dilapidated houses. Why hadn't he taken a picture of the fireflies and the shards of silver twinkling throughout the village at night? Or of the little boy who had insisted on holding his hand, asking him to read a miserably tattered brochure from a travel agency promising work opportunities for Bangladeshi people in Malaysia? And all the grey women who had lined the walls in the garment workshop, where were they? And the food, the food that was the same every morning, noon and evening: fish, rice and daal, and that had been served to them with such obvious pride and generosity – "Here, take it! It's the best we've ever tasted!" – but which eventually had made Janne and Charlotta's stomachs turn. Why hadn't he photographed that? It was a bigger part of his experience of the village and Alor Desh than the colourful bridal party that had passed by during a few short moments, but which nevertheless appeared in several pictures.

And the smells, they were obviously missing. The smell of fried garlic that blanketed the kitchen regions before every mealtime. And the dry, fairly cosy smell of animals everywhere.

Next time, he was going to go about things differently, see things differently, try to get closer to what he wanted to show. Discuss it with Sofia. Because he wanted to go back to Lalpara, preferably with Sofia and the kids. It would have been fun to see if Teo and Tomelilla were able to play together.

His phone buzzed. The display said "Bjarne" and Janne suspected it was about tennis. He'd come to appreciate Bjarne's company more and more, despite his brashness and vulgar attitude. His heart was in the right place.

"Hi, don't you have a job to be getting on with?"

"No thanks, I make a point of giving that a wide berth," Bjarne laughed. "Are you up for lunchtime doubles? Us against two British purchasers, Tesco-Steve and a guy from Asda, Jake. How about it, in half an hour?"

Feeling instantly energised, Janne jumped up from the desk. Fun. Tennis, and maybe a pint afterwards. He missed socialising with adults and was starting to wonder if all the time he spent alone was making him depressed. It was as if he couldn't help dwelling on things in an unhealthy way, and he was upset by little things he normally wouldn't have noticed.

Like the thing about their driver, Nizamuddhin, for instance. There was something slippery about the man, Janne felt. Or was it just a case of so-called cultural differences, which was how he and Sofia had taken to brushing aside anything they didn't understand in their new country?

Didn't Nizamuddhin express himself very oddly? Or was Janne just being overly sensitive? It seemed to him everything Nizamuddhin said in his broken English hid a double meaning. Little messages Janne didn't know how or if to interpret. "No matter what you do in life, you always end up getting out of the car on the wrong side," he might suddenly exclaim, fixing Janne intently. Or "There's only one speed, and it's too fast." The day before, he'd suddenly announced in a grave tone:

"If you don't know where you're going, you might get somewhere else."

Janne had nodded along, and Nizamuddhin had looked pleased. As though there were nothing to add. Also, he had an annoying habit of belching loudly while driving. A habit that had more than once made Janne feel nauseous in the sweltering heat, and which he had no idea how to handle. So far, he'd simply hoped Nizamuddhin would refrain from his habit once he noticed Janne hanging out the window, clearly demonstrating he preferred the heat and exhausts outside to the smells inside the car. But Nizamuddhin had made no sign of comprehending and had happily continued to belch.

When Janne left the house to go to the club, Nizamuddhin came running.

"Good morning, Boss."

Janne climbed into the Jeep and Nizabuddhin immediately turned around and announced solemnly:

"Only Allah knows what's going to happen to us."

Then he settled in behind the wheel and reversed down the driveway. Janne stared at the back of his neck. What was that supposed to mean? If he belched even once during this very short drive, Janne was going to say something. Give him some kind of warning. Yes, he would. But surely you couldn't fire people just for . . . burping? Or could you?

Janne reminded himself he had to ask Sofia what had happened to one of their night-watchmen. The other guards had come to see him when he got back from Alor Desh, upset about one of their number being sacked. But their English was too poor and Hanif hadn't had time to interpret, so Janne had promised to get back to them. If he'd had understood things right, Siv had been sneaking around with a flashlight, trying to catch them sleeping. Odd behaviour, Janne thought to himself. But then again, when it came to Siv, nothing surprised him.

A few hours later, Bjarne and Janne had made short work of the Brits and the four of them were enjoying lively conversation and ice cold pints under the roof of the club's hemp fibre hut.

Bjarne was complaining about an Irish woman he apparently wanted to do business with, who had declined his overtures.

"Short, fat, thick Irish accent. Gwendolyn. She has increased her turnover by five hundred percent since April, employs three thousand women in various villages and refuses to say where they are. They crochet for her, imagine that. Crochet!" He sucked the foam off his beer and shook his head.

"I've told her I'll buy the whole operation right now. Two million Danish kronor, cash in hand. But I want the contracts and the network. Apparently, her order book is full and the work just keeps flooding in."

Steve from Tesco turned to Janne to explain.

"Gwendolyn hangs out at the High Commission Club with her children, so I know her. She was a crafts teacher back in the UK and came here with her husband who's a visa caseworker at the British High Commission. Apparently, she has started a cottage industry by teaching rural women how to crochet. The profits are reinvested in the villages and girls' education."

"It's all Fair Trade and so fucking precious. When I offer to buy her out, she tells me she has principles. 'I have my principles'," Bjarne mimicked a squeaky woman's voice. "What she doesn't seem to grasp is that I have principles, too. Buy low, sell high. That's my principle. Fucking bitches. Gwendolyn, I hate you!"

"She seems to have hit upon a solid business idea, though." Jake countered quickly and Bjarne laughed resignedly.

"You know what they crochet? Disgusting little carrots and cauliflower florets with bells inside. Teething toys for kids. And flags that say "Happy Birthday". And ugly little party hats! Now the whole world's buying her ridiculous toys. Marks & Spencer supposedly put in a big order, Walmart wants them and if the gossip here at the Nordic is anything to go by, H&M is considering ordering their entire summer collection of crocheted bikinis and tank tops from her. She's going to make . . . oh, I don't want to think about it!"

Bjarne collapsed forward across the table and hid his face in his hands with a dramatic flourish. Jake pretended to console him.

"Poor Bjarne, not turning enough of a profit? Maybe you should try some Fair Trade, ever consider that? Sleep better at night?"

"Listen," Bjarne looked up at Jake and shook his head. "I didn't come all this way, from a farm on Bornholm where my dad was a bloody farmhand, to *give* money away. Business is business and charity is charity. I just donated two hundred thousand to a culture fund, didn't I, Janne? But the two don't mix. Business has its own set of principles."

Janne was just about to respond when his phone vibrated on the table. It was Shjuli, Janne and Sofia's aya, and she was crying.

"My Amma has been hit by a bus, she's in the hospital. Please, Boss, can I go home now?"

Janne tried to calm the agitated girl down, and quickly wrapped up his conversation with Bjarne and the Brits.

Nizamuddhin was waiting outside the club. Apparently, he'd already heard about Shjuli. As was so often the case, the Bangladeshi grapevine had proved faster than its bideshi equivalent.

"A mother is a special person. Without a mother, you're no one at all," Nizamuddhin said solemnly, then opened the backdoor for Janne and shook his head, his face troubled. And for once, Janne was in full agreement.

*

Nazreen woke with a start. It was still dark outside. She could hear Reka clattering about in the cooking corner. Before sunrise, they were all free to eat as much as they liked, but once the first rays of the sun had drilled through the morning haze, making the many dilapidated rooftops of Dhaka shimmer orange, abstinence was the name of the game. No food, no drink, no music, just abstinence. That was what the Quran said about Ramadan, the holy month, and Nazreen wanted to obey. But she wished Meena would eat.

"You can't work the way you do all day without anything in your stomach," she'd berated her sister. "You'll faint. You'll make yourself ill. You *are* ill, look how skinny you are. Allah doesn't want sick people to fast, please, Meena!"

But Meena had refused to listen. Quite the opposite, Nazreen thought to herself. It almost seemed like her younger sister was looking forward to fasting with a kind of fervour, like she had longed for the rituals and the cleansing effect of the fast on her body and soul.

"Can it be said that we get closer to Allah during Ramadan?" she'd heard Meena ask Reka. "Is it right to imagine that Allah shows those who fast more mercy? That he is more forbearing?"

Nazreen noticed Meena had already got up, and the smells wafting from the kitchen nook made it difficult to stay in bed. Plus, she wanted to catch her younger sister before she disappeared and before she herself had to rush off to the Radisson.

"Meena, would you mind combing my hair? Have you had enough to eat? Can't we try to meet up later tonight?"

Meena nodded while she filled her mouth with the hair pins that were going to secure Nazreen's bun. She leaned forward, her eyes sparkling triumphantly.

"Two thousand taka," Meena whispered.

"What are you saying?"

"I've invested two thousand taka in a new plan. My business is thriving, Nazreen. I have a new idea."

Meena told her sister about her plan to sell small bottles of shampoo and tubes of toothpaste along the rivers and in remote villages.

"Remember what it was like back home, Nazreen? We could never afford our own toothpaste, we had to share with the neighbours. Remember? I'm selling them in long strips now, twenty mini tubes per strip. I buy them for two taka here in Dhaka and sell them for five. The old men selling them to the villagers, charge seven."

Nazreen hugged her sister.

"The two thousand taka could grow really quickly and become, let me see, six thousand. And maybe I can find some more old men to sell for me. Nazreen, the money is growing, I can see it growing."

"Great, amazing. But you have to eat during Ramadan if you're going to work such long days, sweet Meena-shona."

Nazreen pleaded, but Meena made no reply, just nodded.

"Tonight, I won't be late. I'll be back for *maghrib*. We'll go for a walk and buy *iftar*."

Nazreen let it go at that. She'd fasted many times before so she knew what it was like and how famished they would be come *maghrib*, the prayer that broke the fast around six in the evening. The greasy iftar snacks that were the first thing everyone ate, would taste divine. Fasting days were all the same, year after year. First the contented fullness after the early morning meal. Even though Nazreen normally didn't like eating in the morning, it was different during Ramadan. You had to seize every opportunity to eat. Seizing the opportunity was something Nazreen had in fact always associated with eating, with food. Sometimes, they'd had food, sometimes not. Sometimes, she'd fallen asleep full and happy, as pleased as a belching cow, but it hadn't been uncommon for her stomach to be empty at bedtime.

That being said, the hunger during Ramadan was different, and it started making itself known only when the sun was already high in the sky. It was a good hunger, a healthy hunger. An abstinence that would bring her closer to Allah, which wasn't mingled with feelings of shame or panic, and which she wasn't alone in feeling. During Ramadan, she felt connected to millions of Muslims all across the globe, and for large parts of the day, the faint dizziness and the stretched-out ache in her stomach felt good. But as afternoon turned into evening, around five, the hunger grew hard to endure, for her and everyone else. Everyone started acting prickly. When it was time to break the fast, she sometimes found it difficult not to wolf down her food, giving gluttony free rein. And later, in the evening, when everyone ate and ate and ate, she was overcome with gratitude. With humility in the face of Allah's greatness. It washed over her when she closed her eyes and enjoyed the spices in the biryani often served at night: the gentle cardamom, the fiery chili and the coriander, ever-present. Thank you. Thank you. Thank you, Allah. Thank you for the food. *Laa illah ill-Allah.* There is no god but Allah.

After the early morning meal, Nazreen rested for a while before heading out to Badda Road to wait for her friends Dipita and Salma. Dipita and Salma were exciting. Exactly the kind of young, independent women she'd seen on their neighbour's TV back in the village and longed to get to know. She could hardly believe they were willing to include her. The two of them used nail polish and knew everything about handbags and were always talking about where you could buy the nicest shalwar kameezzes. Nazreen felt a pang of anger at Meena, who was so stingy and boring. Every paisa disappeared into the plastic box. Two thousand taka. Had she said two thousand taka? And she was going to buy shampoo with it?

The CNG, the small motorised rickshaw, stopped and Nazreen squeezed in next to Dipita and Salma. The thirty-minute commute to work at dawn was the highlight of Nazreen's day. The work at the hotel was hard and boring. After clearing away the breakfast buffet, she was on kitchen duty all day and the kitchen manager threw a fit if the girls talked to one another. He was prone to using both threats and his fists.

"I'm going to fire the lot of you, today, if you don't work hard!" he liked to bellow. "There are a thousand other girls who would take your job right now. Am I understood?"

This morning, Dipita was excited, and her meticulous makeup was, if possible, even heavier than usual. She was carefully checking it in a small mirror. Apparently, Dipita had been transferred from reception to the cleaning crew because someone had realised she didn't speak English, but some well-placed baksheesh had saved her from getting kicked out of the hotel entirely.

"Maybe I should go abroad straight away. I have no desire to work myself to the bone in this shit job. Reception was one thing, but cleaning!" She snorted derisively. "No, Dhaka's just too small for me as an actor. I'm going to see the world, want to come with me? First Bollywood, then Hollywood. The United States. That's where careers are made."

Nazreen and Salma both gave their urbane friend a surprised look.

"The United States?"

"My cousin in Bogra has contacts at a company that can sort out visas for India as a first step. It's the kind of work we do now, hotels and restaurants and such. They love people from Bangladesh in India because we're such hard workers."

"What if you don't have a passport? Can you still get a visa?" Nazreen wanted to know.

"Silly, that's where my cousin comes in. But it isn't free, obviously. First, you have to pay an application fee of two hundred dollars, then they buy you a ticket. You have to pay that off the first two years. Then you're free!"

The CNG reached the Radisson, turned in behind the building and pulled up to the staff entrance. Nazreen realised it was late and hurriedly changed into the shalwar kameez that was the hotel's uniform. Dipita pulled on her cleaning smock with a grimace.

"I'm not going to take this for much longer. No, after Ramadan, I'm getting on a plane to Bollywood!"

"But, Dipita, two hundred dollars, how are you going to . . . ?" Salma asked.

"Shh! I can sort it out. If you want to come, I have a suggestion. I'll tell you about it after work today."

"How many dollars is two thousand taka?" Nazreen whispered to Salma later in the day.

"Maybe twenty-five dollars, I'm not sure."

Nazreen felt her heart skip a beat. India? Bollywood? Those were the kinds of opportunities Mokta had dreamed of. What if Dhaka and life in Badda were just the first stop on her big adventure?

11

Bjarne had invited Sofia to his factory several times.

"Just give me a bit of notice and I'll arrange a VIP tour," he'd told her repeatedly. "It's thanks to you foreign aid people I have a factory!"

And now she and Antje were there, standing outside a grey concrete building on the outskirts of Gulshan. Sofia looked up at the countless tiny windows, through which she could make out piles of cloth and ceiling fans. She looked inquiringly at Antje. Sofia had made a half-hearted attempt to reach Bjarne, but was fairly pleased she hadn't managed. Showing up unannounced was more interesting.

"Well, he did invite us, so I think we should have a look inside. No?" Antje took a step toward the factory entrance.

"Sure, after all, we're on our official garment factory tour, right?" Sofia replied, as though to convince both herself and Antje. "It's important to see different types of factories. Don't you think?"

Just from the outside, it was clear to both of them Bjarne's factory was not the same kind of facility as the airy new construction in Ashulia they'd seen the week before. No breezy Ben to receive them here, just a man dozing in a booth, indifferently asking them what they were there for.

"Visitors," Sofia offered, but Antje was slyer than that.

"Buyers. Garment buyers," she said. The man nodded and pointed toward a wide, dark flight of stairs.

Little boys were sleeping on several of the steps, and in a corner of the first landing, a woman was breastfeeding her infant. A small group of young women were sitting on another landing, eating rice wrapped in newspaper. A cat was slinking about, hoping for scraps.

The stairs were wide enough to accommodate both goods and staff. Sofia and Antje had to step aside quickly to avoid two bare-chested men in lungis and untidy turbans huffing past with large bales on their back. The men disappeared through a pair of wide double doors.

Sofia and Antje ascended slowly. The stairwell was dark and Sofia didn't feel entirely comfortable about visiting without an appointment. Antje, on the other hand, was excited.

"This is it," she whispered. "This is when we see the real Dhaka. Not the PR version. Follow me, no one seems to care that we're here anyway. We could be from Walmart. Or Zara. I'm sure buyers come through here all the time."

They opened the doors to the first floor and entered the same kind of factory landscape they'd seen at Hollywood Garment Inc. The difference was that twice as many people worked here and it was considerably darker and filthier. Garments were piled along the walls, and young girls sat hunched over sewing machines in long rows. Bare bulbs dangled from the ceiling, which was covered in cobwebs and irregular damp patches. One section was bulging ominously.

A lot of people looked up at them when they entered, but no one approached them. Bare legs were sticking out from under the tables where the cloth was cut or pressed. People seemed to be sleeping under them.

"Let's pretend we know what we're doing," Antje hissed. "Look like you're interested in the products. Like a buyer."

Sofia obediently picked up a garment and inspected it closely. Behind her, young boys were walking about with piles of garments on their heads, and at regular intervals, a machine made a hissing noise. Everyone seemed to have a job to do, to be on their way somewhere or to be working on something that had to be finished quickly. A strong smell of onions suddenly spread through the room. Sofia spotted a few women cooking over a fire in a corner. Next to them, on a half-finished wall meant to screen off the primitive kitchen, a cat was padding about with a freshly-caught rat in its mouth.

Suddenly, there was a loud crash. Several of the women left their work stations and rushed toward one of the corners of the room. Agitated voiced were raised and a man in a button-down shirt tried to disperse the group. Antje looked at Sofia, who looked back. Then they walked over toward the small knot of people.

A woman lay unconscious on the floor. A young girl was sitting next to her, crying, stroking her hair. Several of the women were pointing at the woman's stomach, speaking angrily to the man. Sofia and Antje could tell they were asking for a doctor.

The man shook his head and turned to the girl sitting next to the woman. They spoke in rapid-fire Bangla and the girl burst into tears. Someone had fetched a glass of water and was trying to hold it to the lifeless woman's lips.

"Ama, Ama," the girl pleaded with the woman who was apparently her mother. She showered her face with kisses and dipped her dupatta in water to dab her forehead. The woman came to but seemed to slip back into unconsciousness again almost immediately. The man in the shirt was visibly stressed. He clearly wanted the woman out of the building. Her co-workers tried to lift her up onto a table, but the man shook his head and pointed at the door. He tried to push people aside and started tugging on the woman's legs.

Antje walked over and tried to speak to the man. His English was poor and he just kept repeating: "No problem, no problem. Just tired, very lazy lady." When Antje said "Doctor?" he just gritted his teeth and shook his head, but he did stop pulling on the woman's legs.

Sofia had squatted down next to the girl and several of the women crowding around them tried to explain. They pointed frantically at the woman's stomach and put their hands on her forehead. Sofia realised she had a high fever. After a while, a terrified harangue in broken English burst out of the girl.

"My name is Rehana Begum, my father is Kalim Pakel from Naobidi and my mother is Moltana Begum from Tirpur. I'm very much sixteen years old and work as a thread cutter at Copenhagen Garments Inc. I love very much my mother who has big pain, big pain. I have two little brothers, we live in Mahendipur, Dhaka, Bangladesh." Then the girl dissolved into tears once more and started rocking her mother back and forth. Sofia stroked her back.

"And I'm Sofia from Sweden. Maybe I can help you."

Dr Hassan quietly closed the door behind him. Rehana, who had been sitting bolt upright clutching Sofia's hand while he examined her mother, let go and jumped up. Sofia and Antje stood up to hear what the doctor had to say, as well.

Half an hour earlier, they'd burst through the doors of Dr Hassan's small private clinic in Gulshan. The embassy car had been pressed into ambulance service and in the small clinic for foreigners, the unusual patient had been greeted with surprise and consternation. American children with sprained thumbs and Norwegian mothers with colds had been forced to wait while the doctor tended to the thin woman in the dirty sari.

"We will pay, just please treat this woman immediately," Sofia had said and the normally grim Dr Hassan had dropped everything.

Now he was looking at them over the rims of his glasses, concern written all over his face.

"This was not a nice business," he said. "The woman, Moltana, is suffering from acute septic shock. We have found dirty rags in her genitals that must have been in there for days. She has a severe uterine infection. It could have developed into peritonitis, sepsis and a quick death."

"Death," Antje repeated.

"Rags?" Sofia was taken aback.

"As I'm sure you know, garment workers aren't allowed bathroom breaks without their pay being docked. So when they're menstruating, they pick up rags from the factory floor and push them into their vaginas."

Rehana looked at Sofia for an explanation. The doctor noticed her confusion and addressed her directly in Bangla.

"Has your mother had stomach pains?"

"Yes, bad ones. Yesterday, she cried and took medicine. Her whole stomach was hard, like this." The girl pressed her thumb into her palm. Dr Hassan nodded. He turned back to Sofia and Antje.

"Unfortunately, this is not particularly unusual. A combination of malnutrition, exhaustion, poor hygiene and a consequent susceptibility to infections. I've read about the phenomenon, but this my first time seeing it for myself. I don't normally treat garment workers."

"Does this only happen to garment workers?" Antje asked.

"Apparently it's most common among them. I read an article about it somewhere. But in theory, any woman who shoves dirty rags into her vagina could suffer the same fate," Dr Hassan replied curtly. "What are they supposed to do when they can't leave? They're expected to have relieved themselves before their shifts and to refrain from drinking all day so they don't have to go to the bathroom."

"They're expected to find an invisible solution. Like with everything else women are forced to do in this country. Without taking up any space," Antje muttered.

Rehana shifted nervously and asked Dr Hassan something in Bangla. The word medicine was mentioned. Dr Hassan answered the girl and put a hand on her shoulder, as though to reassure her.

"We'll pay, of course," Sofia made sure to add, noticing the girl's concern. She turned to Rehana. "Your Amma needs medicine. No problem, money is no problem."

"No, that's okay," Dr Hassan countered instantly. "I'll treat Moltana for free. I'm ashamed of my countrymen, my country. That we in the middle class, who have money and education, ruthlessly exploit our poor compatriots. It's shameful."

He pulled out a notepad, so upset his hands were shaking.

"I've put her on an intravenous penicillin drip and would like to keep her for a few days. I'll let you know when you can come pick her up. I will give her penicillin in tablet form and she will need to rest for at least a week."

He turned to Rehana and they spoke for some time in Bangla.

"Typical. The girl is terrified they will both lose their jobs. And she's nowhere near sixteen, like she claims, you can tell, right? Twelve at most- a child labourer in other words. Moltana has two toddlers who are apparently in the care of a sister-in-law. The girl hasn't seen her father since the youngest boy was born."

Dr Hassan shook his head, still very upset, and mumbled:

"What I should prescribe is nutritious food. Food, light and clean water. For her and her children. They live in Mahendipur. Probably in the worst part of the slum."

Sofia and Antje exchanged a glance over Rehana's head. The girl had slipped her hand into Sofia's again and was squeezing it hard. Dr Hassan looked up.

"Do you know the name of the factory? Can you talk to the owner and at least make sure they don't lose their jobs? Is it the Machiatu Group, by any chance? Or the Bichindura family? Their factories are infamous for sucking both blood and marrow out of their girls."

Sofia shook her head.

"No. It's not owned by a Bengal. It's a Dane. His name's Bjarne. I'll talk to him about their jobs."

*

The numbers were swirling around her head. Had one of the old men tricked her? Twenty times forty-five plus two hundred minus their share . . . no, it all added up. Meena felt slightly faint from her extended fast. It had been a hot, dusty day, as usual, and she and Rifat had parted ways in the afternoon. He was taking a load of cauliflower to Mogh Bazaar and she had promised to spend some time with Nazreen for once. They were going to eat iftar and then do a lap around Gulshan Market to look at all the pretty things for sale.

Meena imperceptibly shook her head at the thought of her sister. She loved that stuff, Nazreen did. The bling. The sparkly sandals they couldn't afford. The handbags they were never going to buy. The combs, the hairclips, the small plastic toiletry kits. The big city luxuries. She smiled slightly at her sister's fantasy world, then her thoughts moved on to Rifat instead.

Rifat. Who looked so much like her cousin back in the village. At first, she had only seen the slum in him, the slum-wallah. His tangled, matted hair with a hint of red in it, the ingrained smell of smoke, dirt and sweat. Then she'd started listening to what he was actually saying, ignoring that sharp voice that didn't seem to belong to his body and always startled her. He was funny, the things he said and the observations he made often made Meena laugh. One day, she'd told him he should eat the fruit sometimes, not just trade it. A mango that was bruised anyway, a banana he wouldn't be able to sell, that's how they'd done it back in the village. Every once in a while, he should crack an egg and drink it. It was better than watery rice. He'd listened. He always listened to her, his eyes warm and happy. And eventually, she'd shown him letters and numbers. He needed to know how to write so they could use their phones to send messages to each other. He caught on quickly and wanted her to teach him more.

Sometimes, when no one was watching, he'd let his hand linger a second too long on her arm. He'd scrape a fleck of soot off her cheek. He kept asking her to go to the cinema with him, but Meena didn't even bother to answer. Of course not. It was bad enough they worked together. The cinema! How would that look? Besides. He was a slum-wallah and she was the daughter of a landowner. Or at least the daughter of a former landowner. She knew some English and had finished high school. She could do better.

While she was thinking about Rifat, she received a text. "Good business happening in Mogh Bazaar. Meet me behind the old storage building. R."

Meena froze mid-step. Good business? She turned and hailed a rickshaw, and while she rattled down the busy street, she texted her sister. "Have to work. Will be back later. M."

Traffic had come to a virtual standstill and stands were being erected everywhere, in the street and on the concrete slabs people used as pavement. As soon as the twilight prayer breaking the long fast was called out from the mosques, they would start selling delicious iftar snacks. The fried aubergines, *beguni*, had been piled high, ready to be served. The smell of onion pancakes, *piazu*, reached Meena in the rickshaw, making her mouth water. The atmosphere was abuzz and impatient. A fight flared up when an iftar stand was erected right in front of a rug merchant's and little boys swarmed around the pots like annoying flies. She wondered whether she should hop off and buy a plate of iftar now and then eat in the rickshaw when it was time.

Suddenly, another text from Rifat. It was blank. Then another and another. Three blank messages in a row. Meena tried to call, even though it was much more expensive, but he didn't pick up. Could the prayer start already so the gridlock would ease?

*

Janne felt big. Big, swollen and pasty. At least compared to the handful of nervous little men crowding around him. To make matters worse, he was a bit hungover after too many pints at the club the night before.

An agitated Hanif had interrupted him while he was indolently flipping through an old issue of *Dagens Nyheter*, a Swedish broadsheet, to ask him to go out and speak to the guards. So now, here he was, squinting in the harsh light. The heat made sweat trickle down his back. He wished he could go back into the cool house. Have something to drink. A beer.

A scrawny little man was standing in front of him, delivering his message in stuttering, broken English. His hair was neatly combed to one side in a greasy wave and he wore an oversized belt in his pressed, synthetic gabardine trousers. Behind him hovered a handful of other men Janne recognised as their security guards. Everyone was trying to help the man with explanations and encouraging slaps on the back. They bowed and nodded at Janne and spouted random English phrases: "always available", "please, Mister, please", "maximum unhappy". Janne didn't just feel big and pasty but also stupid and unwilling to act the big man. The men were certainly behaving as though he was incredibly important.

"How do you mean?" Janne couldn't understand what the man was saying. The man tried again. Nodding eagerly, pleadingly. A new, incomprehensible harangue in incomprehensible pidgin English. Hanif stepped in and translated.

"He's explaining that he supports five children, a sick sister and his old parents. And his brother just lost his wife. He is asking you for mercy."

"How? What happened?" Janne was slowly starting to connect the dots. The guard who had been asleep at his post when Siv had done her nocturnal inspection. This had to be him. And now Siv had fired him.

"Is this the guard who fell asleep?"

"Yes, exactly, Boss. A very bad person, Madame Siv is absolutely right, I think . . ."

Janne had wised up to the fact that Hanif's personal take on things always biased the information that reached him, so he quickly cut him off.

"Hanif. Just translate. Word for word. Would you please ask the man what his name is and to tell me about his family? Don't add anything, don't subtract anything, just translate. Okay?"

Hanif looked offended, but Janne sensed he understood. The skinny man relaxed and started explaining in his own language. He started by saying what village he was from, that his name was Beppin and that he was married to Pushba.

Fascinated, Janne took in the man's expressive story through his body language. First, a list of names, then a short vignette depicting each of his five children, and someone called Alama, who walked with a limp. Then something about old infirm people and the words "medicine, medicine". Then Allah was mentioned and one of his hands rose up toward heaven. Allahu Akbar. Then an accelerated harangue that grew increasingly dramatic and ended with him crying and tearing his hair.

Hanif translated, eagerly cheered on by the guards. If Janne understood the story right, the man had worked as a guard for the Swedish Embassy for over twenty years. He had never fallen asleep on the job and at one point – in 1994, apparently that was important – he'd caught a burglar in the act. This was the first time he'd dozed off at work. Now he was an old man, possibly almost forty, and responsible for supporting about fifteen people. His old father needed drugs and medical care and one of his children was disabled. He would never get another job like this one, at his age, and he was asking Janne to speak to Miss Siv. Could he have a second chance, just one more chance?

Janne felt touched by the man's story and pleased with the solidarity the other guards were showing. The man's answers were a bit vague, but he seemed to live in a nearby slum area called Badda, and apparently one of his children had a problem with her leg. She would never find a husband, that much was clear to Janne.

"What's his salary?" Janne asked Hanif and nodded for him to translate.

"He says he takes home two thousand three hundred taka a month from the security company. But apparently, he owns a plot of land, as well, which makes him some money. But technically, he just works here for two thousand three hundred taka a month."

Janne nodded. Barely two hundred Swedish kronor. He let the little man know he was going to see what he could do, and then turned around and went back into the air conditioning. Hanif, who with his monthly salary of nine thousand taka was apparently a wealthy man by comparison, even though Janne and Sofia had felt his salary was embarrassingly low, followed. Janne slowly started to realise that even within his own little household, there were obvious class differences

*

Sofia and Antje had picked up the recovering Moltana from Dr Hassan's clinic early in the morning. Rehana, who had been waiting for them, squatting in a ditch outside the fancy clinic, had jumped up and run over, looking ecstatic.

"Sofia from Sweden, thankyouthankyouthankyouthankyouthankyou so much, thankyouthankyou!"

Dr Hassan had looked grave and said he wanted to see his patient again in two weeks.

"I've tried to explain to the girl that if her Amma has even a slight temperature, they have to come back immediately!"

In the car, the woman, who apparently was only thirty-three years old, had looked shockingly small. She'd stared mutely out the window, clutching the door handle. Small and old. Sofia would have guessed somewhere between fifty and sixty. Rehana had been chirping excitedly next to her, stroking her mother's hair, kissing her hands and chirping even more.

"Thank you so much, Sofia, my best friend. Antje, also my best friend. From Sweden!"

Antje had explained to the girl that she'd talked to the factory and they would both be allowed to keep their jobs, Moltana as a second seamstress and Rehana as a thread cutter. She'd also managed to wrangle a week's paid leave for the woman. Sofia shot her an impressed look.

"Bjarne didn't dare do less," Antje said airily. "I let him know how I feel about his staff policies and pondered what the newspapers back in Denmark would write about his company if they knew. Maybe that's something I can discuss with that Jens guy. When are you going to introduce me? Is Thursday barbecue night at the Nordic?"

Sofia nodded, slightly ashamed about being beaten to the punch. She was a bit unpredictable, Antje. All her talk about men and hooking up made Sofia liable to underestimate her, mistakenly relegating her to the partying-diplomats category. But just as Sofia had shoved her into that role, Antje would reveal a flash of brilliance, proving she had both integrity and courage. In addition, she was a razor-sharp analyst and adept international actor, with more experience than Sofia. Sofia wanted to work with her and be an ally, but maybe steer clear of her private life. Antje was no Katta.

Instead of commenting on certain Danish bachelors, Sofia had turned to Rehana. The girl had a lazy eye, but when she kept her gaze steady, Sofia was once again struck by how sweet her face was.

"Rehana, we're going to stop and buy food for you and your family. In the market place. So you and your Mum have enough to eat. Okay? Thik ache?"

Their stopover in the marketplace had taken longer than planned. Sofia and Antje had walked behind Moltana and Rehana among stands brimming with wares and pyramids of carefully stacked fruit. Yellow oranges, red apples and green limes. Antje with her wallet at the ready.

Sofia watched with growing respect the way the two women quickly inspected and assessed the food. Moltana's tired eyes lit up at the sight of the beautiful fish and the shiny aubergines. Rehana's eyes scanned cucumbers and tomatoes, her hands darting out to seize individual finds. While they worked, the two women spoke softly and continually to each other, evaluating, pointing, assessing and exchanging observations. There was a warm naturalness to their closeness. Sofia felt a pang of envy. Mother and daughter. So naturally entwined and dependent on each other's hands and eyes. When were she and Noella going to have time to build that kind of relationship? And had she ever been that close to her own mother?

As they were getting ready to leave the market, Sofia spotted a number of stacked cages holding nervous chickens in a corner of the marketplace. The smell emanating from the cages was foetid and sweet.

"Chicken?" Sofia turned to Rehana. Moltana flushed and quickly shook her head. Rehana looked inquiringly at her mother, who lowered her eyes, mumbling something, then replied.

"My mother says it's too much. Thank you, but it's too much."

The merchant made them an offer.

"Two hundred taka each. Five for eight hundred."

Antje leaned closer and announced to Sofia.

"We'll take them. All of them. And the cage. They can eat them or take their eggs. Either way, it's extra protein while she recovers."

On the ride back, Antje had looked pleased, but Sofia had suddenly felt awkward. A line from a song surfaced in her mind, adding an edge of irony to their morning. "It is a good day for charity." She started to hum it. Who'd written that song? And why?

"Antje, this feels too good. Suddenly, we have this urge to be noble, generous, to help the poor wretches living in the slum," Sofia tried to explain her sudden unease. "We swoop in with our big wallets. What had happened if the foreman at the factory had had his way? Just take her out the back! If we hadn't taken her to Dr Hassan?"

Antje sighed and laughed drily at Sofia's line of thought.

"You Swedes are just adorable. Was Olof Palme your dad, or what? That's no way to look at life. I feel good about it. About being able to help, I mean. Did you see how happy they were about the chickens?"

"Yes, that's exactly what I mean," Sofia mumbled. "But what about all the other days?"

*

Dipita stood up and took the money with her left hand. Her right hand was all slimy. She was going to have to borrow the bathroom and rinse off before putting her smock back on and disappearing into the hallway. The Pakistani man had got to his feet and was standing with his back to her, gazing out at Dhaka. He'd done this before, that much was clear.

"I'll be here a week," he said without looking at her. "Maybe tomorrow night? Half past seven. But don't be late, I have a dinner afterwards."

Dipita was smiling triumphantly when she reached the changing room. Asifa and Nazreen were already changing out of their hotel kameezzes. She looked at them and held up a red five-hundred-taka note.

"Side hustle," she said with a laugh. "You know Nurula who oversees the cleaners? She's the one. She sets people up with side hustles."

Nazreen and Asifa said nothing. Dipita could tell Nazreen didn't understand. Asifa, on the other hand, looked pale and quickly gathered up her things. Dipita walked up to Nazreen and looked her in the face.

"For Gods' sake, Nazreen. Why do you think so many young, pretty girls work here? Ambitious girls? What do you think girls do at hotels? They don't just clean, that's for sure. I'm not the only one doing other things on the side. It's not that bad, it really isn't. This way, I'll be in Bollywood in a matter of weeks."

She sat down between Asifa and Nazreen and explained in a lower voice.

"You just tell Nurual you want to give people massages. Massages with happy endings. It's not haram. You're still a virgin, because you only use this. And the men can go home and tell their wives they were faithful. It's like . . . massage. They're nice men, hard-working men. They're tense and need some relaxation."

She held up her right hand and smiled triumphantly.

"Tell Nurula, she'll find you when it's time. Two hundred and fifty taka for her, two hundred and fifty taka for you, easy peasy. I did two old men today. Five hundred taka."

Nazreen's head was spinning. She didn't understand what Dipita was saying. What did she mean by "did old men"? But Asifa looked pale and visibly shaken. She hissed at Dipita.

"Disgusting, you're disgusting, you're a whore. If Allah sees you, if Mullah Ziarful hears about this . . . come on, Nazreen. It is haram, absolutely haram."

Asifa grabbed Nazreen and quickly ushered her out of the changing room, leaving a grinning Dipita behind.

"I'll write to you from India. Or from the US and Hollywood. Country bumpkins!"

Asifa ushered Nazreen into a waiting CNG. Trembling with agitation, she repeated that Dipita was a whore and that it was haram, a sin.

Over the next twenty minutes, Nazreen received her first sexual education. She had never understood exactly how children were made, only that it had to do with the moaning embraces and rhythmical encounters she would sometimes witness going to the outhouse at night back in the village. The bamboo grove, for example, was a popular spot for newlyweds looking for privacy. Or when a bed squeaked against a corrugated metal wall. Then you knew. She hadn't been able to avoid seeing the goats and dogs in the village either, though girls were supposed to avert their eyes when it happened.

But the things Asifa stutteringly told her, about the little twig, so like a tamarind, that little boys had between their legs. That it could turn into a hard stick. That it was supposed to, even, to make children. Nazreen shuddered and thought about Mokta. Now she understood why Mokta had resisted getting married. At the same time, she felt something growing heavy between her legs.

"So it's the stick Dipita massages? With her hands?"

Nazreen didn't see the point but didn't dare ask more.

Asifa flushed a shade darker.

"I suppose you might say that, yes."

Just then, Nazreen's phone dinged: "New business came up, have to work. M."

Nazreen had forgotten she was supposed to meet up with Meena. The events with Dipita had left her shaken, but now she remembered. This was so typical of Meena. She wanted to tell her about this thing with Dipita. And she wanted to talk to her about Mokta. Mokta would probably have done a better job explaining than Asifa.

*

Once they reached the slum area where Rehana and Moltana lived, Rehana badgered Sofia and Antje about visiting their home. Antje clung to her seatbelt and shook her head, looking appalled.

"Thanks, but no thanks. I have to get back to the embassy, but you go! I'll send the car back for you. Can you hold on for half an hour?"

Sofia nodded and helped Moltana and Rehana take their shopping out of the boot. Rehana picked up the chicken cage, delightedly mimicking the nervous clucking of the chickens and calling out at the derelict buildings before them. The car had pulled in between two dilapidated three-storey buildings. Used car batteries, prayer rugs and sugarcane were sold in the street outside. The slum seemed to commence behind the two buildings. Rehana's call drew a small trickle of barefoot children in dirty shorts, who helped them carry. They stared wide-eyed at Sofia.

"Baksheesh," one small boy tried to beg, but Moltana told him off sharply.

Sofia walked carefully in Moltana's wake with Rehana right behind her. Planks spanning the muddiest patches let them cross to a small abandoned lot that had been turned into a landfill. A sweet, sickly smell of decay and filth rose out of the ground, Sofia had to breathe through her mouth. On the other side of the landfill, a row of small shacks was teetering on the edge of one of Dhaka's many waterways.

"Not pretty." Rehana shook her head but smiled from ear to ear.

The shacks were constructed of metal sheets and wood. Tattered sacks and blue tarps hung in front of the entrances. One had a door with mosquito netting. Sofia noticed the shacks were semi-supported in the back by poles and wondered to herself if small children weren't at risk of falling into gaps between metal sheets and wooden boards.

Rehana had rushed ahead into the shack that apparently belonged to them and now had her hands full keeping her younger siblings away from the shopping. Neighbours were congregating from every direction to have a look at the unusual guest. Moltana entered last, balancing a sack of vegetables on her head, issuing a quick series of commands to Rehana. Something to sit on. Something to drink. Keep the neighbours out. Sofia felt she got the gist.

A stool was set out next to the door and Sofia took a seat. The interior looked dark and cramped. Sofia caught a glimpse of a wooden cot and a small, battered cabinet full of kitchen things. There seemed to be a wide shelf running along the ceiling, crammed full of clothes and blankets, canisters and boxes full of junk jostled for space on the floor.

"Many, many people. Not a lot of room," Rehana said as she handed her younger brothers a banana each. Sofia pulled out her water bottle and took a sip.

"Who lives here, Rehana? Who are your neighbours?"

"Almost all of them are garment workers. Garment, garment, garment," she explained, pointing to different shacks. "Different factories. Everyone's hungry, like us."

She handed Sofia an apple, she rinsed it carefully and took a bite. Her every movement was studied by several pairs of eyes. A little girl with a tattered dress and shaved hair tried to climb onto her lap, but Rehana chased her away. A small group of little boys with distended bellies and plastic bags attached to long sticks studied her intently and giggled when she addressed them. Patches of eczema covered the crown of one of the boys' head.

"How much do you pay for your house a month?" Calling the shack a house was a compliment, but the answer came instantly.

"Seven hundred taka to the mustaans and eight hundred taka to the landlord. We have no money left to buy rice. And no money for me to go to school."

She said the last part matter-of-factly and smiled. The tragedy of it would only strike Sofia much later. In that moment, she was more interested in the mustaans, which was to say the mafia. So they blackmailed poor people, too? As though Rehana had read her mind, she explained.

"Protection, everyone needs protection. The poorer you are, the more protection you need. That's how it is in my country."

Before Sofia went back to the car, she took out her phone. A photograph, a memory. People lived so close together here, were so involved in each other's affairs and doings. Neighbours, semi-relatives and family members. Young people and old. Toothless and hunchbacked, coughing and scratching. She had no illusions about it being some kind of idyll, quite the opposite, they were all marked by hard work and poverty. And probably malnutrition. But that closeness, that sense of community, that was something she had never experienced. She watched Moltana and Rehana wordlessly handle the younger children in the cramped shack, helping each other make dinner with little nods and supporting hands. The intimacy she'd witnessed at the market was evident in this, too. Mother and daughter.

"Rehana, I would like a picture of us," Sofia said, holding her phone out to a young man dressed in a loincloth and filthy tank top. She stayed on her stool and put her arm around Rehana's thin waist. Rehana wrapped her arm around her neck. The young man snapped a picture. Moltana came over and stood on Sofia's other side. Moltana, Rehana and Sofia. One more picture? He smiled, flashing big, white teeth, and nodded questioningly to Sofia. She smiled back, of course, he could take more. He turned the phone this way and that, filling her memory card with pictures.

Eventually, Sofia had to go back to the embassy: she had scheduled a meeting with Moberg. This time, she wasn't going to let him slip away. She was going to push him a bit, maybe even be sharp with him. She needed more insight into Dev-Com's work and a clearer position from him on the women's conference.

Her car arrived at the Swedish Embassy at the same time as two visitors from Sweden. She recalled that Rickard was scheduled to meet with a group that had been given a grant as part of SwedeAid's new project Business – Not Poverty.

She smiled gloomily to herself. The contrast between the visiting Swedes and Moltana and Rehana's home in the slum was so stark. Two men in their mid-forties. Both slightly overweight and wearing khaki chinos, sport sandals and socks, short-sleeved white shirts and ties. Both carrying black briefcases. Both with shaved heads and glasses. During the brief minutes it took their driver to unload their bags, they both turned toward the sun. Sofia went over to say hello.

"Jan Lindgren from Lindgren and Möller Innovations," one of the men greeted her. "So good to get out of the blizzards. We haven't been getting a lot of sun lately."

"Klas Möller from Lindgren and Möller Innovations," the other introduced himself. "Yes, it's good to finally get some sun and warmth. I've never been to a third world country before, but it's actually pretty nice."

"Growth market," the first man corrected him. "You never visited a *growth market* before."

"Exactly. That's what I meant."

And then, talking over one another while following Sofia toward the entrance:

"So, we're the ones who . . ."

" . . . wrote looking for more information on Bangladesh. We're interested in inclusive business opportunities."

Sofia nodded politely and showed them to the reception desk. This was Rickard's area, part of SwedeAid's private sector development work that used to apply exclusively to local businesses. But the big new government initiative was to extend the support to Swedish companies. Like many others at SwedeAid, Sofia was sceptical. Why should Swedish companies receive financial support? And why should Swedish taxpayers foot the bill for it? The government's new wave of investments in private companies was ill-conceived and had failed to persuade the foreign aid people.

"So you've been contacting Bangladeshi companies?" Sofia asked with interest while the two visitors pulled out their passports and registered with the receptionist.

"Absolutely. In the leather sector. We have a potential product that could become . . ." one of them began.

" . . . a real bestseller. Really big," the other finished, clarifying to Sofia: "We're looking to create a bit of win-win, simply put. Win for us and win for the poor. Employment opportunities, you know."

"Win-win," Sofia said slowly. "That's great. That it's not win-lose, I mean."

The two men laughed heartily at her comment and then disappeared up the stairs to meet with Rickard. Looking back over her shoulder, Sofia noticed the men stopping halfway up the stairs to gawk at one of the many small lizards darting about the embassy's walls.

She felt vaguely uneasy. She hadn't meant what she'd said as a joke.

12

Farida felt dizzy with the sweetness of triumph, she almost took a wobble. The man took the wad of notes she held out to him, lazily counted the money and then handed her the tattered rope. There! The beautiful goat was hers. And the year-old kid. She whispered to Mostafar, but the boy was staring into space, into eternity, showing no sign of understanding her.

"Blessed girls, blessed, blessed, praise be to Allah, praise be onto him," she murmured and turned back to the village. "Nazreen, Meena, blessed girls, my girls."

She walked along the meandering path from the market place, down toward the houses by the river, with her head held high. Past all the neighbours and past her husband's cousins' plots of land. Made sure all the glittering eyes inside the gloomy houses could see both the goat and the two chickens dangling from her other hand. Stopped and let the goat nibble on the leaves of the *nnem* plant that belonged to the old gossip on the corner. The beautiful goat followed her. And the kid.

Mahmoda had brought her the money. Rustling, crumpled taka notes, more than Farida had seen at once since their last harvest. Since before the flood. Mahmoda had told her. The girls were staying with their second cousin Babul and his wife Reka somewhere in the middle of Dhaka. Both were working, but Mahmoda wasn't clear on with what. It was honest work, that much she could tell her and they were using their English. And apparently, the money was flowing in. They were going to send money as often as they could, a lot of money, enough money. They were both doing well and would have loved to call. Perhaps they would be able to send money for a new mobile phone.

Farida, beaming with joy, had tried to tell their father, Nurul, but he had pretended not to hear. He'd just moaned and rocked his emaciated body back and forth, lamenting and praying by turns, his wrinkled hand raised to the sky.

"I have three dead daughters and a freak for a son. I have no land and no children. I'm going to die like a rat. *Allah shorbo shoktiman.*"

She had gently tried to remind him the mosque committee had received their money. The Bhuia family had handled the catastrophe in a respectable manner, even Mullah Lutfar had been pleased with their donation.

"I'm destitute. I have no land and no children. I'm going to die like a dog."

He continued to lament and rock back and forth.

But. When on the first day after Mahmoda's visit, Farida spent a long time grinding turmeric and chili with garlic, when she fried up the tender chicken meat, poured in the oil, fried the vegetables and let the smells waft toward their neighbours' houses. When she let the white meat absorb the yellow sauce and served several dishes to choose from. When the rice was done. When the fish had been quickly seared in the oil with a few pinches of salt and a squeeze of lime. Then. Then he had come. Hunched over and thin, with a turban carelessly wrapped around his head and his vertebrae visible through his vest. He had come, and he had eaten. And eaten and eaten.

*

"Your husband! You're f-ing accompanying spouse . . ."

Siv burst into Sofia's office without knocking. Sofia had no choice but to quickly get off the phone as Siv continued, her face a deep shade of red.

"There are rules and regulations, and I expect embassy staff to comply with them. Am I making myself clear? He's mocking me, he shows no respect. Are you trying to kill me, is that what you want, the two of you . . . Huh? I'm going to bring this up with headquarters and no one, I repeat *no one* can say I don't do my job right!"

"But, Siv, what happened? Calm down, the night-watchman was fired. I haven't seen him at ours for a week. Janne accepted that you had to fire him, right? He understood . . ."

Sofia felt sure she'd missed something. Countless interminable conversations about Beppin, the sacked night-watchman, had taken place over the course of the past week at Janne and Sofia's house. Janne had felt the man deserved a second chance, and that Sofia should take a stand. Sofia had explained that Siv was the administrative manager, and therefore the only one empowered to make that call. Those were the rules.

"You're supposed to be the one working to make the world a better place, come on!" Janne had argued. "Surely we didn't come here to live a life of luxury and not give a shit about the poor people who might cross our path in our gilded cage? Here's something we can do that would really make a difference for a whole family of poor people."

Sofia had felt both shown up and slightly impressed by Janne's passion. In her family, with her brother the company lawyer and her dad the neurosurgeon, she'd always been the one advocating a gentler approach. The one who cared about the underdogs of this world. Janne's reaction may be far too emotional, but he was right. People should be allowed to make mistakes, at least once. But on the other hand – after so many years abroad, she knew you simply couldn't get involved in every broken life you came across. Besides, Siv was a dangerous enemy. With a few well-placed phone calls to SwedeAid's HR department, she could have Sofia branded a "troublemaker" forever.

"All of Bangladesh is poor. You won't change that by helping Beppin. What about the other guards? Don't they have tragedies in their lives, too?"

Sofia had tried to explain to Janne. They'd ended up entangled in discussions about morality and integrity and she felt she came off as a cold pragmatist and that he always got the last word. Not because she was wrong, exactly, but because he was more right.

"Well, I'm obviously not a diplomat or foreign aid professional, I'm just a history teacher," Janne had said. "And as an historian, I know history is full of brave people who do little things for others. And that good deeds can have a massive impact. Why not us? Why not stick our necks out just a little, an inch, for this man, Beppin?"

In the end, Sofia had agreed to ask Siv if she would consider making an exception and give the man his job back. But the reaction had been exactly what she'd feared. Siv had flown into a rage and told Sofia to keep her nose out of her job, that there were rules and regulations to be followed. The whole thing had turned into an unpleasant confrontation that gave Siv an unnecessary opportunity to take Sofia to task. Ambassador Moberg had studiously kept well out of it.

"I thought you knew the rules and understood that there can be no exceptions. How would that look?" Siv had said, glowering at Sofia. "We have a contract with a security company, and it says, in plain English, that if any guard is caught sleeping, he will be fired. Do I make myself clear? Besides I'm responsible for the security of our Swedish employees and I'm in charge of all administrative routines. How am I supposed to do my job if our guards are asleep? Huh? Or if everyone at the embassy felt free to meddle whenever they pleased?"

Sofia had opened her mouth to counter that one way of improving security would be to pay the guards properly, so they didn't have to work other jobs on the side. But she'd closed her mouth again. Siv was too belligerent. Instead, she'd backed down and been forced to explain to Janne that they had no chance of winning against Siv. She was technically correct. The night-watchmen weren't allowed to sleep on the job. In the end, Janne had yielded and Sofia had thought it was a closed chapter. Until now.

"What did Janne do? What's the matter?"

Siv's face was livid.

"Why don't you come and see? Come on! Come and see!"

Sofia turned her phone off. She had some time before she had to be at the World Bank and was free to come with Siv immediately. Sofia noticed the large woman was shaking with outrage as she marched ahead of her to the carpark. In the car, Siv was evidently too incensed to speak, instead, she snorted and hissed, shook her head and raised her eyebrows.

House 2 on Road 3 in Baridhara, which the embassy rented for Sofia and Janne was surrounded by a high wall. The wall was topped by three rows of barbed wire and the house was accessed through a large iron gate which protested loudly when pulled open. Until today, there had been a few feet of verge between the wall and the poorly paved road. Sofia hadn't given the wall or the grass much thought, but when the embassy car turned onto Road 3, she realised what had Siv in such a tizzy.

Next to the gate, something that looked like a primitive lean-to had been constructed. A stand, like the myriad wretched little stands that filled every inch, every empty surface in the poor parts of Dhaka, propped against the wall. A row of thick bamboo poles had been sunk into the ground and a dirty blue tarpaulin with a sewn-up tear in the middle spread out on top. On one side, sari cloth held down by rocks formed a makeshift wall. Under the tarpaulin, Sofia could make out roughly-hewn wooden benches arranged in a square, already occupied by a handful of men in lungis. A beaming man Sofia recognised as Beppin the night-watchman was standing by some upside-down wooden crates, talking to Janne. Janne waved happily when he spotted Sofia.

"Welcome to Restaurant Beppin!"

"Janne, are you out of your mind?" Sofia was thunderstruck and Siv waited next to her in fuming silence.

"I got the landowner's permission. This is the new plan. I lent Beppin two thousand taka, and he's paying me back over twelve months. He's going to run a tea and snack stand and support himself and his family. Business is already booming!"

Sofia watched the man behind the crates solemnly pick up a large tin tea kettle from a gas burner and pour the brown liquid into small, semi-clean glasses. He carefully measured out spoonfuls of sugar and stirred the white granules in reverently, as though performing a sacred ritual, before prancing over to his customers with their beverages. The men he was serving were deep in conversation. Some of them had parked their rickshaws next to the stand.

Janne looked like he was enjoying Beppin's company immensely.

"Have a seat! Spot of tea?"

Janne turned to Siv, whose face darkened even more. The embassy driver seized the moment and accepted the offer. He was instantly reprimanded by Siv.

"You, back in the car!"

Then Siv rounded on Sofia.

"Like I told you. Your . . . husband! Your accompanying spouse. I'm going to report this. Every last detail. Obstruction. Provocation. Inability to cooperate. I'm going to tell everyone I know, at the Ministry of Foreign Affairs, at SwedeAid . . . I'm going to . . ."

Janne listened with a smile on his lips for a minute, then cut Siv off.

"First of all, this restaurant has nothing to do with Sofia and her professional conduct, it's my own private initiative," he began. "And I have written permission from the owner of the house to use the land. The embassy only rents the house. So what's the problem?"

"It can't look like this! Like a slum. And the guard can't be let off that easily. He needs to be punished for his insubordination, he will not . . ." Siv sputtered, unable to find the words, Janne waited patiently then asked again.

"I don't see how this is the embassy's concern. What exactly is the problem?"

He looked from Siv's crimson face to Sofia's ashen one. Siv turned on her heel and walked stiffly back to the car. Sofia stayed where she was. Janne tried again.

"Sofia, exactly what is the problem? I can't see any problems. Just a terrific solution."

*

Meena looked at her blank phone screen. "Good business", Rifat had texted. Sometimes, landing a shipment of cauliflower at a cut-rate price or a picking up a load of onion before the other traders was a matter of minutes. Granted, Meena had gone without food since dawn, but she was willing to put off eating for another half hour, if that meant securing a good deal. But when the muezzin's strident call to maghrib, the evening prayer, sounded from the central mosque, all of Dhaka stopped. All the iftar stands erected along the walls and outside the shops in the past hour were suddenly swamped with customers. Every devout Muslim man, woman and young person in all of Dhaka thronged to the food, the longed-for iftar, to break the day's fast. Women gathered in their homes to pray to Allah and eat. And in the streets, every single one of Dhaka's more than one million rickshaw-wallahs pedalled to the nearest iftar stand, discarding their bikes willy-nilly along the walls. Then they ate. Silently and with determination. The CNGs, the motorised vehicles that were the next step up from the rickshaws, were parked in clusters on street corners, their drivers confident they would still be there when they got back. Cars mounted the curbs and drivers and passengers jumped out to buy food, leaving doors wide open and radios on, blaring out prayers. Buses emptied in moments. Shopkeepers pulled their doors shut, or drew their draperies, or pulled down their grates, then sat down on the floor with a sigh of contentment and dug into the blessed food.

The irksome buzz preceding the maghrib had been replaced with the sound of contented chewing and grunts of pleasure as food finally filled mouths and throats and stomachs, making the blood flow faster and spreading nutrition throughout skinny bodies.

Meena was unable to persuade her driver to press on toward Mogh Bazaar, he just shook his head and mutely started in on a second plate of iftar. Instead, she counted out the twenty taka a plate of iftar cost and started eating herself while continuing on foot toward Mogh Bazaar.

The streets were empty now so Meena made swift progress. The food filled her with renewed energy. She had never realised how wide the streets of Dhaka were, or how dilapidated. At all other times, they were crammed with rickshaws, CNGs, busses and the occasional car. They were never this deserted. Suddenly, she could move as she pleased, instead of having to push through a flood of other bodies on their way somewhere else. She could walk down the street with her arms out, if she wanted to. Like back in the village. She couldn't resist spreading her arms once or twice during her brisk walk, as though she were about to take off. A feeling of freedom, of having her own space. She, Meena Bhuia, was creating a space for herself, and had access to her own money, in the big city of Dhaka.

Rifat's text had said "behind the big warehouse" and when she reached the marketplace, she understood what he'd meant. The bazaar itself was full of iftar stands now, but in one corner of the open space loomed a big barn-like structure. This was where merchants stored their goods overnight. Meena had delivered vegetables there before.

Crouched behind the big warehouse were, as it turned out, a row of less imposing storage houses. Some of them had tin roofs, others were thatched with reeds. Some had proper walls, others were little more than canopies intended to keep off sun and rain. The area was more or less deserted, since everyone had gone out to the square to eat.

"Rifat!" Meena called out, but there was no answer. A half-naked man who had dozed off on a bench under the eaves of a roof turned in his sleep and a few chickens scattered. A cow tied to a pole looked up at her.

"Rifat, bhai, I'm here!" Still no answer. Meena started walking past the low, ramshackle buildings. The rotting remnants of discarded fruits and vegetables were ground into the mud everywhere. In some places, burlap sacks had been put down so people could walk without slipping. A musty smell of durians or maybe rotten papaya filled the air, swallows swooped anxiously in and out under the low roofs.

Suddenly, she heard a sharp cawing. Rifat's voice.

"Meena!" Just once, her name, and then the sound of something hitting metal: once, twice, three times. She moved quickly toward the sound- maybe he needed help?"

As she turned a corner, she saw him. Miraj was holding his neck in a firm grip and smashing his head into a metal wall. Another man had twisted his arm up behind his back. A third person was covering his mouth with his hand. When he spotted Meena, he bit the man's hand so he could shout.

"Meena, run! Run! Get to where there's people!"

Meena turned mid-step, just as Miraj and his friends let go of Rifat and started after her. She flew through the narrow alleyways between the buildings, but there were a lot of pursuers.

"Spread out! Cut her off! Block all the exits!"

Meena ran, but soon discovered the low buildings formed a horrifying trap, in which she, as the prey, was constantly turned back. Miraj's friends seemed to be everywhere, and through the rushing of blood in her ears and the sound of her own heavy breathing, she could hear Miraj's hoarse voice.

"You fucking whore! I'm going to give you what you've been begging for! Grab her, boys, she's willing. Willing and free!"

From somewhere far away, she heard Rifat:

"I'll get help, Meena! Just keep running!"

In the end, she found herself in a storehouse, out of breath, on top of a pile of onion sacks. Miraj and his friends had her surrounded. She balanced on top of the pile, ready to fight, pressed into a corner of the room. But there were a lot of them.

Miraj seemed to relish having the upper hand and paused, halfway up the mound.

"See how aroused she is. Hear how she's sighing and moaning?" He was talking to his friends, who laughed raucously. He started breathing heavily, moaning, mimicking Meena's rural dialect.

"Look at me, I expose myself to anyone who wants a peek. I sleep with everyone. My name is Meena and I'm a little whore."

He laughed loudly, and Meena saw her chance. One of Miraj's friends had left a gap by one of the walls and Meena resolutely took two long strides and threw herself against the wall. A quick bounce and then back out, toward the door. Just as she thought she'd got by the men, she felt something yank her backwards and she fell and hit her head on the hard concrete. Someone had managed to grab hold of her baggy shalwar kameez and was pinning her to the floor. A split-second later, several of the men were all around her, on top of her. Miraj was straddling her stomach, holding her arms down, laughing. She tried to twist free, kicked her legs and screamed. But Miraj, with the heft of an adult, was impossible to shift. He knew it and hooted triumphantly. When Meena stopped struggling and lay still, with two grown men on top of her, Miraj cleared his throat loudly and slowly gathered spit in his mouth. He paused for a moment with the spit dangling above her face, then let it fall straight into her eye.

*

The structure of the PowerPoint presentation was terrible: page after page of text and pointless stats. The neat but excruciatingly tedious man from Bangladesh's climate commission droned on and on, pointing to the slides. Sofia felt no real need to resist the urge to slump deeper into her comfortable chair. This was the World Bank's conference, she was merely a participant and barely even expected to participate anyway. Antje was sitting diagonally across the large conference table, chatting to Peter from British DfID. They both gave Sofia a friendly nod.

Janne. Darling, stupid Janne. Her astonishment at his Restaurant Beppin initiative hadn't subsided during the drive down to the glass-

and-steel offices of the World Bank. She should have known he was going to do something. The whole Beppin affair was exactly the kind of thing Janne worked himself up over. And he was right, it was a good solution, the problem was Siv was never going to accept it. And Moberg wouldn't lift a finger to help, she was fairly sure about that.

She felt a sharp pang of irritation mingled with weariness at the thought of Janne. The same generosity and overwhelming love for his fellow man that had originally made her love him, now seemed to provoke her no end. His intensity, lack of boundaries and sloppiness. His charm. That nebulous quality that forced her to patrol every border and margin and contour. Much more intensely than she really felt comfortable with. With Janne, everything was so fluid and emotional. At this point in time, she craved structure, she wanted to really focus on her career, without being pulled this way and that by Janne's impulses and needs. The bureaucrat in her was increasingly feeling a need for a plan, a PowerPoint with bullet points and flow charts to explain Janne. She smiled at the notion, but in her heart of hearts, she knew it was exactly what she wanted. She wanted to control Janne.

He was larger than life, a wonderful man. Deep down, she knew that and had fallen head over heels for his spontaneity and warmth. How was she supposed to have rejected a man who after their first night together had declared his love with the words:

"And now, Sofia, from now on, I want to be the most important person in your life. You're the woman I've been waiting for my entire life."

No games, nothing held back. And it had been like that for five years. Close, close. They had been the most important persons in each other's lives. Until she'd become distracted after Teo was born and looked away for a moment. It still hurt to think about how she'd realised he'd lowered himself to having a tawdry affair. An affair with a co-worker. That the two of them were not going to make it, despite the closeness they had shared, despite their intimacy. She was still struggling to come to terms with the betrayal, to put it in into proportion. It wasn't so much about him spending a few nights with that Camilla, it was about the magic being lost. The seal that had guaranteed their honesty and union had been broken. A small hole in the vacuum, which had let bacteria in. Was everything going to have to be thrown away now?

After Camillagate, as they'd come to call the incident, Janne's charm and warmth had suddenly felt less interesting. If anything, it had felt sullied. All the enchanted looks other women shot him. That spotlight he turned on and off, the spotlight that would suddenly illuminate a human destiny or issue that resonated with him. The warm glow everyone wanted to be in, which she had thought was reserved for her alone. How many homeless students had they not taken in over the years? When the teenage crises had swept through his students' lives, Janne had always offered sanctuary in their home. Fun! Had been Sofia's attitude at first. But after they ended up with a self-harming fifteen-year-old in their kitchen in the mornings when Noella was an infant, Sofia had felt obliged to put her foot down.

And all the invitations to visit them in Bangladesh he'd liberally given out before they left. Now she'd been told via email that two groups of backpackers, the children or grandchildren or some of his former colleagues, were taking him up on it.

And the women, of course. The women, who seemed so starved for attention and interest that they fell and fell again for Janne's intense curiosity and presence. Until she found out about his affair with Camilla, Sofia had felt safe with Janne, had seen the women's delight as a compliment more than anything. But that was before she realised how badly he needed to be admired.

She had refused to be jealous for even a moment when he disappeared into the outback with that punk girl from Alor Desh. It was beneath her to interrogate him about sleeping arrangements or what they'd got up to. That's where she drew the line. She had never ever been jealous and didn't want to be. He knew the deal. He had a family to save. It was her turn.

The neat but tedious government minister thanked them for listening and ceded the floor to the World Bank's Country Director for Bangladesh. Sofia pushed the thoughts of Janne aside.

This was Sofia's first meeting with the local head of the World Bank, Anne Wilcott, a woman who made Sofia think of James Bond. Maybe it was her short, blonde hair, her icy, clean features or her short leather jacket that did it. But the woman definitely looked more like an action hero or a film star than the director of the World Bank's programmes in Bangladesh, with a total budget of three and a half billion dollars.

"Well then, dear colleagues, seems there's a lot to do here, doesn't it?" She paused briefly and then added with more urgency: "Doesn't it?"

The World Bank had guaranteed a one-billion-dollar line of credit for, primarily, infrastructure and dams as a means of preventing massive flooding of the entire country. The Bank, as the international institution was known among foreign aid professionals, would also administer the money assigned to Bangladesh by the International Climate Commission. The sums were staggering. A billion dollars, how much was that in taka? How many zeros? Sofia did the conversion in her notepad, wondering if that wasn't too many zeros. She felt compelled to ask the most obvious question.

"How is the country supposed to absorb these kinds of sums? There is neither financial nor technical capacity here to do so. Won't this just fuel corruption? Won't the money just end up in Swiss bank accounts?"

Peter from British DfID nodded and spoke up.

"Right, where are you going to find projects and people to run them? We have a budget of just fifty million pounds, and we have trouble finding projects to absorb *our* money."

Anne Willcott looked around the table. She slowly pulled her handbag, which had been sitting on the table, closer and methodically searched through it for something. A piece of nicotine gum, Sofia noted. Anne Willcott popped it in her mouth and let her powerful jaws work on it for a few seconds.

"There's some risk of increased corruption. Yes. The sums are enormous. Yes. But infrastructure projects are expensive. I envision large international bidding processes. Kickstarting the cement industry. Bringing more engineers to Dhaka. Building new dams. Relocating cities. This is going to give Bangladesh's economy a big boost, increase growth."

She fell silent and looked at them searchingly. The dramatic pause made them all sink deeper into their chairs.

"Realistically, we have twenty to thirty years to save this country from being devoured by its rivers and the sea. Are we going to accept the challenge or not? And what's the alternative?"

No one spoke. Everyone knew this meeting was one of hundreds to be held in Bangladesh, and clearly, the World Bank was firmly in charge this time. They formulated the problems and delivered the solutions.

Peter cleared his throat again.

"Sure, money's needed. But what I'm trying to say is that the efforts to counter climate change in the West have been far too half-hearted. No matter how many dams and embankments we build, millions of Bangladeshi are going to face radically altered living conditions. Human and social adaptation is just as important as technical prevention."

Sofia felt bolstered by his comment and asked for the floor.

"I'm aware that I'm still new here, but there are a number of grassroots organisations working with social adjustment already. With more support, it might be possible to scale up their so-called household techniques."

Anne Willcott smiled briefly and broke in.

"Of course, those are very noble efforts. It's heart-breaking, really, to watch them. But I honestly can't see how the economic growth necessary can be achieved if the land is washed away or salinated, and their response to it is building houses on stilts and raising ducks on tiny islets." She chewed her gum intensely. "Aside from protecting the land in the long term, all the infrastructure projects the World Bank is proposing can also lead to increased productivity."

"I don't think Ms Paulin is saying social adjustment alone will save the land." Peter spoke up and Sofia sent him a grateful look. "But the question is whether dams and embankments can either. People will need to change their lifestyles and habits, both in terms of nutrition and agricultural strategies to survive in a country that's going to look very different from what we see here today."

"Which will require dams and cyclone shelters," Anne Willcott put in quickly.

"Which will also require ducks, floating hospitals and different crops," Peter countered.

Antje asked for a ride back to Gulshan. Sofia felt a bit sheepish, having been reprimanded by the Country Director of the World Bank. She knew, of course, that there was an inherent conflict between the World Bank's large-scale projects and investments and the grassroots work of the NGOs. But she'd never seen the war waged so openly. It was like a kind of pitched battle. She might have assumed both sides had accepted each other's strengths and weaknesses by now. At least that was the conclusion the academic literature she'd read usually came to. Besides, she agreed with Peter's final reflection. The environmental impact caused by the Bangladeshi themselves, their so-called ecological footprint, was the smallest in the world. And yet, they were the worst affected by climate change. With the flooding and the raised sea levels, practically their entire existence was at stake. Whose social and technological adjustment mattered more here?

Antje reassured her.

"Chin up. She's the epitome of a macro economist. Growth, growth, growth. Don't mind her. Plus, she's a frustrated single woman who keeps jetting off to Singapore for another facelift. You noticed her lips, right? I can only say they certainly didn't look like that last year." Antje had pulled out a small mirror and was carefully applying lipstick to her own lips, adding, more softly:

"As a matter of fact, she was sniffing around Torgil last year, at the Glitter Ball, before I made my move. And before that, rumour had it she was seeing the former finance minister, but that would be too good to be true, wouldn't it? The country director of the World Bank and the finance minister in bed together. Hard to ignore that symbolism, eh?"

She laughed heartily.

Once they were in the car, she switched to a professional tone.

"We need to know if we're pulling out of Alor Desh soon. There are a lot of grassroots organisations, but Alor Desh is the most interesting one and Khadija Anam is a legend. I would have loved to go all in with them, have them take the lead on the climate adaptation side of things. Have you heard from the auditors?"

Sofia explained that they were still waiting to hear about the final audit, but that she was going to chase them. Antje efficiently moved on to the next topic.

"I've actually had trouble sleeping since our visit to your friend Bjarne's little factory. That really wasn't okay."

"I know," Sofia replied instantly. "I tried to nudge my ambassador, Moberg, into bringing it up with the Danes on Dev-Com, to ask if it's reasonable for a company receiving foreign aid funding to treat their employees like that. How do Danish tax payers feel about it? Shouldn't companies that receive grants be held to a higher standard? Rather than a lower one?"

Antje chuckled.

"Are you kidding? Talk about a minefield, criticising another country's foreign aid policies. And that Moberg of yours, bringing it up at Dev-Com? Sofia, he never says a word that could possibly offend anyone. Believe me, I sit next to him. He's very happy in his comfort zone. Why would he leave it?"

Sofia felt the increasingly familiar wave of annoyance at Moberg. Why would he insist on keeping her seat on Dev-Com if he didn't want to use it for anything? Couldn't he just go play with the other ambassadors? Attend national day celebrations and brunches and leave the foreign aid work to her?

Antje circled back to Bjarne's factory.

"It was horrifying! Child labour, terrible working conditions, unsafe. And the wages, I suppose one wouldn't even dare ask. Could you check with him? My suggestion is that we raise the issue of the garment workers' conditions within the framework of our Violence Against Women conference. Why not go with the theme 'Violence Against Women, at Home and at Work?"

"Yes," Sofia replied. "Or 'At Home, at Work and in Public Spaces'?"

"Right," Antje replied slowly and then burst out laughing. "But then there's nothing left! What I'm saying is, where isn't there violence? You might as well organise a conference with the theme 'Violence Against Women – Here, There and Everywhere'."

*

Meena stared at the wall and pulled the thin blanket over her. She had lain like this, motionless, for several days, only drinking a bit of water. Outside the open shutters, she could hear Rifat singing. Softly. For her ears only. It was a song by Lalon that her Amma had used to sing to her a long time ago and it made her think about the village.

How was it Rifat knew that particular song?

The unknown bird in its cage,
How does it fly in and out?
I would catch it,
If I could.
I would catch it,
And chain it to my thoughts…

Allah. It must have been Allah. He had saved her at the last possible moment. Lifted her up off the ground. Lifted her up from her helplessness and the men's hardness. Lifted her up toward the light, toward the ceiling, saving her from the evil, evil men.

A force had suddenly thrown Miraj backwards, a thick arm had wrapped itself around his neck and blows had rained down on him. Several of Miraj's men had been thrown into the pile of onion sacks or fled through the maze.

There had been a lot of them, the messengers of Allah. With clubs and truncheons, with their white Panjabis flapping like wings, with their long beards and bare feet. Rifat had filled her in. He'd found the old men sitting on the mosque steps, ordinary men spending the hour after iftar catching up on the gossip. He'd screamed that a woman was in danger and they hadn't hesitated, not for a second. They had dropped their meals, dropped their chickens and grandchildren and rickshaws, dropped whatever they were doing and rushed after him to the storehouse.

They had made it in time. That's what Nazreen had said: they had made it in time. Before.

Even so, Meena hid her head in her hands when she thought of it. Miraj's hands had ripped at her clothes. His friends' eyes had seen her. Their hate and lust had touched her body and soul.

The unknown bird in its cage,
How does it fly in and out?
One day, the cage will fall to the ground,
And the bird will fly away.

Rifat's reedy voice repeated the song, again and again. For days he sat there, singing. This one song, the only song that gave her comfort. The song became a firmament to Meena, became the whole world, turning around her where she lay. The notes and the gliding, grinding rhythm of the notes and the meaning and power of the lyrics. When he sang, Rifat's voice was clear as clean water, no longer croaking. She remembered how her mother had sung it back home, the same song, the same notes. She remembered her own surprise and pride at her mother possessing such beautiful words, at her releasing them into the village, catching and playing with them. That had been in the good old days, when her Amma still sang. Back then, when they always kept double rice stores in the house and her Abba worked at the burlap factory. Before their little brother consumed their mother. Before the river took their land.

She pictured the desiccated yard, saw her great-grandmother sweeping up after the chickens, saw her Amma prepare chard and cauliflower for dinner in the shade on the veranda. She thought she could feel Nazreen and Mokta's bodies, the way the three of them had always held each other, climbed on each other, combed each other's hair, whispered together, batting words and laughter back and forth. A time when they moved slowly in the safety of the village, sheltered by the promise of the fields and surrounded by faces they recognised. A different time. She could sense the village, still living inside her, could feel her yearning for it enduring unabated.

From time to time, Meena heard the song end and noticed darkness falling. Nazreen crawled into bed next to her. At night, Meena was able to use the bathroom and drink some water. With Nazreen's fingers entwined in her own and Nazreen's legs wrapped around hers like the branches of the Banyan tree, Meena was able to sleep deeply.

*

Nazreen stood in front of the wide, ornate door. Unsure whether she would be allowed to enter, she glanced down at her new, red shalwar kameez. On her feet a pair of sandals with glass beads and a proper heel. Her hair was held back by the bright green hair tie. She looked good. But she had never been to such a beautiful house before. Maybe you had to look even better to be allowed inside? This was the kind of house film stars lived in. Film stars, government ministers and factory owners. Foreigners and millionaires. A lot of Badda residents worked in houses like this one, and sometimes in the evenings, people would sit outside on the narrow streets, talking about their bideshi families. Some seemed to love their Western families like their own, bragging about the children's grades and the family's expensive cars. But others said some of the fair-haired children were abused. Beaten and locked up by their dads, treated worse than the Bengalis who worked for them. One had a madame who drank and invited the driver in when her husband was away. Nazreen didn't know what to think. Someone also claimed his boss and his friends had clandestine meetings with little boys when his wife was in Bangkok. And one family had ten cars and a Bengal tiger in the basement. Babul had apparently seen the tiger.

If, if, if she got this job, she would believe in Allah again. She would pray namaz and start saying her maghrib again. The dark events of the past few days had made her question her faith. How could Allah have allowed Meena to be so badly hurt? How could he? Nazreen swallowed hard and blinked away a few tears. Meena just lay in bed staring at the wall. She wouldn't eat, didn't go to work, only had a sip of water from time to time. She would need a doctor soon, or a kobiraj, a witch-doctor, to drive out the evil spirit that seemed to have possessed her. And Reka and Babul, Nazreen could tell they felt Meena had sullied their good reputation. That she had dragged them through the mud. And that little boy Rifat, who just sat there. Outside the house, by the wall. Like a faithful dog.

Oh, mighty Allah, please, please. This job could be their salvation, a rope thrown into the river. Please, Allah, help us. Help us. Allahu akbar.

Nazreen mustered all her courage, took hold of the heavy bronze ring and knocked. A few seconds passed. Just as she was about to knock again, the door slid open. Nazreen shied away from the sight of the big, pale man. His hair was long like a girl's and he was barefoot like a poor person.

"Hi, I'm Janne. You must be Nazreen?"

*

Khadija Anam rubbed her temples and slowly shook her head. Siraj was standing in front of her, looking terrified.

"Madame, I have a family to think about. My little daughter and my wife. If I don't make up lies about you, they'll slit Tomelilla's throat. They came to see me last night."

Siraj, normally so steady, emitted a sound like an animal. Khadija looked up.

"Siraj, this is an outrage. You know that. I need you. Right now especially, I need you."

Khadija sounded first upset, then dejected. A flash of insight suddenly illuminated the bigger picture. The pieces fell into place. Of course they would have to turn Siraj, of course. And they couldn't bribe him, but they could threaten.

"The bastards won't give him a chance," Khadija thought, but said instead:

"Thank you for letting me know, Siraj. I assume you're not the only one blackmailed into making up malicious gossip about me. Are you?"

Siraj lowered his eyes, but eventually nodded.

"Mirjam-apa, Nirmol, Faruk-bhai, old Achbar, Feruz. As far as I can tell, everyone has been bribed to make up stories about you."

Khadija heard him list off the name of every last key person in Alor Desh. They seemed to have targeted her core team, her hand-picked women and men who through years of training and courses had made the organisation what it was today. But at the same time. Poor, vulnerable people from the lower middle class, women and men with scarce resources and many obligations. In a country devoid of social safety nets, a bonus of a thousand taka was not something a person could turn down. Especially if their lives were also in danger. Khadija saw her already tenuous position collapse utterly.

"Do you know who's behind it?"

"It was the usual mustaans from Barikhali, but they didn't say who was paying them. I have my suspicions, though. Land grabbers. Certain mullahs. I think they've teamed up. The landless have grown too powerful."

Siraj spoke quietly, gazing morosely out the window. He watched a young man wobble past on a bicycle and sighed.

"We've made a lot of powerful enemies, Khadija."

"I know. But Siraj, can you tell the donors this? My credibility is non-existent. Assuming that you're planning to hide in Dhaka, that is. Can you at least promise me you'll tell the donors what's happening out here? Can you talk to the Swedes and the British?"

Siraj looked frightened again and started reiterating what he'd said before:

"Madame, I have a family to think about. My wife and my little daughter . . ."

"I know, Siraj. Don't you think I know," Khadija cut him off. "But you have honour, too, don't you? I understand you have to leave Lalpara, but, please, talk to the donors."

"And why would they believe me but not you? You know how it goes. They peer at us and our world through a keyhole and think they know what's in the room. They trust their accountants."

After Siraj left the room, Khadija went down to the river. She'd hidden a packet of Marlboro Lights in her sari. She didn't want anyone to catch her smoking, but she really needed a cigarette. She sat down in the sand by the water's edge, lit a cigarette and watched the almost grotesquely large, deeply orange sun slide into the water in the west. Like a blood orange. Like a drop of blood.

Khadija loved this country, even though it didn't expect it for a second. Even though Bangladesh was so clearly uncomfortable with itself, its rhythm, economically, socially, religiously, biologically and now also in terms of its climate, she never felt more at home than here. Despite the endless disasters that were always the worst in the world, despite the cyclones and shipwrecks and toxic spills, what she found here was an unadulterated feeling of life. Of sincere striving and genuine longing. That was why she had returned and it was why she stayed.

Sometimes, Khadija thought Bangladesh was a bit like a raped woman, the country had a vulnerable quality that she could relate to. That stirred her wrath and protectiveness. The land lay there, exposed and defenceless, its legs splayed, its big, wet delta outraged. Over and over again. By the Mughals, the English, the Pakistani. In and out, in and out, pillage and leave. And now, big capital and the mullahs. She compared it with her own background. The twelve-year-old who was forced to spend her wedding night with a man forty years her senior. He'd held all the cards and had full social backing for his assault, full legitimacy. Her choice had been to run away. What choice did Bangladesh have?

Her own organisation Alor Desh had been active in Bangladesh for almost twenty years and had won countless plaudits for their ground-breaking, innovative work among some of the world's poorest. She herself had been given the Right Livelihood Award and become something of an international celebrity. She had parried and survived many attacks on the organisation over the years. She remembered the early Bush era with a shudder. Clean-shaven American pastors brandishing bibles had strode around the villages, looking for signs of abortions being carried out. When it became clear Alor Desh recommended that women with unwanted pregnancies visit the so-called Menstrual Regulation Clinics in Barikhali, the Americans had cut off all support overnight. But the Swedes had stood firm that time. They had quickly replaced the American money with Swedish funds and publicly supported Alor Desh's work on family planning. It was that kind of courage, that kind of pragmatism that was required if you wanted to effect change.

Every audit ever done had shown that there was a certain level of corruption within the Alor Desh network, as in the rest of Bangladesh. Or maybe the rest of the world, if you looked closely enough? So far, the foreign aid professionals' assessment had been that their ground-breaking results outweighed any minor malfeasance. As long as the big picture was in order. They had overlooked the money that inevitably disappeared when funds were funnelled through so many small branch offices, passed through so many poor hands in one of the world's poorest countries. But in recent years, Western accounting firms had laid into grassroots organisations all over the globe, and the result was devastating. At a large civil society conference in Brussels recently, she had stood up and said:

"Zero tolerance means zero activity. Do politicians understand that? The best way to avoid corruption is to do nothing at all."

Everyone had agreed with her, and she had received a lot of pats on the back. But, as a foreign aid minister from Norway put it:

"I didn't hear that. You can't say things like that. Tax payers shouldn't have to accept that."

She lit another cigarette. Looked up at the village, but no one seemed to have noticed her. She liked this spot. When the tide was out, like now, hollows formed under the trees, perfect places for thinking without being interrupted.

This time, it was unclear what the source of the threat was. This time, it was a devastating combination of reverse bribes and blackmail. Bribes and threats designed to strong-arm people into saying Alor Desh wasn't working the way it should. She wasn't entirely clear on what was behind it all, but when she put the pieces together, a pattern emerged.

The big landowners, whether based in Dhaka or abroad, disliked the organisation's ability to organise the landless. They wanted Alor Desh gone, wanted all Western influence gone, wanted strong, empowered farmers gone and to escape any scrutiny. And in this, they shared a cause with the local imams, who were worried about women's groups and Western gender equality agendas.

"Religion and capital," Khadija mumbled to herself and put her cigarette out in the sand. Always these two together and always the women and their freedoms at the heart of the problem. Now in an unholy alliance with the Westerners' clueless anti-corruption agenda. Why couldn't Westerners recognise that challenging the powerful was expensive and dangerous? Why had they all forgotten to ask the most fundamental question of all – who stands to gain from what's happening?

13

If you look to the north now, you'll see Mount Everest. It's a beautiful day in Kathmandu, where we'll be touching down around 2 p.m. Inshallah."

The pilot's voice crackled out over the passengers' heads in broken English. Karl-Otto Moberg peered over his son's shoulder, trying to catch a glimpse of Mount Everest. And in the far distance, embedded in orange fluff, he could just about make out the peak. He felt relieved. Something to talk about.

"How high is Mount Everest?" he said. "Do you remember, Arthur?"

Wearing headphones as he was, the boy didn't hear him. Moberg tried pulling one away to speak directly into the boy's ear but ended up accidentally poking him in the eye. The boy pulled off his headphones, looking annoyed, and asked his father to repeat the question. He replied with a shake of the head, he couldn't recall how high Mount Everest was. Moberg tried again.

"And K2 is number two, right? Or is it? Well, either way, it's beautiful. Aren't you looking forward to getting to know one of the world's highest peaks?"

Arthur didn't even bother to reply, just put his earphones back on and slumped a few inches further down in his seat. Moberg tried another topic, but when the only response was a few grunts, he gave up.

Vanja had suggested he choose a mantra for his trip with Arthur. She had meditated on it, she'd told him, and come up with a suggestion. "I'm meeting Arthur where he is, at this point in his life, in the middle of life." She had explained how he, as Arthur's father, had a grown man's responsibility to find an energy level where they could meet. Karl-Otto pondered what she might have meant for a few minutes, but got no closer to deciphering it. His son was completely uninterested in meeting him. He made one last attempt.

"What music are you listening to?"

Arthur replied by reeling off a long list of artists Moberg had never heard of and then politely asked if he could put his headphones back on. Moberg heaved a sigh and pulled out the folder Sofia had handed him as he was leaving the embassy.

"I'm planning to bring all the donors together at a conference about violence against women, with special focus on the garment sector," she'd explained. "We're going to keep our thinking broad and create platforms for interaction between employers and the police."

Karl-Otto sighed again. Sofia was extremely competent and brimming with good ideas. Well, with ideas, at least. Karl-Otto wasn't sure, however, a women's conference was something he wanted to host. As Sweden's ambassador, he was ultimately responsible for their country's profile, and women's issues always gave rise to unforeseen reactions. Not least in Muslim countries.

Karl-Otto skimmed the documents. Sofia's proposal looked both realistic and well-thought-out. But ambitious! She'd apparently managed to get the Dutch on board, too. Well, the Dutch foreign aid counsellor was a woman he supposed they had each other's backs. He sighed a little. This would mean more work, he could tell. He was going to have to open proceedings and host dinners and talk about the gender issue.

That being said, he'd taken the time to do some googling on the subject and found fragments of an interesting academic discussion on the subject of gender equality. It would seem there were two schools or approaches. Either, you considered gender equality part of every other issue and let it influence the more general discussion of development. So-called mainstreaming. Or, you dealt with it as a separate issue, in order to call attention to women's causes and make sure they weren't overlooked. Advocates of the different approaches seemed to be at each other's throats. And surely a women's conference would inevitably align them with the separate-track school of thought? Moberg leaned his head back and closed his eyes for a moment. He needed to think this through.

Then he suddenly sat bolt upright. He'd forgotten about the Bengali-Urdu dictionary from the sixties he'd packed in his hand luggage. The book was a rare find from one of the second-hand bookshops by Chandni Chowk. He eagerly pulled out the worn copy. Moberg studied the authors' names, Banerjee and Ahmed. Unfortunately, not names he recognised. But perhaps their hotel would have a computer so he could google them?

The plane set down gently in the Kathmandu Valley and the Swedes made for the exit. The gangly fifteen-year-old led the way. The thin, white cords trailing down his shirt signalled he still wasn't interested in being talked to. He carried a big black backpack and kept tossing his blonde fringe. In his wake followed a tall man with a greying beard, dressed in a brand-new Fjällräven jacket. On his head, a slightly too-small Fjällräven baseball cap, which kept sliding up to rest on the crown of his head.

Arthur had absolutely no wish to be seen with his father. This whole father-son weekend was clearly Vanja's idea. He couldn't believe he'd agreed to it. He could have stayed home over the break and chilled with his mates. Hung out by Aziz' pool. Though, come to think of it, Aziz had gone off on a Singaporean shopping trip.

Out by the taxi rank, Arthur had no choice but to take off his headphones and listen to his dad. The taxi drivers crowded around them. Arthur noted that they were much more used to seeing Westerners here in Kathmandu than in Dhaka. No one stared at them and the drivers asked for dollars and wanted to know if they were going to various temples and city squares. In Dhaka, no one ever took taxis. Everyone had private cars and drivers or rattled around in rickshaws.

"I've booked us into this hotel everyone's talking about, the Kathmandu Guesthouse. It's nothing special, but we can use it as our base while we figure out what kind of guide we need. Don't you think, tiger?"

Karl-Otto made the mistake of putting his arm around Arthur and squeezeing him. The boy angrily slipped out of the awkward embrace and disappeared into their taxi.

The hotel turned out to be located in the middle of Thamel, the old town, and was something like a cross between a hostel and a middling hotel. The mood was relaxed and bohemian. Groups of overly tanned Westerners were hunched over large maps in the hotel restaurant, apparently discussing different hiking routes. Their suite was big and airy and had a private entrance from a lush courtyard. Vanja had probably let the staff know the booking was for an ambassador, which always meant VIP suites or at the very least no backyard views and such. Arthur noted grumblingly that the hotel had neither a pool, a spa nor a boutique area. He would've preferred something swankier, but at least he had his own room. He tossed his backpack on a chair, stretched out on the wide bed and turned up the music in his headphones.

Four years in Asia had given Arthur a taste for luxury. He would never forget the Hyatt in Bangkok, where they'd stayed a few times. Or the Taj Hotel outside Delhi. The Taj chain was actually perfect, a level he was comfortable with. He loved the magnificent lobbies of Asia's luxury hotels, the cushioned efficiency of the lifts. Since turning thirteen, he'd been allowed his own room, too, and he enjoyed spreading out across terraces and sofas, pretending he was a film director. Or a film star. Or just very rich.

Sometimes, though, Vanja got it in her head that all the luxury surrounding him in Dhaka was detrimental. Instead of a shopping trip to Hong Kong last Easter, she'd insisted he go visit her parents back in Umeå, in Sweden's far north. That was after she realised the staff in the residence had taken to calling him "Boss". But Arthur liked being called

"Boss". All the other guys at school were called "Boss" or "Sir" by their staff. And after that Easter with his grandparents, he'd come to a firm decision. The life of an average Swede was not for him, instead, he was going to live somewhere warm and bright and nice. Umeå, no thanks.

That was also why he enjoyed hanging out with Aziz. His dad was a government minister and they were unbelievably rich. Aziz was one of the richest kids in school. His older brother drove a Lamborghini and their palace in Baridhara was sick! It looked like the White House or something, but made of pink marble. When Aziz turned eighteen, he would get to choose any car he wanted. They often discussed which one he should pick. A Jaguar or a Lotus? Within the vast family mansion, Aziz had his own apartment, with a jacuzzi, and on the roof terrace there was a kidney-shaped pool, complete with full-time staff providing foot massages and cocktails. Aziz knew everything there was to know about cool hotel chains in every corner of the world and had a sister who lived in a penthouse in New York.

Karl-Otto appeared in the doorway.

"Want to go for a walk, Arthur? I was thinking we should head toward Thamal Square. I imagine there are quite a few trekking outfits along the way. At least Lonely Planet says you can put together a trekking package deal any time. By the way, are you hungry?"

Arthur slowly got up from the bed where he'd been sprawled. His dad's plan was for the two of them to go on a three-day hike somewhere in the Kathmandu Valley. Arthur knew people who had done that, and it sounded like a cool thing to tell people in Sweden about. If it ever came down to it, he didn't have to let on that he'd done it with his dad.

The level of commercialism that greeted them out in the winding shopping street was completely unexpected and very unlike Dhaka in that it was squarely aimed at tourists. Embroidered scarves, rugs, kites and wall hangings were on display. Every other shop seemed to specialise in trekking and cheap counterfeit North Face clothing. Other shops sold silver jewellery, millions of earrings, pinned to red silk cushions, jostled for space with brass Shiva sculptures, Buddhist mandalas and Buddha faces. The smell of incense hung heavily over the alleyways. The Westerners they saw everywhere were a far cry from Dhaka's clean-shaven consultants and diplomats, these were either tanned adventurers with the Himalayas in their sights, emaciated has-beens or young backpackers with dreadlocks and wooden bead necklaces. Street children and women in saris darted between them, and there were bicycle rickshaws here, too.

"Wow, hippie main street," Arthur mumbled under his breath, pinching a towel with a big marijuana leaf on it. "Mum would love it."

Karl-Otto caught the boy's comment and gratefully seized on it.

"Well, you do know they used to call our mum Mrs Hippie back in the seventies, don't you? Kind of like Mississippi, like the river. I suppose it was a bit of wordplay among her friends. She always wore long skirts, well, yeah, the kind you see here, and earrings . . ."

" . . . and then she went and fell for *you*."

Arthur's astonishment was genuine. He'd never understood what his flaky mother saw in his dull father. He'd asked Vanja about it once, but she'd ruffled his hair, tilted her head and giggled.

"It's not easy being a penniless artist. I wanted to see the world and I wanted to have you."

Now his dad's earlobes went crimson and Arthur could tell he was casting about for a reply.

"Sure, but I'm a nice bloke, aren't I? Right? And who knows, maybe your mother wanted a nice bloke?"

*

Sofia closed the door behind her and turned on the air conditioning. She had to text Janne to tell him she was going to be late tonight, even though they'd agreed they needed to spend more time together right now. Over the past week, they'd only exchanged the bare minimum information needed to keep their lives functional. She could tell Janne was worried she was upset about the Beppin affair. But she wasn't upset, though possibly a little thrown. That being said, she didn't feel she could unreservedly applaud Janne's initiative, either, if that was what he was waiting for. Admiration, admiration . . . he was going to have to look for that elsewhere, Sofia thought wearily.

She did, however, want to hear everything about the new ayah, Nazreen, who apparently had taken the children by storm.

"She plays with them and relates to them, and her English is actually good," Janne had told her early one morning before she disappeared off to the embassy. "I don't have to keep stepping in, like with the other ayah. I think her quitting to care for her mother was a good thing."

Sofia also wanted to talk to Janne about the latest Alor Desh developments. Especially since he was the only one who had actually been there. Had he seen anything?

"Put the kids to bed and I'll be home around eight." The message was too curt. She added a sad smiley. So he'd know she was disappointed, too.

The meeting with the auditors had been worse than she'd feared. She, Peter and Antje knew they had no choice now. Glaring failings in Alor Desh's handling of its foreign aid grants had been uncovered. Large sums were missing from the organisation's accounts and there were signs pointing to a systematic clearing out of assets. The auditors also suspected several of the people supposedly employed by the organisation were so-called ghost employees, employees on paper only. Some of the land rights that had been granted to members of the organisation had been transferred to the head of the organisation, Khadija Anam. And it had been impossible to determine the whereabouts of the many motorcycles and Jeeps the organisation had purchased.

"Seen in relation to the overall financial support, the sums are not significant," the young man from Ernst & Young in Stockholm had said, sounding more than a little appalled. "But this is a matter of integrity. We've heard terrible stories about Khadija Anam's mismanagement of the organisation from her own employees. Plus, the bookkeeping is so deficient we could easily have missed things. I've actually never seen anything like it."

During the meeting, he'd handed out stacks of documents, copies and triplicates, and he'd had a PowerPoint presentation that showed how money could have been moved around different accounts. He'd sighed and shaken his head and said "this is beyond the pale". The British accountant and the two Indian accountants from Delhi, who had done all of the fieldwork, had not spoken. But the message had been abundantly clear. Alor Desh suffered from severe corruption problems and all donors would have to pull out with immediate effect.

"It's your decision, Sofia," Peter from British DfID had said, looking steamrolled by the Swedish accountant's dire assessment. Antje had heaved a sigh.

"I've seen worse, but that doesn't matter. Things were different back then, before our governments decided to hamstring civil society with impossible requirements. You're the one swinging the axe, Sofia, but we're behind you."

Sofia dialled the number of the Stockholm switchboard. It was just past lunchtime back at headquarters and Country Coordinator Bergström should be at his desk. The last time she'd seen him had been at a quick briefing before she departed for Bangladesh. Katta had described Lasse Bergström as "old school".

Lasse had insisted the briefing be held in one of SwedeAid's last remaining smoking modules. He'd sat there with one leg wrapped around the other, stuffing a pipe. Everything about him had been brown, Sofia recalled. Brown corduroy jacket, brown corduroy trousers, brown pipe and brown tan from Africa.

"He's good at his job and wily like an old fox, but usually follows his heart. The world-improvement type. He worked for SwedeAid during apartheid and was given a medal by the ANC," Katta had gossiped. "If he likes you, you're in for an easy ride, if he doesn't, he can throw all kinds of things at your embassy that you definitely won't have time for."

Sofia hadn't made her mind up on whether Lasse was a burden or an asset yet. So far, they hadn't had reason to communicate much and had mostly dutifully cc'd each other when necessary. He seemed more focused on posting angry comments on the internal website than on keeping her busy with assignments from home base.

"When did the poor become irrelevant to foreign aid?" was Lasse's most recent post on SwedeAid's debate forum, Sofia had noted. Answering his own question, he had stated bluntly that the focus of the conservative government's foreign aid policies certainly wasn't the world's poor, much as the taxpayers might be under that illusion, but rather Swedish companies and middle-class elites in the global south. "Simple answers to complex questions are never right," and "The double agendas of the private sector don't benefit the poor," were examples of other posts that had met with some ire within SwedeAid. Not least among the people who had been employed solely to work with private sector issues.

Aside from being SwedeAid's last smoker, Lasse was also an idealist. Something the new generation of foreign aid bureaucrats to which Sofia belonged found a trifle problematic. They preferred to downplay any desire to make the world a better place in favour of a thoroughly professional approach.

"Don't forget that your job is damn important," he'd coughed at Sofia. "I don't really give a shit what you do, so long as you use your mandate to make this wretched world a better place. You have the money, you have the position. Now go!"

Sofia was experienced enough not to underestimate the importance of an ally back at home base and had a deep respect for the consequences a poor relationship with one's coordinator could have. Formally speaking, that relationship was fairly nebulous. Just as the practical relationship between ambassadors and foreign aid counsellors was vaguely defined, SwedeAid had also, whether deliberately or not, left the relationship between foreign aid counsellors and country coordinators hazy. Formally, as a foreign aid counsellor, Sofia was solely responsible for Sweden's foreign aid to Bangladesh and had the mandate to act as she saw fit, but it didn't look professional to ride roughshod over one's coordinator. Or one's ambassador, for that matter. And Sofia wasn't one to make trouble. She had no intention of creating conflict during her tenure.

To Sofia's great surprise, Lasse answered the regular landline immediately.

"Well, hello over there! To what do I owe the honour? A phone call from the foreign aid counsellor herself? What, email's not good enough?"

His chuckle turned into a coughing fit. The phone lined crackled and echoed. Sofia realised banter would be impossible, she had to be direct.

"It's about Alor Desh, you know, Khadija Anam's organisation? The audit shows substantial deviations from the budget."

"Deviations? You're saying they're corrupt?"

"Yes, it looks that way, unfortunately."

"Have you spoken to the other donors? The whole group?"

"Of course, I've just come back from a meeting with them. It's tragic, but we all have the same orders from back home – zero tolerance."

"Zero tolerance," there was a croaking sound on the other end. Sofia couldn't tell if Lasse was laughing or coughing. "You should have seen Afghanistan, they have zero everything. Zero tolerance, zero activity, zero results, zero human value, zero roads, zero houses. Zero peace, zero tolerance of gender equality efforts . . ."

"Anyway," Sofia cut in. "This looks too dodgy, we have to pull out. I just don't see how I could save this."

"Alright, I understand. That's a shame. Do you have a picture of what role Khadija Anam herself has played? She's the kind of person you root for, an icon. A lot of people are going to be very disappointed."

Lasse's voice faded into a buzz and Sofia jumped in, trying to annunciate clearly.

"For now, I just wanted you to be aware. And as far as Khadija Anam is concerned, the buck ultimately stops with her. Has she been embezzling for her own private gain, you mean? It doesn't look like it. It's mostly sloppiness and a thousand tiny leaks."

The phone line crackled, Sofia figured she'd better keep talking while the connection held.

"I wanted you to know, in case the newspapers catch wind. Here or in Sweden. It's a high-profile organisation, after all, so they might write about it. The newspapers, I mean. And now that you've been informed, we're going to put our heads together over here. When it comes to Khadija herself I have no info yet."

Sofia kept talking, hearing nothing but white noise on the other end. No acknowledging noises from Lasse. The line was so bad it was best not to go back and forth, but to deliver large chunks of information every time you had the floor. Lasse knew the drill and only spoke up when there was a longer pause.

"I understand. Well, you've done what you're supposed to, by the book. Informed us. I'll pass it on to the anti-corruption team. Other than that, I'll wait for word from you to see if you need more support. Keep me posted. Is that okay? And while I have you . . . are you still there?"

"Go."

"We've had a request from the Nordic Water Committee to visit Bangladesh. I emailed Rickard about it, but he hasn't replied. Could you chase him for me? And you have to submit materials for the long-term planning by Wednesday next week at the latest. Also, the EU coordinator here wants you to host a lunch in Dhaka on the theme of migration and trafficking and invite the other donors. I'll send you the memo. And, by the way, I heard that you're chargé d'affaires this week while Moberg's away, good. Get stuck in, you're in charge now!"

Lasse kept talking and Sofia jotted down notes. She felt Lasse sounded encouraging and professional. It occurred to her this might be a good time to send up a test balloon about her women's conference.

"I was toying with the idea of organising a conference next spring together with the Dutch. It's not part of the annual plan, but it falls within the framework of our country strategy. The theme is Violence Against Women. We're hoping to get all the donors on board and are currently discussing whether to focus on the garment industry or dowry violence. Or both."

"That's a stellar idea!" Sofia could hear Lasse waking up on the other end. "I've given up on men after my time with the Taliban. Men suck!"

A coughing fit cut him short and Sofia had to pull the phone away from her ear. When he was done, he was all enthusiasm.

"Brilliant, Sofia! Finally, someone who has the guts to do something and not just talk. Bloody hell, it would be good to get something like that done before I retire. But it should be high level, not some sideshow. How can I help you with this? Would you mind writing a memo for me to have a look at?"

"Absolutely! I should've done that a long time ago, but Moberg has been sitting on a draft for weeks . . ." Sofia apologised.

"Moberg! Of course. You have that old coot over there with you, I forgot. How are you going to get this past him?" He laughed and added candidly: "You do realise you're dealing with the roadblock of the century, right? He was stationed in Vienna at the same time as my daughter and didn't lift a finger in five years. What he did do was delay and obstruct her attempts to build a network of entrepreneurs in Central Europe. No, you're going to have to be strategic about this, leave nothing to Moberg."

Sofia absorbed this information with interest. It was news. Granted, Moberg had come across as roundabout and slow, but she'd figured there might be thoughtfulness beneath his handling of various matters. If, on the other hand, the whole act was a stalling tactic, well, yes, then she'd have to change her approach.

"What if I were to sign off on everything myself this week? I mean, I am chargé d'affaires?"

Sofia had no idea where the idea came from, but Lasse let out a cheer on the other end.

"Brilliant! Of course. You're the big boss now! Have a think about what needs to be decided in the short-term and type it up and sign it.

You can list me as 'consulted'. I'll deal with the Ministry of Foreign Affairs on this end. And we're off. Women's conference, yes!"

Sofia's head was buzzing as she left the embassy. She could do with knowing more about Moberg. If he really was the roadblock Lasse claimed, that was a problem. So far, he'd come across as tired and uninterested more than anything else. But was that going to stand in her way? At the end of the day, she was in charge of foreign aid, even if Moberg refused to relinquish Dev-Com. What happened during her tenure as foreign aid counsellor was what mattered. Actions speak, as her old UN boss liked to say.

Unlike in Stockholm, where getting to work could take up to an hour, she was never further than fifteen minutes from home in Dhaka. There was a reason why all the embassies and diplomatic residences were located in the diplomatic zones. True, the traffic could be bad there, too, but you could almost always leave the car with the driver and catch a convenient rickshaw or walk to where you were going.

This late at night, the congestion had eased. Sofia felt like she was flying down the airy streets in her rickshaw. The air was warm and the night pitch black. The electricity scarcity in large parts of the capital meant darkness enveloped her on all sides so her nose was more helpful than her eyes. From time to time, she caught a noxious whiff from the sewer that ran like an open trench along every street, but just as often, there was a wave of the sweet fragrance of night-blooming jasmine. At that moment, only the luxury villas that had their own generators were lit. The power must be out in Baridhara.

Within minutes, they reached streets where she and Janne knew people: the Norwegian admin manager lived in that house, behind him was the gigantic palace of a Korean business man whose daughter was in Noella's class at school, and on the corner of their own street lived the Danish ambassador with his four girls. When the rickshaw turned down Road 3, Sofia noticed a small group of Rickshaw-wallahs and beggars had gathered to buy tea from Beppin. The ragtag band was illuminated by a single lightbulb dangling from the ceiling, and Sofia could see some of Gulshan's street children asleep under the tarpaulin ceiling. Beppin greeted Sofia with a big smile and Sofia noted that Janne must have let him hook into their power supply. So now Beppin could stay open at night, and likely would.

"Assalamu alaykum, Beppin, khub bhalo?" Sofia asked before disappearing into the house.

The living room was empty and the cook had gone home. Sofia walked through the empty rooms where every cushion and carpet fringe was perfect. The children's toys were neatly placed in baskets and a faint smell of cleaner lingered in the air. The new ayah was good.

After some searching, she found Janne on the roof terrace. She stopped short in the doorway. Hundreds of tealights covered the floor and in the middle of the terrace a table set with a white tablecloth and tall wineglasses. It took Sofia's breath away.

"It's so beautiful. Janne, you maniac. It's amazing!"

Lobsters rested on a silver platter and a bottle of wine was on ice in a silver chiller. The table was surrounded by palm trees and bougainvillea in large terracotta pots and the majestic, slowly swaying coconut trees encircling the house were nothing but dark outlines against a jet-black firmament sprinkled with millions of stars. A bone-white moon lent the scene a blueish cast.

"Well, what else am I supposed to do on a regular Wednesday night in Dhaka?" Janne laughed and spread his arms wide. "When I have the most beautiful wife in the world and she's coming home from work?"

He had put on a white linen shirt that was trying to outshine the tablecloth in the gloom. He looked fresh out of the shower and happy. Sofia would have loved to change into something more festive, and wouldn't have minded a shower, either. But that would have broken the spell.

"Darling," Sofia zigzagged her way between the tealights toward the chair meant for her. But instead of taking a seat, she walked over to Janne and straddled him.

"You're . . . Janne, you know I love you?"

"So you say, but are you sure?" Janne kissed her and tried to undo her hair. "Take that hair tie out, you look gorgeous with your hair down." He laced his fingers together behind her back. "Let me see, despite Beppin?"

"Maybe thanks to Beppin?" Sofia said and kissed him. "But I'm going to leave it to you to deal with Siv when she discovers the illegal cable hooking down there. So far, she hasn't been able to nail us for anything, but when she realises the embassy is paying for Beppin's electricity, she's going to have your accompanying spouse grant revoked!"

She laughed and went over to her own chair. Janne watched her, seeming to relish her delight. Sofia picked up her big, starched, elegantly folded napkin, shook it and placed it on her lap. She transferred a lobster to her plate.

"Now I want to hear more about my children. How are they? How are things working out with Nazreen? My god, she keeps the place tidy! That's her name, right, Nazreen?" She chuckled and let Janne fill her glass with wine. "Tell me! How are our children doing?"

Just then, someone cleared their throat loudly, like when a person pulls snot all the way down and then lets it rumble around their throat for a bit. Then the sound of spitting. They suddenly realised a whole family was watching them from their neighbour's roof. Two women in dirty saris with infants on their hips and a couple of bare-chested young men in lungis. The men seemed to have just rinsed off and were airdrying while unabashedly ogling Janne and Sofia. One of the women was holding a large tub of water in her hands, as though frozen mid-chore.

"Must be the neighbours' staff." Sofia giggled. "You didn't seriously think we were going to be alone, did you? In Bangladesh?"

Janne laughed loudly and shook his head.

"Bloody hell! It's just like in Lalpara. They just stare and stare. It certainly is . . . different, isn't it? The way they never look away, it's hard to relate to. Cultural differences . . ."

Janne waved to the little group, which was no more than thirty feet away. No one waved back. Even the big luxury houses were built close together in Dhaka, and life unfolded in parallel on the roofs and in the houses proper. Most people who lived in the big villas had live-in staff, Sofia had been given to understand. Sometimes they lived behind the garage, but often they were on the roof. Waving to each other wasn't normal behaviour. Watching was. If there was something interesting to see, that is. And right now, there was.

Janne tried to pick up where they'd left off. An amused smile was playing in the corners of his mouth and he kept half an eye on their audience.

"Right, you were asking about the children. Nazreen's a gem. Incredible, actually. She's not vague like Shjuli was, she feels solid to the core. Her English is better than Hanif's, she plays and draws for hours with Noella and Teo seems like he can't get enough of her."

Sofia was taken aback. It wasn't usually that easy. Noella often took a while to warm up to new people. And Teo, he was her little boy. But she pushed aside the pang of jealousy she felt at a stranger spending so much time with her children. She'd done it before. And having a nanny who took to the children was obviously better than one who kept them at arm's length. Like Shjuli, she had almost seemed scared of them.

"Amazing! And can she swim? I'm so worried whenever the ayahs are at the pool. You heard about that little Canadian boy who drowned with his ayah just standing there, watching, right?"

"I didn't exactly make her take a swim test. But she's resourceful, Nazreen. I trust her. She's not as wishy-washy as the other ayahs, there's some fire in her. She sets boundaries and takes initiative. Babul at the embassy is her cousin, by the way, did I already mention that?"

"You did, though I'm not sure that's much of a merit," Sofia replied, pulling the meat out of a lobster claw. "He's one of the most unctuous, slimy people we have. The only initiative he ever takes is to suck up to Siv and Moberg. Really, he's the worst sort. He wouldn't jump in the water to save his own mother, take my word for it!"

Janne topped up their glasses and then fixed Sofia intently.

"Tell me! What's going on in your life? What are the auditors saying? And does it feel good to be rid of Moberg for a while?" He took her hand and kissed it. "My beautiful woman, what do you do all day? How do you spend your time when you're not where you ought to be, with me?"

Sofia smiled and took a deep breath. The stress of the past few days had formed little knots in the back of her neck and now she could feel the wine helping her to unwind. She and Janne should talk about their everyday goings-on much more frequently. They had to try to rebuild that intimacy. But where to start?

"I heard Vanja's taking an interest in Beppin? Siv seems to have moved on, now she's remodelling the embassy instead. She has got in her head that we need more room upstairs so now there's cement mixers and architects and . . ."

"Yes, Vanja's fun. She's determined to get Beppin's disabled daughter into a school. She stops by every morning now and buys a cup of tea and a pastry from him. And I showed her my Alor Desh pictures. She got me thinking a gallery around here might want to exhibit them. Vanja's full of ideas."

"Great! But keep the Alor Desh thing on the low burner. The audit is . . . catastrophic." Sofia sighed. "The whole organisation seems to be leaking like a sieve and there are serious concerns about Khadija Anam herself."

"You're joking." Janne looked surprised and disappointed. "My god, Siraj, the children, Khadija . . ."

He trailed off and sat in silence, spinning his wineglass.

"It's not entirely uncommon," Sofia tried to explain. "It's a lot of money for poor people. The bookkeeping is generally subpar. They seem to have a lot of employees on their payroll who don't exist in real life. So who pocketed the salaries? The organisation claims to have purchased vehicles that don't exist. There are a number of bank accounts we didn't know about. Several of the lawyers who handle the land right cases in the local courts report being paid much less than what the organisation has logged. And so on and so forth. I have . . ."

Janne cut her off.

"But Khadija. Have you talked to her yourself? She did imply they were under threat, precisely because the work Alor Desh does is so dangerous. They're challenging both the mullahs and big landowners. I read an independent report written last autumn, did you see it?"

Janne sounded eager. Sofia shook her head.

"Then you really have to read it. It compares members of Alor Desh and regular farmers. The report shows that in areas where Alor Desh is active, people are more literate, they eat better, give birth to bigger babies, are less sick, have higher incomes and a more gender equal view of family life than in other places. The report also makes clear that Alor Desh is, financially speaking, an effective way for the state to handle the land right issue. The landless farmers are given help to protect important land from landgrabbers."

Janne looked enthusiastic. Sofia had heard of the report, but she hadn't had time to read it. She did, however, unlike Janne, know it made no difference how effective and good the organisation was. If it had corruption problems, it wouldn't get financial support. In Tanzania, Sofia had been revolted by the amount of money that ended up in the wrong hands.

"Janne, I know Alor Desh does amazing work. But if the employees also pocket part of the aid money, it's game over. We can't support a corrupt organisation."

Sofia wiped her mouth with a white linen napkin and poured herself a glass of water from a pitcher. "It's disappointing. I really liked Khadija. It's scary to imagine she might have . . ."

"So SwedeAid's position is that all corruption is the same?" Janne's question was belligerent. Sofia looked up.

"Corruption is corruption. Yes. Where else are we supposed to draw the line?"

"You could put a bit of effort into finding out the truth when it's a question of a very successful organisation, for example. Results! Aren't results what counts these days? That you get a good return on your investment? And here they are – outstanding results!"

"Janne," Sofia sighed. "I'm tired. This is part of a bigger discussion. Results, sure, of course, but can you imagine the headlines? The tabloids: Swedish tax money embezzled in Bangladesh. Award winner's corrupt organisation gets funding, despite proven corruption."

"Hold on a minute," Janne broke in and put both his hands up like stop signs. "Are you saying Swedish tabloid headlines determine the fate of the char people? Are you saying *that's* what's happening here? That you foreign aid people care more about avoiding scandal than maximising the impact of the aid? That makes me incredibly disappointed, to be honest, Sofia. I'm convinced that if you asked Joe Regular if he was prepared to tolerate a bit of corruption in one of the world's most corrupt countries as the price paid for some of the money getting to where it's needed, he would understand."

"Ha!" Sofia laughed coldly. "Not a chance! Your Joe Regular has an extremely naïve notion of what we do. People get upset when they realise we have administrative costs, for God's sake – 'the money should be going straight to the poor, not to Swedish bureaucrats'." She mimicked the whinging of an old lady and angrily set her water glass down. "What are we supposed to do? Just hand them bags full of money? How's that working out in oil-rich countries? It would be a disaster! People don't get that the problem isn't a lack of money, it's finding functional ways of distributing it. Administrative costs are what *prevent* things like this from happening! With more admin, in the sense of staff, we would have been better able to keep an eye on the money and support people like Khadija Anam."

Sofia was upset and for a moment forgot how tired she was. Janne had touched on something pivotal, something that had bothered her, too. That there were never enough resources to get at the nuances and complications, the many layers inevitably involved in each individual case. A slimmed-down bureaucracy engendered a black-and-white approach. Like with Beppin. Like now, with Khadija Anam. But at the same time, it wasn't as simple as Janne wanted to claim, either. And to make things worse, she felt like Janne was sticking his nose in her business, again. Once again, like a child, he was pointing out that the emperor had no clothes, while she had to take on the thankless task of trying to prove otherwise. She pushed her plate away dismissively when Janne hurled another question at her.

"Sure, but, Sofia. For God's sake, you can't let the tabloids set the agenda! What do you think is best for the people in the char delta? If you . . ."

"Janne." It came out sharper than she had intended, but at the same time, Sofia felt Janne's overflowing, insistent, puerile, make-the-world-a-better-place questions had to be beaten back. She leaned forward across the table.

"Are you trying to get me fired, or what? Like turning Siv against us isn't enough? You want me take on all of SwedeAid as well? I'm trying to make a career for myself and picking impossible fights is not the way to get ahead. You should know that."

Just then, a grey mass of clouds slid in front of the moon, plunging the terrace in darkness. Of the hundreds of tea lights, only a few were still burning. The silent shadows on their neighbours' roof scattered when the blonde woman got up and left the table. Janne was left to blow out the last of the candles.

14

"Rifat! Wake up!"

Having fallen asleep on the wooden bench outside Meena's window, Rifat was roused by Meena's voice. His face lit up when he spotted her in the window.

"Meena, I've been so worried, please . . ."

"Thick ache, I'm okay. I don't want to talk about it. You saved my life, Rifat." Her face disappeared, a moment later she was standing next to him in the alley.

"You saved my life and you'll always be my brother, understand? Rifat-bhai. I never, ever want to think about it again. Now we're going to do new business, we're going to be rich. Together. So you have time to learn to read properly and so your Amma can go see the doctor. I'm going to save enough to move back to my village."

Rifat nodded eagerly, then looked away.

"Patel doesn't want us working for him anymore. He says he doesn't want . . . well, Miraj seems to have threatened him."

"Good, we don't want to work with him either. Who wants to make money for Patel? Patel has no interest in us getting get rich, does he? I have a much better idea."

While Meena slipped away from Nazreen and Rifat during her days-long hibernation, her thoughts had moved back and forth across time and space like feelers, trying to make sense of her short life. She'd tried to discern how the mosaics formed new patterns, tried to grasp the meaning of those patterns. It was different now. Garishly bright tiles from her time in Dhaka had been interspersed with peaceful, luminous images from back home. She'd dreamt she was back in her parents' house, that she'd sat on the veranda on a sunny autumn day, cleaning fish, or letting her feet slide about in the mud the monsoon brought. Mokta had been there, always Mokta in the foreground. Like a part of the village, a part of their childhood. One moment, her big sister had been sitting on the bottom step by the pond, combing out her long black mane, hair by hair. She had teased Meena, splashed her, the evening sun in her eyes. Squinting. Another time, the picture had been of Mokta helping their mother put the rice out to dry, yelling at Meena for sitting in the big mango tree with the boys. Other times, flashbacks from the abandoned marketplace had shattered the light. The inexorability of Miraj's unyielding strength, the powerlessness she'd felt. The vulnerability. He was so dangerous. So superior. A black, sharp, shard she couldn't afford to forget.

Slowly, some of the pieces had settled into comprehensible, logical patterns. She saw clearly that life in Dhaka provided business opportunities, but also that her business dealings were precarious. They attracted the Evil Eye. Why had Allah made her life so hard? Why had he given her the gift of seeing how money could be made? Boys were supposed to know things like that, not girls. Was he going to let her be successful in the future? Or was he going to use Miraj to punish her? A little while longer, just a little while longer in Dhaka. Fifty thousand taka. Then, she swore to herself, she would return to the village. She pictured what life in the village would be like. A house near her parents where no one could hurt her. A small shop in Rajigonj. A kind, educated husband who let her run a business. A dignified life close to Allah. Maybe children of her own to sit in the mango tree.

That was when the new ideas had come to her, they had seemed so obvious. The plans for how she could do good business in Dhaka quickly and then move back home. Her pulse had started racing. She ran calculations in her head, considered what she'd seen and pondered how to maximise the difference. The difference, that mindboggling space between what she paid for things and what she could sell them for. What goods would get her the biggest difference?

During her many purchasing tours of Dhaka, Meena had visited Sadarghat, the port where goods from all over the world were unloaded, several times. Hundreds of small wooden skiffs steered by means of a single oar jostled with each other, darting hither and thither between rusty ferries and freighters. She'd also wandered around New Market, gaping at its overflowing stands. Dhaka was one big shop, in which one unnecessary commodity after another seemed to find a buyer. Meena was dumbfounded. Vegetables were necessities, everyone had to eat. And maybe plastic sandals and toothpaste. Spices, of course, and salt. But everything outside of that was incomprehensible, riddles that contained answers she couldn't begin to guess at. Doorways to another way of life that made her uneasy. She wanted to understand, but when she asked, people usually brushed her off. It alerted them to the fact that she wasn't from Dhaka.

Keyrings. Trivets. Chew toys for dogs. Mobile phone cases. Foot powder.

"My dear, that's not something you're ever likely to need."

Luggage trolleys. Credit card holders.

"Get lost, you can't afford this."

Sunglasses. Insoles. Laptop bags.

Who invented these things? They didn't exist in the village. There, you could get what you needed, just about. But the deluge of things you could buy and sell in the city seemed endless.

In the end, it was Nazreen who gave her the new idea. She'd come home one night and crawled in next to her as usual. Then she'd started talking about her day.

"I'm an ayah now, do you realise what that means, Meena?" she'd asked. "I make seven thousand taka a month, can you even imagine? Seven thousand! Granted, I have to give Babul his share for recommending me, but I still get to keep six thousand."

Meena hadn't responded, but she'd started counting.

"The family's really nice and the children are adorable. Completely white! And when I work evenings, they pay me overtime. Can you even believe that? More money if I work evenings. Bhalo!"

Meena had noticed Nazreen changing. She was enthusiastically waving her hands about as she spoke. Then a waft of something unfamiliar, a sharp, toxic smell.

"Manicure and pedicure," she'd explained, giggling, when Meena finally turned around and asked what the smell was. "You wash the old polish off and put new polish on. Then it has to dry. Like this." She'd spread her fingers in the air and shown Meena her hands, let her touch the coarse file and shown her how to use a special tool to push the cuticles down.

But the decisive difference wasn't the polish or Nazreen's unfamiliar-looking hands, not the colours and not the shape of her nails. Meena looked into her sister's eyes, looked and looked and noticed something new in them. Nazreen's unadulterated delight. Her desire. An opportunity.

Rifat was trying to tell her how worried he'd been and how happy he was to see her up and about in his hoarse voice, but Meena was already on her way.

"Come with me, I want to show you something."

She hailed a rickshaw and signalled for Rifat to get in.

"I want to show you something I've noticed," she explained when half an hour later they reached a dusty, flat lot next to the main road to Savar. "Hundreds of buses depart from here at six every morning. It's the big garment factories' shuttles. They come back around eleven every night, and the girls are paid once a week."

Meena watched Rifat sceptically take in the pot-holed, dusty lot. A dog was staggering around in the sun and a grey creature approached them with its hand outstretched. Meena ignored the beggar and looked intently at Rifat.

"What are we supposed to sell?" he asked. "Tomatoes? Cauliflower?"

"No, silly!" Meena gave him a shove. "We're going to pool all our savings and make a fortune, isn't that what I just told you? We're going to sell manicures and pedicures to the garment girls!"

And then she added, almost to herself.

"I'm not going to let them break me. I'm going to make my fortune here in Dhaka. And then move back home. Inshallah."

*

Janne hiked Teo up on his hip and decided to forego the lift in the swanky apartment hotel and instead walk the four floors to where the Strömbergs lived. Partly because he didn't want to get trapped if the city suffered one of its frequent afternoon power cuts, partly because he knew he needed the exercise. Tennis a few times a week wasn't enough and right now his weight was on the wrong side of fifteen stone. He felt he'd developed man boobs and his knees were always aching.

He'd planned to do a lot more walking, but the heat and the dust and the constant offers from rickshaw drivers had prevented him. Besides, without sidewalks, there was a constant risk of falling into the sewers that ran along the edge of the asphalt. The few times he'd tried to walk, Nizamuddhin had been offended. Once he'd insisted on driving along behind him. Which is why Janne usually slunk into the backseat even when he wasn't going far at all. And Nizamuddhin's musings on life in Dhaka were both amusing and alarming. Today, his focus had been politics.

"If you have a lot of money, you have to go into politics, it's that simple. Otherwise who would protect your money?" he'd asked in broken English, shaking his head.

Malena Strömberg was the mother of two of Noella's best friends from the club, a pair of spirited twin girls. Their father Olle worked for Ericsson and Malena ran the aerobics sessions at the Nordic Club. Janne had often thought to himself that they ought to be couple friends. Mr and Mrs Strömberg were roughly Janne and Sofia's age, well-educated, from Stockholm and their children were close. Yet even so, it just hadn't clicked.

Malena had told Janne several times she hated Bangladesh and the only reason she was there was her husband's career, and the generous deal the company had been able to offer them as a family. "The Package", Malena had called it. "The Package" would make it possible for them to buy a house in a nice Stockholm suburb when the two years of her husband's contract were up. Malena also told anyone who would listen that she had been inches away from making partner at the big architecture firm where she'd worked before agreeing to move to Bangladesh to further her husband's career. She'd explained that her condition for moving had been that she be allowed a shopping trip to Bangkok every three months, or she would take the children and move back home.

"Isn't it primitive here, Janne? Don't you think? The way they stare, right? And all the strange diseases you see. There's this deformed old crone living in our backyard. Have you seen the lepers? Didn't the invention of penicillin pretty much take care of leprosy?"

Her favourite phrase was that Bangladesh was "like the eighteenth century, but with mobile phones".

Janne always found it hard to breathe after spending an afternoon by the pool with Malena. She was so obviously unhappy about her situation and her negativity was contagious. It made it hard for him to see anything good about Bangladesh. A lot of the things she said were, after all, true.

"This fucking heat, and the dust! Everything's broken and ugly. Everything! All the poor people constantly pushing and prodding you. You can't even go outside. And no one knows any real English. They pretend to, they certainly do that! Pretend, deceive and lie. But understand, no, not so much."

"They're a thoroughly honest people," Janne tried to object once. "They don't deliberately deceive, they're just trying to please. I think it's a privilege to live . . ."

"Privilege! You're not serious! New York's a privilege, London's a privilege, maybe Vietnam and China, maybe, but Dhaka . . . Do you know what Dhaka is? A punishment! If not for The Package, I wouldn't have even considered setting foot in this cesspool. Show me one, *one* beautiful building!"

"Parliament," Janne offered, aware that architects in particular liked Louis Khan's modern brutalist fortress in central Dhaka.

"Fine, maybe. But beyond that?"

Janne's plan was, therefore, to extract Noella quickly so as to avoid Malena and her complaining entirely. But Janne knew he was trapped the second the maid opened the door. She was brusquely shoved aside and the blonde Swede filled the doorway.

"Janne – today is looking up! Welcome! Can I offer you a glass of wine? Or a cappuccino? Yes, a proper cappuccino, home-ground beans brewed in a fancy Jura machine. You have to come in for a chat! And I finally managed to install my Höganäs tiles, that's a legitimate cause for celebration! Vanja's here, we've been doing yoga, haven't we, Vanja?"

Vanja appeared behind Malena, dressed in a purple yoga outfit. Her hair was pulled back into a bun and two mats were rolled out on the living room floor.

"Would you like to do the sun salutation with us, Janne?" Vanja said after giving Janne a hug. "Malena's getting very limber. Yoga's unbelievably good for the circulation, I can just feel my energy levels rising."

Janne declined Vanja's offer but accepted the cappuccino. Vanja asked if she could have a glass of wine instead and Malena disappeared into the kitchen.

Vanja led Janne into the flat, where he'd already been shocked at how Malena had managed to move a piece of Stockholm to Dhaka. Every single piece of furniture was Swedish. Glossy Swedish interior design magazines were spread out like a fan on a low coffee table. Trendy white rugs covered the floor. If it hadn't been for the pink marble floor and a peculiar little stage in one corner of the room, it might have been Stockholm. He could hear the girls playing on a terrace and let Teo run out to join them. An ayah received him.

In the kitchen, Malena was stroking a large wall covered in small, light blue tiles that did look unmistakeably Swedish with a pleased look on her face. A large espresso machine and a red KitchenAid loomed in one corner of the room.

"Now! I can finally breathe again! The Bangle tile in here made me feel sick. We brought a crate of Höganäs tiles in our moving container, but we haven't been able to get hold of grout until now. I thought they'd have stuff like that here, I mean, quality stuff. But . . . silly me . . . I didn't know this was Bangladesh, land of cheap materials. Everything, *everything*, is second-rate here, the people, the materials, the houses, the food." She shook her head, annoyed, and looked back and forth between Janne and Vanja seeking agreement. Janne felt vaguely uneasy and deliberately refrained from nodding. Malena noted his silent protest. She looked at Vanja for a second and seemed to come to some kind of decision.

"Do you think we should show Janne, Vanja? Our secret?"

"I think we should," Vanja replied. "Janne's the kind of man who might understand."

She giggled and burrowed into Janne's arms. Janne put a friendly arm around her. She stroked his stubble. "Janne's in touch with his anima, his feminine side, aren't you, Janne?"

They filed past Malena's new tiles and walked through a room behind the kitchen. Behind two big chest freezers, a small passageway led into darker parts of the flat. In the passageway, the marble floor and white walls turned into grey concrete and Janne glimpsed a bed in a windowless little box room.

"It's a space where the maid and the ayah can rest, which they certainly do every time I turn my back. But we don't want them living here. It's important to have at least a semblance of privacy," Malena commented in passing as she stepped out onto a narrow balcony meant to air out clothes. The balcony was shaded and faced the back of the building. It had an unobstructed view of a slum area consisting of about thirty small shacks. A skinny cow was chewing dry twigs and a man was sitting in the middle of the courtyard, breaking the necks of chickens. When you saw the slum shacks from above it was clear their roofs were used for storage, crammed full of water containers, sacks, tyres and bundles of firewood.

"Look!" Malena turned to Janne, eyes sparkling. "My very own Bangla docusoap. How do you like it? My favourite is that woman over there, see?"

Janne followed her finger and saw whom she meant. Sitting in a corner of the yard was a hefty woman with no lower body. She was propped on a wooden cart with four wooden wheels and wrapped in a dirty sari. Several young children in tattered dresses and trousers were romping around her. An infant was asleep in her cart. She was shouting at the children, berating them, but every once in a while, she burst into laughter. She picked the infant up with surprising tenderness, gave it a kiss and then carefully put it back down.

"I'm mesmerised by them," Malena said slowly. "I don't know what's so compelling, but I can stand here and watch them for hours. Look at how they've done their roofs. As far as I can make out, the metal sheets are basically like lids. It has to be fiendishly hot inside, no? How are the houses ventilated? Doesn't it rain in during the monsoon?"

She continued to point and expound on the design of the shacks and Janne suddenly realised the jumble of metal sheeting, wooden boards and tarpaulins formed seven or eight distinct households.

"They should sort out proper run-off from the roofs. As it is, the water runs straight down from next-door's wall onto their roof. And then straight in through the cracks, I suspect."

Janne could tell she was thinking hard. Vanja was leaning on the railing, letting her wineglass dangle in the air. Now the woman seemed to be playing some kind of game with the children. They threw themselves at her misshapen body, she tickled them and then they tried to get away. Since she couldn't go after them, they fell over themselves with laughter. Meanwhile, the woman was also trying to clean vegetables laid out in front of her.

"Look, corn," Malena whispered. "Every night, she makes dinner and as the sun sets, the older children come back, ten-year-olds and children in their lower teens. And then they all eat together. Isn't that exciting? Or am I losing my mind?"

"I recognise some of the older children from the slum school," Vanja said. "I was here the other night and realised this is where both little Manish and Feruza sleep. But why?"

"No idea. She can't be their mother," Janne, who was watching the woman with interest now, too, replied. "But they seem to have a nice time?"

"Exactly! That's it! It looks homey, somehow. Everyone sleeps in that tiny shack. They all help push her in there when it gets dark. Some nights, they light a small kerosene lamp so I can see inside."

Malena pulled a face.

"Insane, no? I, Malena Strömberg, one of Sweden's most promising young architects, is stalking poor people! To be honest, I feel like going down there to help them set up a run-off mechanism with gutters. Otherwise what will it be like inside when it rains?"

Janne laughed and put his arm around her and gave her squeeze. Vanja seized the opportunity to wrap her arms around his waist and purred like a cat.

"Janne, weren't you considering teaching at the slum school? A bit of English? You can see for yourself how adorable the children are."

Janne laughed quietly and shook his head. They stayed on the narrow balcony in an uncomfortable triple embrace Janne didn't know how to withdraw from. Instead, he focused on the scene below. The deformed woman managed to coax a girl no older than Teo into fetching a tin bowl from the house and put the vegetables in it. She ruffled the girl's hair and slyly poked her belly, making her laugh. Then she yelled at a boy who was holding the matches wrong as he tried to light the cooking fire. Janne smiled at the boy's grimace. Just then, he spotted a familiar figure. With determined steps, a few feet in front of his young wife and with Tomelilla on his arm, Siraj from Alor Desh entered the courtyard.

*

Arthur absently played with his camera. After considering his dad for a moment, his plan suddenly seemed fool proof. The ambassador was sitting at a table by the pool under an umbrella with his laptop open in front of him. Arthur had persuaded his dad to relocate from the middling Kathmandu Guesthouse to the much swankier Yak & Yeti. Now, they were parked by the turquois pool. Books and dictionaries were piled high on the table around the ambassador, who from time to time emitted a pleased grunt. He didn't seem to notice the loud American family occupying the tables around his. His glasses had slipped down to the tip of his nose and his hair was dishevelled.

Arthur got up from his recliner and walked over to Moberg, holding his camera.

"Dad."

Moberg looked up, as though roused from a dream, blinking at his backlit son.

"Yes, my boy?"

"Dad. Do you really want to go trekking? I mean, honestly?"

"Well, I don't know about want to. But I feel like we did promise mum. And it'll be good, don't you think, to stretch our legs a little?"

"Sure, but remember when I was little? When mum made vegetarian lasagne and we binned it and went for hamburgers? Remember? In Vienna?"

Arthur sat down at the table and let his camera rest between his knees. One of his legs was shaking restlessly. Moberg smiled, embarrassed.

"Yes, I remember. We made a pinkie swear we'd never . . ."

"Alright, so now I have an idea. Let's do the same thing again, but here. We're not going to let mum down. But we're going to bin the vegetarian lasagne."

He laid out his plan.

Arthur could tell Moberg was sceptical. He smiled like a schoolboy and abashedly shook his head. It irked Arthur that his dad seemed so scared of his mum. And Moberg really was hesitant.

"You mean we should trick her? No, look, that . . ."

"You're scared of her, aren't you?"

Arthur let the question crack like a whip.

"Scared. Of my own wife? No, really. It's about respect. Vanja really wants us, you and me . . ."

"Yes, you and me. She wants us to do something together, that's what she wants. So we'll take some pictures, and then you can sit here and read and I'll relax by the pool. Everybody wins!"

"What Vanja had in mind was more . . ."

"What mum had in mind. Don't you have a mind of your own?"

Arthur refused to back down. Moberg looked uncomfortable.

"Maybe we could do a shorter trek? Right, Arthur? And sure, why not take some pictures when we do?"

"No. You're in or you're out." Arthur crossed his arms firmly. "Either we spend three days hiking up the Himalayas and you won't read a single book and I will hate every second. Or, we take the next hour and snap some pictures. I'll get the backpacks and zinc paste. I have this whole thing figured out."

Arthur got up and changed tactics. He boxed his dad's shoulder and laughed.

"Dad, come on! One hour, then you can spend three full days with your dictionaries! And I promise, I swear, mum will never find out. I swear . . . pinkie swear!"

He held his pinkie out to his dad like when he was little and they went behind Vanja's back. Moberg smiled, shook his head but then slowly raised his hand and linked pinkies with his son.

"Alright, Arthur. Pinkie swear! But not a word to Vanja ever!"

*

Noella and Teo had several pairs of shoes each, different shoes for different activities, Nazreen had noted. Sandals, trainers, thin shower shoes, plastic shoes, leather shoes, patent leather shoes. Nazreen tried to keep things tidy, lining all the shoes up neatly under the hooks under the stairs. Suddenly, she went stiff. Boss and Madame Sofia were fighting in the living room. Madame Sofia had come home for lunch for once and she and Boss had talked and talked and talked. They'd sounded angry, Nazreen thought. Or was it just the Swedish language that made it sound like they were growling and hissing at each other? Through the hallway, she saw the blonde woman angrily picking up a stack of papers and shaking them in Boss's face. Boss spread his arms and seemed to be trying to explain something.

After a few minutes, Madame Sofia stormed up the large, curved staircase. She climbed the steps in long, fierce strides. Boss followed his wife as far as the bottom of the stairs and called something after her, then sighed and ran his hand through his long hair. Minutes later, Madame Sofia came back down, carrying a briefcase and a handbag. She paused on a step that made her the same height as Boss and unleashed a torrent of words at him. One of her hands chopped the air into pieces in front of her. Nazreen tried to make herself invisible. When Madame Sofia finally left, she slammed the big front door shut behind her. Nazreen could hear Nizamuddhin start the Jeep and drive away.

Boss stayed where he was and sighed again. A few moments later, he spotted Nazreen in the gloom under the stairs.

"Nazreen," he said with a little laugh and shook his head. "I'm sorry, I'm sorry, you shouldn't have to listen to us quarrelling."

He disappeared up the stairs but after a while he came back down, looking for her. He was annoyed.

"Nazreen, I have a few things I want to show you, okay? Something that's been on my mind. You must never, ever feed Teo with a knife again. Like yesterday? That can't happen."

He sounded severe and walked into the kitchen, motioning for her to follow. One by one, he laid out cutlery on the kitchen counter.

"Look, this is a spoon, and they come in two sizes. This is a fork, and this is a knife. Knives are sharp. Yesterday, you fed Teo with a knife. I'm thinking you thought it looked like a spoon?"

He was annunciating carefully. He looked stern. He chopped the air into pieces with his hand. Nazreen knew what he meant. Yesterday, all the spoons had been in the dishwasher, so she had grabbed a flat spoon instead. Same same but different, as people liked to say in Badda. But she didn't say that to Boss, she just nodded.

"So this is a butter knife. We don't use butter knives to feed children, okay? No knives in the children's mouths. Understand?"

Hanif was standing next to them as Boss kept explaining and explaining. Nazreen could sense he was enjoying the situation. He was nodding eagerly, agreeing with Boss, shaking his head disapprovingly when the knife was held out. Why hadn't he told her about the spoons and knives yesterday? He knew she didn't know what they were for. What if she were to tell Madame and Boss how much white sugar he used to make the food tasty? How much rice he pilfered for his own use?

Boss seemed to be on a roll now. He suddenly started talking about the henna tattoos. She wasn't allowed to do *mehndi* on the children's feet, either. She and Noella had had hours of fun tattooing their feet. They had painted dots and stars on Teo's chubby little toes. Both children had been enchanted.

"I've read children can have allergic reactions. Allergies. Do you know about allergies? Anyway, no more mehndi. Madame Sofia and I don't like it." He shook his head condescendingly and pointed to Nazreen's tattooed hands. "Not for the children. Pretty on you, pretty on adults. But not on children."

Nazreen felt confused after Boss left the room. She was making so many mistakes. And yet, no one was beating her. Reka had told her they might beat her, that you couldn't discount it. It made her feel happy and relieved. Surely it couldn't be that bad, then, the thing with the flat spoon instead of the regular one?

Nazreen felt happier than she had in a long time. Her worries about Meena had been weighing heavily on her. Her sister had just lain in bed, staring at the wall, day and night, always with that slum boy Rifat right outside the window. Then she'd recovered overnight. All of a sudden, she'd simply got up and headed out into the city. She'd told Nazreen she needed to take five thousand taka from the plastic box to restock her goods, explaining that she'd spotted a new business opportunity. Nazreen had hesitated at the enormous sum at first, it was almost their entire savings. In the end, though, Meena had agreed that if Nazreen would only say yes, she could take two hundred and fifty taka and buy herself a pair of sandals.

"Two hundred and fifty taka for you and we send seven hundred and fifty taka to Amma and Abba. And I get five thousand, which will turn into ten thousand before you know it. What do you say to that?" Meena had divided up the money in that quick, jerky way of hers and with a determined, almost hungry motion shoved the notes into a small purse clipped to her waist.

"You'll see, while your sandals are worn out, my money will grow," she'd mumbled before striding out the door before Nazreen could have a proper chat with her.

During Meena's long hibernation, Nazreen had heard the rumours among the ramshackle houses of the narrow alleyway. She'd heard Meena's name spoken with horror and contempt and people whispering around the water pump. Was she aware of the scandal she'd caused? Nazreen had wanted to talk to her about it, about the fact that she might be in danger. That she had brought shame on them, even though she'd been saved by the old men at the last second. Back in the village, they'd probably have issued a fatwa against her, but here? In Badda? Were people different here? There was no village court to judge her, but what did the gossip amount to here, in the big city?

"So Meena's resting, eh? Well, I suppose she might need to after working so hard," Reka's best friend had exclaimed when she met Nazreen at the butcher's. She'd sniggered behind the burqa that covered her mouth and got several of their neighbours to join them with a significant look. "I don't want her working my husband!" someone else had called out, flapping her dupatta from side to side. Nazreen had walked away quickly, her head held high.

She'd tried to talk to Reka, but Reka had looked away and then failed to invite her when she and her friends made *pita*, rice cakes. And Babul had started avoiding her eyes and was acting strange and stiff whenever they saw each other.

"She has to get better, soon," he'd said one morning before leaving for work.

And now she was back on her feet. So long as she was alright, Meena could stand up for herself. Nazreen was sure of it. Nazreen smiled and picked up some of the children's Legos, which had ended up in the blue sofa. Everything was going to be fine.

*

Sofia returned Bjarne's serve with a deep, hard backspin. He missed it. Two-three. Sofia felt a wave of satisfaction at besting him. It felt symbolic.

Ever since Sofia and Antje's visit to Copenhagen Garment Inc., Bjarne had been trying to corner her for a private chat. He'd come looking for her at the club's Thursday barbecue, wrapping his hairy ginger arm around her before addressing the elephant in the room.

"Hi there, counsellor," he'd said in greeting. Sofia thought she could almost hear the big, ginger tomcat beating its tail against the ground. She'd felt he might as well have said "Hiya, love". But maybe she was overreacting. After all, Janne liked Bjarne.

"Such a shame you came to visit just when we'd received a bunch of big orders and everyone was working double shifts. The Chinese don't mess around, you know. We only have three weeks from order to delivery. That means bringing in people off the street, you realise. That woman must've been unwell."

"Unwell? Dehydrated, exhausted and starving was the doctor's verdict. And she hadn't been brought in from the street, she'd been working for you for a year. Have you seen her since her collapse? Dr Hassan calls it garment girl syndrome. Acute uterine infection that has spread to peritoneum and can lead to sepsis. She could have died. And your foreman wanted her kicked out!"

Sofia had turned on her heel and marched off, leaving a surprised Bjarne standing with his fork in an imported steak he'd meant to take off the grill. Nevertheless, he'd clearly wanted to continue the conversation. Two days later, Bjarne and his wife Tone had asked if they wanted to play lunch doubles and Janne, oblivious to the tension, had said yes. And so, here they were. She and Janne had a comfortable lead. Six-two, six-three and now two-three, Bjarne's serve.

Bjarne laughed at the lost point and walked up to the net for a bottle of water. He took a few big gulps before pouring the rest over his head. Snorting and spluttering, he turned to Sofia.

"Let me know when you're swinging by the factory next, yeah? I have big plans, we're adding three more floors to make sure we can accept all the orders we get from China. It's going to be nice and bright."

"China?"

Janne joined the conversation. One of the little ball boys handed him a bottle of water, too. There was a brief silence by the net.

"Yes, China. They order from us so they can take orders from Europe in turn. We do basic stitching, a lot of jersey and rib knit, T-shirts, underwear. No fuss. The Chinese do more complex work."

"The Chinese are investing in their garment industry. The Bangladeshi are stuck at the bottom of the pile because no one's willing to pay to train the workers or update the factories. The world's cheapest labour by far. Onwards and downwards!"

Sofia had walked up to them and was explaining to Janne in a cold ironic tone.

"And at the very bottom is where you operate, Bjarne, as I've come to understand."

Bjarne took a long swig of water then let out a hearty laugh. He pointed his bottle at Janne.

"Yes, or 'My servant has a servant', you know. That's what we say in Denmark. Is there a similar saying in Swedish?"

The two couples had resumed their positions on the court. Janne was preparing to serve. Before hitting the ball, he retorted.

"No, but we have 'Don't kick a person when they're down', maybe that's something to bear in mind? Or 'The leaves are flattest at the bottom of the pile'."

The ball sailed over the net, Tone quickly lobbed it back. Bjarne laughed and got into position to counter a quick return from Janne.

"Or, as we say in Denmark: 'The best way to help a poor person is not to be poor yourself', or . . ."

At this point, Bjarne had to back up quickly and missed his shot. Since it was his serve, he paused for a few seconds in the middle of the court, deep in thought. He bounced the ball a few times, a smile playing on his lips. Sofia was relieved to see Janne's impertinence had been taken the right way.

" . . . or 'Give a poor person an inch and they'll take a mile'. That's a nifty one, too. And true!"

Bjarne served and looked pleased with himself. He had to do it over, however, and took the opportunity to turn to Sofia.

" . . . and one for you, Counsellor. 'Give a poor person a fishing rod, not a fish.' Or whatever it is they say."

Sofia joined in Janne and Bjarne's banter. As she hit a hard backspin diagonally behind Bjarne, she nailed the verbal retort, too.

"Right, Bjarne, but aren't you the one who owns the fishing nets?

And hoards the entire catch and pays the fishermen nothing but dry fish tails? Isn't that the way of it?"

Bjarne laughed raucously again and huffed and puffed his way up to the net. He was dripping with sweat. His white tennis clothes clung to his body. He poured the last of his water over his head and shook it violently. Sweat and water rained down on the court. His wife snapped her fingers at a ball boy.

"More water, *paani*, water. *Jao*!"

The boy darted over to Bjarne with two foggy bottles of ice-cold water which he drank in greedy gulps. He pointed the bottle at Janne and Sofia, who had also approached the net to drink. With a sudden chill in his voice, he ended the game and the conversation.

"I'm sorry the woman was ill and would be happy to pay for her hospital bills. But I refuse to apologise for being a businessman. We pay the minimum wage. What more am I supposed to do? I'm not forcing people to work in my factories."

When she got back to the embassy, Sofia noted that Babul had already delivered afternoon tea to her office and realised tennis had taken longer than usual. Even though the exchange at the net had been light-hearted, their ideological differences and disparate worldviews couldn't have been more obvious. Sofia had felt immensely proud of Janne. It had made their victory feel all the sweeter. Like a joint rebuke of Bjarne's worldview. And minimum wage, sure. But what if the minimum wage was impossible to live off? She had to find out more about what the international pressure on garment factory owners looked like.

Sofia needed some time to think. She'd spent the morning preparing briefs for the conference on violence against women. The trick in situations like these was to keep all key stakeholders on board at all times. She'd learnt that during her time as a junior professional officer, a JPO, at the UN. Never make anyone feel run-over or left out, everyone had to feel like they were involved so they would want to advocate independently. Buy-in, she mused. Everyone had to feel like they had some ownership. Lasse had been inspired and engaged his extensive network at the Ministry of Foreign Affairs and SwedeAid. A phone conference with him and the caseworker at the Ministry had made her feel enthusiastic about their plan. Since they were going to invite both the State Secretary for Foreign Affairs and Sweden's Minister for Gender Equality to the conference and thus ensure it was a high-priority event, Moberg would be unable to throw up obstacles. All important emails had been cc'd to Moberg. Sofia had been relieved to note he hadn't even opened them. That officially put her in the clear. As chargé d'affaires, she was free to take his silence as tacit approval and both Lasse and the Ministry caseworker were listed as co-decision-makers in the document.

Suddenly, her phone dinged. Antje was wondering if they could go for a glass of red at the Bagha Club after work and discuss conference formats. The process had accelerated over the past few days and they needed to get on the same page regarding approach and specific topics. After her little confrontation with Bjarne, Sofia had also had a new idea. Would it be possible to designate the extremely low minimum wage within the garment sector a crime against women's human rights? Could "the right to a living wage" be a theme? Or would the government find that too provocative? Probably. Even so, Sofia wanted to pitch her idea to Antje. She did, however, realise tonight was when she and Janne had decided to head over to the American Club for a night of jazz. To do something just the two of them for once. Sofia gave her priorities three full seconds' thought. Then she fired off two brief texts.

"Absolutely, Antje, we have a lot to talk about. See you at eight at the Bagha Club, looking forward to it. S."

"Have to skip jazz tonight, work. Kiss the kids, S"

As the conference prep progressed, Sofia had realised how big an opportunity this was for her and how well her inner career compass had guided her. Again. If and when a high-level meeting took place, she would gain invaluable contacts within the entire UN sphere and be at the centre of Dhaka's donor circle. And who knew? Perhaps after a few more years in Dhaka, there would be a job offer from the UN? She would also get gold stars from both SwedeAid and the Ministry of Foreign Affairs for raising Sweden's profile on a topical issue like gender equality. And violence against women – so spot on! She had, as Mike had urged her at that conference in Nairobi, grabbed the ball and played it well. Back home in Stockholm, they would think of her as ambitious and brave for bringing up gender equality in a Muslim country.

"That'll show them," Lasse had commented from his smoking module in SwedeAid's basement, watching her manoeuvring. "Now we're the ones setting the agenda!"

She felt a twinge of guilt about Moberg over in Nepal, but quickly dismissed the feeling. He was about to retire and any reference from him would be irrelevant the next time she was on the job market. As she turned off her computer and went into the bathroom to reapply her mascara, contrition regarding Janne sitting at home in Baridhara, sneaked into the pit of her stomach. She looked her reflection in the eyes. Sometimes she forgot how livid she was with Janne, his betrayal and her humiliation. Like during the tennis match earlier, when the old warmth had returned. The two of them against the world. But he was the one who had decided to destroy everything, he and he alone. Anger rushed through her again, like so many times before, making the decision easy. It was okay. She wanted to see Antje. Janne owed her. Many times over.

Sofia exited the embassy at a quarter to eight, stepping into a balmy night. The instant fifteen-degree temperature change made her shoulders drop, releasing the tension in her back. The strong scent of the large-flower cacti planted outside the embassy enveloped the shiny embassy Jeeps. A gecko skittered away though the shrubberies. As she was the last to leave, she locked the door carefully with three different keys. The guards working the last few hours of the dayshift opened the gate for her with polite bows. She was immediately surrounded by three or four rickshaws that had been circling in the street outside, probably waiting for the last light to go out in the embassy.

"Madame, come, House 2, Road 3 Baridhara, I know," they told her. Sofia had long since stopped wondering how everyone always knew who she was and where she was going. Just as she was about to climb into one of the rickshaws, a high-pitched voice called out for her.

"Madame Sofia, my friend!"

A thin girl emerged from the shadows behind a tree next to the wall surrounding the embassy. It took Sofia a few seconds to realise who it was.

"Remember me? Rehana, your best friend?"

The girl fired off a radiant smile and for a second, her lazy eye managed to focus on Sofia.

"Rehana!" Sofia climbed out of the rickshaw and greeted Rehana. "Rehana from Copenhagen Garment Inc. Of course I remember you. What are you doing here? How is your mother?"

"I have been waiting for you, Sofia from Sweden. Can I speak English with you?"

"Of course you can speak English with me," Sofia answered the girl's clunky question. "But I'm in a hurry, I'm on my way to a meeting."

"No problem. Can I go with you a little?"

Sofia and Rehana jumped into the rickshaw and Sofia told the driver where she was going. She glanced furtively at the skinny girl, holding onto her seat with every ounce of her concentration. She noticed Rehana's shalwar kameez was less carefully made than her own. The garments weren't a matching set. A floral dress, bright green trousers and a striped yellow and orange shawl. She had no jewellery and no shoes.

"Have you been at work today?"

"Yes, Madame Sofia. I always work. Like you."

The girl beamed with her whole face and her lazy eye shot off into its own orbit.

"How's your mother?"

"Oh, she's tired, very tired. She started working again. But right now she's home taking care of my brothers. When will you visit us again?"

"Not tonight, but maybe on a Friday? Your mum has Fridays off, right? Can I bring my husband?"

"We would be so happy if you came, very really happy!"

Rehana smiled again, her face lit up from inside, beaming in the dark. Her white front teeth shone.

Sofia suddenly had an urge to put her arm around the girl, hug her, buy her a new shalwar kameez. Give her food and vitamins. Comb her long hair. Send her to school and watch her grow up. Yet even so, when Rehana moved her hand, Sofia's instant thought was "just don't beg, please don't start begging". But the girl wasn't begging. Sofia felt her thin hand scratch at her own, and suddenly they were holding hands in the rickshaw. Rehana looked up at Sofia and smiled contentedly.

"Sofia from Sweden, you are my friend. Rehana from Bangladesh is best friends with Sofia from Sweden, thik ache?"

When they reached the Bagha Club, Rehana gracefully jumped out of the rickshaw and was gone before Sofia could say goodbye. At the end of the street, she turned around and waved both arms above her head. Then she disappeared into the night.

*

Janne cursed inwardly. God damnit, Sofia. Here he was, all dressed up, feeling like an idiot. Stood up. He really was in the dog house, banished and rejected. Except when it suited Sofia. Then he was pulled back into the warmth again to enjoy the crumbs from her table.

Her terse text had felt like a swift kick to the shins. All afternoon, he'd been looking forward to the jazz night at the American Club. A really good band was playing and he'd showered and felt good. After the tennis match, he'd felt close to Sofia again, felt that old togetherness. It was the two of them against the world, after all. And yet. He found his mobile, pulled up the text and read it again. "Have to skip jazz tonight, work. Kiss the kids, S." He walked over to the outsized liquor cabinet in one corner of the living room and poured himself a large whiskey.

Sofia. The way she held him close, raised him up with her spirit and brilliance, the woman he never wanted to part with. Her way of approaching the world with integrity, her quick hand pushing strands of hair behind her big ears, her hipbones against his hands in the night. He loved life with her and wanted it back, along with all its constituent parts, exactly the way it had been before Camilla. He wanted to make things right and live close to her clear-sightedness and her obstinance, close to her quick mind and rough edges. All the facets that ensured he would never get tired of her. But he was constantly reminded of his own betrayal.

Camilla had been so unlike Sofia. Much more like his previous girlfriends, women who had laughed at his jokes, been eager to be seen and in exchange had given him a big platform. At least that was his older brother Mikael's analysis. More than anything, Camilla had always been there. Steadfastly by his side when the world around the school fell apart, willing to discuss his problems ad nauseam over lunch. And then over a pint. Sofia had had her hands full with the children and had barely listened to his problems with the school board.

"You're going to have to sort that out yourself, Janne," Sofia had sighed, too tired to pay attention to the details. "Let it go if you can't get people on your side. Don't take it so personally. Move on."

His first night with Camilla had been predictable. Exactly the kind of situation he should have spotted a mile away. They were supposed to go over plans for a staff training day and Camilla had suggested they meet at a restaurant near her flat in Sundbyberg. Sofia had been in Uppsala with Noella and Teo to visit her parents. And just like that, Sofia had faded into the background, yes, that's exactly what it had felt like. That strange displacement that had occurred, the gradual shift in perspective over a number of weeks. Today, it seemed incomprehensible. Sofia had suddenly seemed like a drab, disengaged secondary character who only had eyes for the children, and Camilla had become the main character instead, in luminous technicolour. Her brown eyes and soft curves had felt so uncomplicated, so right. She'd understood Janne, had listened to all his problems and readily offered refuge, sanctuary on a lonely night.

The next morning, Janne had woken up with the feeling of having broken a precious bowl. And yet, a tiny voice had told him: "These things happen. People cheat. You can fix it." And then they had carried on, almost unintentionally. It had been coincidental, happenstance. Camilla was picking something up on Södermalm. Camilla had won a night at Scandic Hotel in a raffle. Camilla needed help putting up a shelf. The whole time, he'd known it would have to end, deep down inside, he'd been hoping Sofia would catch him and be jealous. Because his intention had always been to fix his marriage. The lead role belonged to Sofia.

If only Sofia hadn't been so tired all the time, if only she'd been able to listen to him. Janne felt like she'd pushed a giant pause button in their relationship. He needed more. He needed intimacy and Sofia's attention, she really had kind of driven him into Camilla's arms, he sometimes thought to himself. And yet, he had been determined to end his affair with Camilla. He was never going to step out of bounds again. He was going to fix it. The whole world was full of people who had cheated and found their way back to each other. Right?

That's what he'd told himself. That had been his mantra when he met up with Camilla one last time to end things. If only she hadn't cried, and if only his sister-in-law Helene hadn't been visiting Stockholm with her book club and happened to walk by just then.

It was almost two years ago now. The betrayal had been so brutal.

"You're going to have to do what little kids do, *do* your sorry, not just say you're sorry," Helene had told him when, clearly shaken, she'd called him up later to let him know she was going to tell Sofia what she'd seen. "Why are you kissing strange women in cafés, Janne?"

Helene, who was a teacher at a Christian nursery in Jönköping, and his older brother Mikael had been shocked at what she'd stumbled upon, that much was obvious. Just as shocked as he himself was. It was undignified, beneath the two of them. Sofia was the sun in his sky, his winning lottery ticket.

They'd talked and talked and talked. Sofia had taken him back and he'd tried to *do* sorry in every way he could. He wanted to keep his family together, live with Sofia, at any cost.

It was only months later Janne realised Sofia wasn't just stubborn when it came to work. She was a resentful goat who held a grudge about this, too. Even though she'd officially forgiven him, they hadn't been able to find their way back to each other after two years. What frightened him the most was that Sofia didn't seem very interested in him anymore. He had somehow lost his appeal. It was no ordinary bowl he'd broken, it was a crystal vase that had smashed into a thousand pieces all over their lives.

The ice in his whiskey melted quickly. He'd asked the new ayah, Nazreen, to stay longer, so he had a babysitter. Should he pop by the American Club anyway? Or just go down to the Nordic? His options were rather limited, metropolis or no metropolis. With a wry smile, he got up to pour himself another whiskey. God damnit, Sofia. Was he supposed re-conquer his own wife? Janne paused in the middle of the room with his glass in his hand, unsure, thoughtful, searching. It felt like Sofia needed to find a way to respect him again. Like she'd used to. He had to make himself her focal point somehow, place himself where she would notice him. Build up her interest.

Springing into action, he told the ayah she could reach him on his mobile and called for Nizamuddhin.

"Drive me to Madame Malena's house. But drop me behind the garage, in the slum."

"Okay, Boss. You always know what you're doing, good!"

"I'm not so sure that's true," Janne mumbled.

The area around Malena and Olle's building was full of life. Kerosene and onion and ginger intermingled to form a distinctive smell Janne had started thinking of as an integral part of Dhaka. Out by the road, a group of young men were selling glasses of tea and cigarettes. Janne stopped and bought one of the latter. Why not? He'd been a heavy smoker before Noella was born. He hoped the young men wouldn't notice the whiskey on his breath. What was his plan here? Lingering by the stall, he sucked on his cigarette and ordered a glass of tea.

"Is it raining in Chicago?" the stall keeper tried to converse with him, but his friend shushed him and struck a collegial note instead.

"So, what's your PhD? What university. Harvard? Oxford?"

"Kalmar, top rated, much better than Harvard," Janne replied and blew out a cloud of smoke.

Even though it was late, people seemed to be on their way home from work. He saw people changing out of white button-downs into lungis and T-shirts in the courtyard. The disabled woman in her cart was no longer the only adult. Children were being washed in big troughs and wet clothes were being hung up to dry between the shacks. As the lights in the surrounding luxury flats winked out, one after the other, the people living around them lit small fires. Each family seemed to have their own kitchen, their own fire over which a cookpot balanced. Janne searched the gloom for Siraj and asked the children who curiously flocked around him. When he stepped into the courtyard, he was holding two of them by the hand. The grownups around the fire looked up at him and someone called out toward the shacks, making Siraj appear in the doorway of one of them.

"Janne-bhai," he exclaimed in surprise. "Assalum alaykum, what are you doing here?"

"Wa alaykum assalam, Siraj. Kemon acho? I saw you from one of those balconies the other day. We need to talk. What's going on? What are you doing in Dhaka?"

Siraj let out a clipped laugh and shook his head. He invited Janne into his shack as Fatima and Tomelilla slipped out. Janne greeted Fatima warmly and moved to give her a hug, but she backed away, her eyes bashfully lowered. When he bent down to enter their home, a rusty corrugated sheet of metal almost sliced his face open. Siraj called out at the last second.

"Watch out!"

Janne ducked and hunched over further to squeeze in unharmed. It was dark inside. Dirt floor and corrugated metal walls on three sides and along the one wall formed by the high-rise's white exterior stood a wooden bed. An emaciated woman was asleep on it, wrapped in a greyish sari. She opened her eyes when Janne entered, but soon closed them again.

"My great aunt," Siraj explained, stroking the old woman's cheek. "She lets us stay here, no problem."

"Tell me! What are you doing here? What's going on?" Janne made himself comfortable on an upside-down crate Siraj had quickly placed by the door for him. Siraj himself sat down on a smaller bed.

"I had to leave Barikhali for a while. They said they were going to hurt Tomelilla and even though I'm loyal to Madame Khadija and Alor Desh, I have my limits."

"Hurt Tomelilla?" Janne gasped. "What do you mean? Who's 'they'?"

Siraj gave him a searching look and shook his head.

"You don't know much about the world, Janne-bhai. Or not about Bangladesh. The audit your wife is conducting is not going to show the truth. Alor Desh has become far too powerful and successful, now other forces are striking back. Bad people, evil people."

"What?" Janne didn't understand what he meant. "You work to give the poor more say over the land, you teach women to give birth to fewer babies and you help people survive floods. Why would evil people take issue with that?"

"Because a lot of people in my country want to get their hands on that land. Why wouldn't they be interested in the most fertile soil in the world? And why would the mullahs want us to empower women?"

"You mean landgrabbers?"

"Well, we don't know, but that's our guess. Things are changing. Helicopters are landing. Landowning farmers suddenly sell up. And the courts are becoming increasingly difficult to work with. When we had land right conflicts before, we stood a decent chance of winning. Now, the land is inevitably awarded to big landowners who in turn sell it on. The small farmers and the people in the char area have no rights and so far, we're the only ones standing up for them. Now that we're going to be forced to close down Alor Desh, there will be no one to see to their interests."

"What do you mean close down?" Janne was startled. "Who's talking about closing down? Sofia . . ."

"The audit is going to uncover severe corruption on every level. I've been threatened because I refused to testify against Khadija, but both Mamul and Reihul have told lies about her because they want to stay in the village. Your wife's not going to be able to justify continued support for Alor Desh, it's that simple."

"But when Sofia finds out that . . ."

Siraj cut in.

"Besides, our programme to empower women has put the mullahs' backs up. Things are changing in the char area. Before, we were able to work with the mosques and everyone agreed that the char people needed help and that the women were unable to sustain so many pregnancies. But now . . ."

He trailed off and shook his head. Then he leaned forward and picked up a pinch of dirt from the floor. He held his hand out to Janne.

"The soil, you know. The soil and the food and the water and the women. How many people live in my country? One hundred and forty-five million? One hundred and sixty million? It's never going to work. Too many people want the land and no one's going to allow the char people to cultivate it. No one."

Janne stared at the dirt in Siraj's hand and tried to find something helpful to say.

"But surely, there has to, I mean, I'm sure Sofia can . . . I mean, the world's a complicated place, but we have to fight!"

"You fight! I have to protect my family. The mustaans said they would hurt Tomelilla unless I lie to the auditors. And the auditors, they walk around the village and hold meetings and don't understand a thing. Not a thing."

"So the mustaans are the local mafia?" Janne remembered what Khadija had told him when he visited Alor Desh.

"Yes, usually local thugs controlled by whomever can pay them. If you don't obey the mustaans, you're liable to turn up in a rice paddy with your throat slit. It happens all the time. Every one of our functionaries have been threatened or bribed to paint a picture for the accountants. And sure, some of it is true. Sometimes we have to pay bribes to survive, but, you know . . . this is Bangladesh. If you want to participate and educate and change the lives of the very poorest, you have to work with what is. Right?"

Janne nodded mutely. Siraj fell silent, too. Janne felt sweat trickle down his back and wondered whether the crate would be able to sustain his weight much longer. The woman on the bed whimpered and up by the ceiling he saw a rat scuttle along a bamboo pole. Siraj continued.

"I don't understand it. It's all so strange. We know our country and we know village life and we're doing the best we can to help make life bearable for people. Then you Westerners come in, with your money and your questions. Everything has to fit into your grids and tables, which seem incomprehensible to us. How are we ever supposed to explain all the things that go on in the villages?"

"Yes, for instance, I don't understand where the mullahs fit in?"

"I'm not exactly sure. All I know is that before, we were able to work with women's groups and advocate for allowing women to register as landowners or to have some say over money. But a few years ago, the mosques began to view us as a threat and some imams have been saying we're run by Westerners in their Friday sermons."

Janne let out a mirthless laugh.

"Well, the last part is not entirely untrue."

"But Khadija is Bengali."

"Sure, but the money is Swedish and British far as I know. But go on!"

"Either way, suddenly representatives from the local mosques wanted to sit in on our women's meetings and then their children were pulled out of school and sent to madrassas instead."

"So, Islamification, in other words?"

Siraj nodded.

"I'm Muslim myself, but this is different. A new wind is blowing. Money from the Gulf, guest workers returning from Dubai and the UAE who suddenly want their wives to wear full burqa. That's not Bangladesh. It's new. Before, we were Bengalis first and Muslims second. But now, I don't know."

They sat in silence for a while. Over in her corner, Siraj's great aunt moaned and turned over to ask for water. Siraj called Fatima who quietly entered with a scoop of water. She was carrying Tomelilla, who was wearing a little dress, on her hip. Siraj leaned forward, grabbed his daughter's foot and kissed it. Janne watched them.

"But what are you going to do now? Are you going to live *here*?"

Janne recalled Siraj's simple but bright house in Lalpara, the little veranda and the yard Fatima was always sweeping. The vegetable patch in the back where Siraj had proudly showed off rows of spinach and okra.

Siraj smiled at Janne's question.

"Don't worry, everyone lives like this in Dhaka. We're used to it. I'm going to look for work soon. But right now, I just want to lie low. Not even Khadija knows where I am. But she understands that I have to do what's best for my family."

"You mean you're going to desert Alor Desh?"

Siraj looked at him and his strangely light brown, almost yellow, eyes darkened.

"No, I mean I want to get out of this alive. A better question would be: are you going to desert Alor Desh?"

15

Nazreen picked up the large swimming bag from the floor and grabbed the children's bathing suits from the hooks under the stairs. The clothes smelled strongly of chlorine. Janne insisted on both the children and the bathing suits being rinsed every time they'd been at the pool. And yet, that smell. A proper bideshi smell, Nazreen mused. There were no smells remotely like it in the village.

She was starting to settle into the routines of the household. After lunch, she'd take a rickshaw to pick the boy up from his nursery school and in the early afternoon, the girl was dropped off by the school bus. If she was lucky, Boss might suggest they all go to the club. The children liked the pool and Boss usually played tennis.

Nazreen had got to know several of the other ayahs who frequented the club with their charges. She'd heard everything about the families they worked for. Many had congratulated her on her Swedish family. Scandinavians were the best, then the Dutch, Americans and Britons. But some Britons were apparently awful. Uppity and impossible to please. The worst employers were the Chinese, Japanese and Koreans, and Bangladeshi families, of course. They were the worst of the worst and treated their staff like animals. Unless you were lucky enough to work for a relative, then they were sometimes a bit more decent. It was odd, Nazreen mused. Working as an ayah in a bideshi family was a dream job, but in a Bangladeshi family it was slave work. Everyone knew it. Nazreen realised she'd been lucky.

She did a lap of the big living room and rearranged the big cushions on the sofa. There were photographs of the family on one wall. Nazreen stopped to study them. There was Madame Sofia with baby Noella in her arms in a snowy landscape. The baby was bundled up in red overalls and Madame's hair was hidden underneath a baggy hat. In another picture, Boss was kissing Sofia, standing on steps, surrounded by people. They looked happy and Sofia was carrying an armful of flowers. And in a tiny picture she could see a newborn Teo. All the frames were of different types and sizes. Were they unable to afford nice big frames, despite being so rich? The picture Nazreen liked the best was of the whole family surrounded by old people and several children. Nazreen assumed it was the extended family. She stepped in closer. Yes, Sofia looked like her handsome father, a tall, blond man who smiled broadly at the camera and had his arm around his daughter. Next to him, a fancy-looking woman holding Noella's hand. Noella looked tense. The old people standing around Janne looked older. His mother was a bit thickset and his dad had a beard. Both wore glasses and the man was holding a baby that wasn't Teo. Nazreen could tell one of the men was Boss's brother. Older brother? He looked like Janne but slimmer, more defined. His wife was looking up at him with a happy expression. She was redheaded like the child in Boss's dad's arms.

Nazreen chest ached at the thought of her own family. There was a picture like this of them somewhere. They'd gone to Rajigonj by rickshaw, everyone neatly combed and excited. It must have been when her younger brother Mostafar was born, before they realised he wasn't alright. Abba had been overjoyed at his firstborn son and decided it was finally worth having a proper family portrait taken.

Nazreen remembered how beautiful Mokta had looked, a young woman with two long, black, glistening plaits, her bright, beautiful face smiling into the camera. Nazreen had still been a girl, gangly and angular in her cousin's dress with frill. She and Meena had held each other's hands and their Abba had been seated imposingly at the centre of the picture with their little brother in his arms, like a zamindar, a big landowner. Their beautiful mother had bashfully stood diagonally behind him, with one hand resting on Meena's shoulder. An enormous castle with towers and turrets could be glimpsed behind them. Nurul had chosen it from the many backdrops available in the studio. He'd laughed happily when he picked it.

"This is the start of our royal line. Mostafar is born."

They'd bought a thick gold frame decorated with quotes from the Quran and the picture had been hung in the middle of one of the walls in their house. Later, Nurul had taken it down.

Since she still had some time before she had to pick up Teo at Wonderland, his nursery school, Nazreen went into the kitchen to chat with Hanif, but she soon regretted it. The chef always found things for her to do, as though he were the boss of her. She was never sure how to deal with it. The chef was at the top of the household's pecking order and a man, to boot. But could he order her about? She was employed as an ayah and maid, not as a kitchen helper.

"I'm glad you stopped by. Could you take the bin out? Here!"

The day's refuse had collected at the bottom of a plastic barrel that was supposed to be emptied into the big bin by the front gate. Nazreen wrinkled her nose, but did as she was told. Out by the gate, she emptied the plastic barrel into the big bin and then heard Beppin's voice from the tea stand outside the house.

"Apa, come here. Have a cup of tea on the house!"

It made Nazreen happy. Beppin was always kind and knew all the local gossip. Since she preferred passing the time in the shade with him to being in the kitchen with Hanif, she asked the guards to open the gate. As she walked toward Restaurant Beppin, she noticed a skinny arm reaching in through the bars of the gate to rummage through the refuse. An old, hunched woman disappeared down the street with her hands full of yesterday's food scraps from the Paulin household.

*

Babul was still in a daze on the floor when he heard someone coming. Could it be Meena coming back? Maybe she'd liked it, after all? Maybe this could be their secret? You never knew with girls like her, girls who had been around. There was quite a bit of talk about how they really liked doing it. He'd been overwhelmed by the force of his own lust, how violent it had been. How triumphant he'd felt pushing in between her legs. Like the other men, like a man among men. And she did live under his roof.

Ever since he'd heard about the attack, he'd been virtually unable to think of anything else. Images had kept flashing through his mind, disturbing him, taunting him, egging him on. He'd heard what Miraj and the boys had been allowed to do. He'd pictured her at night, envisioning her face contorted with desire. Felt her hips move in a way Reka's never did, thought about how she'd spread her legs for all those men, receiving them, moaning. Like a woman he'd seen in a forbidden film once. That's what she was like, Meena. A woman who knew how to enjoy herself.

So when she happened to stop by to fetch something while he was on his lunchbreak, it felt like an opportunity that was too good to pass up. He'd been friendly, he had. At first. They'd sat on the bed, talked about her business and then it was as though he'd caught fire. He was overcome with hunger. He'd started by asking her if she liked him. When she just laughed a little and got up to leave the room, he felt silly. Was that such a stupid question? Was there something wrong with him? She was a slut, everyone knew it now. What reason could she possibly have for not liking him? After all, he was the administrative assistant at the Swedish Embassy. And she was nothing but a slut. A slut who lived under his roof and went about with lots of different men. No longer fit to be a wife and mother. A plucked flower, a used up vessel. And yet, he'd wanted her, or maybe that was exactly why? He wanted her to say she liked him. If she'd just said yes, they might have been able to come to some kind of arrangement. He was surprised himself. That such a filthy girl could make him hungry. When he could do it with Reka any time he pleased?

So when she got up without answering, he asked again. And then he cut to the chase. Asked if he could have a go. Like everyone else. Could he have a go, too? Meena had looked at him as though she thought he was joking. Then she'd tried to leave the room. But he'd been faster. With two strides and an outstretched arm, he'd cut off her escape. He'd asked her if she thought he was uglier than Miraj? Was he repulsive? Was that why she was trying to slink away? She'd tried to explain that she was his cousin and a village girl who had never done anything. Then she'd tried to sidle out again.

He hadn't meant to be so rough. He didn't know where the slap had come from. Oh right, she'd started screaming. So he smacked her and then everything had happened very fast. He'd pushed her down onto the bed, her attempts to kick at him with one foot had only goaded him on. He'd forced her down and climbed on top. He'd put one hand over her mouth while opening his trousers with the other. Her thin shalwars had ripped easily. He was surprised at the desire she aroused in him, the force of doing what other men had done was overwhelming. The little slut, did she think he, the administrative assistant at the Swedish Embassy, didn't deserve to have a go? When all the others had been welcome to help themselves. Hardly!

Then it had happened quickly. The explosion had been almost instantaneous and he hadn't had a chance to see if Meena enjoyed it. She hadn't moved like the girls in the film at all and yet he'd felt more than with Reka. A lot more.

Afterwards, her spit had got caught in his hair and she'd heaved him off her onto the floor. He'd noticed she was bleeding. She'd seemed more shocked than satisfied. She'd hissed something between her teeth and looked at him with loathing. Babul felt stupid. Embarrassed and ashamed. He'd been hoping she'd be his mistress, since she lived under his roof and everything. They could have reached an agreement. She could have lived rent-free. But Meena had snatched up her bloodstained trousers and run out. He hadn't even had time to ask.

*

Buddhist prayer flags that Vanja had found somewhere lined the driveway when the embassy Pajero turned in from the street. Vanja had come out to greet them, beaming with joy.

"My Himalayan heroes, welcome home! I want to hear everything!"

Arthur had played along, beaming right back at her, but Moberg had discreetly withdrawn. Guilt flickered inside him. He wasn't sure Arthur's idea had been so great, after all.

Before long, he'd managed to sneak off to the embassy. He enjoyed the silence in the empty building. The power was out in Gulshan, probably all of Dhaka, in fact, but the embassy's diesel generator had obediently sputtered to life. When he turned the kettle on to make himself a cup of tea, a cockroach scurried across the kitchen floor. He never set foot in the kitchen normally, was this where the staff ate? Wasn't it a bit gloomy and austere?

When he got up to his office, Moberg logged into his foreign.ministry email account for the first time in a week. A long series of emails from Sofia. He would never have the energy to read them all. There was also, however, an invitation from the Canadian ambassador to attend a bridge party and apparently a suggestion to make a joint ambassadors' trip to Sylhet to study the tea plantations had been circulating. That might be interesting, the dialects in Sylhet were distinct from the ones in Dhaka. Some scholars claimed they constituted a separate language rather than a dialect. It would be an exciting trip. He'd also been invited to an exhibition in Dhanmondi, an Australian artist, probably something Vanja would be interested in.

While glancing over a quick request from Stockholm, he printed the minutes from the most recent Head of Mission meeting. Everything had apparently been quiet while he was away then, more or less. He was also delighted to discover he'd been formally invited to Delhi to present his paper on the influence of Sanskrit on Bangla. Expected, true, but nevertheless confirmation that he was onto something.

It wasn't until he went out to the printer that he noticed a copy of the letter of instruction from Stockholm. The Government Offices logo on the paper startled him. During his almost five years in Bangladesh, no one at the Ministry of Foreign Affairs and definitely no one at the Government Offices had ever taken an interest in Bangladesh. He read the document with growing astonishment. The Secretary of State for Foreign Affairs and the Minister for Gender Equality were proposing that Sweden host a gender equality conference in Dhaka in the spring. He quickly skimmed the document. He recognised several of the phrases in it as Sofia's. But a letter of instruction?

Moberg hurried back to his computer. All those emails from Sofia. He opened them, one by one. Slowly, a picture emerged. During his absence, the Ministry of Foreign Affairs in Stockholm had apparently caught wind of Sofia's plans to organise a big conference and liked the idea. Now they'd sent out an official letter of instruction. High-level invitations had been sent out. The Dutch were on board. The Dutch ambassador had already been informed and given his approval.

Moberg flushed slightly when he realised she'd actually flagged several of the emails as "urgent". She'd even written "sauf avis contraire" next to several subject headings – which at the ministry meant "silence will be taken as agreement", an expression commonly used when a person wanted to cover themselves vis-à-vis their superiors. How was he supposed to know? Nothing was ever "urgent" in Dhaka. And finally – a decision signed by Sofia, which made it clear she had consulted both Sida and the Ministry of Foreign Affairs.

Moberg gasped. Everything had happened so quickly. Maybe he'd better read through the emails. That reminded him: the decision in-tray, which was normally always full. He rushed out into the hallway and into the mailroom. The orange plastic tray was empty. Had she signed all the decisions?

Moberg slowly walked back to his office, grateful it was a Saturday and not a workday. He needed time to school his facial expressions. As the picture grew clearer, he felt angry at first. Side-lined and angry. But he ignored those feelings, they would only lead to complications. What right did he have to be angry? Sofia had consulted all the proper people and kept him in the loop every step of the way. Maybe she could have held off for a few days, yes, she certainly could have. So he could have stepped on the brakes. He had a nagging feeling that was exactly why she'd pushed everything through so quickly.

When he left the embassy at dusk, he had settled on an approach to Sofia's week as chargé d'affaires. Not for a moment would he let on to Sofia that he'd been oblivious or failed to keep an eye on what she was up to. From now on, he would instead let her have her conference. Let her have her way. He simply wasn't going to lift a finger to help.

Back home in the residence, Arthur had borrowed a projector from Aziz and was planning on showing the Nepal pictures on a wall. Moberg felt he was courting disaster, but Vanja was thrilled and told him in a stage whisper:

"They boy has completely changed! He's been happy as a lark all day, hugging me. saying you had such a nice time. You see, Karl-Otto! You see what a little yang can do!"

Moberg had guiltily padded upstairs. Before long, though, Arthur had found him.

"All the pictures look amazing! You can't tell they're fake. I cropped out the pots from those jungle pictures we took, now it really looks like a rainforest!"

"And the pool? Are mountain streams really that blue?" Moberg's stomach lurched. Arthur was really taking this a bit too far. He should have put his foot down.

"It's fine. It looks like a stream. Calm down, dad."

"Arthur, can't we just say you accidentally deleted the pictures? Do we really have to push things like this?"

"Oh my god, you're such a wet blanket. It's going to be great. I'm a wizard. The pictures are convincing. *Un artiste*!" He said the last thing in exaggerated French and left the room.

Moberg took a deep breath and changed his white shirt for one of the colourful shirts with ethnic patterns Vanja had picked out for him. Anything. Anything to keep her in a good mood.

An hour later, Vanja knocked back her third gin and tonic. She was sitting across from Moberg and Arthur, glowering at the two of them, her eyes glassy. Rocking back and forth.

"You figured you could trick me," she hiccoughed and turned to gaze out the window. "You think I'm ridiculous, don't you? 'Silly, vacuous Vanja. Naïve and gullible, let's dupe her!' That's what you thought, isn't it?"

A tear trickled down her cheek and Moberg leaned forward and tried to take the glass from her. She pulled it away.

"Vanja, that's enough," he said gently. Arthur got up off the sofa and sat down next to his mother.

"It was my fault, Mum. Please." He looked to his dad for help. "I had a blister and we didn't want to disappoint you. We had a good time taking the pictures, didn't we, Dad?"

"At least we did something together, Vanja. Father and son. Wasn't that the point?" Moberg argued. "The yin and yang stuff?"

"You thought I wouldn't notice the edge of the pool? A stream in the Himalayas. Bah! And those were potted plants, they don't grow in the mountains. You think I'm an idiot. My husband and my son think I'm ridiculous- admit it! You find me pathetic and ridiculous."

She sobbed, turned to Arthur and put a hand on his cheek. Arthur looked uncomfortable.

"Mum . . ."

"I want you to become a whole person, my darling son. A human being in whom yin and yang exist in harmony. That's all."

She got up, wobbled, and set her course for the liquor cabinet.

"Now, I'm going to have a . . ."

"It's bedtime for you, Vanja." Moberg put his arm around his wife and ushered her toward the stairs. "You need to sleep."

He looked over his shoulder at Arthur.

"Pack up that projector and return it. Goodnight."

*

Pink with butterflies. Approximately 20 pieces.

The curlicue text extended across a white band of marzipan on the grey frosting. The cake looked like a drab ladies' hat and the text had been copied by someone who clearly didn't know any English. The young man shot Janne a beaming smile and tilted his head.

"Bhalo, very, very nice cake."

The man started packing up the cake, but Janne stopped him.

"No, it's supposed to say 'Happy birthday, Noella!' This is the wrong text, completely wrong. Bhalo-na."

The man waved his hand dismissively.

"No problem, Boss. Same-same."

"No, it is a problem. It can't say that. This is a birthday cake. Show me the note my driver gave you. And the cake is not pink, it's grey. Purplish-grey."

Janne felt irritation creep up his spine and even though he realised what must've happened, he found it difficult to see the funny side of the situation.

The man rummaged around a drawer and at length pulled out a crumpled note. And there it was. On the note, Sofia had written: "Pink with butterflies. Around 20 pieces" on one line and on the second line "Happy birthday, Noella!".

"You see, Boss. No problem," The man beamed at him and resumed packing up the cake. "It's *almost* pink. No problem."

Janne sighed. The difference between "Problem" and "No problem" was an area where so-called cultural differences made a pivotal difference, that much was clear. Earlier that same day, he'd been trying to wiggle into a T-shirt Nazreen must have boiled. She'd also claimed, with a big smile on her face, that it was "No problem".

"What do you mean 'no problem'? My T-shirt doesn't fit me!" he'd mumbled, but he'd let it pass. And now here he was again. This time, it really was a problem.

Noella had carefully chosen a birthday cake from a colourful brochure Sofia had picked up from Gulshan's only patisserie. The cakes in the brochure and the baked goods actually produced apparently shared only a very tenuous relationship, Janne now realised.

The cake looked distinctly unappetising. The grey, artificial frosting was decorated with greenish leaves and droopy butterflies, and the text in the middle was an exact copy of Sofia's handwriting.

Noella was going to be devastated. She'd put a lot of effort into learning how to write her own name. Feeling the pressure, Janne looked around and spotted a large chocolate cake with a big pink rose in the middle.

"I'll take that one, too."

The man behind the counter raised his eyebrows and shook his head as though he couldn't see what the problem was, but in the end, he carefully packed up both cakes.

Janne paid the three thousand taka the cakes cost and hurried out to the car. Nizamuddhin attentively opened the door before the beggar children had time to surround him and closed it again quickly behind him. For some reason, the bakery was a popular spot with beggars, Janne had noticed. Maybe because Westerners often came here in person, instead of sending their cooks. And possibly because they were prone to feel guilty about paying for a cake what a garment worker made in a month?

"Drive me to the club and then take the cake home. Ask Hanif to put it in the fridge, okay?"

Janne sighed and gazed out the car window. It was getting cooler outside. The air conditioning in the car no longer felt indispensable and there were rickshaw drivers with strange scarves wrapped around their heads everywhere. The men had started wearing dirty T-shirts or button-downs instead of going bare-chested, and in the evenings, Janne had seen the guards pull on brightly coloured fleece jumpers. He texted Charlotta when he got to the club and had sent Nizamuddhin on with the cake. It felt good to dispatch the man on an errand. Janne felt constantly guilty for wasting his life. The man spent all day sitting in the car, waiting while Janne played tennis or visited someone, and when Janne and Sofia had events to go to at night, Nizamuddhin just sat quietly in the car, waiting for them to be done.

"He should take an English course. Or read a book, or something," they'd tell each other on occasion, but neither one of them ever did anything about it. And besides, Nizamuddhin seemed content.

"No problem, no problem. I like waiting as much as you like living," he'd replied to their inquiries about taking an English course. "I've been waiting my whole life."

Charlotta had already ordered a cappuccino and was waiting for him. Janne said hi to Rickard who was having lunch in another corner of the outdoor seating area and then joined her.

"I'm glad you could make it," he said. "I went to see Siraj and want to know what's really going on? What's happening with Alor Desh?"

"Thanks for taking an interest! What's happening is that your wife has cancelled all cooperation with Khadija Anam and that one of the best NGOs in Bangladesh, no, in the world, is going to fail."

"I don't know if you should expect me to be able to do much about that."

"I do. You're our First Lady. You have the ear of the powerful." She smiled wryly. "If you can help make SwedeAid and your wife see that zero tolerance is going to have unintended consequences in this particular case, it would be invaluable to the people in Lalpara. If SwedeAid cancels Alor Desh's funding, it would destroy something that is both efficient and functional exactly because it *is* efficient. Idiocy!"

Charlotta spread her arms wide to underscore her frustration.

"My internship at Alor Desh is almost over and I'm about to head home for Christmas. But I've put together materials I think you should show Sofia."

Charlotta had brought a briefcase and now took out documents and pamphlets that she sorted into three separate piles on the table in front of her. Then she quickly opened her laptop. Janne seized the opportunity to leap to Sofia's defence.

"Sofia's just following directives, SwedeAid has clear guidelines for how employees have to act when they encounter corruption. If half of what Siraj says is true, it sounds more like a job for a journalist. This is big politics, violent Islamification and landgrabbing and . . ."

Charlotta laughed drily and clicked through her documents.

"Journalist! You're joking. This is far too complex and . . . shall we say . . . international for them. Who writes about stuff like that? Arundhati Roy, maybe? Some sociologists. But no. It's not mainstream news. It's just a story of how the world works from a bottom-up perspective. Nothing more. Who cares?"

She rested her hand on the first stack of papers.

"These are all the reports, evaluations, independent inquiries and academic reports on Alor Desh's work over the past three years. Everything indicates that their results are exceptional. Khadija has developed methods and programmes that work for these people, and managed to advocate for and broaden their rights very successfully."

Charlotta broke off and patted the documents. Janne asked if he could have a look at the material and flipped through some of the reports. They had titles like "Landrights and Livelihood Amongst the Poorest of the Poor", "Sustainable Cultivation in Flood-Prone Areas", "Measurements of Empowerment Amongst Women in the Jamuni Delta", "Successes and Failures Amongst the Char Population", and then there was an austere-looking book that made the photographer in Janne jealous: *Only the Seasons Change*. Long shadows and yellow light, pictures that had unmistakeably been taken in the char area.

Charlotta noticed Janne's expression as he turned the pages.

"It was a National Geographic photographer, so there's no need to feel inferior," she ribbed him. "It was two years ago, he spent a year with Alor Desh."

Her hand moved on to the next stack.

"This is the audit, the final report as well as the underlying materials. I've gone over every post and question mark. See how I used two colours?"

Janne nodded.

"Yellow means money the accountants consider embezzled or misused where I can personally see where Khadija and the organisation are coming from. Not that anyone cares what I think. The way I see it, this isn't about corruption, it's about pragmatism. In order to solve certain acute problems, Khadija and Siraj have, at times, felt compelled to use money in ways we Westerners don't approve of."

"What do you mean, don't approve of? Bribes, gifts, false invoices?"

"That kind of thing, yes. But nothing out of the ordinary here in Bangladesh. If anything, we should see it as a good thing that they reported it. The donors have to grow up and realise there are many different kinds of corruption. Corruption for the sake of survival and corruption for the sake of greed. You'll find my definitions in the text."

"Seriously, Charlotta, this is a bit hard to swallow. This is exactly how things can't be done. What's difficult for Sofia is that . . ."

Charlotta dismissed his objection.

"I don't know how anyone is supposed to get anything done here without paying bribes. How do you think the embassy got you your house? Do you think your cook gives you correct receipts? Do you think the four hundred million dollars the embassy gives to the thoroughly corrupt water sector via UNICEF are immaculately accounted for? The water sector is infamously corrupt! And what does the embassy do about it? Nothing!"

"But you have to try."

"Khadija is trying. But in Lalpara, just finding people who can read and write is a challenge. The organisation's so-called financial controller is a woman with five years of elementary school, she can't live up to SwedeAid's or Ernst & Young's standards."

"Well, but then you have to try to find . . ."

"Great. Go ahead and try. But these are the facts. Green means posts or information that are outright lies. My educated guess is that they're based on testimony extorted by the mustaans." Charlotta picked up the stack and shook it at Janne, pointing and turning the pages. "Here, here and here. This isn't true. These are lies. Wrong. Fabrication. Slander. Mudslinging. Get it?"

Janne nodded along to Charlotta's fierce staccato while studying the documents. There was a lot of green and a lot of yellow. Many of the organisation's expenses and accounts seemed to have been called into question.

"How is an auditor supposed to know what's true and what's not? They have to work with what they're told." Janne felt a bit overwhelmed.

"Exactly. Accountants only looked at a small sliver of reality, the money, that's what's so problematic and limiting. The other things, the contexts, the risks, the results, the people, the changes achieved, the reality in the villages, none of them matter if there's the slightest problem with the money." She pulled a stapled sheaf of papers from the pile and let it dangle between her fingertips. "Which is why, my dear Watson, I've done my own analysis. Here!"

She flipped through the papers before handing it over to Janne.

"This thrilling treatise is based on over fifty interviews with named employees. The more you dig, the more convoluted it gets."

Janne took Charlotta's report and slowly thumbed through it.

"Yes, Siraj's narrative wasn't exactly crystal clear."

"That's because we don't have all the details. But the big picture goes something like this. For years now, we've been working in a high-tension area with the aim of promoting gender equality, human rights and the ability of poor people to survive. Are you with me?"

Janne nodded and looked up at Charlotta. Her ring-adorned hands were waving about, she was focused and agitated. This was her passion.

"But these are dangerous things in a country like Bangladesh, well, probably anywhere, come to think of it. It's a smidge naïve to think the people in power now would simply be okay with giving it up. Don't you think? I mean, it's not like poor people don't have hierarchies, conflicts, social contexts, religious ideas, dreams, greed, ambition and lies. Everything we have, they have, too."

Charlotta found a specific page in one of the reports.

"Here. An anthropological study done a few years ago in which the mullahs were interviewed about Alor Desh's work. You can sense they feel pressured. All the talk about female empowerment puts their backs up. They're willing to allow women to meet to discuss child rearing and goat husbandry and such, but they *don't* want them to talk about gender equality. That much is very clear from the interviews."

"Interesting. Not entirely unexpected, perhaps, but I guess I figured . . ."

"And here, in-depth interviews with people who have been granted the right to cultivate land through court processes launched by Alor Desh. Almost all of them mention problems with informal village elders and their highly dubious agreements with big landowners. When Alor Desh redistributes the land in a fairer and legally approved way, it causes friction."

"Siraj claimed the Chinese were behind it? Or the Indians?"

"To be honest, we're not sure. It might just be wealthy Bengalis? We think there's a bigger plan behind this, and that local mafia thugs are being paid to make sure Alor Desh and the landless stop causing trouble. No thank you to land rights and empowerment programmes!"

She laughed drily. Janne saw his chance to get a word in.

"I read that in Ethiopia . . ."

Charlotta was angry and well-read.

"Sure, it's the same thing in Africa. Small farmers are driven from their land to make way for big Chinese or German or Indian agribusiness. The Chinese growth rate is making the Chinese want to eat more meat. More meat requires more animal feed, requires more land, requires expansion, requires . . ."

"So we should all be vegans. Like you."

Janne felt weary and cut Charlotta's tirade off with a low blow. Charlotta gave up her grave lecture with a hearty laugh.

"Kind of, yeah. Or at least you shouldn't make the farmers in the char area pay the price for your extreme wealth. Something like that. You don't agree?"

"It's hard to argue with that. Though I still don't understand why Siraj had to go into hiding? And why doesn't Khadija come forward and write to the *Guardian* and the *Washington Post*? She's well-known enough for them to listen, right?"

"Because there *is* corruption in the organisation. She knows she can't claim the paperwork is in immaculate order. Besides, I think she's being smart. She's thinking beyond the foreign aid. She reckons the less fuss she makes now, the easier it will be to resurrect the organisation in a different guise later."

"But Siraj?"

Janne wasn't ready to let it go yet.

"Siraj has been threatened by the mustaans. Since he holds such a central position, they know he would cause the greatest damage if he were willing to provide false testimony against Khadija, because he's the most credible. But he doesn't want to. He wouldn't do that."

Charlotta closed her laptop. She sat in silence for a while, then turned to Janne.

"I'm going back to Sweden. I have some exams I have to do and I'll be working at 7-Eleven in Stockholm. Come by this summer if you're in town."

She started packing up her papers and downed the last of her cappuccino. The one pile of paper she left on the table, she resolutely pushed toward Janne. Then she packed up her laptop and wished him luck.

*

Meena shot out of the room, knocking over a bucket of water sitting in the doorway, and stumbled into the alley. At the last second, she forced herself to go back in and quickly rummage through the jumble in the hallway. A pair of clean shalwars, new trousers, any pair would do, so long as she could change out of the disgusting ones covered in Babul's slime and her blood. Her blood. Her temples were throbbing and her hands were shaking violently. Was he going to come out of the room, come after her? Her breathing was laboured as she fought back her tears.

A small, square, black box. That's how Meena pictured it. That's how it had to be. She staggered out to the water pump with her bloodstained trousers in one hand. A black box. This never happened. It didn't happen. The moment in her life she'd just lived through hadn't happened, wouldn't be included in any kind of pattern, wouldn't be made part of her mosaic. Never. This moment would be pushed into a small, black, square box she would shut tight. In it, she'd seal Babul and his grunting. The blood trickling down her leg, the pain. The incomprehensible hardness that had been pushed into her. A weapon, a baton. The slime from Babul, the smell of his greasy hair when he collapsed on top of her. She didn't understand. Can memories be erased? Can you pretend two minutes of your life never happened? Meena decided she could. Everything would be locked in that box. Water splashed onto her face. She tried to make her heart stop racing. Took a few deep breaths. The pain between her legs and the revulsion deep in her soul. She closed her eyes, let the water rush over her hair, put her whole head under the pump. He'd thrust deep inside something holy, inside the place she barely knew existed, and torn it apart. The slime, he'd left his slime all over her, her body and soul. She took a deep breath and pushed it all into the black box. There was no room for this in her life. It had never happened.

She pushed in behind some barrels, wadded up the bloodstained trousers and threw them in a bin. There, no one would ever know.

She went back to the water pump. This time, Reka was there, washing a sari. Meena started as though she'd been caught stealing red-handed and mumbled a greeting. How long had Reka been standing there? She looked Meena up and down without a word and then went back to scrubbing.

*

The Nordic Club had thrown a Lucia party the night before. Spotting the decorations from the entrance, Siv concluded the shipment from Sweden had apparently arrived on time. The week before, one of the Ericsson employees' wives, Malena, who had twin girls, had stormed into the embassy, demanding decorations be sent from Sweden by courier.

"Surely it's in the embassy's interest that we're able to throw an authentic Lucia event? No? It really should be on you to make the proper decorations available to Swedes who have to live in this . . . hellhole! The only thing they sell here is cheap Bengali tat. It just won't do!"

With tears in her eyes, she'd demanded a meeting with the ambassador and Moberg had after some persuasion agreed to request a few packages of authentic Lucia decorations via the ministry courier. All was well again. Everyone in the colony could breathe a sigh of relief.

Siv had boycotted the Lucia celebration and was hoping people had noticed. Families with young children took up far too much space at the Nordic these days and Lucia was all about admiring little brats in Santa costumes, holding electric candles. They were terrible singers, too, particularly the Danish and Norwegian children who always nagged their way into the traditional procession. No, there were far too many children in the colony at the moment. She was still annoyed her suggestion for a regular child-free day pool day had been voted down. Even though she'd discussed it with Moberg in the days leading up to the meeting and made him admit the pool area was very loud on the weekends, he hadn't supported her suggestion when push came to shove.

Siv walked past the restaurant and stopped to swipe some leftover Lucia baked goods set out on the bar. Someone had left an invitation with balloons on it next to them. Siv glanced at the invitation and almost choked on her pastry. "Noella is turning seven! Join us in Baridhara on Saturday 15 December! Gin for the grownups and ice cream for the little ones! There will be a buffet and Swedish Christmas games!" Siv's head spun as she read the words. And signed, inside a heart, "Janne and Sofia".

She was booked in for a foot massage on the roof in fifteen minutes, but right now she needed a latte and a few minutes to herself, to collect herself. A children's party, true, but one she wasn't invited to. She walked out to the pool area. Rickard and his Australian girlfriend were sitting out there, gazing into each other's eyes. Bjarne was playing tennis and Erik had Swedish visitors. The pool itself was full of teenagers. Two young girls with tattoos were reading at a table.

In the end, Siv joined Bjarne's wife Tone, who was chatting to Vibeke, the Danish ambassador's wife.

"Siv, where were you last night? We had a lovely evening with your Swedish Lucia procession," Vibeke exclaimed, making Siv positively purr with satisfaction. Her little protest had been noted and she gave the reply she'd prepared.

"I get so many invitations, I have to prioritise. You can't go to everything!"

"Well, you missed Vanja falling into the pool," Tone told her eagerly. "It was quite the sight! Sofia's husband, you know, Janne, jumped in and saved her. Proper drama it was!"

"Pardon?" Siv could hardly believe her ears.

"She was going to demonstrate a yoga position and stepped up to the edge of the pool and then . . . in she went."

"Just like that?" Siv's first thought was that Vanja must have been drunk. She was often suspiciously wobbly at major events. Or had the crazy old bat actually tried to do yoga?

Vibeke chuckled and said tolerantly:

"It was fine. The whole thing had a pretty cute ending with Janne dressed as Father Christmas and Vanja with a silver garland in her hair. I'm sure the foreign guests thought the Swedish embassy knows how to put on an entertaining event!"

"Though I'm wondering what you put in that mulled wine of yours?" Tone added. "I don't want to be rude, but really."

Siv watched Tone, waiting for the rest of her sentence. None came. Instead, Tone pressed her lips together and made a show of stirring her Coca Cola. A sense of loyalty crept up on Siv. Embassy people had to stick together; she had no intention of gossiping with the Danes. As the administrative manager, she liked to think of herself as a mother figure to all the Swedes in Dhaka, or at least the ones employed by the embassy.

"These things happen. My God, it must have been crowded here last night, no? No wonder someone was pushed in."

Tone muttered a "sure" and changed the subject. Whether a dinner party ought to be organised for the newly-arrived director of Telenor was discussed, the question was if the Norwegian ambassador was going to step up this time.

Siv only half-listened. There were rules and rules, written and unwritten, and one of the unwritten ones was that one should not gossip about colleagues and their wives. It was a rule Siv prized and made a point of honouring. She enjoyed making it known what she thought of gossip whenever other people at the club got going. No gossiping about colleagues or their wives, preferably ever, but certainly not in a small workplace like an embassy. There, you had to stick together.

Vanja's drinking was awkward, that went without saying, but it wasn't actually against the rules, Siv reasoned. What was definitely against the rules was not inviting her, the administrative manager, to Noella's party. She felt sure everyone at the embassy had been invited, with the possible exception of Rickard. Definitely Vanja. And Anna-Lena. And probably lots of other nice people who would wonder why she had been excluded. These were exactly the kind of rules that mattered and that Janne and Sofia seemed not to understand. Especially Janne. There was something slippery and unpleasant about that man. He was always bending the rules. Like that business with the night watchman and the tea stand. Siv shuddered in the heat. Or when he rearranged all his and Sofia's furniture.

No doubt he was the one who had failed to grasp that when it came to events, she was always supposed to be invited.

16

Rifat walked toward her with a big smile on his face. He was carrying two large tote bags full of little cases. Meena felt anticipation flare inside her and pushed the black box aside. These cases were going to vault their business into a different league.

"Meena-apa. I got the whole shipment, every last case! Are we going to be able to get them ready in time for tomorrow?"

Meena had tested the cases out on Nazreen. She'd been delighted and had helped her set the prices. Nazreen had hugged her several times and said how proud and happy she was Meena was back on her feet. Everything was going to be okay. Nazreen had sent five hundred taka to their parents earlier that week. Everything was working out.

Granted, Meena had woken up at the crack of dawn, sitting bolt upright as the black box spun before her for a few seconds. But then she had recalled her decision and firmly pushed the black box out of her mind. It hadn't happened. Still, should she tell Nazreen? Should someone know? But it would never work, telling Nazreen was impossible. There was no room for difficult truths in Nazreen's bright disposition.

"Do we have enough nail polish?" Meena peeked into the bags.

"Absolutely. Two colours for each case. Can we do it at your house?" Rifat looked happy.

"I'd rather not. Maybe behind the square?"

Meena led the way. Aside from a few half-naked children, no one bothered them. A ramshackle wall and a few bags of cement offered both shade and a level of privacy. Rifat spread out an old lungi and poured their goods onto it. Meena felt her pulse race at the sight of the cases. Exactly. Exactly the kind Nazreen and her friends would love. So far, every kit they'd put together had sold immediately. The tired garment workers lit up at the sight of the gold-trimmed, silver-sparkling or floral cases. They'd lingered by their stand, greed in their eyes. They'd turned the cases over, unzipped the long zippers. Zipped them again. Opened the cases to inspect the miniature tools inside, the file, the scissors, the orange stick, the tweezers. Asked questions. Meena and Rifat had demonstrated, opening bottles of nail polish. Yes, it was real nail polish, no fakes here. Yes, the polish was included in the price. Some girls had reluctantly handed the cases back, mumbling they'd be back once they were paid. Others had squeezed and poked and finally purchased.

"There are three other places where girls get off shuttles from Achulia," Rifat told her eagerly. "Maybe we should try them, too?"

Meena listened. At the moment, they were buying the cases for eighty taka, adding nail polish worth twenty and selling them for one hundred and sixty. So the difference was sixty taka. Could they sell one hundred and twenty cases in each location? It was a staggering thought.

"We need help."

"Why?" Rifat looked puzzled. "Can't we just go around ourselves and . . ."

"Do you have any cousins you trust?" Meena cut in. She started counting the cases in front of them. Forty. That wouldn't last very long. "Rifat, we need a lot more cases and several of your cousins. I know almost no one in Dhaka. If I sell these tomorrow and Thursday, you can go down to New Market and buy more. Then arrange to meet up with your cousins. Here, on Friday, after prayers. Thik ache?"

Rifat nodded. Meena kept thinking. Could Nazreen sell for them? She spent time with other ayahs most every day. Ayahs were rich. Some of them probably already had beauty kits. And Meena was thinking about the old men in the Tongi area. Granted, the village girls never had money of their own, so maybe beauty kits weren't the ideal merchandise. But she'd sold all the toothpaste and toothbrushes. It was a shame to leave the old men sitting idle just because she couldn't hitch a ride with Miraj anymore. While she gathered up the cases and chatted to Rifat, her thoughts hopscotched about, seemingly at random. The old men. The cousins. The cases. The toothbrushes. The buses.

"Have you seen Miraj around?"

Rifat blushed wildly and lowered his eyes. He started fumbling with the cases and mumbled something.

"Rifat?"

"Miraj hangs around the marketplace. You know I live there."

"Yes, and? Do you see him around?"

Rifat stuttered and blushed. Sensing he was avoiding something, Meena waited him out.

"Meena, I would never. I'm really trying. It doesn't bother me . . ." He searched for the right words and then flashed a smile at Meena before averting his eyes once more. And then it burst out of him, that hissing sound that ended in the bird noise.

"To *me* you're not a whore. To me, you're Meena."

"What do you mean, to *you*?" At first, Meena didn't understand what he was saying, but then the truth slowly came out. Miraj had been spreading rumours about Meena all over Badda. Rumours detailing what the boys had done to her and that she had spread her legs for everyone. That Rifat knew it was a lie and had tried to say so made no difference. Instead, men and little children now hurled insults after him, too, as he made his way home in the evenings. He'd had rotten tomatoes thrown at him. His brothers had tried to talk to Miraj and his mother had asked questions. Someone had put a dead rat in his bed. He let the story out in quickfire bursts, looking up at Meena, trying to smile comfortingly at her, but seeming shaken himself.

"I don't care, I really don't, Meena. It'll pass. The most important thing is that we do good business. Meena-apa, don't be sad. I know that . . . we both know what happened."

Meena listened, slumped against the sacks of cement. While she was ill in bed, stories had been made up about her in Badda, that much was clear. This explained Babul's sudden attack and why he'd asked if he could "have a go, too". This was what he'd been referring to. Apparently, he believed Miraj's lies. Meena closed her eyes. In the village, this would've been the end of her. With a reputation like that, she would have been either beaten or stoned. Then she would have been forced to live like a shadow on the outskirts of the village for the rest of her life. She remembered their neighbours' eldest daughter, who had been seen out with a local boy late one night. The next day, the girl's own mother had demanded that she be judged by the shalish. Meena had been no older than ten when it happened, but she still remembered the screams. The girl next door had been sentenced to fifty lashes and had never been able to look anyone in the eye again. She'd been allowed to stay in her parents' home as a servant but a year or so later, Meena had heard she'd hanged herself. There had been no chollisha for her. One day, she was just gone. Meena had trouble even recalling her name.

An icy cold spread through her. She started fiddling with the cases again to dispel the chill. Rifat let out a sob and she realised he was crying. He hastily tried to dry his tears with a dusty hand. So Babul had thought she'd lost her virginity, that she'd committed haram. Everyone thought so now. Flies buzzed stubbornly around her and she waved them away. She should have seen this coming. Badda was really a small village, just in the middle of Dhaka. The same laws, the same judgments, the same people. The freedom the city had seemed to offer had made her forget that the Evil Eye existed wherever there was people. The black box spun through her mind for a split second, but disappeared again just as quickly.

"Rifat-bhai. Don't cry for me. Everyone here in Dhaka knows what good business is and I can do good business. It's different here than the village. We're going to do our best business ever. Then I'll move back home as a wealthy woman. No one can do anything to me if I'm rich."

*

Sofia smelled the sweet, heavy fragrance of tuberose and gardenia and opened her eyes. The flower wreath Rehana had given her was sitting in a bowl on her nightstand. She gingerly reached out through her mosquito-net cage and touched the gift. The small, meticulously wrapped bundle had been waiting for her when she got home the night before. One of the guards had handed it to her and pointed into the dark. Rehana had waved to her from her perch on a gate across the street.

"A present. For you, Sofia from Sweden!" The girl had jumped down from the gate and vanished into the night.

Sofia smiled. It had been her second present of the day. The first had come, very unexpectedly, from Moberg. She'd expected rebuke of some kind for so blatantly circumventing him, surliness or a formal reprimand. She'd prepared a short speech in her own defence and double-checked with Lasse in Stockholm that everything was in order. But Moberg had been nothing but ease and friendliness.

"I've been keeping an eye on things from Kathmandu, of course, but I didn't want to interfere. You seem to have everything in hand," he'd told her in passing, before launching into a remarkably detailed account of how he'd managed to find an outdoor playset for Sofia's children.

"I'm told it's very difficult to find good toys for young children here in Dhaka, so I seized the opportunity. The Canadian ambassador was looking to get rid of slides, swings, bouncy castles and so on. He's moving to Singapore. Just send your driver, the stuff is sitting on the residence lawn for now. Enjoy!"

Sofia was touched by his thoughtfulness. The playset would be perfect on one of their big terraces. Moberg was a difficult man to understand, Sofia mused. On the one hand, he seemed to studiously avoid her and find her irritating when she needed a decision or discussion. She always felt like she was being pushy. He literally shied away physically, backing into the nearest corner and freezing there. Since she'd never before had a superior who didn't value her knowledge and drive, Moberg's attitude confounded her. This was something new, a resistance she didn't understand. Or was this what the notorious glass ceiling felt like? She supposed this was how it happened. When you really came into your own.

But on the other hand, like now. He sounded happy about the conference. Or maybe not? He hadn't so much as mentioned the fact that she'd used her stint as chargé d'affaires to push through all kinds of decisions that had stalled at the embassy. She had probably expected something, either a scolding or a thank you. But Moberg gave her nothing.

Janne shifted in his sleep and Sofia snuggled backwards into his arms. The other day, during the Lucia celebration at the club, he had resolutely rescued Vanja from drowning in her own skirts in the pool. She'd fallen in with a big splash in the middle of the children's performance and Janne had smoothly salvaged the situation and helped her save face. If people at times wondered whether Vanja was a lush or just unconventional, Janne had made the incident come off as the fun lark of an eccentric artist. Janne was at his best in situations like that, Sofia mused. When he raised everyone around him up without making himself the centre of attention. Tenderness for him fluttered briefly in the pit of her stomach.

It was still early. Friday. A day off for everyone in Dhaka and Noella's birthday. Outside, a parrot was relentlessly repeating a sharp, cracking noise that found its way in through the open terrace door along with a fainter backdrop of chirping, cooing sounds. Sofia suddenly realised why she hadn't heard the birds in a long while. The air conditioner was off. It was winter in Bangladesh and only around twenty degrees outside.

Noella's birthday. Deepest winter in Sweden. Sofia remembered staggering through the snow to the maternity ward in the middle of the night seven years ago and how bitter it had been to be sent home again to wait for labour to become more established. She'd taken her time entering this world, Noella. Janne had been a rock, packing the hospital bag, calling their families, arguing with midwives, rubbing her back and mixing energy drinks. And when Noella had finally come out. His tears, his joy and the profound tremors of a completely new protective instinct that bound the two of them together forever. He'd also handled her parents' tactlessness with a great deal of diplomacy. They'd decided they were too young and vivacious to become grandparents and had hurt Sofia's feelings by merely sending flowers. It had been a month before they'd found time to see their first grandchild. Janne's parents had been there hours after the birth. Had thrown themselves in their Volvo and driven all the way from Jönköping in a blizzard.

Janne's hand cupped her breast and his nether regions pressed queryingly against hers. Sofia closed her eyes and kept her mind on Janne as he had been around the time of Noella's birth. There it was. Desire. So different from when Teo was born. She kept her mind on their little flat in Stockholm and let Janne slide into her with the trust that had once been the foundation of their world.

*

Noella was dressed up as Spiderman and came dashing down the stairs when the doorbell rang. The first Korean mother who showed up with a little Min-Ji in a princess dress looked terrified at Spiderman's welcome shriek and hurriedly left her daughter in the grand hallway. Sofia had noticed the Koreans usually kept to themselves. Min-Ji was followed by a long row of little princesses from every corner of the world, each carrying an almost identical present from the only shop in Gulshan that sold toys. Pretend makeup, Chinese-made dolls in bathtubs, sparkly stickers and sari-clad barbies. The best gift came from the twins' mother, Malena, who'd had the foresight of buying presents in Sweden. Sofia was pleased to see a small, hand-made mouse family made of rustic cloth.

"They're wonderful! Thank you. Aren't they lovely, Noella?"

Noella looked sceptical but had manners enough to say yes.

Sofia hugged Malena and showed her into one of the house's sitting rooms while the twin girls threw themselves at the new plastic playset on the terrace. As the hostess, Noella had to stay by the door. The next guest to turn up was Vanja.

"I had a cup of tea outside at Beppin's. Isn't he darling? A wonderful person!" She hugged Noella and asked her to open her present. A strange mobile with feathers and pieces of crystal was hidden inside the wrapping paper.

"It's a dreamcatcher, Noella. With this, all your dreams can come true. I made it myself!"

Janne and Sofia had divided the party into two sections, one for grownups and one for children. The children were going to play Swedish games, the adults drink gin and tonics, and at the end there would be a magic show and goody bags for all. The magician was old Mabob, one of the embassy drivers who insisted on performing his by-now cult magic show whenever Swedish children congregated. Sofia had told him not to use any animals this time, since there was a rumour going around that he'd once broken the neck of a dove behind his back while trying to vanish it. The children had spotted the bloody dove and there had been a lot of drama. Now, he was only allowed to do magic with scarves and flowers. Mabob was already waiting in the kitchen with Hanif, dressed in a large cape and a hat with gold and feathers.

The chocolate cake Janne had bought, and which Noella had graciously approved, held pride of place in the kitchen. Hanif and Nazreen were standing in the doorway, watching as the house filled with guests. Children's parties were important events in Dhaka's expat community, as Sofia was well aware. A combination of diplomatic stagecraft and badly-needed entertainment. She raised her hand to touch the sweet-smelling wreath Rehana had made – a perfect ornament for a special occasion like this one – and asked Nazreen to pick up the gift wrap littering the floor.

High Commissioner Chu's young wife arrived with a sullen five-year-old in tow. She had to pry the girl off her and have Nazreen coax her into the room where the other children played. Then she flung herself down onto the sofa next to Vanja to catch up on some gossip. The Norwegian First Secretary Hans came with two children and no ayah, choosing to personally keep an eye on his youngest. He declined the offer of a drink. Antje came with neither children nor presents, sashaying through the door and throwing Sofia a kiss.

Suddenly, a Bangladeshi boy appeared in the hallway. He was neatly combed, wore a miniature navy velvet suit and carried an enormous present. Everyone did a double-take. The boy's name was Arun and he was Water Minister Choudhuri's child with his most recent wife. The boy had fallen in love with Noella at school and stubbornly demanded a playdate. After careful consideration, Sofia and Janne had sent him an invitation to Noella's party, thinking he wouldn't show. But now, here he was. A large woman in a bejewelled turquois sari swept through the door behind him. She wore heavy black and pink eye makeup and her arms and ankles were covered in bracelets. Her mouth was bright red. She threw her sari back over her shoulder, covering a diminutive grey woman who had followed her in, and shoved her son toward Noella. She barked something in Bangla that sounded like a command to Sofia.

Vanja had noticed what was happening from one of the living rooms. Sofia shot her a grateful look. Suddenly, the birthday party needed a boost in diplomatic status and the wife of the Swedish ambassador smoothly took over the role of hostess. She greeted the minister's wife warmly and whispered discreetly to Sofia:

"I'll take care of her- I've met her before. She's the stepmother of one of Arthur's best friends, Aziz, and we keep being thrown together at various national day celebrations. No worries. I'll text Karl-Otto and make him come over, he can talk to her in Bangla. She doesn't speak a word of English. No need to fret but get the gin and cigarettes out! I'm sure she'll want to seize the opportunity now that she's around Westerners."

*

The crowd was beginning to thin and the dust settled at the bus stop. Meena peered into the sack Rifat had given her. Good, almost everything had been sold. She made her way over to a small stand and handed over five hundred taka. In exchange, she was given a code that she keyed into her phone. There. Send. Mahmoda would collect the money out and take it to the village after Friday Prayer. According to Mahmoda, the mosque had been paid and the mullah had rescinded the half-explicit fatwa against the Bhuia girls. This money would go straight to Amma and Abba. Five hundred taka, that was enough for a couple of chickens and rice and daal for at least a month. Maybe Abba would be able to see the doctor about his sore knee.

Before she heaved the sack onto her back and started homeward, she sent one more text, this one to Rifat. "What did your Amma say?" Rifat had promised to talk to his mother and ask if she would consider taking out a micro loan of ten thousand taka so they could do even bigger business. Meena was too young to be approved and didn't belong to a women's group either. And Rifat was a man. The loans were only available to poor women, if they had a business plan. Meena had plenty of plans.

She was a harsh woman, Rifat's Amma, that had become clear to Meena. She'd yelled at Rifat every day of his life, for being a harami, a bastard whose father had taken off, leaving only a "freak with a voice like a crow". As far back as he could remember, Rifat had been his mother and two older brothers' errand boy. His life had consisted of blows and beatings. He hadn't been allowed to go to school. Instead his brothers had sent him out to steal and beg, until Patel had put him to work in the marketplaces. Because what dowry could you expect to get out of a harami? And who would want to marry him anyway? With that crazy bird voice? It was only after meeting Meena he'd learnt to read and write a little. Now, they were able to send quick messages on their phones and his whole life had changed.

"I never thought people like me could have dreams," he'd hissed once while they were rattling about in the cargo bed of the pickup truck. "But a life near you, Meena. That's my dream."

Meena smiled a little at the thought of Rifat. The question was whether his mother would realise their terms were more than fair. If his mother borrowed ten thousand taka for them, she would get fifteen back later. Would she be able to understand that? Meena had big plans and she needed a lot of money so she could make even more money. She'd go over her calculations at night, almost sleepless by all the numbers swirling around her head.

Meena was deep in thought and didn't notice the little boys who had formed a tail behind her. The first attack came when she turned down a side street in Badda. A strong reek of rotten fish made her back up quickly. A fish cadaver fell out of her hair. The next handful of stinking fish waste flew at her when she turned around. It hit her full in the face. She staggered. The boys disappeared around a corner, giggling, throwing pebbles in Meena's direction. A rotten egg hit her shoulder.

"*Maagi, maagi,*" they jeered. Whore.

One of the little boys made obscene gestures at her and the others burst into shrieks of laughter. The ruckus made several adults turn around. Women in burqas suddenly emerged from their houses. Normally, they stayed indoors. A woman Meena didn't know walked up to her.

"There's this awful smell on my street," she said quietly through the mesh screen of her burqa. "It smells like shit and fallen woman. Why don't you move along to the brothel district where you belong? Go back to Tangaj."

Meena tried to defend herself. She dodged a slimy fistful of fish scraps that came flying at her.

"What do you know about me? I'm from Goalpur outside Rajigonj. I'm the daughter of a landowner. My name is Meena Bhuia. I haven't done anything wrong! I'm not a whore, I run my own business, I . . ."

The woman took a step closer and more women came up behind her for support. A man lounging against a doorpost spat at her and made a gesture like he was shooing away an animal. He yelled something at the woman in the burqa, who nodded and turned to Meena.

"We all think this street has started reeking. You think you can steal our men? Is that what you want?"

Meena quickly walked around the group and hurried on toward Babul's house. Something hit her in the back. Before she could reach the house, Nazreen came running out to meet her. She looked frantic and grabbed Meena's arm.

"They want us to move out." Nazreen was out of breath. "They're saying we have to be out of the house by the end of the day tomorrow. Or preferably tonight."

Behind her sister, Meena spotted Babul and Reka in the doorway. Babul had put his arm protectively around Reka. Nazreen looked terrified and hissed.

"Meena, I think Babul has the plastic box."

17

Outside Gulshan, it was complete traffic mayhem. Rickshaws filled every gap between the big Jeeps and beggars and dogs jostled for space between the rickshaws. Sofia tried to ignore her mounting sense of panic. In two days, they were off to Thailand for Christmas and before then, she had to submit a draft report on the outcomes of the police reform programme and sign two contracts. She'd also hoped to cancel SwedeAid's agreement with Alor Desh before everyone left for the holidays. The audit didn't give her a choice.

They'd moved two hundred yards in the last half hour and were severely late for their meeting with the World Bank. She had an urge to abandon the Jeep and walk. It would've been faster. But she couldn't bear to think how many beggars would swarm her if she did.

Antje, who was sitting next to her in the backseat, was going on and on about her latest fling, an Indian gentleman who worked as a consultant for the Asian Development Bank. Sofia liked Antje, but a real friendship had failed to develop between them. They were nothing more than friendly colleagues. Antje had quickly realised Sofia wasn't going to be her wingman at Dhaka's many clubs and parties.

"I get it, you're sorted. Your husband is a real dreamboat, do you realise that?" she'd said at Noella's party, greedily eyeing Janne who had been busy roughhousing with Teo. "A bit overweight, perhaps, but cute. Hold onto him, or I might just gobble him up."

That last part was meant as a joke, but Sofia hadn't found it particularly funny and had tried to keep her conversations with Antje professional.

The meeting with the Country Director of the World Bank had come at a bad time, but Anne Willcott had suddenly been keen to meet both Sweden's and the Netherland's foreign aid counsellors.

"It's about our violence against women conference. She's heard we're planning a high-level meeting and just wants to be kept in the loop. And that's a good thing, right?"

As far as strategic advocacy in an international context was concerned, Antje was a fully-fledged pro. She had brought a binder with their lists of potential invitees and a draft programme. Now, she was busy setting up a mobile office in the backseat; her laptop was open and plastic folders and binders were stacked between them. Having only brought a notepad, Sofia felt a bit like an amateur. Of course the long hours spent in Dhaka's traffic should be spent working.

"We're going to have to make sure the World Bank doesn't decide to take over, and that Anne Willcott doesn't turn against us for some reason," Antje said. "If she does, she'll simply schedule another big meeting at the same time and take all the wind out of our sails. They have a deep-rooted need to assert themselves, the big movers. Has your ambassador brought up the conference with the EU group, like we suggested?"

"It seems to have slipped his mind," Sofia had to admit. The latest minutes from the EU's Head of Mission meeting should have reflected if Moberg had mentioned the conference. But there had been nothing there, which meant another month's delay before all bilateral foreign aid organisations in the EU would be informed of what Sweden and the Netherlands were planning.

"What?" Antje commented. "Slipped his mind? Oh my God, what if he forgot to bring it up at Dev-Com, too? I wasn't in the last meeting because my parents were here and I took a few days off."

"I can't imagine that would be the case. He's been so encouraging."

Sofia felt a twinge of concern and had to resist an urge to tell Antje about her doubts concerning Moberg. "He just needs to be reminded sometimes."

Sofia decided to continue to be loyal to Moberg and changed the subject.

"Would you mind if I brought up WSNP 11 with Willcott? We have a lot of money tied up in water and sanitation."

"Not at all, do it while we have her attention! We have no money in either, but I'm curious to hear more about it. Leaks like a sieve, right?"

Sofia had been planning to bring up the funding given to the Ministry of Water and Sanitation with the World Bank for a while. The Water and Sanitation National Programme, or WSNP II for short, was coordinated by the World Bank and UNICEF and had a dismal reputation in donor circles. But it was also one of Sweden's biggest financial commitments to a government agency, and the contract had been raising a number of concerns. SwedeAid had questioned whether Bangladesh's civil service could really handle the vast amount of money involved. Bangladesh was, after all, one of the world's most corrupt countries and the integrity of the minister in charge was under question.

New winds were blowing in the foreign aid sector. No more small projects and programmes. These days, grants of less than ten million kronor were rarely awarded. The macro economists who had come to dominate the field advocated giving large sums directly to government departments and ministries, so the money could subsequently be disbursed as the countries themselves saw fit. Vast sums, big impact. The analysis and competence of economists applied to the real world, Sofia thought to herself, not without annoyance. Big mistakes when things went awry. In the field of law, what was needed was small, targeted investments with long-term effects. Working with human rights required a completely different analysis and worldview.

The ideology behind the enormous sums given directly to foreign governments, the so-called budget support, was that developing countries should be shown more trust, in the name of democracy, and that it would give them so-called ownership of their own development. It sounded reasonable to a lot of people, while others felt it was lunacy. Reasonable because it inevitably took a long time to effect change by means of small, diverse investments. Lunacy because the elites in many developing countries had no interest in making things better for the majority. Large sums risked disappearing into Swiss bank accounts, and accountability risked being negligible. The usefulness of budget support and sector funding was an ideological watershed in international aid circles.

"Yes, I've been told the sector funding is leaking," Sofia replied to Antje's quick conclusion. "But the audits come back flawless. So what can we do? How do you handle your enormous health support? How much is that again? Fifty million Euros from you, right? It's the same thing there, that leaks like a sieve too. What do you do?"

Antje rolled her eyes and covered first her eyes, then her ears and finally her mouth with her hands. She shook her head. Then she made the sign of the cross.

"That's what I do. Inshallah. I have a career to think about, and no one back home is interested in bad news. We're talking about an ideological decision – we have to take it on faith. And the government ministers, well, they're laughing all the way to the bank. But we're not allowed to talk about that."

"Unlike Alor Desh, then," Sofia mumbled. "There's no ideological war to protect them. They're caught up in binary systems, zero tolerance, Swedish accounting standards, requirements their barely literate employees can't live up to."

"Yes," Antje slowly shook her head and let her finger meet the hand of a beggar child on the other side of the car window. The child laughed with delight and then the car inched forward a few feet. "I've thought about that, too. We have completely different set of rules for poor grantees, small organisations with limited capacity, than for government agencies. It's ridiculous, when you think about it."

After almost two hours in traffic, Sofia and Antje crawled out of the Jeep's backseat, vaguely nauseated and hunched over after the bumpy ride. The World Bank offices were located in central Dhaka, far from the relative peace and quiet of Gulshan. It was a glass building and a quick, quiet lift with a cracked mirror took them upstairs. Sofia could feel the temperature change as they stepped into the hallway. What Antje had told her about Anne Willcott had been true. The Country Director had ordered the whole floor to be kept at sixteen degrees, and since most people found that unbearable, a lot of international experts had relocated. Her only company now were two Dobermans who came to greet them, along with a Bangladeshi woman wearing a fleece jacket over her sari.

"Ms Willcott has been expecting you," the woman commented curtly and showed them to a frigid room.

Anne Willcott looked like Sofia remembered from the brief meeting with the Climate Commission. Elegant, waifish, sharp features. Close-cropped hair and a waist-length leather jacket. James Bond.

"Sofia from Sweden. Delighted. Antje, lovely to see you again."

Remembering who else had recently called her Sofia from Sweden, Sofia smiled a little. Anne Willcott nodded toward a couple of visitor's chairs and Antje and Sofia took a seat. It was difficult to shake the feeling that they'd been called to the headmaster's office. Anne sat down behind her massive desk. The wall behind her was all glass. On the other side of it, a crumbling city centre spread out toward the horizon.

"Your conference. I want to know all about it. When? Where? How? And why?"

Sofia let Antje take the lead. Her well-prepared binders and documents came in very handy as she listed off the guests and experts they wanted to invite, what speakers they were considering. Their proposed budget. Desired outcomes. Possible impact. Sofia studied Anne Willcott while she skimmed the documents. She'd seen that efficient look before, among the top brass at the UN. Had seen directors cut to the heart of a problem after just a few quick questions. As though they had the ability to step into a mental helicopter for a moment, from which they had a view of the whole picture without getting stuck on details. Then they offered their analysis. "Like this, and this and this. Done." It always made Sofia feel deeply impressed and a little concerned. The larger picture wasn't always obvious to anyone but them. That was very much the case here, Sofia soon realised.

"Good." Anne Willcott had finished reading and put the papers down on her desk. "But I suggest we postpone. That you postpone."

Sofia leaned forward. She really felt the cold now. The room was freezing and Anne Willcott's words sent a shiver down her spine.

"I'm sorry, but why? This isn't a World Bank initiative and we already have the support . . ."

"I'm planning a major donor meeting on climate change this spring, and our equality unit wants women's issues represented there, too. It would be a shame to run two big conferences at the same time, don't you think? Dhaka's not that big, after all. Let me make myself clear," she scratched one of the dogs behind the ear and paused briefly. "I won't be supporting your conference."

She clicked her tongue at the dog.

"Quite the contrary, in fact."

Sofia gasped. She asked politely but with an edge of defiance in her voice why the World Bank hadn't advertised their conference sooner. Wasn't this slightly short notice? She was quickly interrupted by Anne Willcott, who fixed her sternly.

"Your ambassador, Moberg, was at the Dev-Com meeting where this was decided, and he was on board. He doesn't seem particularly anxious to get violence against women on the agenda, put it that way. He didn't so much as mention your conference, which I'm sure you agree is rather remarkable."

Antje shot Sofia a look. All Sofia could do was shake her head in bewilderment. She felt her cheeks flush and deflated in her chair. She'd dropped the ball.

Anne Willcott got up, walked around her desk and sat down on it, diagonally in front of Sofia and Antje. She was considerably more focused now. She'd moved on to more important matters.

"On the other hand," she said, addressing Sofia, "On the other hand, I remember you saying something about an NGO working with climate adaptation when you were last here. Is that correct?"

"You mean Alor Desh?"

"Exactly! That was the name of it! We don't work with grants that small, or with civil society at all, really, so you'll have to excuse me for forgetting the name."

"That's fine," Sofia replied lamely. "But we're actually about to pull our support. The organisation appears to be corrupt."

"But I'm told they're having a tremendous impact in the char area? In the lead-up to the conference, we've had clear directives from Washington to invest more in adaptation and social change. Well, what you said when we last met. What was it? Ducks and stilt houses? Could someone from Alor Desh give the keynote address at my conference? I don't want to be known as an infrastructure enthusiast in a context like this. Our reputation is bad enough internationally as it is."

"To be perfectly honest, I'm not sure what's going to happen. We practice zero tolerance of corruption, so our orders are to pull out."

Antje chimed in. Her voice trembling with cold, she tried to explain:

"There are big problems we don't have the resources to tackle, to put it simply. The auditors have uncovered severe malfeasance."

"Zero tolerance. Is that what you call it? When you have something that's proven to work?" Anne Willcott laughed out loud. One of the Dobermans padded over and pressed himself against her. She stroked the animal with an immaculately manicured hand.

"You minor donors are so touching in your efforts. The Swedes and the Dutch, fighting corruption together. Adorable." She seemed to be talking to the dog, but then she turned to Sofia and Antje.

"Nothing wrong with fighting corruption, I guess, but you have to pick your battles. You have something the whole world needs: how are people going to survive when the flood comes? You should nurture that. Be proud that you found and financed something that yields results, for God's sake! Look at the big picture, the forest, not the trees. Don't you ever wonder where all the money goes? Do you know how hard it is to squeeze real results out of the billions of aid dollars inundating this country?"

She stood up, walked over to the big window and gazed out at Dhaka. Most of the skyscrapers surrounding the World Bank were poorly maintained. Large patches of damp darkened the walls. Far below, between the buildings, the slums sprawled out in every direction. From above, it was clear how congested the streets were. An Asian megacity. A yellow haze hung low over the buildings.

Neither Sofia nor Antje answered the Country Director's rhetorical question, but they followed her gaze out the window. She turned back to look at them.

"No, you don't. But I do. Make it your business to save this organisation from the clutches of the anti-corruption lobby instead of taking the easy route and pulling out. It's no coincidence the anti-corruption lobby in Washington consists of Republican thinktanks. Anti-corruption is their number one tool for tarring all foreign aid. They point to any aspect that's not working and then demand every programme be cut. As though foreign aid's to blame for the world being the way it is! Talk about shooting the messenger. Or the assistant."

The Country Director looked agitated and started digging around her handbag for something. A piece of gum calmed her down.

Antje and Sofia said nothing. The feeling of having been chastised was not lessened by the fact that Anne Willcott made it clear there was nothing to add. Her attention turned to the dogs and she mumbled soothingly to them.

Antje regained her composure first. She stood up and grabbed her bag. Sofia followed suit. They took their leave of Anne Willcott as politely as they were able and were shown to the lift by the woman in the fleece jacket. They stared at each other in silence in the cracked mirror on the way down. Somehow, Sofia's questions about corruption in the water sector had got lost entirely.

"Can you imagine why Torgil would choose her over me?" Antje smiled wanly.

*

It was amazing how modern computer programmes were able to create graphics with just a few clicks of the mouse. Moberg inputted the percentages. Sixty percent of Bangla consisted of native words, but as many as twenty percent were totshom, borrowed from the Sanskrit. And then a small group of bideshi, foreign, ones. Click. A pie chart filled the screen. A nice illustration for his article.

He glanced at his watch, but it wasn't time to go to the Norwegian reception yet. A number of Norwegian oil companies had started to drill in the Bay of Bengal. He and Vanja had been invited by the Norwegian ambassador to meet representatives from the companies in question and lend some diplomatic heft to the lunch. The Norwegian ambassador had a skilled cook and he could probably count on both imported fjord salmon and those delicious Jarlsberg cheese tartlets.

He'd seen in Notes that Sofia was online. He should pop over to her office, he really should. The thought of it made his stomach clench. Sofia had, in a sharply worded email, demanded to know why he hadn't raised the matter of her women's conference in Dev-Com "as we had agreed". She had cc'd Country Coordinator Lasse Bergström and the caseworker at the Ministry of Foreign Affairs, but thankfully left out the State Secretary and the department heads. Still, it was aggressive, Moberg thought. He'd prepared himself for her ire, had weighed it against the inconvenience of having to host a women's conference. He skimmed a notepad full of notes, stood up, held his breath for a second or two as though to brace himself and then set his course for Sofia's office.

Sofia listened and Moberg talked. Sofia looked determined and tried again:

"You've misunderstood, Moberg. I've worked with gender issues for five years and my assessment is diametrically . . ."

Moberg could tell Sofia was having a hard time finding the right words and took the opportunity to sum up:

"That's why I figured mainstreaming the issue was a more relevant approach, which is why I supported Anne Willcott's proposal." Moberg spread his arms wide and smiled warmly at Sofia. "I think it would be most regrettable if we were to launch small, individual initiatives and end up segregating the women's issue, don't you?"

"This is a contentious issue within academia," Sofia emphasised *academia* and inhaled, searching for words. She had stood up and was facing Moberg with the desk between them. "But *in practice*, there are many who claim it's in fact the mainstreaming approach that makes the gender equality issue *invisible*. Are you clear on that? I'm in charge of Sweden's foreign aid and my assessment is that making violence against women *visible* is highly relevant in Bangladesh at this time."

"If you say so," Moberg tried to sound friendly and play for time. Sofia was clearly upset. If he wanted her to believe he was acting in good faith, he had to sound more convincing. He made another attempt.

"Sweden has committed to working with gender equality and not just women."

"Yes? And what do you know about the difference in methods? Pardon my asking, but can you expand on your way of thinking at all?" Sofia waited without taking her eyes off Moberg. The question threw Moberg off balance.

"Well, my thinking was that the World Bank's initiative to organise a climate conference with a gender equality angle was more in line with that. You have to start somewhere, right?"

Sofia stared at him, unable to hide her annoyance. She started gathering up documents.

Moberg could sense the already thin veneer of respect Sofia had had for him had thinned considerably. And maybe cracked.

He stayed where he was, waiting for further instructions. But none came, if anything, she seemed to be ignoring him. Relieved, he carefully backed out of the room, mumbling:

"Okie dokie, so that's great then."

*

Meena watched Babul hurry down the alley through the mesh screen of her burqa. Reka had left for work at the crack of dawn and her parents were sitting in the marketplace as usual. She and Nazreen had been staying with one of Nazreen's friends who worked as an ayah for a Canadian family. The guards had let them in and kept quiet in exchange for a bit of baksheesh. But it wasn't a long-term solution, the room was too small.

Meena slipped out into the alley. A burqa among burqas. No one noticed her, no one whistled or jeered. No one paid any attention as she walked up to Babul and Reka's front door and tried the handle. Locked, for once. She kept walking like nothing had happened and turned down the next narrow passage, toward the water pump. No one noticed her.

Nor did anyone notice when Meena walked up to the back of the house and pried the wooden shutters open. It was quick work. She knew where the hook was on the inside. Meena quickly looked around, decided no one was watching and a second later, she was inside. The plastic box.

Her hand fumbled behind the dresser. Not there. Had it fallen to the floor? Meena's hand searched, but no. She let her eyes scan the room but there weren't a lot of places to hide things. While she rummaged through the linens on the bed she'd shared with Nazreen, her eyes fell on the shallow wardrobe angled in one corner. Babul's meticulously looked-after work clothes.

Having to touch his clothes made her feel sick; something about the smell of them made her scrunch up her nose and hold her breath. The black box was spinning nearby, so nearby. In the end, she found the plastic box under a pair of carefully folded gabardine trousers.

The money, their money. She counted it with the efficiency of habit. Filthy, torn taka notes of various denominations. It was all still there. Warm relief spread through her body. She stayed seated on the bed for a minute with her eyes closed. Allah lil-ahl inna, you look out for me, Allah.

When she opened her eyes, she knew what she had to do. She silently removed the hangers with Babul's white, carefully ironed shirts. One, two. He was always boasting about owning three shirts, he must be wearing one now. Her heart was racing. She hid the shirts under her burqa and quickly scrambled out the window.

Badda was deserted at this time of day. A rat scurried ahead of her down the alley and disappeared into a hole. There. The open sewer of the houses next-door, hidden behind a crumbling wall. She looked around furtively and pulled out the blindingly white shirts. Then she heatedly threw them both in the sewer and stood staring at them for a second. It wasn't enough. She picked up a stick and fished the shirts out. She kicked them where they lay on the ground, let her sandal grind them into the muck and filth. Her heart was pounding faster and faster. She quickly looked around. Still alone.

She hitched up the skirt of her burqa, squatted down over the shirts and let her steaming urine soak them.

*

The wet cement reached halfway up his calves. Janne looked around. Twenty scrawny, dark-skinned men were staring back at him, aghast. Janne lifted up one foot. The cement slurped. He lifted the other. More slurping. He closed his eyes and counted to ten. When he opened them again, he was still standing on the embassy roof, which had been turned into a construction site, and the men were still staring at him mutely. No one moved. One of the men was gaping, slack-jawed, at him. Janne heard Sofia come up the stairs and pause in the doorway as though to take in the entire scene.

"Janne. Are you okay?" Then she burst out laughing. "Oh my god, what happened?"

Janne had no trouble suppressing his mirth.

"Would you mind fetching a newspaper or something for me to stand on? I have to get this off."

"Sure." She said something in Bangla to the men and suddenly febrile activity broke out. One person helped him out of the cement, another brought pieces of wood to scrape off the muck. A third fetched a basin of water.

"This," Janne exclaimed. "This is sick. This is proof positive that Bangladeshi society is sick, do you understand me?"

"What?" Sofia couldn't help laughing at the whole thing.

"Don't laugh! You should be crying! Don't you get that not one of these men, not a single bloody one of them, dared, *dared* to stop me. Even though they could all see I was about to step into wet cement, they said nothing. Do you get the level of subjugation? Do you get the kind of walking abuse of power people like you and me represent here?"

Janne felt both annoyed and uncomfortable:

"The difference they make between people is bizarre, how can anyone live like this? Sofia? Here's how I interpret what just happened: since I'm a white man I'm a god and here comes the god. No one dares to interfere with a deity, so he steps right into the cement. Get it? They don't have the confidence to put up a hand and say: "Stop!" Or: "Don't step into the wet cement!" None of them *dared* to stop me. Get it? No one said a word. Do you understand the extent of . . ."

"Come on, Janne, I think you're reading too much into this. They didn't realise you had no idea there was cement. Wet cement. That's all."

"Ha! That's all! So this would've happened in Sweden? Are you seriously saying that . . ."

"Janne. Let's put your sandals out to dry here. Babul will bring up coffee. Do you think you can make it *around* the cement this time, to the terrace? Come on!"

Sofia's sarcasm was friendly but Janne grumbled under his breath. They had a lot to talk about and he sensed the cement incident might have more to do with his own relationship with Bangladesh than anything else. That feeling of always being on top. Every relationship was impossibly unequal and that was increasingly irksome to Janne. What did this feeling of superiority do to people? Not to mention the feeling of inferiority?

Babul servilely served them coffee, careful to point out a cake Sofia had ordered. Sofia gave him a stiff smile.

"That one, he's the opposite of your cement guys," she said in Swedish. "Ever since I got here, I've had to ask him to start up the copier whenever I want to make photocopies. And then it turns out he's *removed* a lever, which he keeps in his pocket. That way, we always have to ask him before we use the copier. Talk about artificially creating a position of power. Just like Moberg and Dev-Com. I'm so sick of all these idiots throwing spanners in the works! I told you the conference is off, right?"

"You mentioned it. But next year, when Moberg has moved back home. Then."

Janne had grasped the embassy dynamic and shot Sofia an encouraging smile while he picked at the cement stuck in his leg hair.

"The important thing is to make sure it doesn't dry." Sofia leaned forward and kissed him. "Where do we start? Are we packed for Khao Lak? Did we get Christmas presents from your parents?"

"Yes, it's all under control, trust me. But there's something we need to discuss."

"Discuss?"

Sofia eyed her husband suspiciously. Janne took a deep breath.

"Don't give me a kneejerk now, promise?"

"Okay . . . ?"

"Good. I want Nazreen and her sister to move in with us."

"Forget it. We always said no live-in staff." Sofia's reply was instantaneous.

"Listen, Sofia. Nazreen and her sister live in Badda and have been evicted. Nazreen is wonderful with the children and the children are the best thing we have. Right? There are five small staff suites in our house. Did you know that? Five! Two on the roof, three behind the garage. They're completely self-contained. According to Hanif, you can cook on a gas stove outside.

"But we agreed that . . ." Sofia had crossed her arms and did not look amused. Janne cut her off, annoyed at her lack of flexibility.

"Sure, fine, we agreed. Back in Stockholm, where things were simple and straightforward. But here! Sofia! Dhaka is the world's most overpopulated city and we have empty rooms. Is it morally justifiable not to let people live in them? How do you defend that?"

Sofia said nothing. He pressed on.

"I know we agreed, but that was before we knew Dhaka. Of course they should stay with us!"

"Janne, those are horrible, dark little cupboards! Not even fit for animals! Damp, mouldy. Have you seen them? Are we supposed to live in our palace and keep them in the backyard like slaves? How is that going to feel?"

Janne was slightly taken aback.

"What's the difference? Other than you have to *see* how they're living?"

"It feels so . . . old-fashioned. Upper class. Upstairs, downstairs, you know."

Sofia sighed at her own lack of logic, which Janne had quickly exposed.

"And? Do you have any idea how they're living today? Let them decide what's unfit!"

"Fine, the slum might not be great, even I get that. But I don't like having people living so close. We have to be able to cope here, too. When they walk down the stairs from the roof, they can look straight in."

Janne raised his eyebrows.

"Sofia, listen to yourself. I'm going to pretend I didn't hear that last part. You're telling me that from a *certain* angle when they're climbing up to their rooftop, *if* you were to be standing in front of the mirror, getting changed, they *might* catch a glimpse . . ."

"I actually appreciate having the space to relax every once in a while in this country. I work really hard and I always have to be nice to everyone, and now I'm suddenly supposed to have people in my home."

"Not your home. Our home. And not even in our home, on our roof. Like neighbours."

Janne got up and gave Sofia a look. "This time you can't hide behind the official rules. This time, it's actually just our rules. And who is going to interpret them? What kind of people do we want to be?"

He walked over to check on his mucky sandals, scraping the last of the cement off his feet. Sofia sighed. Janne left her on the roof without giving her time to answer his question.

*

As usual when she arrived in England, Khadija was struck by how many expensive things she saw everywhere. Not people's private possessions – well, that, too – but in the public spaces. Pavements, traffic lights, central reservations, planters full of flowers, squares. Signs, poles, streetlights. Tunnels, aqueducts, roundabouts, whole traffic systems that must have cost the taxpayers billions but everyone took for granted. So different from Bangladesh where the only expensive things were the mansions of the wealthy and the hotels, and all public goods were deficient and broken. Where the one modern, two-level motorway in the capital was called *The* Flyover. She would never forget the time when Siraj came back to Lalpara after a visit to Dhaka. Visibly exhilarated, he'd told her he'd taken the bus across The Flyover.

"The view! It was dizzying!"

Khadija had been reminded both of his complete lack of experience and of how flat her native country was. But now he was there, Siraj, somewhere in Dhaka. Protecting her by going into hiding.

She glanced at her son, who was expertly manoeuvring his small Fiat out from the chaos at Heathrow and onto the M4 toward London. Nirmol, her only family. He was a looker, she could see that. Thankfully, very different from the young men in Bangladesh who, with their gabardine trousers and ironed shirts and old-fashioned haircuts, always looked like someone's cousin from the country, she mused. Nirmol had long hair. He wore a black T-shirt with a Metallica print and his wrists were covered in bracelets from last summer's many festivals. Ratty jeans. Stubble. Three more terms until he was a doctor, three more tuition fee instalments. How was she going to tell him it might not be possible anymore?

She'd always been determined about one thing: she would give her only son an international education. The same opportunity she'd been given. The Metallica shirt, the rock concert bracelets, the tiny car. The difference university studies in England made was ever so pivotal. Nirmol was a young European.

"So, how's your struggle to save the world coming along? I'm not hearing any reports on the BBC that you've solved global injustice? Is the world still unfair?" He was teasing her and pulled down a pair of sunglasses that had been dangling from the rear-view mirror. "Mum, come on. Why don't you move here and teach at a university instead of living in the swamp? Theory instead of practice? Stop swamping around in Bangla."

Khadija ignored that last part. "Swamping around" was what he called her work with Alor Desh. Half in jest, half serious. She hadn't managed to pass on her love for Bangladesh to her son. He'd reluctantly agreed to work as a doctor in Bangladesh for a period equivalent to his time at university in England. That was the deal they'd made. Three more terms. How was she going to tell him? She still had a few days so she decided to hold off.

"Can I meet Sara? She looked very sweet in the pictures you sent."

"Absolutely! I was thinking we might go for a curry tonight. Are you up for that? And then her parents in Islington want to have you over. You'll love them." He gave her a warm look and wiggled his eyebrows playfully above his sunglasses. "Politically correct, naïve idealists. Just like you."

18

Nazreen pushed Meena ahead of her. The big gate slid open and the guard, who recognised Nazreen, nodded indifferently. Meena heaved the bundle containing all her wares onto her back and stepped into the driveway, which was strewn with toys. Nazreen walked behind her with a hand on her back.

"It's okay. We're allowed to walk here. We're safe. Come on, there, behind the garage."

The house was white and silent. A large entrance not meant for them was held up by white columns. A marble staircase that poured out onto the driveway ended in a glassed-in entrance with a carved wooden door. On the top step were neat planters. Next to them, someone had parked a tiny plastic truck. Meena registered all the unfamiliar things.

The smell of urine greeted them as they rounded the garage. A temporary concrete staircase behind the privy led up to the roof. They had to step over rebar sticking out of the wall. Nazreen led the way, eager to show her sister.

"Here! Come, look!"

On her way up the stairs, Meena could see into the bideshi family's garden. She glimpsed a veranda with large bamboo furniture. Big windows opened up onto it. Was that where the family slept? Nazreen had said she liked the family. The man in particular seemed nice, the woman was apparently always busy. The children were blonde, she'd said, white-haired like old people. Meena craned her neck curiously.

Did they ever play in the garden?

Two concrete rooms had been built on the garage roof at some point, directly against the main house. Outside the rooms ran a poorly constructed wall topped with a corrugated metal sheet that covered a small cooking area. The rooms were narrow and windowless, it took Meena's eyes a few seconds to adjust to the gloom. The only light came in through a gap at the top of the wall where the bricks didn't reach all the way up. There was a bed and a metal footlocker in each room. And there were ceiling fans.

Meena couldn't believe her eyes. So much space! For just the two of them! And fans! And a lightbulb! She also noted a power outlet where she would be able to charge her mobile phone.

"Here," she went over to the doorway of one of the rooms. "Our storage room. It's enormous. And we have guards, no one can steal our things." Then she took a step over to the doorway of the other room. "And we can sleep here."

Nazreen, looking pleased, nodded and explained.

"The guards will give us gas for the stove, and they might be able to connect our electricity to the family's diesel generator when there's a power cut. That would make the electricity a lot more reliable than in Badda!"

"Nazreen, this is amazing! And you said we don't have to pay rent?"

"Yes, I think it's included in my salary. They didn't seem to want any money."

Meena had disappeared into her appointed storage room and eagerly begun to unpack her bundle. Nail polish and toothbrushes were put in piles on the bed and she measured and assessed the space.

"We can feel safe here. I can keep a lot of goods here. Nazreen – Allah shorbo shoktiman – the power belongs to Allah. Look how he cares for us! Maybe I should consider buying in proper bulk, straight from the docks? Nazreen, this is incredible. This means . . ."

"This means we're together and safe. That's the most important thing. We don't have to depend on Reka and Babul anymore. Miraj and the neighbours can't get to you."

Nazreen walked up to Meena and hugged her from behind. Meena was halfway into her sack. She had something she wanted to show her sister. A black, synthetic piece of cloth fell out.

"No, no one is going to get to me. I've bought one of these."

She unfolded the burqa and pulled it over her head. "What do you think? Now who's going to have opinions about what I do?"

She spread her arms and waved them about so the black fabric shimmered. Nazreen sank down onto the bed and slowly shook her head.

"No, Meena-shona, not that." She looked at Meena's face, which she could just about make out behind the mesh screen, but didn't feel as happy as her sister seemed to think she should be. "We're not that kind of family. What would Amma think, and Mokta? This is giving up everything. Mahmoda would never forgive us."

She gestured resignedly with one hand. Meena sat down next to her on the bed.

"But Nazreen, I'm *not* like that. Like the burqa women, like the mullahs want." She searched for words. "I'm Meena. But I need protection. You have no idea how relaxing it is to wear a burqa, it makes you invisible." Meena was trying to explain. "Everyone thinks I'm devout and leave me alone. Which is exactly what I need. I walked past Miraj yesterday and bought an enormous jackfruit right under his nose. Do you see what I mean?"

Nazreen fingered the cloth and said nothing.

"You're going to die of heatstroke," she mumbled, then raised her hand and stroked her sister's back through the fabric. She looked sad. Meena tried again:

"It doesn't mean the same thing here as in the village. Amma and Mokta have never been to Dhaka, they don't understand it doesn't have to mean you're devout. It just looks like you are."

"Nazreen nodded, looking thoughtful. Then she jumped up, saying she was eager to introduce Meena to the people in the house. Nazreen wasn't in the habit of dwelling, and Meena seemed to know what she was doing.

"Well, you won't get me to wear one, that's for sure," she said firmly. "I'm thinking of buying jeans. You know? Blue, thick shalwars? We live in a bideshi house now, under the protection of Boss and Madame. I've asked people not to tell Babul we're here."

"And you don't think they will?" Meena shook her head, dived back into her bundle and fished out the plastic box with their money. She carefully placed it at the bottom of the metal footlocker before wiggling out of the burqa and placing it on top.

Meena sat down on the bench next to Nazreen and waited for Beppin's tea to come to a boil. She felt good. A new home and a new start in Dhaka. The plastic box was safe. She'd reclaimed what was hers. The thought of Babul's soiled shirts sent a jolt of smugness through her.

Suddenly, a redheaded Western woman unexpectedly ducked in under the tarpaulin. She called out "Assalamu alaykum. Kemon acho?" in every direction and dashed at the embarrassed, lungi-clad men on the benches, hand extended. Her arms and shoulders were bare and her bare legs stuck out below the hem of her dress. Many of the men had never seen a Westerner up close and gawked unabashedly.

Beppin dropped what he was doing and asked her to have a seat. She'd apparently been here before, Meena realised with astonishment.

The introduction to the rest of the house staff had gone well. Hanif, the cook, had been welcoming, handing her a dry piece of dough that tasted like cinnamon.

"The children's favourite," he'd explained with an air of expertise. "Swedish. *Kanelbulle*."

"He's trying to ingratiate himself so you won't tell anyone he brings rice home every night. He buys double of everything and lets Madame and Boss pay," Nazreen explained. "Sometimes he shares, though, so it's a good thing."

The gardener, old Sirul, had told her she had to jump over the flowerbeds if she was cutting through the yard on her way to the garage roof at night, and the family's driver, Nizamuddhin, had told Meena a joke she didn't understand. The two guards had greeted her politely and she'd realised she enjoyed a certain amount of respect as the ayah's sister. The ayah worked indoors and was higher-status than the people who worked outdoors.

Meena watched in fascination as the redheaded, slender Western woman tried to balance on Beppin's home-made bench. Her wrists rattled with Hindu bracelets and she wore large sunglasses on her nose. She seemed intent on making friends with Beppin.

"A Christmas present, for you. Do you know about Christmas? Happy Christmas?"

Meena understood her English, but realised Beppin was clueless. The woman handed him a parcel and Nazreen stepped in, explaining in Bangla. Beppin listened attentively.

"It's their annual holiday, which is called Christmas. They give each other presents as a sign of friendship. Boss and Madame gave me a gift before they left. A handbag."

Nazreen held up her handbag and pointed at it. Beppin lit up. The redhead looked to Nazreen for further assistance.

"Can you translate, please, Nazreen? Your name's Nazreen, right?"

"Yes. We're not exactly used to celebrating Christmas, so I had to explain to Beppin. Beppin is very happy, he says thank you. Dhonnobad."

Beppin unwrapped the gift. There were several layers of colourful wrapping paper. He turned it over and over before managing to get the paper off to reveal a biscuit platter rimmed with gold.

The Western woman smiled and turned to Nazreen.

"You're Janne and Sofia's *ayah*, aren't you? I've seen you at the club a few times. Anyway, I just wanted to show my appreciation. Beppin has really . . ."

The word "Sofia" made a young girl who had been slumped at the edge of the small stand rouse herself.

"Madame Sofia? Sofia from Sweden?" She switched to Bangla. "I've been waiting and waiting, where is she? She's my friend!"

The redhead looked up in surprise. Where had the girl come from?

"She's my friend and I've been waiting."

Nazreen turned to the girl and stepped in again. Vanja studied the girl with interest.

"Madame and Boss are on vacation. In Thailand. I work for them. Can I help you?"

"No, I was just wondering. When will she be back? Sofia from Sweden? Can you tell her Rehana was here? Rehana from Copenhagen Garment Inc."

The girl got up to leave. But now Meena was suddenly paying attention. She looked the girl up and down.

"Copenhagen Garment Inc. A garment factory? Where is it?"

"Behind Gulshan-2, Copenhagen Garment Inc., next to the Landmark Building. My Amma works there, I'm not really old enough . . ." She shot the Western woman a concerned look. But the woman was busy trying to talk to Beppin about the platter she'd given him.

"I have a job as a thread cutter, mostly to help Amma. But when I'm older . . ."

"You can get into the factory?"

"Yes, of course I can get in. I know everyone there."

Meena nodded, intrigued. She contemplated Rehana for a moment and then said in a warm tone:

"Would you mind doing me a favour? I would like to sell some things. I need to get past the factory gates. Can you help me? I'll pay you good money."

*

Siv got up from the massage table. The girl put her hands together in front of her chest and bowed deeply to her. Was she satisfied?

Indeed, was she satisfied? Most of the masseuses at the spa on the club roof did a good job the first three or four times. But then it was as though they slacked off. The massages became half-hearted and weak.

No feeling. But this had actually been good. She gave the girl a curt nod.

"Yes, I'm satisfied. Good, thank you."

Siv retreated to the changing rooms and was overcome with the feeling of loneliness she sometimes felt after a massage. As though her need for intimacy and skin contact had been thrown wide open only to slam shut again. She was suddenly reminded how starved she was of physical contact. She needed those hands. Needed the rush of pleasure the hands induced. Bought and paid for pleasure, granted, but still.

This Christmas, she was just going to look after herself. That's what she said when people asked. Work and look after herself. Like now. Slip out during her lunch hour and indulge in a spa treatment.

Last Christmas had been a disappointment. She'd used one of her complimentary trips to Sweden to go home to Vallentuna, figuring people would be at least a little bit interested in her life. But no. She'd gifted her mother and older sister silk scarves and shown them pictures. But after admiring the scarves and glancing at the photographs, they'd launched into a discussion of a TV programme apparently called "Let's Dance". They hadn't asked her a single question, and when she had brought up Bangladesh, they'd listened politely and then changed the subject. At one point, her sister had pulled her aside and hissed:

"Mum's slowing down, in case you haven't noticed? I'm wondering if it's getting to be time to put her in a home. Things would be a lot easier if you'd move back soon. From Dakar."

While Siv walked the short distance between the club and the embassy, she pondered her next move. Taking care of her aging mother in Sweden was distinctly unappealing and there was no chance she'd keep her administrative manager title back at SwedeAid headquarters. Dakar had, as a matter of fact, closed down, but maybe somewhere else in Africa? Kenya? Or Tanzania with its beaches and Zanzibar? Because Siv was moving on, she was. This summer. At the same time, though, she liked living in Dhaka. If Moberg had signed on for a sixth year, she would have considered staying on as well. Managing his embassy suited her. Ever since she realised you have to take charge in a workplace, she herself felt she'd done an excellent job. That being said, without her and Moberg's unspoken agreement about how to run the embassy, she didn't dare to stay. She countersigned all his expenses without asking questions. He didn't meddle in her running of the administrative side of things. Siv shuddered when she thought about the horrors a new ambassador and Sofia could inflict on her between them.

As the guards opened the embassy gate for her in exchange for an aloof nod, she noted that Babul was waiting for her by the entrance.

"Madame," he said, bowing. "Has Madame had time to . . ."

Babul was always flapping about, doing things to draw her attention. She was smart enough to know his strategy was to do his job visibly. Make sure he was seen. Put the tea out on time. Remove a crumb-covered tablecloth. Always with a smile and a bow. A few weeks into her tenure, she had promoted him from kitchen assistance to office assistant. That had prompted him to expand his repertoire to constantly emptying her bin. Putting pens out for her every day. Making sure she got her afternoon tea before anyone else. Then he'd suggested she might want to make him administrative assistant. Since he was ambitious and unfailingly solicitous, she'd agreed. And now, he was angling for more.

"Babul. I don't know. Media Distribution Officer? Is that really necessary? Isn't delivering letters and newspapers part of your duties as administrative assistant?"

"I don't think so, Madame. I have been given a big responsibility. What if the post is lost? Who would be held responsible? An *officer* feels that responsibility. An assistant . . ."

He shook his head and made a face that seemed over the top to Siv. She sighed and opened her mouth to speak, but Babul cut in.

"So, excuse me, Madame, but maybe the best thing would be for me to have both titles. I don't mind. Both administrative assistant and media distribution officer. Both."

Eventually, Siv managed to get Babul out of her office without promising too much. But his suggestions had made her think about her own career. She'd heard that in some embassies, the administrative manager could step in as deputy. Become a counsellor. Should she suggest that? Though she supposed Sofia had already been appointed deputy.

The thought of Sofia made her get up from her desk. Sofia and her mess of a family were in Thailand for the holidays. Perhaps she should have a look in her office while she was away. Water a plant, perhaps.

Siv entered Sofia's office. Stacks of paper on the visitor's chairs. She'd had the temerity of removing the embassy's poster from the Museum of Modern Art in Stockholm and hang a lithography instead. Siv had to step closer to make out the name . . . no one she recognised. There were pictures of the children on the windowsills and on the wall behind the door she had put up several children's drawings with thumbtacks. Siv frowned. That was unacceptable. An embassy was a Swedish government agency and had to maintain a certain polish. What would visitors think?

On the desk sat a stack of papers stamped Confidential. Siv took a closer look. "Forensic Audit of Landrights Organisation Alor Desh". *Forensic.* Wasn't that a criminal term? She recognised the word from watching *Midsomer Murders.* She glanced over at the door, but the hallway outside was quiet.

"Misuse of funds", "Possible embezzlement", "Ghost employees", "Bribery", "Immediate legal action". Siv read on. Next to the Alor Desh papers, she found Sofia's notes. Something in them made her look again. She squinted. It took her a minute to decipher the scrawling handwriting, but then she discerned a pattern. "Extremely good results, should be given a second chance. Have to acknowledge the complexity, difficult context. Who else works there? Khadija high profile, person with integrity. Gossip/land grabbing/violent Islamification, extremism/climate. Where are we leaving them??" And then, underlined three times: "Meet with British asap" and an arrow pointing to "Stockholm" and "Build argument!!"

Before her thoughts had time to form fully, Siv carefully detached the cover page from the stack of papers. Registration number, date. Then she picked up Sofia's notepad.

A few quick strides took her to the photocopier. Copies rattled out. She had just finished arranging the papers into a neat pile when Babul appeared around the corner and with a bow asked how she wanted her tea.

*

The hammock on the veranda was rocked by the mild breeze. Sofia closed her eyes. From inside their hut, she could hear Janne reading aloud to Noella. They tried to make sure to read all the Swedish classics now that the children were growing up in an international environment.

Teo had fallen asleep next to her in the hammock. In one hand, he was clutching a seashell and in the other, two dummies. They had to put a stop to the dummies, Sofia thought to herself. Those dummies were health hazards.

Their stilt hut was located on the beach in Khao Lak. Sofia could see the ocean and the waves below. She needed this, a family get-away. Distance from Dhaka. She and Janne had had good conversation, good love-making. They'd giggled when they realised their neighbours must have noticed their hut shaking when they made love. The children's tanned little bodies under the fan in the next room.

The days on the beach were intense and between jungle excursions and playing with the children in the sand, her mind kept turning recent events over and over. Moberg had managed to nip the conference in the bud. She was trying not to be paranoid, but how deliberate had his actions been? How was she supposed to do her job if her superior didn't want anything done? Any ambition on her part was perceived as a threat. The day after their confrontation, he'd popped by her office, the epitome of pleasantness. Suggesting she travel to Manila for a conference and adding that she should feel free to stop by Cambodia on the way to support their embassy there in their access-to-justice work. He would be happy to endorse and sign the decision if she wanted to go. Stunned, Sofia had said she'd think about it, her anger suddenly seeming out-of-place.

The debacle with the conference on violence against women set her back twelve months or so, but Moberg would be gone next year. And Willcott would still be at the World Bank – she'd checked – and she'd reviewed their plans and deliberately squashed them.

"She owes us now," as Antje had put it. "We'll back off for now and give her Khadija Anam. That means she's obligated to support our conference next year, and throw the full weight of the World Bank behind it. Don't worry, she knows how it works."

Khadija Anam, yes. Sofia cringed inwardly. She'd gone from picturing herself in an international arena, as a person who picked the right battles, asked the right questions and had the right people on her side, to being the person left holding the bag. Defending the corruption would be difficult. No free points in Stockholm. She would be thought of as naïve and soft for not taking a hard-line stance. The fact that taking a hard-line stance was a lot easier than acting responsibly wouldn't occur to many people.

Colourful lights dangled above the veranda. One green, one blue, one yellow. Below them, the sea, whose waves had once turned into a deadly tsunami ravaging thousands of families, lapped peacefully against the sand, pushing up friendly little fluorescent foam breakers.

Sofia gazed out into the darkness. Khao Lak. Christmas time, just like now. Children who had gone to sleep, just like hers, after a day of beach fun. Her then-colleague had gone out for a dive on Boxing Day morning and never returned. Last summer, she'd seen her husband and their two children in town. How do you go on living after that kind of loss? She squeezed the boy sleeping in her arms. She sniffed his hair. Child sweat and salt. Why couldn't life be simpler? How were you supposed to grab the ball and play it and make a difference when no one seemed to appreciate it?

She'd changed since moving to Bangladesh. Who was she? Upstanding and spineless at the same time, as often strict and moralising as completely permissive. Sometimes dead certain, equally often deeply insecure. It had been easier to be a clearly-defined person back in Sweden, at the cool, remote policy level. Position-taking was inevitably easier when there was no reality to make everything complicated. Reality forced out nuances that didn't quite fit into a bureaucratic system. Outside of work, she could feel her self-image slowly eroding. She was a good person. She tried to do the right thing. She sided with the weak and voiceless. But now. On the same day that she gave a fiery speech about every person's equal value, she could also give her driver a good dressing-down for pretending to know how to read a map and getting lost. And while she fought for women's health at work, she didn't want Nazreen and her sister living on their garage roof. She even liked having someone fold all the laundry and enjoyed not having to cook.

And Janne, it was the same with him. She simultaneously kept him close and pushed him away. Loved him and wanted to punish him. How was that going to work out in the long run? Everything was unstable. She hugged the little boy again. But the children, at least they existed. They were real. Her's and Janne's little miracles.

Janne stepped out onto the veranda.

"Do you want me to take him? You stay there."

He carefully picked up the boy and disappeared back into the house. When he came back out, he was carrying two wineglasses. He climbed up on the wooden railing and leaned back against one of the columns supporting the hemp-fibre roof.

"What are you thinking about?"

"If I say work it'll just make you angry." Sofia looked at him and reached out to push off against his leg. "Being here's good. I need some distance."

Janne nodded and gazed out at the sea. They sat in silence. A group of swift bats moved among the trees. Sofia went on:

"I was just thinking about what's *right*. About doing what you think is right. It's not easy." There was a long pause. "It's easier to be a good person in Sweden. I'm going to try to be a bit kinder to you too, Janne."

"Well, that does sound like the right thing to do." He smiled at her. "But you mean at work. Something about the gap between theory and practice, right?"

"Yes, sort of. Everything's always so extreme in Bangladesh: all my decisions, all my choices, everything I say and think is loaded and immediately put to the test in reality. Here we are, on a hardship trip. Swedish tax money pays for our holiday because it's considered so hard to live and work in Bangladesh, but since when are we the ones experiencing hardship? You should have seen where Rehana and her mother live. That's real hardship."

She sipped her wine.

"So what are you going to do? About Alor Desh? I assume that's what this is about?"

Sofia continued to sip while she thought and spoke by turns. "Yes. I'm changing my mind. I think. There are a lot of grey areas. Would I be wrong to go to bat for them?" She stopped and held her glass up to one of the lights, studied its light through the wine. "Life's short. I could die tomorrow. Maybe this is my chance to make a difference? I mean, real difference. Pulling out would hurt a lot of people in the char area."

"Well, you know what we think. Me and the Country Director of the World Bank." Janne smugly crossed his legs. He held up two crossed fingers and joked.

"Me and her, *this* tight."

"It's career suicide, though. You're going to have to be prepared for this to be my last international posting. I'm not going to have a friend left at SwedeAid. Do you still have the documents Charlotta gave you?"

"The whole lot is sitting on my desk in Dhaka. Go over them and you'll see what you have to do. Regardless."

"Regardless of what? The consequences?" Sofia snorted derisively. "That's easy for you to say." Sofia fell silent and stared into the night. Janne brought her back.

"So what are you going to do now? Concretely?"

"I think I'm going to skip even consulting Moberg from now on. This is my job. I feel I've consulted him enough. And I'm going to have to go to Stockholm fairly soon. Call a meeting. Explain to the corruption advisors. Advocate. Swear on my life that Khadija Anam is honest."

She turned to him and pointed her wineglass at him.

"Would you? You've spent time with her in the village. Is she honest? Would you swear on your life?"

Janne didn't answer. Instead, he jumped down from the railing and took the glass out of Sofia's hand. He put both glasses down on a small table and pulled her out of the hammock.

"Beautiful, darling goat woman. The only think I can swear on my life is that I love you. And I'm proud of you! What was it you said, you were going to be a bit kinder going forward?"

He kissed her tenderly. A playful tongue. He butted his forehead against hers and whispered. "Can't we be friends again. For real. Can't you just . . . forget?"

Janne's question about being friends had two dimensions. Firstly, the Camilla dimension, ever-present. Secondly, the everyday dimension. They'd quarrelled earlier in the week. Janne had suddenly struck up a conversation with some German families and when Sofia came back from a foot massage, she found out he'd arranged to have dinner with them that night, and to go on a boat excursion at a later date.

"Incredibly interesting people," Janne had beamed. "One guy just had his tenure as head of education for all of eastern Düsseldorf extended, which means he's overseeing both the east and the west district."

Sofia had sighed and scowled at Janne. Were new friends really what they needed? She'd managed to cancel the boat excursion but had compromised about dinner. Instead of the cosy family dinner they so sorely needed, they'd joined the families from Düsseldorf, who'd laughed raucously at Janne's jokes and let him be the centre of attention. Sofia had gritted her teeth and focused on helping the children with their satay skewers. Teo had needed constant supervision, he'd been more interested in a stray cat than the German children. Sofia's irritation had reached peak levels when they realised after the dinner that they wouldn't be able to get the deposit back for the sailboat they'd rented.

"You might have asked me before you paid a deposit. I would have had said no," Sofia hissed.

"Maybe that's why I didn't ask," Janne had replied, adding sullenly. "You're not the boss of me."

That little skirmish had passed, but it had been so typical. He needed so much attention it made her exhausted. Because what if he didn't get it? Would there be another Camilla?

Sofia still went black inwardly and had trouble breathing when she thought about how Janne had betrayed her at her most vulnerable. She, tired from sleepless nights with an infant, he, in bed with a colleague. Was the fact that she was still holding a grudge pathological? How did people go from symbiotic lovers to battered and flawed, yet durable? They had talked and talked and she had raged and been furious. But in the end, she'd said she wanted to carry on, that she wanted her family and Janne. Janne who was so much more than his charm. It was just that it always stood in their way.

But forgetting? Sofia didn't know how to perform the kind of volte face that would let them land back on their feet. Was forgetting the key? Because that was what she wanted, right? To live with Janne? She liked discussing her work with him and share everyday life with him and the children. She enjoyed having sex with him, liked his smell and his grunting, enthusiastic manliness. It was when he had to be Wonderful Janne, friend to all, that she put up a wall. She didn't want to be one of his admirers. She wanted to keep him on a short lead and continue to punish him.

Now he was kissing her face, starting to lick salt off her neck. Let his thumbs flutter around her nipples through her bikini top. She stood with her feet wide and her eyes closed and her face turned to the sky, accepting his tenderness.

"We're always friends, no?" she mumbled. "But you always need so many friends. Why aren't the children and I enough?"

Afterwards, they lay entangled in a sweaty, white sheet, listening to the tropical night outside. The mosquito net swayed under the fan. After Sofia fell asleep, Janne answered her question in a whisper.

"It's always been just you, Sofia. You're enough. But am I?"

*

Moberg had defended himself. As had Ericsson-Olle. The Boxing Day dinner had turned into a blackmailing scene where the two wives, Vanja and Malena, had pressed their husbands hard. Ericsson-Olle had crawled deeper and deeper into the Josef Frank fabric of the embassy sofa and at several points over the course of the evening, he'd bravely tried to change the subject. Bangladeshi politics. Swedish politics. The telecom infrastructure in Asia. He'd even tried asking questions about the origins of the Bengali language. Moberg had gratefully seized on each attempt at distraction. But their wives had been relentless.

"This is a unique opportunity. Something that only happens once," Vanja had pushed.

"It's just a fun thing, the way I see it. Come on!" Malena had explained. "It would be something to write home about, for once. The ayah can watch the girls."

An internationally renowned shaman was visiting Dhaka and the P.E. teacher at the American school had personally invited Vanja and Malena to some hocus-pocus ritual. Moberg had barely been able to bear to listen, but he knew his negotiating space was minimal. After the faux pas with the photographs from Nepal, Vanja had a hold over him. And she was determined. New Year's Eve was going to be celebrated with drums and a sacred fire on the P.E. teacher's roof.

And now, here they were, holding hands in a big circle around a fire. It was almost midnight and the drums were deafening. The shaman had walked around the circle, asking all participants to breathe in the smoke from his torch. Moberg had anxiously scanned the other participants and been relieved to find he didn't know anyone. This was neither the rich Bengalis' nor the diplomats' scene, he noted. The group appeared to consist mainly of the wives of international businessmen. And a teacher or two from the American school. He and Ericsson-Olle were the only men and Ericsson-Olle was unlikely to say anything. This was equally mortifying for both of them.

The shaman leapt and mumbled. His eyes were closed and his body swayed rhythmically to the beat of the drums. Moberg glanced at Vanja. She had let go of his hand and was extending her arms toward the fire at the centre of the circle, staring into the flames. Ericsson-Olle was holding his wife's hand. The shaman suddenly threw himself to one side and started hyperventilating. He was bare-chested and wore a skirt of animal pelts around his waist. A profusion of leather thongs were tied around his upper arms. Sweat was streaming down his torso and his naked skin reflected the dancing flames. Then he threw himself in the opposite direction. He held the torch up high above his head and chanted in unknown languages, which interested Moberg for a second. Was that syntax familiar?

The compelling beat of the drums grew louder and louder. The shaman had thrown his torch into the fire and was flapping his arms about, still hyperventilating. Vanja started to step to the rhythm of the drums and Malena followed suit. The shaman walked up to Vanja and held out a tattooed arm. He took her by the hand and Vanja turned to Moberg.

"Come on," she said. The shaman saw what she wanted and pulled Moberg along with his other hand. Moberg followed on stiff legs. Enveloped in the pounding drum beat, the shaman showed Vanja that she should squat in front of the fire, and that Moberg should stand with both arms stretched out above her.

Moberg felt like he stood there with his arms over his wife for an eternity. He didn't dare to so much as glance in Ericsson-Olle's direction. When the shaman came over and urged him to find a bass note and sound it into the drums, while slowly flapping his arms, he felt he was already making such a fool of himself, he might as well do as the shaman said.

It was only when he got back to his place in the circle and his eyes adapted to the surrounding darkness that he realised what had happened. At the stroke of midnight, a small group of revellers had come out onto the roof of the house next door. They were holding champagne bottles and flutes and ogled the spectacle in astonishment. Someone snapped a picture.

To his horror, Moberg recognised Peter Lewis from British DfID. Peter slowly raised his glass to him and even though he was some distance away, Moberg could see his lips move.

"Happy New Year."

19

Meena let the burqa cover both her cloth bundles. There, now no one would know what she was doing. She asked the guards to open the gate, quickly looked both ways and then slipped out. Beppin wouldn't say anything. But would Nizamuddhin? So far, no one in Badda seemed to know where she'd gone. They'd either stopped caring about her or it was only a matter of time before they realised she was the one tracing her own footsteps in a burqa. Since Rifat was under strict orders not to risk leading Miraj and his posse to the house in Baridhara, they now always met up in the marketplace and communicated primarily via mobile phone.

Meena prayed inwardly to Allah. La hawla wa la quwwata illa billah. Let him protect me and keep the demons at bay. Allah is the greatest.

Rehana had appeared at just the right time. It hadn't taken her long to grasp how Meena's business worked. They'd spent several days walking around the docks together, buying things the garment workers might like. Sparkly hair ties. Underwear. Tiny bottles of neem oil. Pain killers. Hemp bags. Eye shadow. Meena had taken a deep breath and paid. Since Nazreen stopped counting the money, deciding to trust her implicitly, Meena had been freer to act as she saw fit. And her business was thriving. Maybe Allah approved of her wearing a burqa? Maybe he wanted to reward her? With more money and Rehana's contacts, she had entirely new ways of reaching the garment workers.

Now the small room in Baridhara was crammed from floor to ceiling with various goods and she had put in orders for a lot more. Rehana had known as much about garment workers as she herself knew about village life. You had to have genuine insight into people's lives and dreams to understand what they would want to buy.

"You can only sell manicure cases to the women who have more qualified jobs in the factories. The lead seamstresses," Rehana had explained. "They end on time most days, so you'd have to be there at eight. The junior seamstresses would never be able to afford beauty kits. They don't have the time or the money, but that's what's great. We can sell them knick-knacks they don't usually have the time to buy. They work all the time, so you have to catch them around eleven at night. My Amma's one of them." Rehana had said that last part with her eyes on the ground. Otherwise, she was always happy and sweet. Always punctual and kept close track of the money.

Like now. Meena checked the time on her phone. Half past five in the morning. And, true to form, there Rehana was. The gates to Copenhagen Garment Inc. were about to open.

*

Janne felt himself going cold. Not another beggar. Like stubborn flies, they were. He quickly rolled up his window and sighed heavily. Thailand had been so restful. Clean, tidy. Sweet-smelling and easy. He closed his eyes and reminisced. Sofia had been so open and relaxed, they'd talked like they used to. Close. They'd had time to listen to each other. And he'd lost at least seven pounds, maybe more. Long swims and lots of salads. The children tanned and happy, recharged by the closeness and saltwater. After two weeks in Thailand, Dhaka felt almost painfully chaotic. Wasn't there a layer of grey dust covering everything, too? Didn't the men dragging themselves around in their pyjamas look utterly depressed, and weren't they all completely misogynistic?

"Dad, are the twins going to be there? If they're not, I don't wanna go!" Noella's shrill little voice from the backseat snapped him out of his reverie.

Nizamuddhin had the day off for once and Sofia was working late, so Janne had decided to take the children to the club himself. Enjoy the barbecue and listen to a Norwegian folk singer playing "Oldies and Goldies", talk to adults for once. He'd brought Nazreen to look after the children so he would be free to make conversation.

"Let's hope the twins are there, sweetheart. Otherwise, I'm sure there are other children . . ." Janne cursed inwardly. He'd forgotten to text Malena to ask if they were going to the barbecue. Noella was fixated on playing with the twins.

"Otherwise, I'm not gonna," the girl announced and stuck her nose in the air.

Janne didn't reply. The traffic was ridiculously congested. They came to a standstill in a roundabout. All around the, cars were reversing and manoeuvring out of seemingly impossible tangles. Half of the cars had entered the roundabout going the wrong way so now there was a struggle over which direction was the correct one. Janne sighed again.

Eventually, the traffic scrambled loose and after a few more minutes of drive-brake-drive-veer-brake-zigzag, they were able to turn down road 55, home to the Swedish embassy and the Nordic Club.

Janne suddenly heard a thud. Then someone screamed. Janne spotted a young, agitated man, who urgently signalled for him to stop and pointed to something in front of the car. He banged his hand on the bonnet. Janne stopped and opened his door.

"What's going on?"

They were surrounded in seconds. In front of the car lay a man with no limbs. Janne recognised one of the lepers from Gulshan market, who was always fairly aggressive about his panhandling. The lepers often dragged themselves across the streets in groups, shouting their "Allahu akbar, Allahu akbar". But this time, this man was alone. His torso was wrapped in rags and someone was trying to heave him back into the cart he'd apparently toppled out of. While the leper screamed and sputtered, people were giving Janne accusing looks.

"Nizamuddhin, if only Nizamuddhin were here," Janne cursed. "What do I do now?"

Then Nazreen was suddenly standing beside him. She said something placating in Bangla to the growing crowd and listened to the hissings of the leper.

"Boss," Nazreen said, turning to Janne. "He says you ran him over. He was begging on the corner. Maybe you didn't see him?"

"Oh my God, Nazreen. Tell him I'm so sorry. Can I . . . ?"

Janne felt a hundred pairs of eyes turning to him. Were they threatening? He walked over to the man and tried to help him get settled in his little cart. The man smelled strongly of infection and filth. Janne felt the blood drain out of his face. He looked at Nazreen.

"Please, Nazreen. What do we do now? What am I supposed to do? This is terrible, I could've killed him. Can I pay?"

Nazreen nodded and squatted down next to the man. They seemed to negotiate, quietly and efficiently. Janne perspired and tried to calm the children, who wanted to know what was going on.

"Don't worry. Daddy just has to see to something."

Nazreen was done striking a deal.

"Two thousand taka, Boss."

"That's it? Tell him I can pay more, five thousand. Maybe he needs medical care? Is he hurt? Ten thousand?"

"Two thousand will do fine. Do you have money on you?"

Janne nodded and dashed back to the car, but couldn't get the door open. People were pressed up against it and the handle slipped out of his clammy hand. The crowd watched his every move. Eventually, he managed to get the door open. Noella was bored and had turned on a Pippi Longstocking DVD. Teo was sucking his thumb, slumped against the side of his car seat. They seemed completely unperturbed by the faces pressed against the windows.

Janne rooted around his bag and at length found his wallet. Rummage, rummage, there, two thousand. It was nothing. He could've killed the man! He could've been killed himself. Crowds could be dangerous, he'd been told.

Janne jumped out of the car brandishing the money, sticking them under the leprous man's nose. Since the man had no arms, he just hissed. Janne felt a new wave of perspiration break out. Nazreen calmly stepped in and took the money from Janne. She handed it to the young man who had first banged on their car. Then she signalled to Janne that they should make a swift retreat. Get in the car and leave.

Once they were back inside the car, Janne caught Nazreen's eye in the rear-view mirror. Was everything okay? He felt shaken. Nazreen looked happy and placid as usual. She met his gaze, nodded her head slightly and smiled.

"It's the poor man's business plan, no problem, Boss."

When they got to the club, Janne realised his legs were shaking. He needed a drink. He made sure the children got in the pool with Nazreen sitting on a chair next to it, then went to the restrooms. Thankfully, there was a large bottle of alcogel next to the sink. He scrubbed himself clean. His arms, hands, face and neck. First soap, then alcogel. Bloody hell. Poverty reeked. He felt infected by his physical contact with the leper.

Bjarne, standing out by the bar, quickly picked up on Janne's agitation.

"Having a Dhaka crisis? Whiskey?"

Janne was relieved at the chance to unload. Bjarne was facing the restaurant, his elbows propped on the counter. He half-listened to Janne while scanning the people who had gathered to eat and listen to music. Janne was still shaken. He spotted his own reflection between a bottle of Cinzano and another of gin. It was ashen.

Bjarne nodded along to the music.

"I'm sure your ayah's right, it was a setup."

"You think?" Janne sheepishly turned to him.

"Sure, they hang around street corners, waiting. And when they see a bideshi driving . . . bam!" He illustrated the collision with a hand gesture. "Well, and usually, it works. We're so upset we're prepared to pay whatever they ask. Right?"

Janne stared at Bjarne.

"Are you yanking my chain?"

"Hell no. I know you think I'm an old cynic, but this time, I'm right. Last year, someone heaved their old grandma onto Gulshan Avenue. After she was already dead." He sipped his drink and laughed. "They managed to get money for her twice in one day! Imagine that! That's what I call an entrepreneurial spirit! Private sector development."

He laughed and Janne felt sick. They were interrupted by Malena, who appeared with a crying Noella in her arms. Janne took the girl, who'd come straight out of the pool and was soaking wet.

"She collided with Felicia. She's fine, but I figured you'd want to comfort her since you're here. Your ayah is keeping an eye on Teo."

Malena nodded to Bjarne and Janne mumbled, "see you". Then he followed Malena to the pool. They sat down on a lounger and Janne inspected Noella's forehead. He could see the beginnings of a small bump.

"How was Thailand?" Malena asked. "Not as filthy and horrible as delightful Dhaka, I bet? We went to Hong Kong. It was so good to have some proper food! Walk on proper pavements, not have to step around faeces and muck."

Janne recoiled from Malena's whinging. He had his hands full dealing with his own internal griping. Tonight especially.

"It was nice. Good to spend some quality time with the family, Sofia's always working so hard. But I think we're going to be leaving now . . ."

"Janne." Malena leaned forward. "I haven't had a chance to tell you about my backyard. I've ordered gutters. And a few joists."

"Okay?"

"Before Christmas, Vanja and I went down there to check the roofs of those little shacks. And I was right, the metal sheets are just placed on top, like lids on boxes. Do you know how warm that'll make the interiors? And the water from the wall runs straight into people's homes. We used sign language to communicate and they knew exactly what we meant. The way the roofs are, the water can trickle straight in. Get it?"

Malena sounded enthusiastic. Janne was only half-listening. He was trying to corral Teo and wrap him in a towel. He just wanted to go home.

Malena pressed on.

"The next day, I went down there again, this time with measuring tape. And I started talking to some of them. And now. When we got back from Hong Kong . . ."

She lit up, tugging on Janne's T-shirt to get his attention.

"It was like coming home, Janne! When I went down there the day before yesterday, people flooded out to see me. Everyone wanted to talk and show me their homes. They gave me food and asked me to sit. They call me Malena-apa."

"That's nice." Janne got ready to leave. "Did you meet a young man called Siraj, who has a little girl called Tomelilla? He's a good friend of mine."

"What? You know Siraj?"

Janne nodded and started looking for the children's bathing suits and toys, which were scattered around the pool. Nazreen took the hint and started packing up.

"Janne, give us a hand, will you? With the new roofs? If there's a few of us, we can definitely get it sorted before the rains come. Can't you . . . ?"

Janne felt his patience run out. Not today. Not now. No roofing in the slum and no Malena. No Bangladesh and no goddamn poor people. He declined politely but firmly, put a writhing Teo under his arm and strode out of the club.

When they reached their car, Janne realised that in his haze, he'd parked with one front wheel in the open sewer. He looked around for help. It had been a big mistake to give Nizamuddhin the night off.

*

Send, send and send. Sofia's fingers danced across the keyboard and she was pleased to note that she was a week ahead, despite just being back from her vacation. She had never missed a deadline in her professional life and always felt calmer when she had wide margins. Now the evaluation report on the measles vaccination campaign with her added comments would soon land in the UNICEF manager's inbox, the final report on the police reform programme had been read through and commented on long before the British expected it back and a job description for the new caseworker position had been sent off to Lasse Bergström in Stockholm. Everything was checked off and done. Some of the caseworkers, on the other hand, seemed to take a different view of deadlines than she did. Sofia had noted that Aisha was supposed to have completed a report by the start of the week and that Anna-Lena should have submitted her part of the embassy's operational plan long ago. The thought of their tardiness made Sofia frown, but before she had a chance to send reminder emails, Babul appeared in the doorway.

"Madame, your car is waiting. British DfID."

Babul remained stooped in a bow until Sofia had grabbed her bag and exited into the hallway, giving her irritation a new target.

"Stand up straight, for God's sake," she mumbled in Swedish as she passed the genuflecting man.

Half an hour later, Sofia sprinted up the stairs to the British foreign aid office in Gulshan. She had got stuck in traffic and was late, and this was an important meeting. After careful consideration, she had decided to make an honest attempt at saving Alor Desh, even if that meant defying every directive from her own bosses. The organisation was too good to close down, so now she would have to start pulling every string at her disposal. The result agenda versus the anti-corruption agenda. She had devised a plan together with Peter and Antje. The UKs local anti-corruption advisers were going to assess the audit and provide their Swedish colleagues with a recommendation, then Sofia would go to Stockholm to convince them in person.

Before entering DfIDs offices, she had to go through a security check.

"The Iraq War, you know," Peter apologised while Sofia's briefcase was meticulously searched by a guard and her body scanned with a wand. "Something's happened in Baghdad so the threat level is up at all offices and high commissions in the Muslim part of the world."

Peter led her to the lifts and up to the fourth floor, which was home to the Department of Support for the Civil Society and Democracy. People were clustered behind frosted glass and meetings were advertised on large whiteboards. Between the meeting modules, a vast office landscape spread out. Sofia nodded left and right as she trotted along in Peter's wake.

There was Noella's friend's mother, Sheila, who was the director of a large women's organisation. And there, she caught a glimpse of Rick, a climate researcher who played tennis with Janne sometimes. Kamrul, who was married to Habiba, a local consultant for SwedeAid, was sitting in a corner. Dhaka was a tiny pond. That thing about it being more like a big village was in fact rather accurate.

It was true, what someone had told her before she moved out here. The British still held great sway in their old colonies and other countries were ill-placed to understand their interests and agendas. Colonialism in a new guise. Compared to the UK, Sweden, Norway, the Netherlands, Canada and Denmark were peripheral actors in Bangladesh.

She would have preferred to work for the British. Or the UN. Big offices, big questions, big opportunities to effect change. Power. Was it wrong to want it?

The UK was world-leading when it came to foreign aid. Sofia wasn't the only one who thought so. Well-educated, influential, knowledgeable and fighting poverty was always their official overarching goal. At least until recently, when "growth" had begun to climb up their foreign aid agenda. But at least they called it "pro-poor growth", growth intended to trickle down to the poor and not get stuck higher up the food chain. Like in China. The World Bank preferred the simpler term "growth" and Stockholm was on the fence. To fight poverty or promote growth? Or were they the same thing? Was it necessary to focus on the poor, or did they eventually get their share of any potential growth as a matter of course? There were endless seminars and workshops on the subject.

"We're letting the private sector have a go now, too, since they're growth creators," Peter had commented with reference to his country's shifting priorities. "Private companies used to be banned from foreign aid, but now, they're suddenly being invited to claim a share of the billions. Makes you wonder who's going to build hospitals and schools from now on."

Sofia's priority when it came to foreign aid was human rights. With all this money, shouldn't human rights be built into the terms and conditions better? What happened to including poor people, to antidiscrimination and to transparency when the private sector became an actor? What kind of results could be expected of private companies?"

"Highlight the *results* our funding of Alor Desh has yielded," Lasse Bergström had told her in an email that also contained a brief apology and a private addendum claiming the Ministry of Foreign Affairs suffered from Obsessive Quantifying Disorder.

"I'm retiring soon, thank God. This is madness. Good luck quantifying those results!"

Attached to his email was a forty-page document full of matrices and tables, in which Alor Desh was to be quantified in relation to signed contracts, focus areas, policies, guidelines, impact and global agreements.

SwedeAid needed to demonstrate to the Ministry of Foreign Affairs and the taxpayers that the money invested in foreign aid made a difference. Sofia understood the game and wanted to email back – "if quick results are what we're after, we should reconsider working in difficult environments altogether". But who would appreciate that kind of reply? The demand for measurable results had led to everyone looking for quick, simple fixes. Eager to pick low-hanging fruit, as the saying went. Bridge building. Further education for the already well-educated. Tunnels. The much tougher task of working to change attitudes and empower the poor so they could stand up for their rights was difficult to measure and therefore under threat.

Behind the donor countries' seemingly reasonable demands for results and a zero tolerance approach to corruption lurked an ideological agenda that in all important respects was hostile to foreign aid. The market was going to solve all of the developing world's problems. Foreign aid was doomed to fail. Sofia was starting to discern the patterns.

Instead of emphasising the countless good things Sweden's foreign aid had made possible, in spite of the difficulties inherent in attempting to develop sound societies in a fundamentally unfair world, Sweden's Minster for International Development Cooperation was bent on pointing out SwedeAid's every failing and shortcoming and complaining to the press. Katta had been sending Sofia links to provocative statements made by their most senior boss all autumn. Most recently, Katta had written an email.

"I give it five years- five years from today, he will have shut down SwedeAid and cancelled Sweden's foreign aid. Want to bet? You should give some thought to what you want to do after you're made redundant."

So . . . results. It was, in fact, Lasse Bergström's email about results that had finally tipped the scale for Sofia. Fuck her career. A flood could sweep in any day and put an end to it. You never knew how much time you had to make a difference. Results? She'd give them results. That was why she'd requested a meeting with the Brits. She needed to sit down with the other donors supporting Alor Desh and discuss a possible rescue operation, despite the disastrous audit. It was time to grab that ball.

Three hours later, Sofia was in the car on the way back from DfID. Antje was sitting next to her. She nudged Sofia gently.

"You see. Sometimes, reason prevails. Now you go book a ticket back to Stockholm and talk them into it, too. Then Khadija Anam can continue to function as a trusted and exceptional tool to fighting poverty."

Sofia was relieved. With the UKs local corruption advisers on her side, she would have an easier time convincing her colleagues in Stockholm. And yet, she wasn't sure. SwedeAid's corruption team was made up of lawyers and accountants from various government agencies. They'd never set foot in a developing country and had no intention of ever doing so. They had made it clear the audit conducted by Ernst & Young was all they needed. Their mandate to "drain the foreign aid swamp" had come from the minister himself, and they took their duty very seriously. Sofia wasn't sure their grasp of ambiguity and complexity was as well-developed as the highly experienced local British team's. In a memo Sofia was bringing with her to Stockholm, the local auditors and the representatives of the other donor countries had expressed their opinion on the matter clearly and eloquently.

"The demand for quantifiable results from our foreign aid investments requires us to weigh this overarching goal against any potential malfeasance. Alor Desh has consistently demonstrated good, not to say exceptional, results and represents a set of values and store of knowledge that have been built up over a long time. We judge that the organisation has sufficient integrity to be granted increased administrative and financial support rather than a suspension of funding, which could prove devastating to its mission. The overarching aim of fighting poverty among some of the world's most vulnerable groups must not be sacrificed on account of temporary shortcomings in the organisation's bookkeeping.

We demand that any decision to withdraw Alor Desh's funding be preceded by a thorough analysis of the vacuum such a withdrawal of funds might create. There is good reason to believe such a vacuum could create a recruitment opportunity for the violent jihadists already thought to be active in the area, and leave vulnerable groups exposed to criminal elements and local mafias."

After the meeting, Peter had invited Antje and Sofia for a cup of coffee in his office. Unlike the Nescafé and dry crackers Siv so generously allowed them to have at the Swedish Embassy, the British understood the pivotal importance of "a nice cup of tea". Peter had fussed with his teapot and conjured up cappuccinos with tall foam for Antje and Sofia.

Antje and Peter had discussed the most recent gathering of Dev-Com, where they represented their respective countries. As usual, Sofia felt excluded and found out she hadn't been kept properly informed. Once again, Moberg had hoarded all information.

"Excuse me? The Canadians are working with UNESCO? In the education sector? What does UNICEF have to say about that?" Sofia wanted to know more.

Peter explained patiently.

"You didn't get the memo?"

"No, not yet."

"Yet? It was sent out last Monday! Sofia, Sofia," he shook his head. "You're going to have to circumvent Moberg and ask to be put on the cc list. Hold on, I'll email Tim, the Dev-Com secretary, right now."

He turned to his computer and started typing.

"There! He'll put you on the list straight away. It boggles my mind Moberg hasn't done it already."

After sending the email, he shot Sofia an amused look and mockingly bobbed his foot up and down.

"You'll never guess who I saw on New Year's Eve, by the way, flapping his arms about like a lunatic in some king of voodoo dance!"

"No, who?" Sofia's interest was piqued.

"Sweden's Dev-Com representative. Mr Ambassador himself. Moberg. Your boss, love."

He laughed delightedly and moved his foot in big circles, he was so pleased.

"Ambassador Moberg sang and they had a big bonfire. And a man dressed in animal pelts was hopping around the fire, yes, indeed. It was a sight to be seen!"

Antje had opened her eyes wide and now burst out laughing. She looked over at Sofia whose jaw had, quite literally, dropped.

"I'm sorry? Moberg?"

"The very same. Sweden's ambassador. They were on the roof next to ours. On New Year's Eve, at midnight. They were hard to miss," Peter said smugly. "Someone actually snapped a picture with their phone."

"What? Now you have a hold on him!" Antje nudged Sofia. "You could strategically leak that information when you're back in Stockholm. 'Swedish ambassador attends voodoo party.'"

Sofia looked at her and Antje carried on, giggling.

"He is here in an official capacity, after all. He doesn't just represent himself. I think that party sounds well dodgy. And if you could rustle up a picture . . ."

Peter stepped in.

"Sofia is far too nice to do anything like that, she's Swedish. Don't forget! We Brits can be nasty buggers when there's need for it, and I'm sure you Dutch have it in you, too. But Swedes. No, they're good people. Always top of the class. No funny business."

He laughed loudly and nudged Sofia playfully with his foot.

"Excuse me?" Sofia felt provoked.

"Sofia." Antje leaned forward and adopted a pedagogical tone. "There's an opposite to 'if you scratch my back, I'll scratch yours'," she explained. "Moberg is making your life difficult so you can make his life difficult. He ruined our women's conference. An eye for an eye, a tooth for a tooth. A seat on Dev-Com for not exposing his life as a voodoo priest in Stockholm. Sounds about fair, no?"

Peter laughed.

"Outstanding. I love how to-the-point you are, Antje. And she's right, Sofia. It does sound fair."

*

Rifat made a face and jumped about like something had scared him. Then he lunged at the plate and devoured a *fuchka*, a crispy chick-pea ball, looking caught out. Meena laughed at his antics. She often laughed with Rifat. He was funny when he did impressions, identifying those tiny movements and sounds that made people recognisable. Patel. Miraj. His angry mother. The mullahs.

Meena was sitting on top of a wide wall at the Sadarghat docks in Old Dhaka. From her perch, she had a good view of the entire marketplace and was able to keep an eye on the boats as they docked, as well. Rifat climbed up to join her. No one knew them here and they were surrounded by the hubbub of the harbour. Two men were fighting over a cage of chickens on the steps leading down to the boats, four women in burqas swept past, their arms full of pineapples. A clutch of street children were playing with bottlecaps on the steps and an old man with a defective megaphone was urging everyone to give generously to the local mosque.

"Allahu akbar, Allahu akbar."

Meena's burqa was balled up in one of her tattered sacks. At Rifat's suggestion, they'd bought fuchka as a reward for doing so well. They slowly emptied the plate of crispy delicacies. An unnecessary indulgence, Meena thought, but business had been outstanding the night before and Rifat had proposed rewarding themselves. He felt Meena worked too hard and in the end, Meena had acquiesced.

Meena felt her belly fill with mashed chickpeas and potato, but it was the sharp coriander and chili that together with the tamarind juice and eggs created a flavour sensation she enjoyed sharing with Rifat. She felt better than she had in a long time and the thoughts of what had happened in Badda no longer weighed as heavily on her as before. It had worked. Shoving all the horrible things in a black box. Soiling Babul's shirts and then sneaking back in and putting them back on their hangers. He'd probably got the point when he discovered them. She smiled a little. After her act of revenge, she'd breathed more freely and been able to fall asleep without the black box spinning before her.

The taste of chili and coriander was strong and pure. Not long before, though, as they'd been scurrying about the quayside, coming across a large shipment of cheap wristwatches, Meena had retched as a man walked past, pushing a cart of fresh meat. Flies had buzzed around the meat and a wave of nausea had forced Meena to turn away. The same feeling as the morning before, when the smell from the open sewer had seemed unusually overpowering.

"Meena-apa," Rifat hissed suddenly. "Have you thought about what I said?"

He looked serious. A chapped hand quickly stoked Meena's cheek, but she pulled away.

"No one makes me feel like you, Meena. Before I knew you, I didn't know I was human, a man. I ran around like a stray dog. If you . . . If we . . ."

"Stop it, Rifat. You have to stop talking like that. I'm going to earn my own dowry and marry someone from my village, you know that. Someone who lets me keep a shop. Stop talking like that."

"Meena, there's no other girl like you, no one who makes me feel as much. I just want to be close to you, I can't explain it . . ."

"Then stop trying. Either way, I'm going back to my village."

Meena jumped down and Rifat followed. What Meena couldn't tell Rifat was that she was hoping to do better than him. Someone from a good family with education and maybe a real job. With a solid dowry, she could make that happen.

She started sorting through the washcloths they'd bought a sackful of. Light yellow, blue and green. The garment workers liked cheap washcloths. Three for twenty taka.

"I would let you do business," Rifat said, bending over the sack. "We could do business together. Like now."

"We're co-workers, nothing else, Rifat. Look at me. I'm not staying in Dhaka. I'm going to make money and move back home. There's no place for you in the village. Find someone else if you want to get married so badly."

Meena saw Rifat's thin body deflate. He'd never before been so explicit about what he wanted, and she had never shared her plans with him. Working side by side, she'd often felt his eyes on her face and noticed a longing in his eyes. No one cared about her like Rifat. But he didn't fit into her plan. True, she liked him and he made her laugh, but that was still a far cry from wanting to marry him. She would have preferred not to get married at all. In fact, she recoiled from the thought of it. Did she really have to get married? Subject herself to the painful thing Babul had done to her? And that she knew Mokta had wanted to run away from. She shook herself imperceptibly in revulsion.

Rifat grabbed a hemp sack, heaved it onto his shoulder and gave Meena a long look.

"What you don't get, Meena-jaan, is that I don't just want to get married like everyone gets married. I want to live with you every day. That's what I want. I never want to be away from you."

They parted ways once they'd left the docks. It was crucial they not be seen together anywhere near Gulshan or Badda. Meena slipped in behind some houses and quickly pulled on her burqa. There, safe.

It was stifling inside the burqa. The heat and odours emanating from her own body hit her when she jumped on the bus and squeezed in with the other women. A sour smell of sweat and urine. She was going to have to have a proper wash tonight. Even so, she felt grateful for the burqa and Allah. He gave and he took away. She obeyed him and he made her business prosper. That much had been established. So long as she wore the burqa, he would protect her.

When Meena reached Baridhara and the guards opened the gate for her, she saw, to her surprise, that Madame Sofia and Rehana were chatting on the wide marble front steps. There was no sign of Nazreen.

"Meena-apa, come sit with us!" Rehana's elated face beamed at her. "I have a gift for you. One for Madame Sofia and one for you!"

She handed her a small, hand-embroidered purse. Meena noticed Sofia had been given an identical one. Madame Sofia studied the curlicue flower on the case with interest.

"Dhonnobad, Rehana! Who taught you to embroider?" she asked. "It's very pretty."

"My mum and aunt were better than anyone in the village, before we moved to Dhaka. I think I get it from them."

Meena said nothing, just gingerly sat down on the steps. The small purse with its two compartments and little zippers was nice, but absolutely not something she would be able to sell. Every village woman in Bangladesh made similar ones. Meena wasn't impressed. She was, however, slightly touched by Rehana's joy at giving them away.

Rehana and Sofia almost seemed to be friends. Madame Sofia asked questions about Rehana and her mother and younger brothers. It gradually became clear to Meena that Madame Sofia had visited Rehana's home in Mahendipur. Meena wondered why a bideshi would ever want to go to the slum. Incomprehensible. Then she saw that Madame Sofia had brought out several bags of used clothes.

"Maybe for your brother, Sohel? What do you think?" She held up a pair of tiny denim shorts. "They used to be Teo's."

Rehana took the shorts and a pile of shirts. Sofia dug into another bag.

"Here, some medicine and fun plasters for the children and such. Some pills for headaches and upset tummies. This you use if you have a small wound." She held up a bottle. Meena studied the items carefully. Rehana looked happy.

"Bhalo, the boys really need clothes. Mum will be very happy."

"Right. Moltana, yes. When we were having curtains made, I bought far too many saris, would you like to have a look? Your mum might like them? Because you mostly wear shalwar kameezzes, don't you?"

Sofia disappeared into the house and Rehana hugged Meena.

"Isn't she wonderful. Madame Sofia? She's my friend."

When Sofia returned, she was carrying an armful of fabrics. Meena was stunned. Saris made of georgette and saris with prints. A sky-blue silk sari. Saris that cost over a thousand taka, a whole pile of them, completely unused. Meena's hand reached out of its own accord to touch the beautiful fabrics. Sofia handed the pile to Rehana but noticed Meena's movement and turned to her.

"And you, Meena, stand up."

Meena got to her feet. The two women faced each other in the driveway. Sofia reached out and touched Meena's arm.

"You're as scrawny as me, but a bit shorter. I think I have some shalwar kameezzes your sister shrank in the wash." She laughed. "Would you like to try them? And by the way, I've noticed you're always lugging those big sacks around. I have a suitcase I was going to throw away. One of the wheels is a bit broken. Maybe you could use it?"

*

Janne was lying under the ceiling fan on the big double bed, sipping a beer. He'd tossed his tennis shoes and racket into a corner. He was watching Sofia, who was rushing back and forth between the walk-in closet and the regular wardrobe. She tore clothes off hangers and rummaged around for shirts.

"Where are our winter coats? Didn't we pack them away in a box somewhere? My parka? And socks, when did I last wear socks?"

Janne smiled at her excitement. The goat in her had been roused. She was climbing treacherous cliffs, pushing upward, forward, onward. Her high cheekbones were more marked than ever and Janne thought he could almost see her bracing to make the jump to a higher ledge. That determination, he admired it. She'd wrapped a bright green hair tie around her blonde ponytail.

"Nice, no? Meena gave it to me. It's supposed to give me luck. I gave her my old wheelie bag."

"Tell me about Moberg again. How did you break it to him?"

Janne had asked earlier and Sofia had explained. But Janne wanted to hear it again.

"I'm not sure how it happened. At first, I just mentioned that Peter had seen him and asked if it had been a good night."

Janne nodded in gleeful anticipation. Sofia continued.

"Then Dev-Com came up several times when we went over what I'm going to be doing in Stockholm. In the end, I just said it."

"What? What did you say?"

"Something about how I thought it was an odd choice for an ambassador to be seen in two contexts as different as a shamanic ritual and Dev-Com. Both were bound to raise questions in Stockholm. Then I pretended I'd seen the picture."

"And what did he do?"

"He went bright red and tried to make light at first. But then, just before we wrapped up the meeting, he suddenly announced, out of the blue, that he was planning to nominate me to Dev-Com. 'And I will give you my full support, really, my full support.' That was the end of it."

Janne smiled smugly and sipped his beer. Sofia had mimicked Mobergs overly enunciated, timid way of speaking and Janne could just picture it. Sofia was a brightly shining star next to the drab Moberg. But she needed space to twinkle and shine. Hopefully now, she'd get it. She'd filled her suitcase to the brim. At the top were embroidered cushion covers, silk scarves and a few embroidered jewellery boxes. Gifts for their friends in Stockholm.

"Oh, by the way," Janne jumped up. "I have something for you, too. You can't open it until you get to Stockholm. Promise!"

Janne handed over a wrapped present and got a hug in exchange.

"Thank you, my love. Take good care of the children, now. And the staff. And I have the USB stick."

She held up the small stick, and Janne watched her put it in one of the suitcase pockets.

The memory stick contained one hundred of his photographs, taken in various locations in Bangladesh. Sofia had promised to give it to their friend Martin who worked for South Reporting.

"It would be neat to hear what he thinks. Are they of professional quality? Could there be an exhibition in Stockholm? Are you going to have time to have dinner with him and Katta?"

When they lay next to each other an hour or so later, Janne felt calm. Calm and content. Sofia was his woman, he was invited and included. It was the two of them against the world again.

A strand of her curly hair slipped into his mouth. He didn't bother to take it out and they fell asleep that way.

20

The rust red five-hundred-taka note was worn and must have come from the pile of stuff from Boss' trouser pockets sitting on the mirror table. Holding the vacuum cleaner in one hand, Nazreen bent down to pick up the note. It was almost hidden under the big table. They were careless with their money, the Swedes.

For a few seconds, she stood there, motionless, the note in her hand. Then, suddenly, her pulse began to race and her knees trembled. She did it. Let the note disappear into her apron. Her cheeks flushed and it was an effort to breathe calmly, good thing the vacuum cleaner was so loud. She could still put the note back. Five hundred taka. She didn't put the note back. Five hundred taka.

She tried to act natural in the kitchen. Hanif was telling her Madame was going away for a while and that it might mean more baby-sitting money for Nazreen. He droned on and on. Nazreen smiled and nodded, her mind spinning.

She could feel the banknote burning in her pocket. Meena confiscated every taka Nazreen made, she was in charge of the money. Nazreen wasn't allowed to keep anything. Well, two hundred taka, which Meena doled out on Fridays and which was supposed to cover food and soap. Anything else was inevitably the subject of lengthy negotiations because Meena couldn't understand that sometimes Nazreen wanted a new dupatta or some fancy shampoo.

It seemed to Nazreen Meena's obsession with the plastic box had grown more intense since they moved in with Madame and Boss. She counted the money every night and logged the total in a small notebook. The money was growing, it was. But were they having fun? Like the other ayahs? Five hundred taka, more than they sent their parents the other day. Nazreen wet her lips. Hanif asked her something, she looked up but didn't understand what he meant. He had to repeat the question.

"Hello? Anybody home? I was asking if you shouldn't get going to pick up Teo?" Nazreen nodded and took off her apron. She stealthily transferred the money to her handbag. Of course she was going to go pick up Teo.

Boss was in a good mood and told Nazreen she could leave early. Nazreen flinched. Was he on to her? Was he suspicious? But he just seemed happy where he sat reading to Noella on the big sofa.

Nazreen sneaked up the stairs behind the garage. She quickly changed into her prettiest shalwar kameez, a red one with embroidered trouser legs and a sparkly dupatta. She went into Meena's storage room and tried on sandals until she found a pair that fit. There was also lipstick and earrings in Meena's stores. She detached a pair of shiny gold earrings from a piece of cardboard and put them in her ears. The lipstick felt thick and dry and was bright red. She found a pen that looked like her mother's kohl and drew lines around her eyes. There. She examined herself in the small mirror. Like a married woman around the eyes. The lipstick, on the other hand, the big red mouth, that felt risqué. She grabbed a rag and violently rubbed it off. She had looked too much like Dipita from the Radisson Hotel.

One night, on the way back from the club with Madame and Boss, their car had ended up behind a military Jeep on its way to the base just outside Gulshan. Suddenly, someone had thrown aside the tarpaulin covering the Jeep's cargo section and Nazreen had caught a glimpse of a woman's face and a sari among the dusty soldiers. After a few seconds, she realised it was Dipita. She'd looked more sad than scared and she hadn't returned Nazreen's wave. Her face had been powdered white and her mouth flaming red, like blood. Nazreen had heard the gossip about Dipita being sacked from the Radisson and was curious what Dipita was doing at the army base. Maybe her acting career had taken off?

Back in the village, Nazreen had come to understand that she was considered beautiful. *Shondori*, a beautiful girl. Not radiant like Mokta and their mother, perhaps. But beautiful. Pale-skinned. She stared at her face in the little mirror. Who decided what beauty was? Was being beautiful a good thing? It hadn't brought Mokta anything but suffering. She pulled out the glasses she'd worn at the Radisson, the zero power ones. Beauty wasn't what she was aiming for, not primarily. Though she might put on a teeny tiny bit of lipstick.

One of the guards did a double take as she walked through the gate. But he said nothing. Nazreen jumped straight into a rickshaw and said where she wanted to go.

Several Jeeps were parked outside Coffee Star in Banani. Nazreen's pulse began to race again. She made a hash of paying the rickshaw driver and had to force herself to walk up the stairs slowly and nonchalantly. There they were, sitting in the big windows overlooking the street, the girls who looked like they could be on TV.

She opened the frosted glass doors. Although she was taken aback by the cold air rushing to greet her she intrepidly set her course for the till. Big pictures of coffee drinks hung from the ceiling. Three hundred and fifty taka, five hundred taka. Did she have enough? She mustn't look hesitant! She pointed resolutely to a picture of a tall glass topped with whipped cream.

"A Frappuccino Hazel?" the girl behind the counter asked lazily and Nazreen nodded. "Four hundred taka."

She paid without hesitation and even went so far as to shoot the complimentary white bread on the counter a slightly bored look. No, not her thing, she signalled to the girl behind the counter.

A seat at a bar table next to one of the walls seemed unoccupied. Nazreen walked toward the stool, balancing her tall glass. Once she'd climbed up, she didn't know what to do with her handbag. It would look abandoned on the floor and in her lap it would be in the way. It was going to have to be her lap. She recognised the smell of coffee from Boss and Madame's house, but it was sweeter than she'd thought it would be. And tastier. And the whipped cream.

Her pulse had slowed down. She looked around the room. This was going splendidly. Some of the young women at Coffee Star wore jeans under their kameezzes instead of shalwars, she noted. A small group of Bangladeshis her own age, two guys and two girls, were huddled in a corner. She looked around for their older relatives, but couldn't see any. Everyone at Coffee Star was young and there was a cluster of Western teenagers playing with their mobile phones in one corner.

Then she caught her own reflection in the window. Her handbag in her lap, her mouth around the straw of her coffee beverage. Her glasses and the casual way her dupatta was draped. The clearly outlined lips.

She blushed. She'd seen herself like this in her dreams, like the girls she and Mokta had fantasised about. She was one of them now.

It looked both very good. And very bad.

In the wee hours of the following night, Nazreen slipped out of bed. She hadn't slept a wink. She kept reliving the moment her hand reached out and picked the red banknote off the floor. She relived bending down, lowering her hand toward it. The crazy impulse. The hand that suddenly, as though of its own accord, reached out and picked up the banknote. The floor pitched and swayed, the red banknote in her pocket.

Nazreen tiptoed across the room. Quickly glanced back at her sleeping sister and sidled over to the metal footlocker in the corner. Ever so quietly, she opened the lid and found the plastic box. Meena's plastic box. Meena's and her plastic box. There. Red. Five hundred. She was going to put everything right. She, Nazreen Bhuia, was not a petty thief.

*

Stockholm's Hötorget Square was deserted. A cold wind blew across the cobblestones. The wind cut through Sofia's jeans and she cursed herself for forgetting to put on long johns. She kept her hands clenched like claws in the sleeves of her parka. She had to buy gloves.

"This cold. It does something to a person's body, it's inhuman," she mused. "Does everyone walk around tensed up like this all winter?"

It was dark, even though she'd just had lunch. Her meeting at the Ministry of Foreign Affairs had gone well. The Asia Director and the State Secretary had supported the idea of co-hosting a large women's conference in Dhaka. She'd explained why it would be better to push it back to after the summer, they hadn't asked any questions.

Once he'd caught on to the fact that Sofia was posted in Bangladesh, the Asia Director had invited her to give a talk about climate change. It was a hot topic, that much was clear. The room had quickly filled up with young, ambitious diplomats. Her insight into the country's efforts to bring about major climate adaptation had aroused people's interest. Their questions were shrewd and troubled. Fifty years, in fifty years, half of Bangladesh would have been washed away. Where were thirty million people supposed to go? Brows furrowed.

So different, Sofia thought to herself. Gender equality never aroused this kind of interest. When she gave talks on gender, gender and health, gender and conflict or gender and work in various context, it inevitably drew no more than two or three people. And it was always the Ministry of Foreign Affairs' in-house adviser on gender issues, Gudrun, and some new employee she'd dragged along.

She had mentioned the corruption crisis at Alor Desh to the Asia Director and the relevant caseworker, but neither had shown much interest. It was a foreign aid matter, and foreign aid was handled by SwedeAid.

Friday was the big day. A meeting with everyone involved. She would have one hour to save Alor Desh. That gave her a few days to work on her pitch and she'd already made plans to spend the next day at the public library so she could work in peace. There was no desk for her at SwedeAid when she was in the field and open-plan offices made her feel stressed. Besides, colleagues would want to say hi and hear about how she was getting on. No, work had to come first. The main branch of the Stockholm Public Library was calm and quiet and Sofia had booked a computer so she could work without distractions. There was a reasonable chance the corruption advisers would agree to look beyond the ones and zeros if she played her cards right.

Sofia headed down to the metro to go over to Södermalm, her old home turf. A feeling of being on her way home. Should she swing by their flat? Their small three-bed by Södra Station? But what was she supposed to do there? There was nothing of hers in it now. A grateful family with young children from Janne's neck of the woods in Småland was renting it. She was suddenly overcome with an odd feeling she recognised from her years in Africa. Of being completely free and untethered. No real connection, a fleeting visitor, a guest in an old reality. It was a dizzying feeling, full of possibilities and the rush of freedom. She was having dinner with her parents in Uppsala the next day, but that was it. They were busy with their own things. She'd emailed her friends to say she'd be down the local pub, Kvarnen, from seven. Anyone who wanted to should stop by. Certain friends she wanted to meet up with individually, but this was her way of ticking off as many people as possible during her brief visit.

As she entered the pub, Katta waved at her from a table. Then she spotted Annette and Johanna. And Cecilia and Lisa had come, too, and Martin and Johan. They all turned to her when she stepped through the door and joy unexpectedly washed over her at the sight of them. So friendly and familiar. So unlike Antje and Vanja, the people she spent her days with now.

"Sofia, it's so good to see you!"

"Tell us everything!"

"Thank you for your emails, Noella is so big now!"

"How's Janne?"

"Is it true he lost weight?"

"Sit down- a pint for you?"

Her friends looked winter pale and a bit weary. Had they all grown so much older in just a few months? The group was a mix of her old friends from Uppsala and colleagues from SwedeAid and Johanna, a neighbour. Johan was Janne's best friend. One of Janne's cousins was potentially joining them later.

"Why aren't you tanned? I thought we were in for a charter holiday tan!" Katta laughed. "And did you bring back any horrifying diseases? Is it safe to hug you?"

She laughed loudly, significantly. Sofia did in fact still have a fading tan from their Thailand trip, but since Katta worked at SwedeAid, Sofia knew her questions had been rhetorical. They were the two questions everyone back home asked when you were posted abroad. Why aren't you tanned? Because around the equator, everyone avoids the sun like the plague and make sure to stay inside where there's shade and air conditioning. Did you bring home any nasty diseases? Nothing worse than the flu doing the rounds around in Sweden. They have vaccinations and drugs abroad, too.

Sofia hugged everyone. To her surprise, she realised Lisa was pregnant and was just about to give her an extra hug when her phone rang.

"Hold on. It might be Janne."

She got up from the table and turned away. She pressed her hand to her ear, asking if she'd heard the caller right.

"*Kvällspressen*. The newspaper? What do *you* know about Alor Desh?"

*

Moberg studied Anna-Lena's agitated face. Her hair, normally a smooth, grey helmet, was dishevelled. She was so upset she was getting entangled in her long Bengali shawl and her wooden earrings were swinging wildly back and forth.

"Who could have leaked it? Poor, brave little Sofia. Alone in the clutches of the tabloids. What are you going to do, Moberg? Who could have sunk so incredibly low? Yes, low!"

Anna-Lena glared at him from across the table.

Moberg sighed. The Sunday meeting had started out so well. Everyone except their water caseworker Rickard had been present. And Sofia, who was in Stockholm. But Siv, Anna-Lena, visa caseworker Erik and the local employees – Aisha, Zakia and Manik – were there. Briefing the staff about Professor Malcolm Davis and Dr Ahmadiya's report on the violent Islamification of the countryside, he'd made it sound like he'd read the whole thing from start to finish. The summary had been exhaustive. Several grassroots organisations were working with moderate imams to counter the extremist, militant influences creeping in from the Gulf and Pakistan. Among them Sweden's partner organisation Alor Desh.

The agenda item "applications for leave" had gone well, too. All local employees were given leave whenever they wanted around the Bengali New Year. The different cultural traditions were a blessing. The Bangladeshi didn't mind working Christmas, the Swedes happily worked on Eid and Diwali.

But then Rickard had come bursting in. He'd been contacted by Swedish tabloid *Kvällspressen*.

"They're asking questions about the Alor Desh audit. Definitely smelling blood in the water. Front page and substantial article inside the paper. They go to print in exactly six hours. The headline is going to be something along the lines of "SwedeAid's Funding Scandal. Laureate's aid money used for bribes and luxury Jeeps."

Rickard had been unable to conceal his excitement. Finally, some action at the Swedish embassy in Dhaka. Moberg looked nonplussed. Anna-Lena's question about what he as the head of mission was going to do was left hanging in the air. He needed time to think things through.

"You know I can't investigate leaks, Anna-Lena. This is a government agency."

Moberg was floundering. There was going to be trouble now. His embassy would become associated with scandals. He cowered inwardly. Anna-Lena pressed on, looking at each of the others in turn.

"Well, she'll have my support. Someone at the embassy must have sent the Alor Desh audit to the editors. Personally, I have my suspicions, but I hear you, Moberg. No going after the source."

"They are right in saying Swedish tax money can't be used for illegal purposes," Moberg put in lamely.

"Luxury Jeeps," Anna-Lena sneered. "They haven't seen the Lamborghinis the sons of the government ministers drive or all the garages with those Hummers they have in Hollywood! That! That's corruption, but everyone's afraid to talk about it. It really irks me! In the cultural sector we don't work with that kind of money. In fact, I think if we just supported cultural endeavours, the rest of the work would fix itself! Culture and human rights, that would sort out everything else, too."

Moberg shifted uncomfortably. Rickard shot Anna-Lena an interested look.

"So you're saying the funding for clean water and sanitation should go to dance troupes and art instead?"

"That might be taking it too far," Anna-Lena backpedalled. "But the son of the Water Minister drives a Lamborghini, explain that if you can! Alor Desh is neither more nor less corrupt than any other organisation. We swallow camels and strain out gnats. That's what we're doing. It reflects well on Sofia that she's going to bat for the little people, for the grassroots! How can we help her?"

Once again, the question was left hanging while Moberg looked around for help. Erik glanced at his watch and the local employees squirmed in their seats. Old Zakia suggested inviting *Kvällspressen* so they could see the cars driven by the ministers' sons with their own eyes. Siv sat very still with her eyes on her boss and her hands folded on a stack of papers. Moberg turned to Rickard again.

"Would you, Rickard, mind jotting down some language guidelines?"

"Pardon? Language guidelines?"

Moberg sighed inwardly. The SwedeAid people were clueless about even the most basic diplomatic jargon.

"That is to say a few official statements from the embassy. Like talking points. That we always inform and act on any knowledge of corruption. Sweden's anti-corruption policy is online, use something from that."

"Surely we can be more proactive than that?" Anna-Lena's voice was impatient. "Sofia has thought this through, that's why she's in Stockholm. To try to save the organisation. Are we going to let ourselves be pushed around by a tabloid? Has anyone talked to her?"

"It's not morning yet in Sweden," Rickard put in. "Judging from an email I had, Sofia spoke briefly to a journalist before going to bed. She wrote that this doesn't change anything, and that we have to keep our cool."

Anna-Lena sighed. An annoyed silence fell, Moberg started fiddling with his papers. Anna-Lena suddenly pointed to the sheaf of papers in his hand.

"The report!"

"Pardon?" Moberg looked up.

"The report you just briefed us on. What were you actually saying? Didn't you just mention the work Alor Desh does?"

Anna-Lena reached across the table and snatched the study on the Islamification of the countryside from Moberg. She read the summary page, nodded and quickly skimmed the rest of the report. From time to time, she lingered on a passage, emitting astonished noises. Rickard got to his feet and went to read over her shoulder.

"Here! And here. In writing, exactly what Sofia needs." She showed Rickard and then turned to Tulsi, their secretary." Would you mind scanning this immediately? So it's in Sofia's inbox when she wakes up. And I'm going to be placing some calls the minute SwedeAid opens."

*

Meena looked into the foggy mirror hanging by the door to her and Nazreen's room on the garage roof. She pulled a comb through her thick fringe.

He'd been so happy, Mr Janne. He'd offered to give her money, but there was no way she could accept a wad of cash, just like that. Once he realised that, he'd purchased a shipment of ladies' sandals instead. Twenty pairs for five thousand taka. No negotiation, he'd paid her asking price without question. Was he maybe a bit simple? What was he going to do with twenty pairs of ladies' sandals? Meena looked into her own eyes in the mirror and smiled.

The water barrels had been changed, she'd spotted that straight away. Bideshis didn't boil their own water, they bought it in large plastic containers that were delivered to the house ever week. Big, round, blueish containers of drinking water were brought by pickup truck straight from the factory. And right now, a lot of Baridhara's Westerners were in bed with stomach cramps and diarrhoea after drinking that water. But not Mr Janne and the children.

Meena had come home late the night before and stopped by to see Beppin, who had offered her a glass of tea. While sitting there, she'd seen one of the night watchmen lugging around a water container that must have been delivered that day. The next morning, she'd noticed the container's lid was a different shade of blue from the week before, and just as Hanif was getting ready to carry the water inside, Mr Janne had walked by. She didn't know where she'd found the courage to address him, but she had.

"Bad water, they've swapped out your containers. Don't drink it!" she'd said as they crossed paths in the driveway. Janne had looked surprised at first, then angry. He'd marched out to Hanif in the kitchen. Meena had grabbed her new suitcase and disappeared down the street.

That night, a grateful Mr Janne had come looking for her.

"People are sick all over Baridhara. It's terrible, the little ones could've died. Apparently, there's a criminal gang that steals the clean water and sells it on. I'm very grateful, Meena, how can I thank you?

Madame Sofia is in Sweden and she is grateful, too. Can I give you money?"

Meena looked in the mirror. Give away money, just like that? No, she hadn't allowed that. But she'd been happy to sell him the sandals. Twenty pairs with plastic rubies on them.

Meena headed south. Via a complex succession of rickshaws, buses and CNGs, it took her an hour to get to the rendezvous point where she and Rifat started their work in the evening. An intersection on the road to Naragonj had become the place where they felt safe to meet up without anyone from Badda recognising them. Meena made herself known by an impatient wave of her arms that made the cloth of her burqa billow.

While Rifat did a quick inventory of their wares, she told him about the sandals. Five thousand taka, cash in hand. The difference between what they'd paid down in New Market and what Mr Janne had given for them was a staggering four thousand five hundred taka.

"It's too fast," mumbled Rifat, who didn't look nearly as happy as she'd thought he would.

"What do you mean, too fast?" Meena peered at him through the mesh screen of her burqa.

"Before you know it, you're going to have your fifty thousand taka and then I'll lose you."

Rifat had become increasingly open about what he wanted. And this time, Meena's reply was different.

"Maybe you don't have to lose me. If it's true that you want to, if you really mean . . . ?"

The last part of her sentence was drowned out by the roar of a lorry that narrowly missed them.

"What was that, Meena?" Rifat leaned in closer, his voice cut through the dust. "What do you mean?"

"We need to talk. After the factory. Okay?"

Rifat had to make do with that cryptic response, they started walking toward Naragonj. Meena led the way with a sack on her back.

The suitcase she was also carrying hit the ground with every step she took. One of the wheels was broken. Rifat trotted after her lugging two bursting hemp sacks.

After a while, they managed to catch a ride with a pickup truck that slowed down long enough for them to be able to hurl themselves and their goods onto the cargo bed. Rehana was waiting for them by the factory gate.

During the day, she'd taken orders from the factory girls for everyday items the hard-working women never had time to purchase. Miniature bottles of shampoo, salt, spices, Vaseline, hair ties, soap. But also the kinds of things the girls coveted, that made their eyes widen in the gloom. Nail polish, sandals, handbags, mobile phone cases, perfumes, colourful hairclips and little makeup sets. Bleaching lotions, mascara.

Rehana helped carry the goods up the stairs to one of the unfinished floors. A scrawny cat that had been sleeping up there meowed and disappeared into the main room. Meena and Rifat took their wares out and arranged them in neat piles according to their customers' orders. Rehana read the women's names out from a piece of paper. The steps served as their shop counter. Meena was impressed by Rehana, even though she was so young and barely knew how to write, she had performed her task efficiently. She had a head for business, Meena could tell. Lots and lots of women, lots and lots of goods.

"Next time, you can pick the goods up and hand them out yourself. You're really good at this, Rehana," Meena praised her. "The more you sell, the more money you get. Understand?"

Rehana smiled. She understood very well.

Twenty minutes after Rehana let Meena and Rifat into Copenhagen Garment Inc., the charge commenced. A shrill bell announced the end of the last shift of the day. It was eleven at night. Tired women hurried home to hungry children and angry husbands to see to the family's needs behind walls of corrugated metal and plastic sheets. Some of the shadowy figures paused. Hands reached for the small piles and eyes glinted in the dark in momentary delight. Rumpled taka notes exchanged hands.

Then the shadows quickly moved on.

*

Moberg closed his eyes. What a taxing day. He lay down on the bed to rest his eyes for a minute. A spot of Swedish talk radio and some peace and quiet before the dinner at the Water Minister's house. What a taxing day. Anna-Lena had marched about, tearing through the archives in search of documents to send Sofia. She was angry, that much was clear. Everyone seemed to expect him to do something. But what?

Either way, tonight, he was having dinner at Water Minister Choudhuri's residence. Vanja and the minister's wife had apparently hit it off at Noella's birthday party and since Arthur spent so much time with Aziz, the minister's teenage son, a dinner seemed appropriate. The good thing about dinner at a Bengali house was that there was never any alcohol. Only endless glasses of Fanta and Coca-Cola and usually a host of friends and relatives who wanted a good look at the Westerners. At least he wouldn't have to worry about Vanja.

Moberg heard the clatter of Vanja's shoes on the stairs moments before she appeared in the doorway. Moberg fumbled around for his glasses. He felt caught out.

"You're in bed?" She sounded reproachful.

Moberg continued to look for his glasses. They must have slipped off the bed. He peered at his wife, her eyeliner seemed blacker than usual.

"I figured I'd have a quick nap before dinner. It's been a stressful day."

"So I gather. Have you seen the papers online?" She sounded upset and was eyeing him critically. She found his glasses on the floor and handed them to him. "I assume you're giving Sofia your full support?"

He put his glasses on and sat up drowsily.

"I don't know about full support. We've written a language guide and posted a statement on the website. I don't know how you . . ."

"I ran into Anna-Lena at the club," Vanja cut him off. "She claims this is an unheard of double-standard. Corruption among the poor is excoriated, but no one says a word when it's rich people doing it."

"What do you mean?" Moberg tried to argue. "Sweden can't accept corruption in any shape or form. If we see evidence of wrong doing, we act by immediately freezing all funding."

"Then I suppose some people are simply better at hiding the evidence than others," Vanja snapped. "This minister, Choudhuri, Konika's husband, whose house we're going to tonight. Anna-Lena says he a much bigger crook than Khadija Anam. Much bigger. A *proper* crook. Uses his government position to line his own pockets with money that was meant to give people in this country clean water to drink. Apparently, lots of Swedish tax money is going into that. But no one says a word. Not a word!"

Moberg started to look for his shoes. Vanja was on the warpath again. He realised she was talking about WSNP II, the budget support for Bangladesh's water sector, which was administered by the World Bank, to which Sweden had contributed several hundred million kronor.

"Vanja, diplomacy is not about scolding one's host country. Diplomacy is . . ."

"Yes, tell me, what is diplomacy? To never under any circumstances do anything that could possibly offend? What if the people in power exploit that? You diplomats see nothing, say nothing? But you're implicitly legitimising the system."

"I think you're exaggerating, Vanja," Moberg had found his shoe and realised he had to confront Vanja's ire. "I would say that in this case, diplomacy is . . . the exchange of information. Dialogue. We tell them how we see things back in Sweden. They listen and slowly, slowly, their attitudes may change."

"But it's my tax money. You people in your fancy gentlemen's clubs, Head of Mission and Dev-Com and whatever they're called. Do you at least ask questions? Of the government? Of the ministers?"

She'd crossed her arms and was studying Moberg while he put his shoes on. He looked up and noticed her swaying.

"Have you been drinking, Vanja?" Moberg studied his wife and felt the conversational tide turn back in his favour.

"No one gets drunk off two glasses of wine. There won't be anything but Fanta tonight. Don't worry about me."

"That's enough, though, Vanja. No more drinking now. Okay?"

"Either way," she calmed down. "I've meditated for Sofia and sent her light."

"That's lovely."

"Arthur's ready. I'll let the driver know we'll be ready to leave in fifteen minutes."

Vanja disappeared down the stairs. As he was trying to pick out a tie, Moberg heard a clatter from the liquor cabinet downstairs. He suddenly had a sinking feeling in his stomach.

Half an hour later, the ambassador's Mercedes pulled in through an ornate metal gate on Road 23, Baridhara. A security camera watched them arrive. Arthur waved to the guard who checked their car's undercarriage. The driveway curved gently on its way up to the palatial house and well-kept red and pink hibiscus bushes were neatly lined up on a golf-course short lawn.

"Crikey," Moberg exclaimed. "This where you spend your afternoons, Arthur?"

"We actually mostly hang out on the roof. There's a pool area and a spa. But check out the cars."

Moberg leaned forward to look out the window. On one side of the building he caught a glimpse of a low garage and a line of sportscars.

"There, the white Lamborghini. That's Aziz's big brother's. Sick, right?"

"But where do they drive them?" Vanja said. "There are virtually no roads here. Do they just sit in traffic on Gulshan Avenue?"

She giggled, Moberg shot her a look. Had she had time to have more than one drink? When they climbed out of the car, it became clear to Moberg she must have. She swayed and lost one of her shoes.

The minister and his wife were effusively welcoming as they received them in the opulent hallway. A large, round fountain was splashing in the background and as if to underscore that this was a Western evening, Brahms was being played at a high volume. The hallway was like an atrium, several floors and rooms overlooked the fountain.

Moberg gasped, the house was even bigger on the inside than you'd think looking at it from the outside. Vanja handed over a hostess gift, a tray with a moose roadsign on it and "Sweden" written in black letters.

"Amazing," the minister said with a chuckle. "I visited Skansen once in my youth, so I've seen this beast up close! Come in, come in!"

Arthur and Aziz promptly vanished upstairs and the ambassador and his wife were led into a large room where an assortment of relatives were waiting. Events hosted by upper-crust Bangladeshi people were never completely relaxed, they knew that by now. The relatives were stiffly lined up in sumptuous sofas and armchairs timidly placed along the walls. The women were dressed up in glittering saris, wore heavy makeup and looked uncomfortable and anxious. They weren't used to socialising with men and spoke no English. In Bangladesh, it was more common for men and women to socialise separately. The women had in all likeliness been pressed into attendance and scattered about the room to make the Western guests feel comfortable, Moberg mused. The Western way of greeting didn't come naturally, either: limp little fingers were held up to the Swedes while nervous eyes darted this way and that. They sipped their Fanta and seemed to wish themselves miles away.

Vanja, by contrast, had warmed up and was at her most charming, Moberg noted with a measure of relief. She made good use of a young woman in a yellow sari as an interpreter to converse with the ladies and ignored all the men. As she should.

Moberg was relieved. Vanja was a pro when it mattered and there would be nothing for her to drink here. Tonight was going to come off well. It would also give him an opportunity to speak shodhobangla, classical Bengali, and investigate the existence of different versions of certain typical idioms. This magical language never ceased to fascinate him and among the elite there were people capable of reflecting on their own linguistic habits.

The minister and his two brothers and a handful of brothers or sons-in-law gathered around Moberg and praised his Bengali. The conversation revolved around Arthur and Aziz's education at the American international school and which of the world's universities would best serve them afterwards. Harvard Business School or Oxford? Columbia or Stanford? It turned out the minister had three sets of children with three different wives, though it was unclear whether he was divorced or polygamous. Moberg didn't ask. Aziz belonged to set number two and Noella's little friend to the third and final one. The older children were apparently studying in London and New York respectively.

At the other end of the room, Vanja and the small clutch of sari-clad women were now on their feet, walking around, studying the art on the walls. Vanja considered signatures and paintings with the air of a connoisseur. Moberg noted out of the corner of his eye that she asked questions and was given answers, pointed with her Fanta glass and nodded. After disappearing into an adjoining room filled with even more paintings, she returned and walked straight up to the minister. The small huddle of women watched her from a distance.

"Incredibly impressive collection," she said admiringly. "I see you were the mystery bidder who claimed the Chagall in the auction at Sotheby's last year. And the triptych in the gallery can't have been cheap. Pardon me for asking so bluntly. But where does the money come from? Who pays for the art? And the cars and the house itself?"

She made a sweeping gesture encompassing the entire room and smiled placidly. Tilted her head. Moberg cleared his throat and grabbed his wife's arm. But Vanja calmly pulled herself free and continued.

"In Sweden, a government minister makes, maybe, well, what would be a good guess? Four or five times more than a schoolteacher. What's the equivalent difference in Bangladesh? Ballpark? I mean, surely you don't mind exchanging a bit of information? A dialogue about pay gaps, perhaps? I could tell you how I see things and you could maybe tell me how you think? Yes? Karl-Otto? How does that sound?"

*

Sofia hurried out through the hotel lobby and across the street to a corner shop. She could tell from afar that *Kvällsposten* had dug up a picture of Khadija Anam receiving the Right Livelihood Award. "SwedeAid's Funding Scandal. Award winner's money was used for bribes and luxury Jeeps."

Inside the paper, Rickard had offered a very brief comment on behalf of the embassy.

"All funding has been frozen."

SwedeAid's press department referred to the meeting later in the week.

"It goes without saying that Swedish taxpayers have a right to feel confident their money is used correctly. We are looking into these allegations. An embassy representative will be meeting with our corruption team in Stockholm later this week," said a press officer Sofia had never met.

The first thing she did when she got back to her hotel room was to open her laptop. Though it was still early, her inbox was already full of messages from people who had heard about the allegations. From her dad, the neurosurgeon, came an exhortation to keep cool, which Sofia replied to by saying she wouldn't be able to make it to Uppsala as planned. They understood. They always understood when she prioritised her work over everything else. From Anna-Lena at the embassy, an email with a red flag. Urgent.

"Sofia! What a mess, eh? I've asked Tulsi to scan a report that was apparently commissioned by the British on the radicalisation of the Bangladeshi countryside. Alor Desh is mentioned as an example of effective cooperation with moderate mosques to counter the spread of violent extremism. I've attached the report below. Maybe you can find something useful in it? Is there anything else I can do for you? I'm here if you need anything. Best, Anna-Lena."

Sofia skimmed the report and reached for her notepad. She was going to have to spend a few hours reading and planning. She might need to ask Anna-Lena for more information as well. Maybe Lasse Bergström could help provide nuance? With his experience from Afghanistan? But he was pessimistic.

"You're in for it now," he coughed from his smoking module down in SwedeAid's basement when Sofia called. "The anti-corruption lobby finally feels it has the upper hand. They're not interested in complexity. And how were you planning to throw the tabloids off the scent?"

"I have to at least try. If you could just back me up with an example or two from Afghanistan, that would be helpful," Sofia pleaded. "How much was it the UN estimated had ended up in the wrong hands there? Fifty percent of the foreign aid? With Alor Desh, we're talking no more than ten percent, depending on how you count."

"Yes, fifty percent, if not more. We would have done better if we'd limited ourselves to the countries where we were actually making a difference," he replied, seamlessly segueing into his favourite subject, "instead of being a medium-sized dog trying to act like a big dog. Laos, Vietnam, Nicaragua, there, *there*, we were somebody. There, we could make a difference. Talk about results . . ."

Sofia had to cut him short.

"Are you coming to the meeting?"

"Yeah, I'll be there. But Ulla and her gang have the wind at their backs, the minister's blessing, you know. It carries a lot of weight. You're not going to make friends doing this."

"I know."

She flipped through the pile of reports Charlotta had given Janne, which she'd only had time to glance at before. There was a lot of useful stuff in them. Before the meeting on Friday, she would have a comprehensive strategy in place.

*

"Come, come," Nazreen took Meena by the hand, but Meena hesitated. She was tired after her trip to the factory. Her back ached and she would have liked to have a serious talk with Nazreen, curled up on the bed they shared. Five hundred taka were missing from the plastic box, but Meena had also made a much more terrible discovery. Something had been slowly dawning on her. She needed her big sister. She missed Mokta.

But Nazreen was excited. She pulled Meena along the back of the house and over to the kitchen door.

"Just wait until you see what it's like inside. Boss gave Hanif the night off and he'll be gone with the children overnight. I'm in charge of the house."

"But the guards?" Meena glanced over at the guard hut.

"I'm their boss now. I work inside. They won't say anything."

Nazreen led her through the kitchen, which was lit by sharp electric lights and filled with tall worktops and running water and machines. Nazreen went over to the tap and turned it on and off a few times to show Meena.Then she opened the large fridge and showed her all the food. Two newly-slaughtered chickens lay plucked and ready in a bowl, but there seemed to be mince and lots of jars and boxes as well.

A long passage led from the kitchen to a room where an arched ceiling rose high above the girls. It took Meena's breath away. In the middle of the room was a table and row of beautiful matching chairs, beyond that, a doorway leading to even more rooms. Meena looked around. For a moment, the height and size of the room made her dizzy. The feeling of being so small in such a large room was new to her. She could tell Nazreen had felt the same way. Her sister was standing in the middle of the room, her long hair down and her arms spread wide. Slowly spinning in circles.

"Look at what our life is like, Meena. Imagine if Mokta could see us now." She was holding her dupatta in one hand, dragging it across the floor as she twirled. She tilted her head to the side and spun faster. She tried to pull her sister along, but Meena felt a heavy hand across her chest. She tried to smile at Nazreen, but her face had gone numb. She really needed to talk to Nazreen tonight.

A few days earlier, Meena had realised she was pregnant. It had suddenly occurred to her she hadn't used the cloth strips in a long time. Then the black box had reappeared one morning and she had understood. The slime, the blood. Babul.

Meena had sunk through the earth, falling, falling. The same way she now watched her sister fall. Meena said only two words.

"I'm pregnant."

Nazreen froze mid-movement. She looked stunned. She stared wide-eyed at Meena and then let out a howl. She collapsed on the blue sofa, rocking back and forth, racked with sobs. She tore her hair.

"It's not true, no! Do you understand what you've done? Tell me it's not true. Did it happen with Miraj, after all? Did he come at you again? I'm a poor, wretched woman, my sister has sinned, we're only useless women, useless, not worthy. Allah, Allah, koro."

Nazreen moaned loudly, turning her face to the ceiling and howling. She fell into the ancient lament that was Bangladeshi women's strongest expression of grief. The words came without thought, pouring out. Meena recognised them. It was the village *bilap*, the lament of the women, so strange here in the big city. And yet so familiar.

"I'm a useless woman, Allah, see my sin. See my sister's sin, give us mercy. I'm just a wretched woman, give me mercy, a useless woman, Allah, Allah, koro!"

Meena hadn't expected this. She had expected reproach and anger, then comfort and help. In the village, she'd heard it was possible to remove a child from the womb. But here? Maybe Nazreen knew. But Nazreen was overcome with her own despair.

"Is it that slum boy Rifat?" Nazreen grabbed her hair again and howled. "Give us mercy, give us mercy, we're just useless women." She fell silent but continued to rock and stare vacantly into space. Her moaning faded into a whimper. "Why couldn't he leave you alone? Did you let him . . . ? Why do you have to ruin everything? Everything! We're useless, you're useless. Allahu akbar."

"Nazreen," Meena put her arm around her sister's shoulders to console her. Nazreen cried like the women did back in the village when someone died, when tragedy struck. Meena had planned to tell her about Babul, had wanted to ask her big sister if it could be true, that the blood and the slime had done this to her. Could it be true? She missed Mokta so much it hurt. She'd always been able to share her secrets with Mokta. Mokta had always been able to comfort her, to receive Meena's despair. When Baba smacked her for being disobedient, when she cut her fringe and the whole village avoided her. Mokta had known what to say, she would have known what Meena should do now. But Nazreen wasn't Mokta. Nazreen had no comfort to give, just the bilap.

"Meena, what have you done? Things were just starting to work out for us. Do you realise you're going to be an unmarried mother? Do you understand that we can never go back to Goalpur? You're going to destroy Amma and Abba. This is what they're more afraid of than anything else in the world. Allah, give us mercy."

Meena looked at Nazreen and in that moment, the glass mosaic rearranged itself. Nazreen would never be able to handle knowing what Babul had done to her, she was alone with her secret. New patterns and new solutions were appearing. Rifat. Harami. Dowry. Fatwa. The village. Amma and Abba. The child.

"Nazreen, it's okay. We're getting married. Rifat and I are going to get married now. It's going to be fine, we're both happy about this child."

21

Janne read the text and smiled. He had email and text bombed Sofia since she left for Sweden. He'd sent flowers to her hotel room. This was when things were best between them, when the old feeling of them against the world sparked back to life. He knew he was her rock when she needed one. When the going got tough for her, he stood strong. It was when she didn't need a rock that he floundered. Now he'd had a reply from Sofia. "Love you too. Fuck the papers, the last word hasn't been spoken yet. I'm honing the plan. How are the kids? Scary with the water containers. Thank Meena!"

The children were with Malena and the twins for a movie night playdate. Thankfully, the twins hadn't had time to drink the contaminated water, so they were fine. Their dad, on the other hand, was in bed with severe stomach pains, as were several other people at Ericsson.

Janne had planned to have dinner at the club, but first he wanted to take some twilight photographs. The light when the sun set over Dhaka was breathtaking. A heavy, orange sphere which, unfortunately aided by the air pollution, cast a shimmer of gold over everything, setting people's eyes and skin aglow. He wanted to capture that. Maybe when Sofia came back, they could visit Rehana's family together. Sofia had told him about their house in the slum, about how they lived like animals behind the factories. He would love to capture it on film.

The moment he opened the front door, Nizamuddin came running, looking hopefully, generously sharing his wisdom.

"A lonely man is a dangerous man," he said with emphasis. For a second, Janne considered asking him to expand on his thinking, but then he dropped that idea and instead replied defiantly.

"I'm not a lonely man, Madame Sofia will be back soon."

"Maybe some lady company? No man should have to sleep alone." Nizamuddhin tried again. Janne glared at him.

"No, no lady company. What do you mean?"

"Or maybe little boys?"

Nizamuddhin nudged Janne and smiled conciliatorily. Janne froze mid-step. What was he playing at? That comment was not okay, it opened up a bottomless chasm in front of Janne's feet. He gasped. Sofia and he would have to deal with this when she got back, this was cause for dismissal. Janne stared incredulously at Nizamuddhin.

"No, absolutely not."

The Jeep pulled out of the driveway. Janne tried to shake off his unease and wondered if this was a matter for the embassy. Siv? Or was the driver their private employee?

Sitting in the car, he realised the heat was slowly returning. For the first time in a long time, air conditioning was needed. As winter, with its comfortable climate and temperatures between twenty-five and twenty-eight degrees, turned to spring, it had started to get warmer at night. There was a new sweetness in the air, a warm humidity that forced crawling insects and spectacular flowers out of trees and bushes that had not long before looked grey and drab. The seasonal changes in Bangladesh were subtle, but Janne had had time to notice them. Maybe he'd travel down south to Sundarban, the world's largest mangrove forest, full of tigers and crocodiles, later in the spring. A group of Norwegians he knew were renting a boat and had asked if he wanted to tag along. Take pictures. Find inspiration. Sofia would be busy all throughout the spring and he felt the best way to balance out her tour de force and regain her respect was to create a good life for himself. He hated feeling clingy and whiny about not having enough to do and not getting enough attention.

Nizamuddhin suddenly came to a full stop in the middle of the road. They hadn't made it out of leafy Baridhara yet. Janne looked up and saw Sofia's friend Antje come bursting out of another car that had stopped with its bonnet against theirs. She waved her arms around and jumped into the backseat next to Janne without asking. When she turned to him, he realised she looked distraught.

"I just had a call. A factory in Gulshan has collapsed, lots of girls probably crushed to death. I think it's your Danish friend's factory, the one Sofia and I visited. Copenhagen Garment Inc. I have to make sure Rehana and her mum are okay. Come with me, please, I can't bear to go by myself."

At what had once been Copenhagen Garment Inc., utter chaos now reigned. The building had collapsed completely. The five floors sat on top of each other, like stacked dominos. The walls had buckled like pieces of cardboard, rebar was jutting out at the sky like fragile antennae. A cloud of smoke and dust still enshrouded the scene when Janne and Antje arrived.

They threw themselves out of the car and asked Nizamuddhin to park somewhere nearby. A crowd had gathered on the street outside the factory, people were jostling to get a better look. As they got closer, they could hear the agonised screaming and dismayed sobbing coming from the debris.

Janne climbed onto the cargo bed of a pickup truck parked next to a building to get a better view. He pulled out his phone and called Bjarne. Half-naked men had started to drag away the debris and the factory gates were about to be breached any second. The crowd kept pushing forward. Bjarne didn't pick up.

Four dead bodies had been laid out in the factory yard, draped in dirty lungis. Next to them lay a woman who was bleeding profusely from a cut on her leg and moaning loudly. Up on what had used to be the factory roof, a lone man was walking around, tugging at corrugated metal sheets. Police officers in ragtag uniforms arriving at a run were doing their best to cordon off the area, but the desperate crowd defied the barriers. Before long, people were climbing onto the pile of cement and lifting sections of wall and floor.

"Oh my God, like a fucking house of cards," Janne was pale when he looked down at Antje who seemed to be in shock and merely shook her head. "Check out the walls, about as sturdy as a regular fence. And almost no rebar, see?"

"I can't look. This isn't happening. We were here, Sofia and I. We saw it, but we never thought that . . . Tell me this isn't happening, Janne."

She had to jump out of the way of a group of men in dirty white button-downs who could potentially be paramedics. A troupe of lungi-clad men with gurneys that looked like they'd been hastily crafted out of bamboo poles and cloth followed in their wake. Janne called her back.

"Bjarne's not answering. What do we do? What do all the, well, foreigners do? Diplomats? Foreign aid organisations? Can we help? You know this world, Antje, come on . . ."

Janne looked around. No one seemed to be in charge. No diggers or technical equipment to be seen. No Westerners, no Jeeps, no lamps to light the scene. Just screaming and crying and women's voices howling for help. Janne and Antje looked around helplessly. A big embassy? The Americans? Would they have the resources? For lack of better options, Janne called Siv.

"Are there no emergency networks? No helicopters? Who can we contact?"

"We're only responsible for the safety of our Swedish employees. I think you should get out of there as quickly as you can, Janne," Siv said before Janne ended the call in the middle of a sentence. Antje had the same message from her embassy.

When Janne finally got through to Moberg, he stammered something about "putting out a statement of support" and then Vanja grabbed the receiver. She listened for a few seconds and announced that she, at least, would come down to the scene.

"When things like this happen, the Bangladeshi are on their own, it seems," Antje said quietly. "Maybe we're just in the way? Sadly, they're used to dealing with disaster."

During the minutes that followed, Janne watched, like in slow-motion, as scrawny, anxious men pulled and dug and heaved to find their missing women. He could taste their panic in his own mouth. Frightened, half-naked children darted this way and that between the piles of bricks, sobbing. Janne silently picked up his camera and took picture after picture, as though in a trance. People were joining the fray, brandishing shovels and digging bars. Everywhere, hands prying and backs bending, bars seeking leverage and shovels heaving cement and bricks out of the way. This, Janne had time to think several times over, this must be hell. Bodies trapped under rubble, no healthcare, no help. It was only once the initial shock had subsided and they had acquired an overview of the situation that he and Antje thought to lend physical assistance. Antje wandered off to try to find Rehana and her mother. Janne handed his camera to Nizamuddhin and walked over to a group of men trying to shift a beam. A dusty, haggard old man looked up at him in gratitude. Tears were making tracks down the man's cheeks.

As darkness fell, help continued to arrive. Big lights were brought in to aid the rescue efforts. Diesel generators had been installed and electric drills and saws roared and squealed. There were now more than twenty bodies laid out in the yard and the police had managed to cordon off the scene. A medical team had set up a makeshift emergency point under some tarpaulins and big Jeeps were ferrying injured women to Dhaka's hospitals. Small groups of shadowy figures clustered around the stretchers, small children, hugged by slightly older children. Thin shoulders wracked with sobs.

Janne worked as though in a trance. He was covered in mortar and dust and barely knew what was going on around him. He had been focused on a man with a scruffy turban who seemed to know what he was doing, Janne's powerful body at his service. They'd moved beams and pried aside rebar. Hacked open brick walls and moved sections of floor. Janne had shut his eyes when they raised a big slab of concrete floor under which the corner of a sari had let them know a woman had been crushed. Another time, he'd managed to free a frightened girl who had found an air pocket next to an inner wall.

When he stepped off the mounds of debris to get something to drink, sometime much later, he heard Antje's voice through the racket. It sounded broken. When he looked up, he was blinded by the glaring construction lights at first, then he saw a dark silhouette approaching him. When Antje got closer, Janne realised she was carrying a scrawny girl in her arms. Next to her walked a stooped, grey woman who seemed to have shoved her whole fist into her mouth, as though to stop a scream. Her face was twisted in pain.

"Janne," Antje stumbled and Janne realised she was crying. "This is Rehana. She's dead."

Janne took the lifeless girl from her. A child, Janne was holding a dead child in his arms. He closed his eyes and felt his knees almost buckle. Blood had trickled out of Rehana's mouth and dried. Two long plaits. Antje cried and shook her head. She put her arm around the hunched woman.

"A wall fell on her. Moltana, her mother, only just survived. She's in shock. She can't talk. Do you know where your Meena is? Moltana says Meena was with Rehana before the collapse. I haven't seen her. Have you checked the bodies?"

Several weeks later, when Janne woke up in the middle of the night, he remembered. There had been a plaster around one of Rehana's fingers. A Swedish children's plaster.

*

Evening had fallen when Sofia exited the public library. A lot of the things she was looking for had been available online. Even the corruption advisors at the Christian Michelsen Institute in Norway advocated distinguishing between *development damage* and *reputational damage*. Whenever corruption was discovered, which was unfortunately common enough when working within flawed systems, the two had to be weighed against each other. In other words, the damage done by an abrupt withdrawal of funds had to be weighed against the damage done to the donor's image as it became associated with corruption. There were many examples online of instances when foreign aid donors had elected to save an organisation like Alor Desh, increasing their resources rather than closing down and pulling out. Maybe, maybe, maybe. Friday afternoon was the moment of truth. Two more days. She was approaching this like the lawyer she had been trained to be. Methodically building a defence.

She turned her phone back on as she left the library. Fifteen texts from Janne. A bit over the top, she thought with a smile and opened the most recent one. It was a continuation of a previous one. " . . . so now Antje's sleeping here and Nazreen's out looking for Meena.The children are staying at Malena's tonight. I have to sleep. Why aren't you answering?? Turn on your GODDAMN phone. I need you!!!"

Sofia stared at the message. What was he on about? Why was Antje spending the night? Suddenly, there was a knot in her stomach. And why wasn't Nazreen minding the children? Sofia went into Espresso House on Odengatan and sat down.

She opened the earlier messages, which seemed to have been delivered out of order. She tried to call Janne, but his phone was off. "Bjarne's factory has collapsed, panic over here. Check Reuters. Do you know anyone who can help locally? Can Sweden do anything? Siv's an idiot, Moberg just mumbles at me." Then she opened the text that finally made the penny drop. "Antje found Rehana's body, you know, that little girl. Dead. Antje in shock. Meena missing. CALL ME!"

She sat frozen on her chair, phone in hand. Rehana scratching at the side of her rickshaw. The flower garlands and her lazy eye. Sofia had to hold onto the table. The world lurched on its axis. Bjarne's fucking factory. They should have done something.

A group of teenagers came into Espresso House from the snow and asked Sofia if the empty chairs around her were taken. When she didn't respond, they gingerly moved the chairs from her table to theirs.

Sofia closed her eyes, mind hard at work. Then she slowly unlocked her phone again. Yes, they were still there. That one and that one and that one. She clicked around. And that one. She had a plan.

*

Anders Fullén was pleased with his effort: a front page headline and three full pages inside the paper, plus a follow up on day two. That should make SwedeAid sweat a little. Best case scenario, he'd be able to get an account of the Friday meeting of SwedeAid's anti-corruption group into the Saturday paper. Apparently, a representative from the embassy was going to be there, which meant he was going to be able to hold those responsible to account and get beyond the official statement and press releases. Surely they weren't contemplating wasting more money on supporting this organisation? It was always like that with SwedeAid, an obscene amount of money, right down the drain what with corruption and all the rest of it. Fat cats in Africa and Asia lining their pockets with Swedish tax money. He'd seen it, travelling around South America when he was twenty-four: pudgy aid workers and emaciated kids. Bloody hell.

He entered the newspaper office and was handed a yellow piece of paper by the assistant editor. "Traffic chaos last night, check in with the county!" He sat down to dial the number of the regional emergency command but was immediately given new orders.

"Hey, Anders." The assistant editor was waving a piece of paper around. "SwedeAid is calling a press conference this afternoon. Your story seems to have stirred things up. Want it?"

Anders Fullén climbed the stairs to SwedeAid's conference room two steps at a time. He was annoyed about the press conference. He was the one who had broken the story about the corruption in Khadija Anam's organisation and he would have preferred for it to remain an exclusive scoop a little while longer. The audit and other materials had been sent in anonymously, all he'd had to do was read it. Bribes, ghost employees, hidden accounts, fake contracts. But now, the rest of the press was suddenly joining the fray. He spotted colleagues from all major papers.

Journalists were torn about SwedeAid. There was this ambivalent feeling that having a go at the agency was a bit like kicking someone when they were down, just too easy. The indignation of certain groups of readers was always simmering beneath the surface, was it really a good idea to stir it up? Over issues like global poverty and famine? The online comment sections for articles on foreign aid always left a bad taste, much like when the subject was immigrants: the same indignant tone, the same bigotry.

Being well-educated, most journalists realised the agency was working with difficult issues in difficult areas and that sometimes, that means big risks and big losses. On the other hand, things were often incredibly incompetently managed. Like in this case. If you started turning over rocks, something always crawled out. But you didn't want to start playing into the hands of neo-liberal thinktanks, either. Any exposé on foreign aid risked bolstering the anti-foreign aid lobby's cause.

As a consequence, journalists usually avoided going after SwedeAid. Partly, also, because the material was dense and time-consuming, the sums involved enormous and the distribution channels myriad. There had been a radio journalist who was on top of it all, but he had retired. Swedfund, the Ministry of Foreign Affairs, the National Audit Office, the National Export Credits Guarantee Board, the Swedish Trade Council, a jungle of agencies and NGOs. It was easy to slip up and start hammering the wrong nail. And in the end, who cared? Really? Anders Fullén had had a hard time persuading his assistant editor to run his story. Money going missing in Bangladesh wasn't exactly a blockbuster. What was the point?

But Anders Fullén had stuck to his assessment that this particular story needed to be told. It was a slam dunk. Clearly defined, easy to understand and with a famous name to draw attention. Not publishing when the audit was literally sitting on his desk would be ethically reprehensible. And judging by the attendance of this press conference, he'd been right, this story was a slam dunk.

The blonde woman at the podium looked efficient. Her long, blonde hair was gathered in a loose plait tied off with a bright green hair tie. It wasn't one of SwedeAid's press officers, he knew all of them. Probably someone from the embassy in Bangladesh. They must have panicked when he published his article. The woman cleared her throat and looked up. Ander's looked appreciatively at her svelte figure. A bit on the skinny side, perhaps, but other than that, nice. Her eyes were ice blue and her face angular, interesting. She was good-looking, but not cute. She wore a blue scarf across her chest, Indian style. Pity, Anders Fullén had time to think before she got going.

"Hi, it's good to see so many of you here today. My name is Sofia Paulin and I'm in charge of Sweden's foreign aid to Bangladesh. In the past few days, there has been controversy about one of our partners, Right Livelihood Award winner Khadija Anam. Today, I'm going to tell you how we at the embassy plan to address the alleged corruption but I also want to take this opportunity to share a slightly more nuanced perspective with you. There are inevitably many shades of grey when you work in difficult environments."

Everyone in the room was paying rapt attention as she leaned forward and pushed a key on her laptop. A large picture of her on a chair next to a scrawny girl with two long plaits appeared on the wall behind her. The blue scarf Sofia was wearing was the same one she had on in the picture.

"I want to tell you about a friend of mine, this twelve-year-old girl whose name is Rehana. Rehana died last night when a garment factory a mile or two from my house in Dhaka collapsed. Rehana was working in a factory funded by Danish foreign aid money. A model for international development that is becoming increasingly common in Sweden, too."

The room was silent. Sofia clicked to the next picture. The girl with the plaits with a naked toddler on her hip. Another picture. Sofia with her arm around a stooped older woman and the girl beaming with joy next to them.

"I heard a garment factory collapsed in Dhaka, it was on the wires this morning," a colleague sitting next to Anders Fullén whispered. "If it's not a ferry sinking it's a factory collapsing. Or burning down. Poor sods. And they always die in droves."

"The first time I met Rehana was a few weeks ago when I visited the factory where she and her mother work. Or worked." Sofia took a deep breath before pressing on. "Now I'm going to show you pictures taken last night of the factory, or the scene of the accident, but I want to warn you. You may find the pictures disturbing."

The wall behind Sofia filled with a photograph of a grey factory building that had collapsed. The floors lay stacked one on top of the other, shrouded in dust. Sofia showed picture after picture without comment. She didn't look at them herself, she had averted her eyes. People in shock, their faces were twisted with horror, half-naked toddlers standing in the rubble. There weren't a lot of pictures from the scene, but the ones displayed on the wall were stark. Powerful, close-up and clear.

"Unfortunately, those are all the pictures we have. My husband, he's the one who took them, chose to help with the rescue instead."

Sofia's voice suddenly sounded thin, she gratefully took a question from Anders. He was seeing a new potential angle for his SwedeAid story.

"Powerful pictures, thank you. This is a tragedy. Will they be made available to the press? And the pictures of you and the girl, what was her name? Johanna?"

"How can we reach your husband?" another journalist asked.

"What was the name of the factory? Was it under Danish ownership?" The questions kept coming.

"The girl's name was Rehana. And of course you can use the pictures. But one step at a time. First, please listen to what I have to say about Alor Desh. During the main slideshow later, there will be sandwiches and coffee."

*

Nazreen had looked. Boss had looked. They'd spent the entire day after the collapse searching the rubble. Nazreen had forgotten to eat and drink. When the sun reached its zenith, Boss had forced her to sit down in the shade to rest and have a bit of water. The odd lady with the red hair Nazreen had seen at Beppin's had brought them food.

Every time a section of floor was raised up, Nazreen had stopped breathing, her eyes darting this way and that among the bricks and mortar, searching for Meena's blue-and-yellow shalwar kameez. Moltana had said both she and Rifat had been with Rehana minutes before the collapse, doing business, as usual. But there had been no sign of Meena and Rifat's bodies where Rehana had died.

When dusk fell, Nazreen thought she'd found her sister. A familiar-looking hand sticking out of the debris. Nazreen had felt her legs buckle. First Mokta, now Meena. Pain had pounded through her body, she'd held her breath and whimpered, like a wounded animal. Boss had held her and rocked her like a child, covering her eyes with his big hand. It was only when she saw the long hair that she knew. It was someone else's sister.

She exhaled.

Janne shot Vanja a grateful look. She'd been there all day, helping the doctors, dispatching the embassy car to the hospital again and again. In her extravagant way, she'd soothed children, made calls and ensured the small street stands had enough food ready at all times to sustain the people digging and lifting. Wearing a pair of oversized sunglasses and military trousers that looked like they might belong to her son and with her red hair like a halo around her head, she'd become central to the rescue effort. Bewildered police officers had done her bidding.

Now she put her arm around Nazreen and gave her a gentle squeeze. It was past midnight and a digger had arrived at the scene. Nazreen had charged up to it, banging its side, trying to stop it.

"They're crushing her, they're crushing her!"

Vanja had gently coaxed Nazreen away, explaining that they would have heard Meena if she'd been alive.

"But what if she's unconscious?"

Vanja wrapped a shawl around her and tried to pull the reluctant girl toward the car. She needed to sleep. Janne needed to get back to the children and he wanted to talk to Sofia in Stockholm.

"Nazreen, sweetheart," Vanja soothed. "Don't feel there's no reason to hope. There is. We haven't found her, so she's not here. I can feel that she's alive, I can feel her presence on a higher plane. Would you like us to take my car and drive around to look for her?"

"She would have come here if she was alive. She would have known I'd be worried. Meena thinks about things like that, about not making people worry. She has never not answered her phone before."

Nazreen was shivering in the warm night. Vanja and Janne exchanged a look over her head. As she ushered the girl toward the embassy car, Vanja said softly:

"You go home to your children, Janne. And call Sofia, send her a hug from me. Girl power! Tell her that." She thrust a defiant fist in the air. "I'll look after Nazreen. We'll drive around and look for Meena."

The emergency was over. Janne had spent nearly two full days and nights labouring at the scene of the accident. Nizamuddhin was quiet for once. He'd been transporting injured people and dead bodies all day. Now he was driving Janne home. Janne's jeans were ripped and he was bleeding from a large gash on his thigh. His hands were full of cuts and his arms ached. His hair and face were covered in dust.

Sofia. He missed her so much it hurt. They'd only had minutes to talk after Sofia woke up in Sweden, She'd been furious and distraught. Rehana must have meant more to her than he'd realised.

"Goddamn fucking Bjarne!" she'd sobbed. "Where is the bastard? We knew, Janne. Antje and I saw the factory, why didn't we do something? Your fucking tennis buddy! He's a murderer, you know! A child murderer!"

"Bjarne has run away to Bangkok. Made himself unavailable," Janne said lamely, which only made Sofia more upset.

"It's always, always like this! The biggest rat is the first to leave the ship. I'm going to make sure he pays. Somehow, he will pay."

"Someone saw him and Tone on the way to the airport about an hour after the collapse. They've probably gone into hiding in some luxury hotel in Bangkok. Apparently, the Danish press is looking for him."

"It's people like Bjarne who are an outrage, I'm telling you. Not people like Khadija. He thought it was worth rolling the dice, knowing the building was probably deficient."

Sofia's voice had cracked. Janne had tried to console her. Sofia wasn't often thrown off balance.

"What happened is horrible, and he will pay, but try to stay calm. You have a job to do. You can cry with me when you're done."

Eventually, Sofia's breathing had slowed and when they finished the call, she had sounded collected. They'd agreed to have a proper talk after Sofia's press conference.

Which was in half an hour. At seven, Swedish time. He would have time to shower.

Janne pushed the phone against his ear so hard it hurt. Sitting on the bed, fresh from the shower, the gash on his leg cleaned up, he'd listened as Sofia told him about her day. She had pulled off a veritable coup, he could barely believe it. That she'd been able to keep cool enough, even though she was in shock. She'd circumvented SwedeAid's press office and pre-empted the anti-corruption group's report. The defence of Alor Desh she'd mounted had been worthy of the craftiest lawyer.

"I went with my gut, Janne. Bet everything on one card. I just figured I couldn't let Rehana die in vain." She sounded tired and sad. "There's no guarantee it'll work out. But the press bought my spin, hook, line and sinker. They're toning down the rhetoric around Alor Desh, choosing to see the nuances instead. The report on violent Islamification, the material from the British anti-corruption team and then the factory and the new private sector aid model. Different risk profiles for different kinds of support. And your powerful pictures from the scene. All the papers will be running them, just so you know."

"And the pictures of Rehana?"

"I happened to have them on my phone. I didn't like using them, but I figured anything to distract them from Khadija Anam."

Her voice trailed off and Janne felt a wave of tenderness for his wife.

"Are you okay?"

"I think so. A bit hyper. You?"

Sofia's question made a lump swell in Janne's throat. Her soft voice, the concern in it. Was he okay? While he tried to figure out if he was, he suddenly remembered hanging out in trendy cafés in Stockholm, sipping lattes and nibbling on sourdough bread. He'd been so self-important, going on and on about seeing the world, starting fresh, trying his wings. "Time for new horizons." Was he happy now?

The reek emanating from the collapsed factory by the second evening had attracted stray dogs. Big, yellow dogs that fought and copulated and smelled blood. Predators. People had made bonfires to keep them away. He could still feel the cold of the dead girl's scrawny body in his arms. He realised just how far from home he was. The thread tying him to his old life was so thin, so fragile. The hand holding the phone trembled. His leg might need stitches.

"It was like hell on Earth," he said quietly. "Remember when we talked about evil? I think that's what it looks like, evil. Recklessness.

Ruthlessness. The trampling of the weak. I could throttle Bjarne, we're both lucky he slunk away. When I left today, sixty-four women were dead and as many critically injured. The death count is still rising."

Sofia replied quietly.

"I read that on Reuters. It's insane, I can't believe it actually happened. How could it happen?"

"Bjarne did mention adding more floors, remember? It seems all the bricks for the expansion were stored on the roof. In the end, it got too heavy. The walls were like the walls of a playhouse. You didn't have to be an engineer to see they were nowhere near strong enough."

"We should have known. I can't believe we were there and failed to see it." Sofia sounded like she was on the verge of tears, but then continued softly. "You've been back there, helping out?"

Janne answered on an inhalation.

"Yes."

Sofia was quiet for a long time. The phone line crackled.

"And Meena?" she asked finally.

"Still no word. But on the other hand, no body, either. Nazreen and Vanja are going to drive around to look for her tonight, she might have stumbled across a business opportunity that . . ."

Janne faltered, unable to finish his sentence. He wanted to cry. The small body in his arms, so light and cold, almost like a ragdoll. Lifeless. He recalled Moltana's twisted face and Antje's horror at all the bodies. The man in the scruffy turban, whom Janne had been working alongside, had eventually found his wife. He'd pulled her out of the rubble with a roar, unconscious but still alive. Her lower half had looked flat. Janne had shut his eyes. The images kept flashing before him; he couldn't make them stop.

The next question came from the bottom of his heart, in a whisper:

"Sofia. Why did we leave our life in Stockholm? Why did we come here at all? What are we doing here?"

*

The mock-up on the night editor's screen was striking. Good pictures, good layout. The managing editor had seen what he was trying to do, how much sexier this was than yet another corruption scandal at SwedeAid. The cool, blonde woman, squatting next to a barefoot girl. Shacks and a dirty stream in the background. And the text, poignant. About the Swedish aid worker's shock at the sudden death of the girl and her thoughts on life and work in Dhaka. Her thoughts on the corruption scandal, how it wasn't black and white. The headline added an extra dimension, as well. A lot of people were going to read this carefully. Anders was more than pleased. "She lost her friend in the rubble – now she refuses to bow to the fundamentalists."

Sofia Paulin's story was solid, she was solid. Authentic and plain-spoken. She had outlined different approaches to foreign aid and the risks and possibilities inherent in each. Apparently, every model had its pros and cons, and her point seemed to be that the contexts in which the aid was needed were challenging. She'd told them foreign aid should be viewed as venture capital and that its social impact stood in direct proportion to the resistance it met from conservatives. The more dire the need for aid, the greater the risks. He'd turned the info she'd given them into a sidebar he was actually properly proud of. There! That was how you explained complicated things. Inside every good journalist there is a true pedagogue, he thought to himself. That thing about how money given to grassroots organisations helped counter terrorism and violent Islamification. Spot on! And about how this new kind of aid to the private sector was problematic, too. She had tried to explain to them that changing the world was complicated. Apparently, it had more to do with grappling with dilemmas than finding simple solutions. Anders Fullén smiled. *Really*. But he laid it out clearly for his readers.

Sofia Paulin was media-savvy. Attractive. She'd worn the same blue scarf at the press conference as in the pictures with the dead girl. Shrewd. And the Danish angle. What Swede didn't enjoy having a go at the Danes? The night editor had wanted to go big, as well, had asked if he had more. Anders Fullén had been right – compared to this, the corruption scandal was uninteresting.

"Maybe we should do a whole series of articles on Bangladesh?" the night editor had mused, proposing a headline on the spot: "Sofia Paulin and her fight for the people of the delta? An article series about 'The almost drowned', what do you reckon? Fuck, that's brilliant – 'The Almost Drowned'. Let's go with that! And do you think she'd be willing to blog from the embassy?"

*

Nazreen stared out the car window. Meena-shona, darling sister, where are you? The last fires around which Badda's poorest gathered at night were dying down. There was no electricity in the area and the car's headlights were soon the only source of light. Nazreen was sitting on the edge of the backseat, peering into the dark. She'd barely moved for three hours straight. If only she hadn't taken money out of the plastic box, if only she hadn't been so angry with Meena . Her guilt was as heavy as her worry.

"Nazreen." The kind woman stroked her back. "You have to go home and get some sleep. Tomorrow's a new day. Who knows, maybe Rifat's mother . . ."

Nazreen whipped around. She held up a trembling finger.

"One! Let's go by one more time. Please, please, Madame. One!"

Rifat's mother, a woman she'd only glimpsed in passing once, was Nazreen's last hope. She knew the woman's name was Jalula and that they lived somewhere near the Badda Bazaar bus station. They'd been by several times already, asking for her, one person had claimed to have seen Jalula buy banglanod – moonshine. But no one had seen Meena or Rifat.

The driver parked the car so its headlights illuminated the empty marketplace. A handful of rats scurried across the square. Bundles of people were sleeping next to the ramshackle buildings enclosing the open place. Nazreen jumped out of the car and walked up to one of the bundles. An old man. Behind a parked lorry was another bundle. When Nazreen saw it was a woman, she hissed. "Jalula, are you Jalula?"

The bundle rolled over. The woman's hair was unkempt and she seemed to have thrown up on her sari. She reeked of vomit and something sharp. Nazreen studied her for a minute, then she was suddenly sure the woman was Rifat's mother – she was clutching Meena's mobile phone.

"Jalula! Wake up!" Nazreen made another attempt at rousing the woman, this time with an edge of panic in her voice. She pried the phone from her grasp. "Jalula, I'm Meena's sister. Please, please, wake up!"

Missed calls. Sixteen missed calls from her. How long had Rifat's mother had Meena's phone, and why?

"Wake up!"

The woman seemed under the influence of something. She slurred her words and was unable to sit up unaided. When she opened her eyes, they were crossed and she soon closed them again. Nazreen gave her a kick.

"Jalula, look at me! Where is Rifat, your son?"

Jalula roused herself, fixed Nazreen for a moment and then laughed hoarsely. She triumphantly pulled out a bottle that had been hidden behind her back. Banglanod. Then she started fumbling around for something, seeming confused.

"Is it the phone you want?" Nazreen was speaking loudly, holding the phone up in front of her face. "Tell me how you got it! Why do you have Meena's phone?"

"Dowry," Jalula managed. "My disgusting harami, I finally got a dowry for him. Ten thousand taka and a mobile phone. The weird girl married my weird son."

She laughed and closed her eyes again. Nazreen shook her and screamed in her ear.

"When? Jalua, when? Where are they now?"

Jalula opened her eyes, laughed and closed them again. After that, she was dead to the world.

*

It had been a long time since SwedeAid had received this kind of positive press coverage, that much was clear to Sofia. She walked up to the hotel's breakfast buffet and poured herself another cup of coffee. She hoped no other hotel guests were looking to read the morning papers, she needed to go through them. Open newspapers covered her table. Sofia's blonde hair could be seen in *Kvällspressen*, its main tabloid rival and both morning broadsheets. *The human angle*, Sofia noted with mixed feelings.

Her meeting with SwedeAid's anti-corruption team was scheduled for eleven and the new Head of Public Relations Percy Bengtsson had been in touch to say he wanted to attend. He'd woken her up, hollering on the other end of the line:

"This is some spin, Sofia! Exactly what SwedeAid needs! I'm going to back you up today. We can't pull our support!"

"That's what I'm saying." Sofia could tell he was going to play his part in the meeting.

"*Kvällspressen* called, they want to do an article series about your work in Bangladesh. Outstanding! 'The Almost Drowned'. The attention this is getting is unbelievable! I would also like you to blog from the embassy and . . ."

"One step at a time," Sofia cut in. "First we have to straighten this out. Until the anti-corruption team agrees to reassess, we're nowhere. You're coming to the meeting, as is Ola Björnberg from the Conflict and Security Department and Katta from the Gender Unit. Just so you know. And Lasse Bergström, our country coordinator."

"I have full faith in you! This is some wicked spin, me likey!"

Sofia had managed to get SwedeAid's conflict advisor Ola Björnberg, a bluff former reserve officer whom she had called earlier in the week, on board. For years, he'd done his best to demonstrate to the agency that foreign aid could counter extremism and prevent conflict through careful, targeted investment. The case of Alor Desh had made him hopeful the agency might finally listen. Sofia hadn't had time to go over the details with him, but had referred to Charlotta at Alor Desh and the written material. And Katta would be there, for both moral and professional support. It was the best backup she could muster for her cause.

It might work. Sofia drank one last cup of coffee and headed out in the snow. Before entering the SwedeAid building, she mumbled under her breath: "Inshallah". It would work if a force greater than her wanted it to. The notion that some things were out of her hands was oddly comforting.

The young, well-tailored Head of Public Relations hurried toward Sofia as soon as he spotted her in the hallway. He was waving a copy of *Kvällspressen*. She greeted him politely and then turned to Ola Björnberg, who was waiting outside the meeting room. He was early.

"Did you get hold of Charlotta?"

"Yes, I spoke to Charlotta Malmström and I read the British report. I think I have a good handle on the situation. Spot on. These are exactly the types of grant we can't afford to terminate."

The anti-corruption team arrived together. Sofia recognised Ulla Magnusson, lawyer and head of the team, and two accountants, both recent hires. A pasty woman with strawberry blonde hair and white eyelashes and a portly man in his forties. Sofia greeted them with brief nods and hellos while pulling binders and printouts out of her briefcase and placing them in front of her on the table. Katta was the last to arrive and she walked over to Sofia and gave her a hug.

"Good luck!"

After the obligatory introductions, Ulla Magnusson took the floor. She had a stack of papers in front of her on the table, which she straightened fastidiously while she spoke. She weighed her words carefully.

"It's always regrettable when SwedeAid is forced to acknowledge that one of our partner organisations has mismanaged the funds received from us. In the case of Alor Desh, the corruption must be deemed severe. We have studied the audit conducted by Ernst & Young's New Delhi office and see few or no prospects of saving the organisation. We want our cooperation with Alor Desh to be terminated with immediate effect."

Conflict advisor Ola Björnberg and head of public relations Percy Bengtsson simultaneously tried to cut in, but Ulla Magnusson pressed on, unperturbed.

"We don't feel the potentially extenuating circumstances presented to date are enough to warrant a reassessment of our recommendation."

Sofia had prepared for this. She set about her task methodically, refusing to get worked up. A PowerPoint presentation showed the composition of Alor Desh's funding over the past ten years, with arrows linking various accounts and donors. Then a summary of the organisation's striking results. Declining maternal mortality rates in the area where Alor Desh was active, increased literacy rates among children in villages where Alor Desh ran schools and measurable improvements in a range of social indicators. Not to mention that land had been registered in the names of both men and women, a big step forward for gender equality. Sofia also mentioned the organisation's innovative approach to helping farmers cope with ever-rising water levels in the delta.

"Climate change is an everyday reality for the people in the char area. They adapt as best they can, even though their own carbon footprint is negligible," she explained.

While she talked, Sofia tried to read the faces of the three people on the anti-corruption team. Did they understand what she was trying to tell them? Did they understand how hard it was to get any results at all in this part of the world? Were they capable of assessing anything other than numbers and columns? Sofia doubted it, but stuck to her plan.

She methodically outlined what the consequences of a funding gap would be. No emotions, no pictures. Just cold, hard facts. Madrassas would multiply, for better and for worse. Alor Desh's self-help groups would be hijacked by radical religious elements. There would be no boats to help women access hospitals. She matter-of-factly described Khadija Anam's unique network and fortitude and emphasised her own personal conviction that Khadija Anam's integrity was unimpeachable.

"Khadija is a strong woman whose work threatens to undermine the existing power structures in the char area. As a consequence, she has made powerful enemies who want her gone at any cost. We have reason to suspect a majority of the allegations of corruption are part of a smear campaign aimed at her."

"Do you have any proof of that?" Ulla Magnusson intervened brusquely. "Otherwise we have to assume the information uncovered by the auditors is correct. This seems to be an unholy mess."

"Reality tends to be messy," Lasse Bergström commented drily. Sofia shot him a grateful look.

She'd been right to invite so many people to the meeting. She wouldn't have to do all the heavy lifting herself. When the pasty-faced accountant spoke up, questioning Alor Desh's payrolls and "certain irregularities with regards to receipt management routines", conflict advisor Ola Björnberg was unable to hold his tongue.

"I'm sorry, all due respect to you . . . number crunchers, but the fact is that what we're talking about is global politics. Global issues, global problems. Have you heard of 9/11? About the link between violent radicalisation of the countryside in Muslim parts of the world and an increased threat of terror attacks in the West?"

Ola Björnberg leaned forward and fixed Ulla Magnusson intently. Then he went on:

"Sweden has an international obligation to act conflict-sensitively and perform thorough risk analyses. The Bangladeshi government has adopted an anti-radicalisation policy and is expressing strong support for foreign aid donors who work to counter radicalisation. Do you have any idea what's going to happen if Alor Desh is forced to seek financing from radical jihadists in the Middle East or Pakistan? Or if the self-help groups are taken over by violent extremists?"

The two accountants looked pale but the more experienced Ulla Magnusson stepped into the breach.

"It goes without saying that all foreign aid is well-intentioned, but that doesn't mean this is acceptable. We have committed to a zero-tolerance approach to corruption and in the case of Alor Desh, the audit has established that the organisation has failed to adequately account for at least ten percent of the aid received. That money may have been used for bribes."

"Ten percent?" Ola Björnberg struggled not to yell. Instead, he jabbed the table with his finger. "That's bloody nothing! *No-thing.* A risk margin. Have you been to Bangladesh? Any of you?"

Ola Björnberg turned to the pasty woman who had spoken.

"I demand that the embassy and the anti-corruption team perform a thorough risk analysis to assess the consequences of cancelling our aid to Alor Desh. What will become of the organisation if we decide to pull out? What will become of Bangladesh's one hundred and fifty thousand landless?"

He was addressing Ulla Magnusson now, but was interrupted by Lasse Bergström, who so far had said nothing.

"In Afghanistan, we informally expect a fifty percent loss, at least. Foreign aid is no picnic, don't make the mistake of thinking it is. And I haven't even mentioned Somalia and Sudan."

Katta asked for the floor and drew their attention to the existence of a gender dimension in which poor women were pitched against wealthy, powerful men. Grassroots programmes aimed at poor women were easy targets for anti-corruption advocates, while the much more substantial grants given to predominantly male government ministers were left unchallenged in the name of diplomacy. Following the priorities set out by the Swedish government, foreign aid programmes aimed at empowering women were to be promoted, but that required an improved understanding of the type of programmes likely to actually reach women. She sounded professional and authoritative. Sofia smiled down at her papers.

The new head of public relations said nothing. He didn't know much about foreign aid, had just been hired from a flashy PR firm, Katta had told Sofia in a whisper. Sofia started to outline her proposal for reforming of the organisation, but was interrupted by Ulla Magnusson.

"Sofia, in all honesty. I think it's too late. We've made statements to the press, promising the taxpayers we're going to deal with this."

That roused the head of public relations.

"I'll handle the press! The public relations team has formulated a strategy and I'm sure Sofia won't mind helping out. *Kvällspressen* has expressed interest in dispatching a reporter to Bangladesh to write a whole article series about Alor Desh. 'The Almost Drowned', they're calling it, it's going to have its own logo and this bloke . . ." he glanced down at his notes, " . . . Anders Fullén, will be heading down there as early as next week."

Sofia looked up. Support from yet another direction. Percy Bengtsson spoke with intensity and rhetorical flair. A spin doctor.

"We've finally found a human angle on foreign aid, people who are relatable, who we can get to know. Sofia, Rehana, Moltana. Let's work that! Believe me, SwedeAid needs all the good press we can get. Today's paper . . ." He opened his copy of *Kvällspressen* to a page dominated by the picture of Sofia and Rehana. "This is what we want! We have to give the papers something other than tedious corruption stories. We want people to associate SwedeAid with . . . well, with saving the world. Get it? *We are saving the world* – that's what we need to communicate!"

Ulla Magnusson opened her mouth to speak, but was again interrupted by Ola Björnberg.

"Ulla, seriously. The government has explicitly instructed my department to counter radicalisation and mainstream anti-terrorism efforts within SwedeAid's broader mission. Now you're impeding that work by recklessly pushing *your* priorities," The word "reckless" dialled the rhetoric up a notch and drew a soft gasp from Sofia. Was

Ola Björnberg the one being reckless? Sharp words were unusual at SwedeAid, where everyone strived to reach consensus at any cost. But Katta immediately jumped on Ola Björnberg's bandwagon.

"I have to say I agree with Ola. At Gender, we take a similar view of the situation. What we have here is an organisation that despite delivering extremely good results for vulnerable women risks being wiped out because SwedeAid's anti-corruption team is pushing a clueless agenda of zero tolerance . . ."

"Let's not lose sight of the fact we are under direct orders from the minister to comply with this "clueless agenda", as you call it," Ulla Magnusson countered sharply, cutting Katta short.

Sofia could sense the steel in her resistance. Ulla Magnusson was no fledgling, she was going to go to the mat for this. Sofia recognised the intransigence of a lawyer.

Lasse Bergström, cleared his throat loudly and leaned forward ponderously.

"I've worked for SwedeAid my entire life and I'm retiring next year. I expect you to respect my professional knowledge and judgment. Today, we have a minister who uses allegations of corruption to discredit all foreign aid programmes, with the aim of redistributing funds to the private sector." He paused, looked around the table and sneered. "As though there's no corruption in the private sector. I've seen ministers come and go, but this one! His agenda is unabashedly ideological and he has no interest in helping the poor. But remember, at the end of the day, we're in charge, the minister doesn't have the authority to micromanage SwedeAid. Let's show people we're equal to the responsibility by making prudent decisions. Let's save Alor Desh!"

Ulla Magnusson licked her lips, looking harassed. She was suddenly intensely interested in making sure the papers on the table in front of her were neatly stacked. Her accountants were looking at her.

"We have made statements to the press, promising the taxpayers . . ."

That's as far as she got. Percy Bengtsson broke in.

"I'll handle the press, thank you! Sofia has managed to turn their attention to larger, global issues, matters of justice and fighting poverty and promoting human rights. They've moved on from the corruption scandal. Thankfully," he beat back Ulla Magnusson's final objection once and for all, then looked around the table.

"Friends, let's turn this around! SwedeAid saves *The Almost Drowned*. We care about real people and aren't afraid to take risks to make the world a better place. Could it be any better?" Sofia looked down at her papers and mumbled.

"No, this is as good as it gets. Inshallah."

22

Janne had slept for fourteen hours. The news that Sofia had managed to persuade the anti-corruption team had come via email while he was asleep, and now she was asleep back in Sweden. He wrote her an affectionate email and ordered flowers to be delivered to her hotel room when she woke up. Competent, wonderful, brave Sofia. Janne missed her so much it hurt. She needed to come home now.

Nazreen was downstairs with the children. The girl had finally found her sister's phone and then a letter. The letter had apparently been placed on Nazreen's bed but must have fallen in under it at some point. Beaming with joy, Nazreen had told him her sister was getting married and that she and her fiancé had gone back to their village. She'd seemed calm and relieved.

Janne packed up their swimming gear and called Noella and Teo. The plan was to have lunch at Malena's and then go to the club. As they were leaving, his phone rang.

"Hiya, Rickard here, from the Swedish embassy."

Janne had asked Rickard to find out more about Bjarne. What was going to happen to him? What was the Danish embassy doing? Was Bjarne likely to be held to account by the Bangladeshi authorities? Or Denmark's foreign aid agency? The *Daily Star*, Bangladesh's largest English-language newspaper, had put the death toll at sixty-seven. Sixty-seven women. Sixty-six women and one girl.

"Any news?" Janne wanted to know.

"Not so much as a peep from Bjarne, but I'm given to understand there are systems in place for this kind of thing. It's not the first time something's gone wrong, put it that way. Fires, collapsing buildings, accidents involving machinery, the work environments here aren't exactly safe. The Danish embassy has washed their hands of it. As far as they're concerned, they gave Bjarne a start-up grant ten years ago, and that was the end of their involvement. According to some contract between garment factory owners and the government, however, factory owners are obligated to pay compensation when a factory worker is killed. About one hundred thousand taka per family."

"Eight thousand Swedish kronor. Well, I suppose that's a fortune here."

"If it's paid out at all, sometimes it takes years. Sometimes it doesn't happen. I found out online that the families of the workers who died in the Startex collapse five years ago are still waiting for compensation. Legally speaking, Bjarne gets off scot-free. The law considers the collapse an accident."

"And there's nothing about neglect or mismanagement?" Janne wasn't a lawyer, just incensed.

"Nope. In theory, he could fork out a few hundred thousand in damages and carry right on. If I've understood things right. But the Danish newspapers are laying into him, have you seen it?"

"No, I haven't had time. There's a lot going on right now, what with Alor Desh and everything. You heard, right?"

"I did, nicely done, Sofia. And I've been told your efforts at the scene were beyond impressive. A couple of heroes, eh?"

"So Bjarne can just hide, pay and carry on?"

"In theory, yes. But that's not going to happen."

"What do you mean?"

"Well," Rickard chuckled. "You're here. As am I. And a few others with a bit of backbone. He wouldn't be able to show his face in the club for years, and without the club he wouldn't want to be here. Am I right?"

"I suppose you are." Janne laughed drily. "Who would Papa Bjarne be without the Nordic Club?"

"So it's probably best to let the press take care of it, let them rip him apart."

"Sure, but a media takedown doesn't compensate the families for the loss of a breadwinner. They need money to survive."

The children, fed up with waiting for their dad, were shouting at him from the car. Janne asked Rickard to let him know if he heard anything from the Danes and then ended the call.

"Sooner or later, he has to come back to clean out his house. It's hard to imagine him steering clear of the club all together if he's in town. And when he turns up, I have a thing or two I'd like to discuss with him."

As Nizamuddhin turned into Malena's garage, Malena appeared with a twin in one hand and a gangly boy in shorts in the other. The slum area where Siraj and his family lived was right on the other side of the garage wall. Noella and Teo slipped out of the car, seemingly unperturbed by the chaos of the past few days.

Malena led the way to the backyard and the children skipped after her. Malena had used the sandy patch between the garage and the slum shacks to draw pedagogical squares with numbers in them. A whole gaggle of children were jumping from square to square.

Janne walked over to Siraj's door, which stood ajar. Siraj came out.

"Janne-bhai, assalamu alaykum. Come in!"

"Kemon acho, Siraj-bhai."

Like last time, Siraj's great aunt was lying on the bed. Tomelilla was asleep at her feet. Janne told Siraj the news from Sweden in a low voice, told him about Sofia's research efforts and how even Charlotta had contributed. Siraj listened and filled in the gaps where Janne's story faltered, but the reaction Janne had expected wasn't forthcoming. Janne noted that instead of looking pleased, Siraj had gone quiet and was shifting uncomfortably. At length, Janne felt compelled to ask.

"Aren't you happy? It looks like Alor Desh is going to keep its funding? You can go back to the village and do your job?"

"Yes, of course I'm happy, of course I'm happy."

But he didn't look happy and his pale eyes avoided Janne's. He awkwardly began to collect the laundry that was drying in the room.

"But?"

Janne waited.

"But." Siraj stopped working and gave Janne a searching look. "But. It's not that simple."

"What?" Janne felt annoyed. What now? Always another layer. Was nothing ever straightforward in this country?

"I've been back to the village. The auditors missed a few pay-outs our financial director found in conjunction with the audit. There is an account in Khadija's name that none of us knew about."

"And?" Janne fixed him intently, Siraj sighed and turned his attention back to the laundry.

"And." He paused for a minute, searching for the right words. "And, it turns out she has used aid money to pay for her son Nirmol's university studies. Twice a year for three years. Tuition fee payments to ITM, the Institute of Tropical Medicine in London, one of the world's best medical schools."

"Goddamn it!" Janne closed his eyes and leaned back.

Siraj nodded and turned back to the laundry. Janne tried to understand.

"I can't defend it, I can't. It's corruption, no two ways about it. But I do understand. Khadija's more educated than most bideshis who come here, and yet they take home salaries she can only dream of. She's passionate about her country and her people and is prepared to work for a Bangladeshi salary. But she's not prepared to rob Nirmol of his future."

"Goddamn it!" Janne was still in shock and only half-listening.

"Nirmol is the only family she has, a smart, upstanding guy. She must have decided it was a risk worth taking."

Siraj fell silent and slowly sat down on the bed next to Janne. Janne was silent, too. Seconds ticked by. Janne tried to fathom what he'd just been told. For Sofia, this was a disaster, an unmitigated disaster. She had staked her reputation on Khadija Anam's integrity. The case for continuing to support Alor Desh would fall apart.

At length, Siraj sighed and spoke again.

"I understand it all. I understand Khadija's thinking, I understand how she justifies it to herself. She can't risk her son's future and education just because she's an idealist. That's where she draws the line. She's not like me, a regular Bengal. She has a degree from Oxford, why would she not want the same for her son? But . . ."

"It's unacceptable." Janne finished with a heavy sigh.

"Yes, exactly. It's unacceptable. Corrupt. Khadija must be held to account for her actions."

Malena stuck her head in through the door. The sudden movement made Siraj's great aunt stir. The bed creaked and the old lady's knees banged against the metal wall.

"My goodness, don't you just look ever so gloomy! Come out and play with us, Janne! There's a bunch of people here I want you to meet. Asma, over there in the corner, is going to . . ."

"Not right now," Janne declined. "I'll be out in a minute."

He turned to Siraj. He made a decision.

"Siraj-bhai. We can't let this get out. Sofia can't know. Please? Is there any way to persuade your financial director to keep quiet?"

*

Katta leaned forward and topped up her wineglass. She had set out a small cheese board on a wobbly end table in Sofia's hotel room. Grapes, pears and cheeses, sitting on their own packaging. Trendy miniature crispy breads with sesame seed and spelt. Fig marmalade. Delicacies Sofia had been yearning for for six months. Katta was curled up in the only armchair in the room and Sofia was reclining on the bed.

They'd analysed their meeting with the anti-corruption team from every angle, trying to figure out if this was the end of Sofia's career. Sofia had run into SwedeAid's director general in the hallway. He'd turned around abruptly to avoid her. At least that was how Sofia had interpreted the situation.

"Maybe he didn't see you? Don't read too much into it!"

"My career is over. I just know it!" Sofia had no doubt in her mind.

Katta had suggested it might only be starting. Her first steps outside her comfort zone.

"I'm sure you've made enemies," Katta acknowledged. "But so what?"

"Well, that's not great, is it? Next time I need references, people will say I'm trouble. You know as well as I do, you have to keep your head down at SwedeAid. Making a fuss comes at a price. Don't argue, don't question."

This was Katta and Sofia's favourite subject, the Rubik's cube they kept turning over and over. How were they supposed to contribute without stepping on anyone's toes or being critical? Any criticism of SwedeAid's work was liable to be suppressed for fear of it being used to attack foreign aid work in general. Being critical and yet *for* foreign aid, for *better*, more qualitative foreign aid, was difficult. The merest hint of criticism could get you labelled as disloyal. At SwedeAid, everyone was terrified of putting a foot wrong. The neo-liberal thinktank Frihetsbron had over the past five years brashly appropriated the right to define the problem and maintained that all foreign aid was a waste. Both Katta and Sofia were convinced Sweden's foreign aid work could be improved and made more efficient through a deeper understanding of local realities and grassroot perspectives, but that was a hard notion to sell.

Suddenly, Katta fixed Sofia intently.

"Okay?"

"What?" Sofia met her eyes. Something about Katta's tone made Sofia's hand slip imperceptibly down to her stomach.

"Are you pregnant?"

"What makes you think that?" Sofia played for time and held her breath.

"Everything. You're distracted, you're running to the bathroom every two minutes and you've barely touched your wine. I know you."

Sofia continued to hold her breath. She'd planned to keep this to herself. She'd had an email confirming her appointment to have an abortion at a local clinic. No big deal, a pill, wait twenty-four hours and then go home. It would barely have happened. If she didn't have to talk about it, it would barely have happened. She exhaled.

"I'm having an abortion. Tomorrow, as it happens."

"Okay?" Katta held her gaze.

"It wasn't planned and it couldn't have come at a worse time. You know I'm happy with what I have. Two is enough."

"What does Janne say about it?"

"You know what he's like. This was an accident, we're not having another baby. But I can't tell Janne, you know what a drama queen he is," Sofia smiled wanly and shot Katta a pleading look. "Everything's always such a big to-do with him, there would be no end to the drama. He would feel rejected and run over. He always wants so much of everything. Attention, love, children, good food . . . you know."

Katta leaned forward and picked up a piece of cheese. She nodded. She was familiar with Janne. Sofia looked miserable.

"Whatever I do, it comes out wrong. We're just getting back on track after the whole Camilla thing. I'm starting to like him again, he's a great dad. We've almost found our way back to each other. I don't want another pregnancy right now. The timing is . . . catastrophic."

She trailed off. That hadn't sounded good. She tried again.

"If he found out, he'd blow it out of proportion. It would be about his ego rather than the viability of a third child. Besides, there's no time. Could I even have an abortion in Dhaka? I really don't want to be talked into it, I don't want . . ."

Sofia felt tears burning in her eyes. How inconvenient.

"Fair enough." Katta leaned in and squeezed her arm. "It's your decision. I won't tell anyone. You don't have to . . . justify it. It's okay."

Sofia prodded a piece of cheese with her fork, grateful for the silence. She popped a grape in her mouth. Two lovely children, two blonde little tykes who looked like their father. She was going to leave work earlier from now on, enjoy their playfulness and chubby cheeks. She was going to stop punishing Janne, be more generous, warmer. Her phone was beckoning her. It had been for days. It went without saying she should call. She wasn't alone in this. Tenderness washed over her, Janne, the children, her little family. At the same time, everything would become so complicated if she told him. She was absolutely certain she was happy with her life the way it was, or at least that she could be. If she was a bit more forgiving toward Janne, gave him that second chance she hadn't really given him yet. Teo was just becoming manageable, Noella was a delight. They could handle two children. Her first impulse had been to tell Janne, but then she'd had second thoughts. She really didn't want to be talked into it.

As though she could read her mind, Katta said simply:

"It's ultimately your decision, Sofia. Your body. You're not the first woman on the planet to get pregnant at a bad time. You choose which children you give birth to. Pro-choice, right?"

Sofia smiled at Katta. Exactly. What did *she* want? She closed her eyes for a moment, trying to listen to her gut instinct. It oscillated between extremes. The shame of keeping something so big from Janne, the joy of the growing life inside her, the weariness at the thought of caring for an infant. The inadequacy of wanting contradictory things. The clarity she felt about who she and Janne were and what they could handle. The dream of who they could become. The panic she'd felt when she found out she was pregnant. Her triumph at work. The feeling of just having picked up the ball.

Yes, she knew what she wanted.

She wanted to go back to Bangladesh, wanted to continue the work she'd started and be closer to Janne and the children. She was going to keep her appointment tomorrow, then follow her doctor's orders and rest for a day.

And then fly home.

*

Meena watched Rifat with a smile on her face. Her heart, her body, felt light. It had been good to visit Mokta's grave with him, to place a single hibiscus flower on the unmarked stone. He'd stood there, serious, still, had held her when the tears came. Then she'd showed him the mango tree where she'd used to hide as a child.

The mosaics were in perfect harmony now, bright colours forming a radiant star. Rifat and her Abba had walked down the slope toward the parked rickshaws. Rifat was listening politely and attentively to the older man, nodding sympathetically as the older man griped about the carts. Meena knew Rifat would be able to help her Abba. From time to time, Rifat glanced over at Meena and smiled.

"What an incredible husband," Farida had come up behind Meena, putting her arms around her waist and looking down the slope, too. "What an amazing son-in-law we have, shonamoni. A proper Dhakaite."

"His voice . . ." Meena said, but her mother cut her off:

"He uses it to say wise things. His eyes light up when he looks at you."

Surrounded by the dry huts and untamed verdure of the village, Meena realised Rifat really did look like a Dhakaite, a young man from the big city. His new haircut, the blindingly white shirt, the pressed beige trousers and the belt. Her husband. Meena watched him squat down to inspect something on the rickshaw's wheel.

"Your father is happy for the first time in a long time," Farida said softly in Meena's ear. "We're so looking forward to the wedding. Two goats, six chickens. We're going to have to ask the neighbours to help with the slaughter. And the mangos, it seems we'll have mangos again this year."

Afterword

Most things in this book resemble reality, but nothing is entirely true. It's a novel. For three years, I worked as a development analyst at Sweden's embassy in Bangladesh and many of the scenes and stories in *Sisters by the River* stem from that time. The environments, discussions, work descriptions, conflicts, buildings, food, flowers, frustrations. The questions that pose themselves and the answers everyone is looking for. All of this is Dhaka. Or at least the Dhaka I experienced.

That being said, the characters in the book are made up, and any similarities with people who happened to live in Dhaka while my family and I were there are accidental.

A special thank you to my Bangladeshi friends Khuchi, Sohel, Raihan, Tasneem and Afsana for showing me your Bangladesh and teaching me to see and respect your aspirations. I also want to thank my colleagues at Sida, the Ministry of Foreign Affairs and the Government Offices who thought this was an important book to write. Thank you to my amazing circle of friends who have been my cheerleaders and critics and mirrors for a long time. My lovely children Edward, Harry and Laura and my extraordinary husband Nick have endured my mental and physical absence while I worked on this book. Thank you! Writing a novel has been infinitely more profound and transformational than I could ever have imagined. You gave me the time and space to experience it.

Finally, thank you to Lisa Christensen at Lund University's Creative Writing Program, who helped me trust my voice and instilled me with confidence and enjoyment all the way to the finish line. And thank you to Sigrid Combüchen at the same programme, who used her pitch-perfect ears to listen to my story.

Helena Thorfinn
Lund, January 2012

Glossary

Amma and Abba—Mum and Dad
Apa—sister
Assalamaleikum—'Peace be upon you', common formal greeting phrase
Ayah—nanny
Bhai—brother
Baksheesh—tip, bribe
Bilap—lament song of women
Bideshi—foreigners, Westerners
Chollista—memorial service
Chula—fire pit
Dai—traditional midwife
Fuchka—crispy chickpea ball
Iftar—meal to break fast during Ramadan
Kemon ache?—How are you?
Khub balho—I am fine.
Kobiraj—witch doctor
Maagi—whore
Maghrib—first prayers at dusk
Shalish—the village court
Shonamoni—darling
Shondori—beautiful girl
Thik ache—okay, fine

About the author and this book

Helena Thorfinn is a Swedish writer and development practitioner who lived in Dhaka between 2005-2008 where she worked at the Embassy of Sweden. Bangladesh, its people and challenges, was for her an unforgettable encounter that later became this novel.

This book however, is a work of fiction. Every character is fictional and has never existed, and every situation is made up and has never happened. This is important. Any resemblance with real life is entirely unintentional. The Embassy of Sweden, where a large part of this book is played out, was and is a place where hard working diplomats and dedicated colleagues from Bangladesh are working side by side to combat poverty and support Bangladesh in turning its challenges into opportunities. Every single day.

This said; the beautiful country of Bangladesh, its green fields and the huge, orange sun that sets over paddy fields and expanding cities alike, its amazing people, women and men, girls and boys, have been an endless inspiration. Bangladesh is more complex and rich than an outsider can grasp. This book can only capture a small slice.

Washington DC, January 2020

For more information:
www.helenathorfinn.com
www.meshewe.org

Printed by Amazon Italia Logistica S.r.l.
Torrazza Piemonte (TO), Italy